"Damn it, Grace.
You shouldn't be here."

"Lord Ruthveyn," Grace answered, "did I give you leave to use my Christian name?"

A mocking smile lifted one corner of his mouth. "No," he whispered. "You did not, *Grace*. Shall I stop? Is that what you want, Grace? For me to stop all this? Because I'm not sure that's an option now."

He towered over her, a beautiful, untamed beast of a man, and something deep and treacherous began to twist in the pit of her belly.

Grace tried to pull away. He softened his grip, but his gaze was still drifting over her face. Wariness and something that looked like yearning warred in his eyes. Grace let her gaze drift down to his mouth and her breath caught.

"I think, Mademoiselle Gauthier," he said softly, "that I am about to do something for which I *will* owe you an apology."

By Liz Carlyle

ONE TOUCH OF SCANDAL

Coming Soon

ONE WICKED GLANCE

LIZ CARLYLE

One Touch of Scandal

AVON

An Imprint of HarperCollinsPublishers

This is a work of fiction. Names, characters, places, and incidents are products of the author's imagination or are used fictitiously and are not to be construed as real. Any resemblance to actual events, locales, organizations, or persons, living or dead, is entirely coincidental.

AVON BOOKS
An Imprint of HarperCollins*Publishers*
10 East 53rd Street
New York, New York 10022-5299

Copyright © 2010 by Susan Woodhouse
ISBN 978-0-06-196575-3
www.avonromance.com

First Avon Books paperback printing: October 2010

Avon Trademark Reg. U.S. Pat. Off. and in Other Countries, Marca Registrada, Hecho en U.S.A.
HarperCollins® is a registered trademark of HarperCollins Publishers.

Printed in the U.S.A.

10 9 8 7 6 5 4 3 2 1

One Touch of
Scandal

Rise of the Guardians

Paris, 1658

*T*he fine haze crept over the Marais in silence, a gossamer thing that settled softly into the cobbled lanes and grand *allées* alike, deadening the night like so much straw cast down before a hearse. Along the Seine, the lamplights of Paris turned one after another to a rheumy amber, their beams barely piercing the night.

It little mattered. The storm that had rained down upon *la cité* for all of three days and nights had driven both man and beast to shelter, and in the Marais, neither stirred. None heard the hoofbeats that pounded out of the brume, at first a mere rumble of sound. But the sound gathered and quickened, became a cacophonous clatter, then rang and swelled into a roar neither fog nor death could still and no man could ignore, until the narrow lane of rue St. Paul was filled wall to windowsill with horses dark from sweat and foamed with lather.

Casements screeched and sashes thudded up as, all along the street, the good citizens leaned out to see what despot's army bore down upon them. But as quickly as they had come, the horsemen passed through, clattering down onto the river road, along the Hôtel de Sens, then onto the Pont Marie, their thick black capes streaming out behind as they fairly leapt over the Seine to vanish into utter darkness.

Later it was whispered by those who had seen them that the horsemen had been inhuman; that the heavy hoods had concealed naught but cheeks of pale, bleached bone with bright, burning sockets above. That the hands which fisted the reins were without flesh or substance; indeed, that the riders came thundering forth in the wake of the storm and down upon the quiet pastures of the Île Saint-Louis as emissaries of the devil himself—and that all that was to come afterward was naught but a righteous punishment.

In the darkness beyond the Pont Marie, the foremost of these devil's minions drew up his steed, a snorting, wheeling mass of muscle and temper, and hurled himself from the saddle in one motion. His cloak of black wool billowing about his boots, he strode through the mud and weeds, then lifted his fist—of bone and flesh—to pound upon the door of an old stone cottage with the strength of his whole of his arm, and much of his shoulder, too.

Within, the knock was heard too well, as was his intent. Indeed, the horsemen had been heard and their purpose surmised long before they had come thundering across the bridge.

A second dismounted, his torch held aloft. "They are within?"

"Aye, stench of guile carries," said the horseman. He pounded upon the door again. "*Ouvre-moi!* Open, you scurrilous dog! In the name of the *Fraternitas Aureae Crucis*!"

As if his words had willed it, the arched and weathered slab of a door creaked open on stiff hinges, the rusted iron ring that served as its knob clunking impotently as it stopped.

"*Oui?*"

"The Gift," rasped the horseman, planting a wide palm upon the door. "We've come for the Gift."

A round-faced friar, his vestments a dull brown in the flickering light, his eyes feverish with agitation, looked up at the intruder.

"*Now*," the horseman bellowed, laying the opposite hand to his sword hilt.

The friar shook his head. "*Je ne sais pas ce que vous veux!*"

"You, sir, are a bloody liar." The words were lethally soft. "The Gift, man. *Now*. Or by all that is holy, I shall bind you by the wrists and drag you back up to St. Paul's to stand before our Jesuit brethren. And what will you say for yourself then, eh?"

The friar's visage twisted with vehemence. "*Très bien*," he snarled, spittle flying. "Let the sin of this be upon your head!"

And yet he did not move. The horseman stood stalwart, saying no more, his sword hand eagerly twitching. "I am sworn to God," he said, "not to peace. You would do well to heed me."

After a slow exhalation, the friar turned from the door, rummaged in the gloom but a few moments, and returned with a large bundle set high upon his hip.

The horseman leaned across the stone threshold and

pushed gingerly at the folds of wool until a small, drowsy face peeked out at him beneath a tumble of brilliant red curls, one fist set squarely to her mouth.

"Nay, Sibylla!" said the horseman gently. "No' the thumb, lass!"

He reached for her, his tall leather boots creaking in the stillness.

But at the last possible instant, the friar hesitated and withdrew a pace into the gloom. "*Imbécile!*" he hissed. "Think what you do! She is *le antéchrist*! You will rue this day in hell."

"The only day I rue," said the horseman, shouldering his way inside, "is the day she set sail for this place."

The friar spat onto the flagstone between his firmly planted boots.

"But now we return," the horseman went on, drawing his sword, the sound of steel on steel ringing through the night. "And the only question which remains, *mon frère,* is does God let you live to see us go?"

CHAPTER 1

Only the Good Die Young

London, 1848

Blood. Blood, everywhere.

Oblivious to the whispers and the quick, soft footfalls up and down the passageway, Grace Gauthier lifted her hands, studying them with numb dispassion in the flickering gaslight. It felt as if the fingers and palms—indeed, even the ruined cuffs of her nightdress—belonged to someone else altogether.

Guarded whispers drifted from the study across the corridor.

"In shock, in't she?"

"Aye, and this 'un dead soon after 'e hit the carpet."

Grace shuddered.

Had he suffered? She prayed not. She dropped her

hands, shut her eyes, and leaned back against the sitting-room wall to stop the shaking, but her trembling, she realized, was bone-deep and would not be so easily stilled.

Somewhere downstairs, a woman was sobbing. Indeed, *she* should be sobbing. Why was she not? Why could she not make sense of this?

"Miss Gauthier?"

This voice came as if from a distance, mangling her name. Grace did not care. She felt as if she stood in a tunnel, far, far away from this quiet chaos. But she did not. She was here, and Ethan was gone, and this—all of this—would soon seem all too real. Long months spent upon the battlefields of North Africa had taught her that numbness in the face of death was but a fleeting respite.

"Miss?" said the voice again.

An English voice, but not a cultured one. Yet not like Ethan's, either. Not hard with the confidence of a self-made man.

"*Oui?*" Grace forced her eyes open.

A warm, heavy palm slid beneath her elbow. "I am afraid you must come into the library with me now, miss."

She came away from the wall and went down the corridor with him like an automaton. What was his name? He had told her upon bursting into Ethan's study, this broad, ruddy-cheeked man who had seized such a firm grip on her elbow. And told her again when he'd dragged her from the body, his voice shushing and gentle, as if he spoke to a child.

Or a lunatic.

But the name had escaped, along with all hope. And now he was drawing her swiftly past the study, where the men in blue, brass-buttoned uniforms whispered, then down the sweeping staircase where the draft from the gaping front door stirred at the hems of her wrapper. The sobbing from within the house deepened to a wretched, inhuman moan.

She hesitated, the newel post cold as Ethan's body beneath her hand. "I should go," she murmured. "I should find Fenella—Miss Crane."

But the man ignored the suggestion. "Just a few more questions, miss," he said without slowing, "then we—"

His words were forestalled by the appearance of yet another man; the fourth, Grace thought. Or perhaps the fortieth. She had been too stricken to count.

But unlike the others, this man was no uniformed officer. Instead he was dressed elegantly, as if for the theatre. A black opera cloak swirling about his ankles, he materialized like a specter from the London fog, coming up the front steps and through the open door as if he owned the house and everyone in it, stripping off a fine pair of kidskin gloves as he came.

The incongruity of this threatened to at last shove Grace over the edge of hysteria. Ethan lay dead in a pool of his own blood, behind his own desk, in his own home. And the rest of London went about its business? They went *to the theater*?

The man swerved gracefully around the pile of luggage sitting in the front hall and headed toward them, his footfalls ringing sharply on the fine marble floor.

"Evening, Assistant Commissioner." Grace's escort stiffened as he tucked his tall top hat neatly under one arm.

The man halted a few feet away, his quick gaze flicking over Grace, then back again. "Evening, Minch. This is Mademoiselle Gauthier?" He pronounced the name flawlessly—*Gaw*-tee-aye—as if he were a Frenchman born.

"Yes, sir," said Minch. "Did the capt'n brief you?"

"No need. Sir George saw fit to drag me from the opera himself." The man—the commissioner, or whatever he was called—dipped his head to catch Grace's eyes. "Mademoiselle, I am sorry for your loss. The deceased, I collect, was your affianced husband?"

Grace tried to hold his gaze, but it was cold as ice. "*Oui*, I . . . we . . . we had—" Suddenly, the swell of grief and horror came up to nearly choke her. "W-We had an understanding."

The man took charge. "Sergeant Minch here will escort us to the parlor, where we may speak in privacy," he said. "If you would kindly follow him?"

It was the first order given Grace that had not sounded quite like a military command. Indeed, it sounded rather more dangerous than that. He took her arm, and, in an instant, Grace was seated in Fenella's favorite chair by the hearth and a brandy pressed into her hand.

"Drink it, mademoiselle."

After a time, she looked up to see that she was now quite alone with the dark man with the thin blade of a nose. He had tossed down his opera cloak along with his gloves and was staring at her quite intently.

"Where is Miss Crane?" she whispered, plucking nervously at her bloodied cuffs. "I . . . I should change and go to her."

The commissioner turned his eyes away. "I am very sorry, mademoiselle, for your loss," he said again. "The trunks and baggage in the passageway—I understand they are yours?"

Grace licked her lips and tasted the brandy she did not remember drinking. "Yes, I was going to my aunt's," she managed. "So that Ethan—Mr. Holding—might send the announcement to the papers tomorrow."

"The announcement?" His eyes narrowed. "Of your betrothal?"

"Yes." Her voice caught. "His year of mourning, it . . . it was over."

And hers had just begun—yet again.

"I am afraid, mademoiselle," said the man, "that I cannot permit you to remove the baggage tonight."

"Tonight?" Grace blinked. "I—why, I had no intention of doing so."

He regarded her in silence a moment, one finger rhythmically stroking the edge of a leather folio he held balanced on his knee. And as she watched him, beginning bit by bit to return to herself, it dawned on Grace that this was the very thing Ethan had most feared. Scandal. Speculation. The tawdry bits and pieces of a less-than-genteel life; things a former tradesman with social aspirations did not dare trail past the hallowed white portals of Belgravia. All of Ethan's efforts to fit in, to be one of them, would be for naught.

But then she remembered. It did not matter now.

The commissioner, however, was speaking. "One of the housemaids will be assigned to repack under supervision those things which you shall need for the next few days," he went on. "Have you any family in London? Where were you to go tomorrow?"

"To my aunt's," Grace answered, puzzled. "Lady Abigail Hythe in Manchester Square."

"Hythe." He puzzled a moment over the name, but no recognition dawned. "Well, I shall ask you to be so kind, ma'am, as to walk back over the events of this evening with me. Then, once you have changed, and your valise is packed, Sergeant Minch will escort you to your aunt's house."

For the first time tonight, Grace fully grasped the horror of being dressed in her nightclothes amongst all these strange men. She should have been embarrassed, but on her next breath she realized just what the man had suggested.

"Leave *tonight*?" she said sharply. "Why, this is not possible! The children will need me. Miss Crane will want me. *Mon Dieu,* sir, they have lost their father, and Miss Crane her brother. I would not dream of abandoning them at such a time, no matter my own loss."

He set his head slightly to one side and studied her, his eyes as cold a shade of gray as ever Grace had seen, his gaze boring into her, and it was then that she felt it. That faint frisson of fear. It ran down her spine, chilling her.

Inexplicably, the realization brought her courage. Or perhaps it was indignation. Ethan was dead, yes. None-theless, she had borne up under far worse. She was the daughter of a commandant, for pity's sake. She did not feel fear—not from a mere bureaucrat.

"*Monsieur,*" she said stiffly, "a fine man and good friend to Her Majesty's government was just cut down in cold blood. I should hope the police have a vast deal more to worry about than where a nobody governess lays her head tonight. Indeed, I should hope you would have every man in Scotland Yard turned out on the streets within the hour."

"Oh, I am quite well aware, ma'am, of precisely how valued a citizen Mr. Holding was to the Government," the man replied. "Had I not been, the visit I received tonight courtesy of our Home Secretary would most assuredly have made it plain."

She came swiftly to her feet. "Excellent, then," she said. "You have much to do. I must bathe, change, and see to Fenella and the children. Really, sir—I did not catch your name—"

"Napier," he said without rising, a terrible breach of etiquette. "Assistant Commissioner Royden Napier, Metropolitan Police. Now kindly sit back down, Mademoiselle Gauthier."

Grace drew herself up to her full height. "I shall be but a few moments," she said with as much Gallic hauteur as she could muster. "I fear I must insist."

He hesitated for only a heartbeat, as if weighing something in his mind. Then, "Mademoiselle, I am very sorry," he said. "You cannot go yet, nor can you see your fiancé's sister. We have advised the household that no one save perhaps one or two servants can remain here tonight. Interviews must take place, and the property must be searched for incriminating evidence."

"Evidence?" said Grace. "In the *house*? But a thief would have come from outside. Wouldn't he? Some sort of—what do they call it?—a cracksman? And the children—who will comfort them?"

Something that might have been pity sketched over his face then. "I believe their late mother's sister—" Here he consulted his folio, "—a Mrs. Lester, is coming to collect the children and take them down to her country house below Rotherhithe. So it would be best, mademoiselle, under the circumstances, if you went as planned to your aunt's."

"Tonight?"

"Yes, mademoiselle." His finger still stroked the leather of his folio. "Tonight."

And at last Grace heard what was *not* being said. This was not about grief, or about sympathy, or even about what she might have seen. This man did not trust her. She might even be—God help her—a suspect.

With a hand that shook, Grace drained the rest of the brandy.

The frisson of fear had returned.

* * *

As the morning sun rose high over Westminster, Adrian Forsythe, Lord Ruthveyn, tipped back his head to allow his valet to scrape the last swath of black bristle up his throat, half-hoping that this time the fellow's wrist might twitch and slit his jugular vein.

This prospect was followed, however, by the ring of Fricke's drawing the blade clean across the rim of his basin.

Alas, not today.

Ruthveyn straightened in his chair and took the steaming-hot towel Fricke offered. "Well, get on with it, Claytor," he grumbled to his waiting secretary as he wiped the last of the soap from his face. "What else has gone wrong in the last twelve hours—other than the two shattered windows, Teddy's concussion, and that little contretemps with the bailiff?"

Claytor stood in the open door of his bedchamber, still clutching his hat, his expression colorless. "What *else*?" the secretary echoed. "I daresay that's enough, isn't it?"

"Then you are dismissed." Ruthveyn tossed down the towel and uncoiled his lean frame from the chair. "Tell Anisha I shall hope to be home for dinner. I'll look in on Teddy then."

"Very well." Claytor seemed to wring his hat brim. "B-But the bailiff came round yesterday afternoon, sir. And today is . . . well, *today*."

The marquess stripped off his dressing gown. Naked to the waist, the fall of his trousers but half–done up, he stretched across the bed for the fresh shirt Fricke had just laid out. He knew what the man was getting at, and it would not do.

"Have you a point, Claytor?" he finally asked.

The secretary's eyes widened. "I've done what I can,

sir. I told Ballard to call the glazier, and little Teddy's stitched up, but what ever am I to do, sir, about the other? About Lord Lucan?"

"Let him rot," Ruthveyn suggested, dragging the shirt over his head.

"B-But in a sponging house?" sputtered Claytor.

"Every young man must learn to live within his income," said the marquess, adjusting his collar and cuffs. "I merely prefer that my brother should do it sooner rather than later."

"But sir, your sister was quite beside herself! Indeed, Lady Anisha was in tears! You cannot think what it was like, sir! You weren't *there*."

You weren't there.

The phrase hung in the air but a moment, laced ever so lightly with accusation—but it was only a hint. Claytor knew better. Ruthveyn paid well—very, very well—and his black moods were notorious. And yes, he was almost always away from home nowadays.

"The boy got himself into debt, Claytor," Ruthveyn answered. "He can bloody well get himself out again."

But it would not, of course, be easy. Lord Lucan Forsythe received a quarterly allowance from the estate, with the next payment due at Michaelmas—which would be just long enough, Ruthveyn hoped, to learn a lesson. But not so long as to contract blood poisoning from bedbugs, keel over dead from dysentery, or worse, fall in with an even lower class of associates than those he'd already befriended since arriving in Town. Ruthveyn sensed none of this would happen, but even he could be wrong—and sponging houses were vile, iniquitous places.

A little ruthlessly, the marquess stabbed in his starched shirttails, then hitched up the rest of his buttons. Perhaps he should have watched Lucan more carefully, but

Ruthveyn had believed what was to come inevitable. And as Claytor pointed out, for the last six months, Ruthveyn had made his home, more often than not, here in an upstairs suite at his private club, fetching down from Mayfair his valet and his secretary and whatever and whomever he wished—and whenever he wished it. Ruthveyn did not much care to be inconvenienced, even in exile.

Claytor conceded defeat. "For dinner, then, my lord," he murmured, stiffly inclining his head. "I shall tell Lady Anisha to expect you."

The secretary turned to go just as Fricke thrust out Ruthveyn's cravat. Ruthveyn snatched it and relented. "Look here, Claytor," he said over his shoulder. "I'm sorry, but I've a morning head and an ill temper. Still, no young man ever died of a fortnight spent in a sponging house. Indeed, I daresay it will do my brother a world of good."

"But do you mean ever to get him out?" asked Claytor a little bitterly. "Or do you mean to grease his skids straight into debtors' prison?"

At that, Ruthveyn whirled about. "Careful, old boy." His voice was deathly quiet. "Do not mistake an explanation as a license to make free with your opinion."

Claytor dropped his gaze. "I beg your pardon," he replied. "But I can tell you, sir, what will happen. After another four or five days—after the bailiff has come round again with his demands, and a few more duns have piled up, Lady Anisha will go down to Houndsditch and start selling off her jewels. That, sir, is what will happen."

The galling thing was, Claytor might be right. But that had to be Anisha's choice.

"My sister will not be made a prisoner in my home," said Ruthveyn quietly. "Her jewels—and her life—are now hers to do with as she pleases. I only hope and pray that she means to raise Tom and Teddy a little more strictly than our stepmother raised Lucan."

"But, my lord, it cannot have been so very—"

"You cannot know what it was like, Claytor," Ruthveyn cut in. "You weren't *there*."

But turn poor Claytor's words against him as he might, the truth was, Ruthveyn hadn't been there either. Not very often, at least. He had been in the early years of his diplomatic career, and, like his father before him, haring about Hindustan risking life and limb in service to Her Majesty's government and its well-shod bootheel, the East India Company. Then, as now, he had avoided his family. He had avoided *intimacy*. And he was not fool enough to confuse intimacy with sex or even with love.

He did love them—even Lucan, cocky young fool that he was. He loved them more than life itself. But their coming out from Calcutta some six months past had taken the life he'd tried so desperately to hold together and rattled it at its very foundation.

But Anisha was now a widow with two little hellions to raise. As to their half brother . . . well, Lucan simply needed a father. Pity he did not have one.

"Which coat, sir?" Fricke enquired as the door closed behind Claytor. "I brought down the dark blue superfine and last year's black."

"The black," said Ruthveyn, stripping off the half-tied cravat. "And I want a black stock to go with it."

"Indeed," murmured Fricke, carrying away the offending linen. "We're in a black mood, I collect."

"It was a black night," said Ruthveyn.

There was no need to say more. The detritus of a difficult evening lay cast about the room: an empty decanter of cognac, a corkless apothecary's vial, filthy ashtrays, and the sharp scent of spiced tobacco and charas still hanging in the air.

Fricke finished dressing him in silence, touching his master as little as possible. Ruthveyn's odd quirks in this regard were made plain early on to anyone employed to serve him, and the marquess was beyond caring what was thought of it.

His toilet thus complete, Ruthveyn gave one last neatening tug on his cuffs, then went downstairs to order a freshly pressed copy of the *Morning Chronicle* and a pot of the particularly strong tea always kept on hand for him.

He found the club's coffee room empty, save for Dr. von Althausen and Lord Bessett. The latter was leaned over one of von Althausen's specimen boxes, studying it through the doctor's gold monocle. Ruthveyn nodded at Bessett as he passed, and Bessett motioned him nearer.

"We had word from Lazonby last night," he said quietly. "His father's affairs have been put in order. He's taking the child to his mother's people. She will be safe there."

"An excellent plan," said Ruthveyn. "Good morning, Doctor. What have you there?"

"A rare African tumbu fly," said von Althausen, now peering at it. "Have a look. The larvae, you see, burrow under one's skin, and the resultant oozing boils are—"

"God spare me," Ruthveyn interjected, wincing. "I haven't had my breakfast."

"If that does not pique your interest, old chap, he'll repeating his experiments in galvanism this afternoon," Bessett suggested. "The electromagnetic generator has been repaired."

"Thank you, but I am not sticking my finger in that contraption," said Ruthveyn. "I believe I shall leave the mysteries of my brain precisely that."

"One must occasionally sacrifice in the name of science, Adrian," von Althausen grumbled. "Especially you. After all, if the brain of the *Electrophorus electricus* can generate an electrical field outside its body, then just imagine what—"

"No," the marquess firmly interjected. "I am not an eel. Thank you. Gentlemen, carry on."

Von Althausen waved him away distractedly, and the gentlemen returned to their examinations.

Ruthveyn took up his usual position—alone at a table in the centermost bow window—and sipped at his tea while absently perusing the paper. The tea was hot, the opulent clubroom comfortable, and the day ahead as rich with possibility as any wealthy, titled nabob might wish. Yet the night still chafed at him.

He was going to have to dispense with Mrs. Timmonds.

It was a shame, really, when his mistress was so very beautiful. But Ruthveyn was beginning to feel the stirrings of an attachment to her. Worse still, the lady had begun to ask too many pointed questions. She had not heeded his initial warnings, and warnings they had assuredly been. And now . . . well, he was simply too fond of her to give her the backhanded emotional slap he reserved for those who disobeyed him.

But he was angry—at her, a little, but most of all, at himself. How long had he imagined he could perform the intricate steps of this dance, which time and again had tripped him up? A mere six months, and he'd begun to feel the tug. That seductive wish to throw caution to the wind and look past the chasm he'd placed quite deliberately between them. Not because he'd fallen in love—of that, he was not capable—but because, as with Anisha and Luc and the boys, he wanted to take care of Angela Timmonds. To make her happy.

But he had never in his life made a woman happy. Not for long.

On impulse, he snatched up the little bell that sat in the center of the table. One of the footmen instantly materialized, his expression emotionless. "May I freshen your tea, my lord?"

"No. Fetch me Belkadi."

The footman inclined his head. "He is with the vintner at present, sir, but I shall tell him."

The decision made, Ruthveyn scanned the front page of his paper, reading but not really absorbing the words as he burned with impatience. God's truth but he did not need another night like his last. He did not need to touch a woman and have himself torn apart in the aftermath. Or to coolly walk out on her as if she were no more than a discarded rag. To leave her sobbing alone in the darkness.

Even he was not so heartless as that. And yet it was precisely what he had done.

On that thought, Ruthveyn flung aside the newspaper, rigid with suppressed emotion, until at last Belkadi deigned to appear. The club's majordomo gave a slight bow, his black suit immaculately pressed, his black hair drawn severely back in an old-fashioned queue.

"You wished to see me?"

Belkadi never said *sir*—not unless it was laced with sarcasm—so Ruthveyn did not expect it of the arrogant devil. "Sit down," he said, gesturing at a chair. "Have a cup of Assam."

"Von Althausen's hybrid?" he replied in his faintly accented English. "Thank you, no. I should prefer to keep the lining of my intestines." But Belkadi sat, all the same.

Ruthveyn pushed his paper a little away. "So tell me, old chap, have you ordered your vintner to cease sending us that red rubbish he calls claret?" he asked. "Or did you simply behead the poor bastard?"

"I think you did not call me here to discuss the cellars," said Belkadi.

Ruthveyn smiled faintly but did not quite hold the man's gaze. "I did not," he agreed. "I wish to dispense with Mrs. Timmonds. Will you arrange it?"

Belkadi's surprise was betrayed by the merest lift of one eyebrow. "Why do you wish this?"

"Why?" Ruthveyn echoed. "What business is it of yours? Perhaps I have grown tired of the lady. Perhaps my intcrests are otherwise engaged. Whatever my reasons, you brokered this arrangement. Now un-broker it."

A dark look passed behind Belkadi's eyes. He rose smoothly to his feet, and bowed. "But of course, *sir*."

Ruthveyn watched the man turn to go, his spine rigid. "And Belkadi," he said, "one last thing."

The majordomo turned back.

"Offer her the use of the Marylebone house for her lifetime," Ruthveyn added. "And an annuity of whatever amount you think fair. Tell Claytor to make it so."

Again, Belkadi gave his stiff bow, his black gaze revealing nothing now. "I shall extend your generous offer," he said, "but Mrs. Timmonds is not without pride."

Or suitors, Ruthveyn silently added.

The lady would not long grieve his absence, he was sure. Indeed, in a week's time, she'd be glad to be shut of him. He ruthlessly pushed the vision away and somehow forced his attention to the newspaper, radical rag though it was. A wise man knew his enemies. He read in silence for a time until, on page three, a name caught his eye, and his mouth twisted sourly.

He looked over his shoulder at von Althausen. "It would appear our favorite reporter has run out of salacious drivel to print and resorted to astronomy," he said. "He claims Lassell has found another moon round Saturn."

"Hmph!" said the good doctor. "I shall send William my congratulations on his discovery. But as to the whelp, I should have assigned him the obituaries."

Ruthveyn gave a grunt of agreement, then turned back to his table and his window. It was at that instant he chanced to see her: a tall woman dressed in black and gray turning purposefully into St. James's Place from the main thoroughfare.

Ruthveyn could not have said why she caught his eye; he so rarely looked at anyone. Perhaps it was the veil of black bobbinet, which covered all but the tip of her chin and lent her an air of mystery. Whatever it was, once he'd begun to observe her, he was loath to turn away. Her neat, quick steps carried her closer and closer until, at the point just opposite the half dozen steps that led to club's entrance, she paused to look up as if studying the symbols etched into the pediment.

At least Ruthveyn *thought* she was studying them—but it was difficult to say with any measure of certainty given the veil. Indeed, it was as if her whole inner being—her purpose, her persona, her emotions—were similarly veiled, for she radiated no sense of her inner self whatsoever. Save for what Ruthveyn could see with his two eyes—a lithe, youngish woman with impeccable taste in clothing and hair the color of honey—she was a mystery. How very odd.

A shaft of frustration pierced him unexpectedly. Or was it fascination? Ruthveyn wanted to get up and go down the steps to lift the veil so that he might touch her face and look into her eyes.

What madness. On his next breath, he forced himself to relax into his chair. Forced his respiration to slow and his mind to focus on the ceaseless, fluid motion of the air in and out of his lungs.

He had had a bad night. He did not need a bad day to go with it.

The lady in black bobbinet was none of his concern. Perhaps she was merely wandering St. James's and had paused to admire the strange symbols. She might be a tourist. Indeed, that was likely the case, for though her black hat and dove gray walking dress were elegant, they were not *à la mode* in London. And Ruthveyn should know. He'd bought a great deal of fashionable ladies' clothing of late.

The thought of Mrs. Timmonds served to push the veiled lady from his mind. Ruthveyn poured another cup of tea and snapped out the *Chronicle* again. Out of sheer perversity, he began to read the article about Saturn's moon, though the celestial sky was more Anisha's forte than his. But he was scarcely halfway down the column when something of a clamor arose downstairs in the entrance hall.

Ruthveyn could hear Belkadi speaking firmly—and rather brusquely, too, which was odd. Belkadi rarely spoke harshly to anyone; like Ruthveyn, he did not need to.

Just then a woman's voice echoed in the corridor, sharp and faintly angry. Ruthveyn cut another glance at von Althausen. The doctor lifted one shoulder and tilted his head in the direction of the clamor. *Your turn, old chap,* said his eyes.

Thus appointed, Ruthveyn sighed, pushed back his teacup, and rose. The nature of the Society's research did bring the occasional raving lunatic to their doors. No one liked it, but there it was. One had to deal with it.

He went out and down the wide marble staircase, which poured a story and a half down into the reception foyer like a wide, white waterfall, and was immediately taken aback to see the lady in black and gray just inside the front door. Her black wool cloak lay over her arm, and she was tugging off her gloves with short, neat jerks, as if she meant to stay.

As with the lunatics, it was rare to see a woman within the club's portals but not unheard of. The Society maintained scientific reading rooms and vast libraries, which were occasionally made available for the public's use. But she hardly looked like a bluestocking.

Just then, the lady lifted back her veil to reveal a face as elegantly classical as her attire—and an expression as ashen as Claytor's had been earlier this morning. Ruthveyn came smoothly down the stairs, his gaze steady upon that face with its wide blue eyes and full, rather tremulous mouth. And still, despite all the emotion she radiated, there was nothing. It was dashed disorienting.

Just then the argument escalated. The lady threw up a small hand, the palm thrust into Belkadi's face. "I thank you, sir." Her voice was sharp, with a faint French accent. "But really, I shan't be put off. I must see Sergeant Welham with all haste."

"If madam will but listen," said Belkadi haughtily, "I shall endeavor to again explain—"

"May I be of some help, Belkadi?" Ruthveyn interjected.

The majordomo held out a card on a salver.

Ruthveyn glanced down. "Mademoiselle Gauthier?" he said, reading aloud the vaguely familiar name. "How may the St. James Society be of service to you?"

"In no way whatsoever," she said tartly. "And in any case, if this is the St. James Society, why does the pediment say F.A.C.?"

Ruthveyn lifted both brows in his most arrogant gesture. "Some obscure Latin phrase, I believe, ma'am," he answered. "Might I ask what brings you? One of our rare book collections, perhaps?"

"A rare book?" she echoed incredulously.

He managed a tight smile. "I confess, you do not look quite the type for our card room or the smoking salon."

Agitation sketched over her lovely face. "I have come merely to see a friend," she said. "An old and dear friend who—"

"Yes, I heard a name. Sergeant Welham." Ruthveyn permitted himself to hold her gaze very directly, carefully assessing her eyes. "This friendship, however, is not so old and so dear as to make you aware that Sergeant Welham is now Lord Lazonby, I collect? But it little matters. He is not in Town at present."

The insult flew past her. "Not in Town?" The lady set a hand just beneath her throat, a telling gesture. "How can he be away? How long shall he be?"

"Some weeks, I daresay," said Ruthveyn. "He caught the train up to Westmorland two days ago."

This seemed to send the lady reeling, and it occurred to Ruthveyn that her bravado was more than a façade. It was desperation.

Ruthveyn wondered what manner of trouble the young lady had got herself into—or what sort of trouble Rance Welham had got her into, damn him. There was a hollow, haunted look about her eyes, and the hand remained at her throat, frozen.

And despite all this—the barely suppressed anxiety, the veiled fear in her eyes, and the fact that Belkadi was going back up the wide staircase, leaving them quite alone together—Ruthveyn could not read the lady at all. He could see only with his eyes, and see only that which any neutral party might observe.

"*So he is gone . . .*" the lady whispered. "*Mon Dieu!*"

Then her head flopped back at an odd angle, the cloak fell, and her hand came out, flailing blindly for the reception counter.

"Belkadi!" he shouted.

But it was too late. The lady's knees were buckling. Despite his grave reluctance, Ruthveyn was obliged to touch her, scooping her up in a froth of skirts and petticoats to prevent her collapsing onto the marble floor.

"Belkadi!" he said again, cradling the woman almost gingerly.

In an instant, Belkadi was at his elbow. "Fresh air," he said. "Follow me."

Her gray silk skirts spilling over his arm, Ruthveyn carried her down the short flight of steps that turned and descended to the ground floor, then followed Belkadi along the corridor. Belkadi threw open the double doors that led to the club's portico and rear garden.

Ruthveyn settled the lady on one of the wicker chaises. "Fetch Lazonby's whisky."

Belkadi vanished. Ruthveyn knelt to further examine the lady's face, which was pale as milk beneath the swath of black netting that had half tumbled down again. She was not as young, he realized, as she'd first appeared. There were perhaps the faintest hints of lines about her eyes, as if she'd spent some time in the sun. But her cheekbones were high and strong, her forehead aristocratic and very English.

He wondered again at her French name, and at the faint stirring of recognition he'd felt upon seeing her ivory calling card. Already, however, the lady was coming round and muttering something in French.

Ruthveyn tore his gaze from her face, and stood. "I am going to prop up your feet, ma'am," he said. "I beg your pardon in advance."

"*Wha . . . happened?*" she whispered.

"I believe you swooned," he answered, seizing a pair of pillows from a nearby chair. "It was likely Belkadi. He occasionally has that effect on females."

The lady merely blinked her blue eyes at him in stupefaction as he lifted her ankles—her very slender, well-turned ankles—then propped her feet upon the pillows. Suddenly her gray hems slithered away to reveal her foamy undergarments and rather too much of her fine ankles. Against his better judgment, he twitched them back into place again.

Elegant ankles, thought Ruthveyn. *Gorgeous eyes. Beautiful, strong cheekbones.*

And still, he felt was nothing.

Nothing, that was, save good, old-fashioned lust . . .

CHAPTER 2

It Must Be Magic

Spirits. Again.

Did men imagine them the solution to all the world's ills? Grace wondered, choking down another swallow.

"Merci, I am feeling quite myself again," she lied, pushing the glass away.

But the two dark-eyed men still knelt beside her, their gazes affixed on her face. Absent the rush of panic, Grace looked at the first, the more broad-shouldered of the two. He looked almost satanic in his severe, obviously expensive attire, with eyes that burned black as night. The second—the one who had admitted her—was younger; his face less harsh and strikingly handsome.

"Belkadi," she muttered, recognition dawning. "A Kabyle name."

"It can be."

As if he found her words intrusive, the man's face shuttered, and he rose to go.

The second man stood as well, but instead of leaving, drew a rattan footstool to the foot of her chaise, its legs rumbling over the flagstone terrace. Grace looked about, not at all sure where she was. The man settled himself on the stool, set his knees wide, then propped his elbows upon them.

"Now," he said, his voice quiet but commanding, "tell me who you are and why you are here."

Grace looked about, blinking against the sun. "Wh-Where is *here*, precisely?"

A look of frustration passed over his face.

"I mean, is this still Sergeant Welham's club?" she clarified. "Indeed, I very much fear you had to carry me out here."

"Quite so. On both counts."

Grace felt her cheeks flush. "I did not know gentlemen's clubs had gardens," she said inanely. "And I never swoon. How mortifying."

The man smiled faintly, but it did little to soften his face. "How long has it been, ma'am, since you slept?" he asked. "Or ate?"

"I had dinner." She tried to think. "But that was yesterday, I suppose. And last night . . . *non,* I did not sleep."

The faint smile turned inward, then melted. "I know the feeling."

"I beg your pardon." Grace extended a less-than-steady hand. "I am Grace Gauthier. Thank you for your help."

After an instant's hesitation, he took it but instead of shaking it, bowed his head and lifted it almost to his lips. "Ruthveyn," he said, his voice low and a little raspy. "At your service."

"Thank you," she managed. "Tell me, do you know Sergeant Welham?"

"Very well," said the dark man. "I believe I can safely claim to be his best friend in all the world."

Grace lifted her eyebrows at that. "Can you indeed?"

"How long has it been, ma'am, since you last saw him?" the man asked. "My esteem of him not withstanding, Rance—Lord Lazonby—is not the sort of man gently bred ladies ordinarily claim to know."

Grace lowered her gaze. "You mean because he was once in prison."

"Amongst other reasons, yes."

"I *never* believed him guilty," she said hotly. "I *never* did. Nor did my father. Sergeant Welham was a gentleman through and through."

"Ah!" said the dark man.

Grace looked up to see recognition dawning in his eyes.

"Your father was Commandant Henri Gauthier of the French Foreign Legion in Algiers," said the man. "That is why you recognized Belkadi's name."

Grace wriggled up a little straighter on the chaise. "Yes, I lived there for many years. But you . . . you are not Algerian."

"I am not."

The man—Ruthveyn—seemed disinclined to say more, and Grace resisted the impulse to ask anything. Save for his thick raven hair, sun-bronzed skin, and a nose that was perhaps a tad too strong, he could perhaps have been an Englishman—or Satan in a pair of Bond Street boots.

But wherever his fine clothing had come from, he was no ordinary Englishman; she sensed it. There was an air of otherworldliness about him that defied description, and an almost chilling sense of dispassion, as if he observed but gave up nothing of himself. He did not radiate evil, precisely, but something far more complex.

Or perhaps she had fractured her skull on the marble foyer.

Really, how fanciful she had become. Her mission was far too pressing to allow for silly speculation. Besides, for all his claim to be Rance's friend, Grace was not at ease with the man.

She pulled her gaze away and stared into the depths of the small, symmetrical garden beyond the elegant portico. "Sergeant Welham served under my father for many years," she managed. "They were very close. Indeed, he once pledged Papa a debt of honor. I . . . I need to collect that debt. I need to see him quite urgently. But now you say . . ."

"That he is away," the man finished.

He rose unexpectedly, unfolding himself from the footstool like some lithe black bird of prey. He was very tall, Grace realized as she sat up. Very tall, and very dark—and in a way that had nothing to do with his coloring. He wore an elaborate gold ring set with a cabochon ruby that must have cost a king's ransom. It glinted in the afternoon sun as he extended a dark, long-fingered hand down to her.

"If you have quite recovered yourself, mademoiselle," he said, "I believe the rest of our conversation might best be had in private. And you should perhaps eat a little something."

Unable to contemplate food, Grace glanced about to see that at least thirty windows overlooked the garden from the back side of one tall building or another, most of them open to the cool September breeze. He was right. There was no privacy here.

Left with little alternative, she took his arm, which felt warm and thick with muscle beneath his black coat.

"Do you feel steady enough to walk, mademoiselle?" His·voice was low and solicitous.

"Yes, quite," said Grace. "And I am just a miss. Miss Gauthier. It will do."

He gave an acknowledging tilt of his head, then Ruthveyn led her back inside, through the house, and up half a flight of stairs. Grace could see the front door at the first turn, and already she could hear the man called Belkadi barking orders to someone above them.

"Welham wouldn't give you the time of day, even if he were here." The steely tone carried down the stairwell. "Now kindly take yourself off before Ruthveyn or Bessett catch you, and give you a proper thrashing."

Grace's escort suddenly stiffened. Then, on a soft curse, he pulled away and hastened up the stairs. "Out!" he ordered, turning the next corner. "Out of this house, sir!

Grace turned across the landing to see Belkadi standing by the tall reception desk, and Ruthveyn stalking across the foyer area.

"You've been warned, Coldwater!" Ruthveyn stabbed his index finger in the face of a young man dressed in a dull-colored mackintosh clasping a tattered folio under one arm. "Leave now—or this time, I'll hurl you headfirst into the street."

"*Namaste,* Lord Ruthveyn," said the young man, setting his hands prayerfully together and giving a mocking bow. "How do you do? I was hoping Welham might care to comment upon his ascension to the family earldom. Our readers do so love to follow the intricate twists and turns of his life."

Lord Ruthveyn?

Lord Ruthveyn. Lord Lazonby. Grace's head was beginning to spin from it all, and she felt rather as if she'd been dropped into some bizarre theatrical production. In the last two days, her predictable life had turned into a nightmare, and now she was beginning to fear tripping over yet another corpse as she fled the stage, for Ruthveyn had seized the young man and was frog-marching him toward the door, a look of unadulterated malice etched upon his face. The lad was doomed—and he had come here for the same reason as Grace.

"Mon Dieu, is everyone in London looking for Welham?"

Grace scarcely realized she'd muttered the words aloud until the young man twisted round to shoot her a look over his shoulder. "Jack Coldwater, ma'am, with the *Morning Chronicle,*" he said, his eyes aglitter. "Know Welham, do you? Care to comment? Answer a few questions?"

Ruthveyn jerked to a halt, then set his lips very near the young man's ear. "You begin to try our collective patience, sir," he said in a voice as still as death. "Go quietly, and let it be the end. For your sake."

The young man appeared undaunted. "All I'm saying, Ruthveyn, is that it is quite a coincidence Welham gets released from prison, and but a few months later, his father is dead. Wanted to ask him about it, that's all. Does he blame the Government? Or himself? Or *you?* The timing, you must admit, is poignant."

Suddenly, Ruthveyn seemed to explode—but in a cold, controlled sort of way. In an instant, he had slammed Coldwater around, fisted his hand in his coat, shoved him against the door, and hefted him six inches off the floor. And still the top of his head did not reach Ruthveyn's.

"Poignant?" Ruthveyn's voice was dangerously soft. "I'll give you poignant. I'll throttle you here where you stand, you little shi—"

"B-But I'm n-not standing," the young man gargled, toes dangling. "Have done, Ruthveyn! I'm just doing my job."

"And your job is to hound an innocent man?" Ruthveyn returned. "To turn up every rock and stone in London to see what manner of filth slithers out, then print it?" He gave the man a sharp jerk. "Is *that* your job, Coldwater?"

"My job—" Here, the young man paused to swallow, "—is to ask hard questions."

"Then expect hard answers," snarled Ruthveyn. "Let's start with the answering side of my fist."

Grace must have made a sound. Ruthven cut a glance over his shoulder, then relented and let the man slither back down the door and onto his feet. Then he turned abruptly to seize Grace's arm.

"Throw him down the steps, Belkadi," snapped Ruthveyn, practically hauling her up the wide marble staircase. "And don't ever let him in again."

"Certainly." Belkadi stepped briskly round the desk as if he'd been asked to dispense with a piece of baggage.

"Good heavens," said Grace, hastening to keep up with Ruthveyn.

"I beg your pardon," he said tightly. "I am not accustomed to a lady's presence."

"No, I meant—" Here, she cut a glance over the banister as Belkadi quite literally pitched Coldwater out—and rather effortlessly, for the fellow likely wouldn't have weighed ten stone tarred and feathered and looked scarcely old enough to shave. Coldwater landed on his arse somewhere near the third step, his notebook flying, then staggered to his feet just as the door thumped shut behind him.

Ruthveyn jerked her to a halt on the next step. "I beg your pardon," he said again, his eyes still flashing dangerously. "No lady should have witnessed that."

Good heavens, thought Grace. One would not wish an enemy of this man. "I'm a daughter of the French army, sir, not some frail English flower," she managed to answer. "I've seen men knifed to death in the bazaars of Algiers over a chess game gone wrong. I meant only that everyone on earth seems to be looking for Rance. And I wonder why."

His dark gaze burned into her again. "It is complicated," he gritted. "Why? What do you know of him?"

Grace lifted her chin. "Everything that matters."

"*Everything.*" He echoed the word dubiously. "If you believe that, then you are naïve, Mademoiselle Gauthier."

"There are some things worse than naïveté," she returned, drawing up her courage. "Indeed, Lord Ruthveyn, perhaps we've had rather enough conversation. It does truly seem as if Rance is gone, so there can be little reason for me to remain."

"Just come with me," he said in a voice that brooked no opposition.

She would have to be a fool to go with him anywhere, this man of whom she knew nothing and who already frightened her. The words *dark* and *dangerous* seem to have been minted just for him. But, inexplicably, Grace found herself following him up the steps and down a short passageway. Perhaps because she had no better option. Or because he professed to be Rance's friend. Scant hope indeed, but it was all she had.

A few steps farther on, Lord Ruthveyn pushed open a door. After a deep breath, Grace stepped inside and found herself in what appeared to be a small library or study, the walls of which were packed carpet to crown with massive, gilt-titled books, many cracked with age. The room smelled pleasantly of old leather, beeswax, and men.

"The club's private study," said Ruthveyn, motioning toward a pair of sofas that faced one another before the hearth. "Pray take a seat while I send for refreshments."

Grace did not bother to protest. "Are not all the rooms at a gentlemen's club private?" she asked when he returned. "Mightn't your members take exception to my being here?"

Lord Ruthveyn settled himself on one of the leather sofas, keeping the light of the window to his back— deliberately, she thought. He stretched a taut, well-muscled arm across the ridge of the sofa, then crossed one knee languidly over the other in a posture that with any other man might have looked effeminate but on him looked faintly intimidating.

Ruthveyn's dark gaze again caught hers, and Grace felt suddenly as if he were trying to see straight to the depths of her soul. It was a chilling thought. And a fanciful one, too. What had she said to set him on guard so?

"What, precisely, do you know of this house, ma'am?" he finally asked.

Grace shrugged. "Nothing save the address, to be honest."

"It is not, strictly speaking, a club," he said. "It is a sort of society."

"A society?"

"An organization of men who share similar . . . well, let us call them intellectual pursuits."

"What sort of men?" she asked warily.

"People who have traveled the world, primarily," he said, waving a languid hand. "Adventurers. Diplomats. And yes, mercenaries, like Rance Welham."

"When my father's end drew near, Rance wrote to us in France," said Grace. "How he got a letter out of prison, I cannot say. But it was almost as if . . . well, as if he somehow sensed Papa was failing. And he suggested that should ever I need his help, I might call here. And that is all I know."

"So you have not seen him?" Ruthveyn snapped out the question like a whip.

Grace drew back. "Not since he was captured in Algiers," she said.

"Yes," said Ruthveyn tightly. "I was with him in Algiers. I followed him back here."

"Oh," said Grace softly. "We were frightfully worried for him. But Papa soon fell ill, and I took him to Paris. I have been in London less than a year myself."

"Why?" he asked. "If not to see Welham, why did you come?"

"To take employment." She was growing weary of his high-handed questions and hard, glittering eyes. "Really, my lord, what did you imagine? That I followed him? That there was something between us?"

It was his turn to look away. "You are a beautiful woman, Mademoiselle Gauthier," said Ruthveyn. "And Lazonby was never able to resist . . . well, much of anything he desired."

"But I have *always* been able to resist a rogue," she said waspishly. "And that's precisely what Rance is—a fine soldier and a good friend, yes—but a rogue all the same."

"I merely wished to be certain," said Ruthveyn.

"Why?" she demanded.

He looked at her and crooked one impossibly black eyebrow. "Let it go, Mademoiselle Gauthier." Again, he waved a languid, graceful hand. "Querulousness becomes neither of us. Now, what sort of employment, ma'am? Did Gauthier not provide for you?"

Grace drew herself up an inch. "That's hardly your business, either," she said testily. "But yes, my father did provide for me. I am not wealthy—barely comfortable, I daresay, by your standards—but nor do I believe in idleness. It pleases me to work, and I have been the last several months in the employ of Mr. Ethan Holding of Crane and Holding Shipbuilders."

Ruthveyn seemed to stiffen. "Crane and Holding," he murmured. "The largest shipbuilder to the British Navy. They've yards in Liverpool and Rotherhithe."

"And Chatham," Grace added. "Ethan—Mr. Holding—recently forced out a competitor." She dropped her chin and stared at the floor. "I am—or was—governess to his stepdaughters, Eliza and Anne. Their mother died in a tragic accident last year."

A long silence held sway over the room, and through the row of open windows, Grace could hear the clatter of carriages and carts in distant St. James's Street. In the lane below, someone was sweeping a doorstep, and farther along, a doorman was calling out to a passing hansom. And all the while, Ruthveyn was looking at her with his cold black gaze.

"The *Morning Chronicle* reported Holding's death this morning," he finally said. "It was suggested someone slit his throat."

And just like that, Grace felt the loss well up anew, choking off her breath. *Suggested?* There had been nothing so vague about it. Ethan's death had been swift and horrid and real, and his throat most definitely slit.

She fell forward a little, one arm wrapping round her abdomen. She felt suddenly clammy with nausea, the whole of that night rushing back to the forefront of her memory. Good God, had it only been little more than a day ago? She could still see Ethan there, gurgling upon the floor, his fingers clawing into the carpet as if he might drag himself away.

She needed to go. This man—this peer of the realm—could not help her find Rance. He was gone. There was no help for her here. Worse, she had not missed the uniformed policemen posted at either end of the square this morning, nor the fact that one of them had followed her all the way down to St. James's. And suddenly it occurred to her—how ever was she to explain her presence here? And she would have to. It would not take the police long to retrace her connection to the notorious murderer, Rance Welham. That thought was becoming acutely clear to her now.

What a fool she was! Grace dug her fingers into the arms of her chair and attempted to rise, but even the ability to command her muscles had seemingly abandoned her.

"Mademoiselle Gauthier?" Lord Ruthveyn's voice came as if from a distance.

"Mademoiselle?" The voice was sharper this time.

"*Oui?*" Grace managed to release her death grip on the chair. "Yes, I beg your pardon."

"What is your involvement in Mr. Holding's death?"

Somehow she forced her gaze to his. "My . . . involvement?"

"Is Holding's murder the reason for your visit here today?" His eyes flashed like black diamonds. "Were you there? Have you been questioned? Are you a suspect?"

"Yes," she cried, finally jerking from her seat. "And yes, and yes, and yes to all your vile questions! I very much fear I *am* a suspect. I do not know. No one will tell me. I have been shut out of the house. Forbidden the children. A policeman is following me, for God's sake. So yes, my lord. I think we can safely say I'm up to my neck in it."

Panic surging, Grace lifted her skirts and rushed for the door. But Ruthveyn was so fast, she never saw him move. Grace slammed against him, chest to chest, and felt something inside her give way. He caught her shoulders surely in his elegant hands, and Grace sagged into him, all her strength and will dissolving on a single, choking sob.

Then Ruthveyn did the strangest thing. He enveloped her in his arms, gingerly at first, as if he'd never held another human being. As if she were blown from spun glass and might shatter at the merest touch. For an instant, he held her thus, then suddenly his arms went fully around her, warm and incredibly solid, holding her with all his strength.

"My dear girl," he murmured, his breath warm against her temple. "All cannot quite be lost."

Such tenderness—and from a man who looked anything but tender—was almost too much for Grace. She bit back another sob, knowing that the deluge was but barely subdued. "Oh, sir, you cannot know what I have lost," she managed. "But you . . . you are kind. And I thank you for that."

"*Kind*," the marquess echoed, as if the word had never before been applied to him.

Somehow, Grace set the heels of her hands to his shoulders and pushed herself away. He let her go, his face still unreadable. But the loss of his warmth was almost painful, like the stripping away of something as emotional as it was physical.

The timing, however, was fortuitous, for just then the door flew open, and a manservant appeared, rolling in a mahogany cart that held a tea service and three small platters. She turned to face the window, blinking back tears as the tea was set out.

"You must stay, Mademoiselle Gauthier," Ruthveyn ordered amidst the clacking of porcelain and silver. "I insist you eat, and tell me what, precisely, you wanted of Sergeant Welham—or Lord Lazonby, I should say."

Five minutes later, Grace found herself urged back

into her seat, her bloodless hands warmed by a cup of tea strong enough to peel paint. She lifted it, sipping almost gratefully, as Lord Ruthveyn filled her plate with bits of food she would never eat. It was a ridiculously early hour for tea, but he did not look like a man who much cared about convention.

The china, Grace noticed dispassionately, was of the thinnest porcelain imaginable, while the tea service was of heavy chased silver that bore the same odd crest she'd seen etched into the house's pediment. Indeed, the house and its every appointment spoke of quiet, well-heeled masculinity. Whatever the St. James Society was, its members apparently wanted for nothing. Grace found it hard to reconcile such opulence with the gruff, hard-bitten soldier she'd known as Rance Welham.

Lord Ruthveyn flicked an appraising gaze up at her, severing Grace's musings.

"We have got off to a rather curious start, have we not, *mademoiselle*?" he murmured as he pushed a lemon biscuit onto her plate with a pair of elaborate silver tongs. "What with Lazonby away, and you stuck with me. And then there was my appalling loss of temper downstairs."

"I'm not sure I blame you." Grace took her plate, grateful for the mundane conversation that was designed, she knew, to put her at ease. "That frightful young man—what was his name?"

"Coldwater," said Ruthveyn. "He has become rather a thorn in our side, for he keeps dredging up Lord Lazonby's old murder case and airing it again in the press. But I will deal with Coldwater. Now pray be so kind as to explain what you wished of Lazonby."

Grace set her teacup down. "Why?"

He looked at her pointedly. "So that I might help you."

"But why should you?" Grace felt her brows draw together. "You are under no obligation to me. You never met me before in your life."

For a moment, he hesitated as if measuring his words. "Perhaps it is fated, Mademoiselle Gauthier," he finally answered. "Fate, after all, has brought you here today."

"I believe one makes one's own fate, Lord Ruthveyn," she returned. "You owe me nothing."

"And Lazonby does?"

"He seemed to think so," she returned.

"And is not my brother's debt my own?" said Ruthveyn. "Lazonby would do the same for me, and has. So I ask you again, Mademoiselle Gauthier—what was it you wished him to do?"

Grace opened her mouth, but nothing came out. "I am not perfectly sure," she finally confessed. "I just thought that . . . that he might advise me. After all, who better to do so? Rance was unjustly accused of murder. Indeed, he had to flee his own country because of it and sell himself as a soldier of fortune. But at last he has prevailed. He has been cleared of all wrongdoing."

"In Her Majesty's courts, perhaps," Lord Ruthveyn interjected. "But in the court of public opinion? That is less certain."

"I don't give a tuppence about the court of public opinion," said Grace.

"Alas, my dear, this is England." He cut her a strange glance. "I very much fear you *should* care."

"Well, I don't!" she said sharply. "Really, I cannot *think* why I ever came back here to begin with! My English relations are of no help, the police see only a suspicious Frenchwoman—the French are always suspicious, you know—and now my fiancé is dead. There is little else to care about, sir, save my father's good name. And that is all I shall fight for."

Lord Ruthveyn's black eyes hardened. "Your fiancé?"

Grace looked down and took up her teacup again, but her hand shook, and it chattered ominously on the saucer. "Yes, Mr. Holding and I . . . we were secretly betrothed."

"Secretly?" Ruthveyn's voice was sharp. "How secretly?"

"Not terribly." Grace took a fortifying sip of the strong, black tea. "His sister, Fenella Crane, knew. His late wife's family had been told. Officially, however, we were waiting out his year of mourning—but we did tell the girls." Suddenly, she felt her face crumple. "And they were *so happy*! I was so afraid they would not be. That it was too soon. But they—they were—*so happy . . .*"

She had not realized she was crying until Ruthveyn slid onto the sofa beside her and produced a handkerchief. "Oh!" she whispered, awkwardly putting down the cup. She dried her eyes and blew her nose. "Oh, you must think me a frightful watering pot!"

"What I think, Mademoiselle Gauthier," he murmured, "is that you are a young lady who has seen much tragedy. And in too short a space of time."

Embarrassed, Grace turned away. There was something about Lord Ruthveyn that was simply . . . too intimate to be borne. But to her shock, he set his hand to her face, cupped his long, incredibly warm fingers round her cheek, and gently turned her face back to his.

And then the strangest thing happened. It was as if the heat of his touch seeped into her, through her jaw and up into the muscles of her face, until there was a flood of warmth through her body that felt something like the sizzle of nearby lightning, and yet nothing like that at all.

It felt as though Grace had turned her face to the brightest sun imaginable, and drawn from it not just warmth, but something that felt vaguely like peace. Grace held herself perfectly still to it and let the hush fall all around them. The noise from the street below, the faint autumn breeze from the window, even the sound of her own breathing; all of it faded away, but for how long, she could not have said.

When she returned to herself, Grace heard a voice saying, "Open your eyes."

She tried to remember whose voice it was.

"Look at me, Mademoiselle Gauthier."

She had not realized her eyes were closed. "W-Why?"

"Because I wish to see your eyes," Lord Ruthveyn murmured. "They are, after all, the window to one's soul, are they not?"

At that, her gaze flew to his, almost against her will. But once their eyes met, Grace forced away the strange lethargy. She had nothing to hide. She would not be afraid of this man and his black, glittering gaze. And so she watched him as intently as he watched her. They sat so close, Ruthveyn had one hard thigh pressed to hers. His heat and scent swirled in the air—a mélange of exotic spices and smoke and raw, unadulterated male.

Grace drew it in, the strange sense of calm and the otherworldly silence still pervasive. A moment passed, a heartbeat in time in which she felt utterly alone with Ruthveyn, as though nothing beyond this room and this moment existed.

And then his hand fell from her face.

As if nothing unusual had occurred, he turned his attention to the tea table, plucked one of the lemon biscuits from her plate, and set it to her lips.

"Eat," he murmured.

"Why?"

"You have lost all your color again," he said.

As if mesmerized, Grace found herself doing as he bid,

biting off half and chewing it slowly. It was as if her taste buds had been jolted to sudden awareness. The morsel was tart as a slice of raw lemon, yet sweet and buttery. A crumb almost fell, and unthinkingly, Grace caught it with her tongue on a low sound of appreciation.

Ruthveyn's eyes narrowed approvingly. "Our chef's special recipe," he murmured. "Monsieur Belkadi raked all of Paris for him—then had his sister completely retrain the poor devil. Wait until you taste his saffron couscous."

"Couscous?" Grace took the second half with her fingers and finished it off. "Truly? Oh, I shall be his slave."

"I shall let him know," said Ruthveyn. "Now a sandwich."

"I . . . I am not hungry."

"You are," he commanded. "You are starving. You need the clarity of mind that food will bring."

It seemed a strange thing to say. But Grace ate a bite of the tiny sandwich he presented, almost without considering how odd it was to be fed by a man she'd just met—or any man at all, come to that.

The sandwich held a thin slice of cucumber atop a pink pâté, which tasted of salmon and lemon and dill all at once, then finished with the taste of purest cream. "My heavens," she said after swallowing. "I wonder any of you can waddle up the steps."

Ruthveyn said no more but simply handed her the plate, then refilled her tea, slowly stirring in a dollop of milk just as she liked it. She finished off every bite, working her way round in a meticulous, clockwise fashion until, to her shock, the plate was empty.

"Excellent," he said again, setting the plate away.

He returned to the opposite sofa, leaving her feeling oddly bereft and a little cold. He occupied himself for a moment freshening his own tea, which, Grace noticed, he drank with nothing in it. For no reason in particular, she made a mental note of that fact.

After a time, Ruthveyn set his cup away, then resumed his almost feline posture on the sofa. "Your color has returned again," he said calmly. "So let us return to the pressing business at hand, mademoiselle, and to my questions."

Grace was beyond quibbling with him. "Very well," she said on a sigh. "What do you wish to know?"

Some nameless emotion sketched across his face, so swift and so vague she might have imagined it.

"I wish to know," he said quietly, "if you loved Ethan Holding."

Grace looked at him in surprise. "Do you indeed?" she asked. "Does it matter?"

He lifted one shoulder a fraction. "Perhaps I am merely curious," he answered. "But one might argue that a crime of passion looks far less likely when there is . . . well, little passion."

She gave a withering smile. "How cruelly practical you are, Lord Ruthveyn," she said. "No, I did not love him. Not in the way you mean. But I had a deep respect for him. And while some might have believed him hard, I knew him to be a fair man and a good father."

"I see," said Ruthveyn. "And who is the Crane in Crane and Holding? Surely not the sister?"

"Oh, heavens no!" Grace tried to relax against the sofa. "Ethan's mother believed women had no head for business. It is his stepcousin, Josiah Crane."

"A cousin?" said Ruthveyn. "That seems an odd arrangement."

"The business was begun by the Crane family," Grace explained. "Ethan's mother was a widow who had inherited Holding Shipyards, a failing business. She married one of the Crane heirs when Ethan was small, and he accepted Ethan as a son. When his mother died some years after Mr. Crane, Ethan inherited the controlling interest."

"Now that is what I call a marriage of convenience," said Ruthveyn. "And the noncontrolling interest?"

"Mr. Crane left 40 percent to his nephew, Josiah Crane, in his will."

Ruthveyn's mouth lifted at one corner. "I wonder how Josiah Crane felt about that?"

"Bittersweet but grateful, I daresay," said Grace. "Josiah's father was the elder of the Crane brothers, but he proved to be a wastrel and had to sell his share of the family business to his younger brother. For a time, Josiah was just a junior clerk, working for his uncle. But there, that was a long time ago. It is old history now."

Ruthveyn set his head to one side and looked at her assessingly for a moment. "Yet what is time, Mademoiselle Gauthier, save an invention of man?" he finally said, his voice pensive. "Time can span into infinity. On the other hand, sometimes it is no more than a platitude—*Time heals all wounds!*—is that not what the English say? But envy—oh, trust me, mademoiselle. Envy can be eternal."

Grace managed to smile. "You are a far more esoteric thinker, Lord Ruthveyn, than I could ever hope to be," she answered. "And I must hope, for my own sake, that time does indeed heal all wounds."

"Sometimes, Mademoiselle Gauthier, it does not," he said quietly. Then Ruthveyn seemed to stir from some sort of reverie. "And so Josiah Crane's father sold his birthright, did he?" he murmured. "He was dashed lucky to get it back again."

"Forty percent," Grace reminded him. "Not the original fifty."

"Ah, so the control Mrs. Holding wielded during her widowhood was significant."

"I gather she wielded nothing more significant than a darning needle," Grace replied. "Ethan's mother believed a lady's place was in the home. From what Fenella says, trustees managed everything until Ethan and Josiah were experienced enough to go it alone."

"Fascinating," Ruthveyn murmured. "How did Ethan Holding get on with his minority partner?"

"Quite well," said Grace. "They argued at times, as strong men will. But on the whole, they were close."

"Who handled the money?"

"Josiah Crane," Grace answered. "He had the head for numbers. He and Fenella. I think it must be a Crane family trait. Ethan is—*was*—the public face of Crane and Holding. People liked him. They trusted him."

"Certainly Her Majesty's government trusted him."

"Yes," said Grace simply. "There had been talk, even, of a knighthood."

"Indeed?" murmured Ruthveyn. "So you might have become Lady Holding?"

Grace laughed a little bitterly. "As if that would matter to me," she said. "There are titles aplenty in my late mother's family, and none of them the better off for it. One cannot eat a title or live in it. A title cannot keep one warm at night. A title is just for show—your pardon, my lord."

"No pardon needed," said Ruthveyn.

Grace felt embarrassment warm her face. "I daresay you were born to the purple," she murmured, "and that the marquessate has been in your family since Domesday."

"No, just a minor title, I'm afraid," he replied. "My forbearers, however, managed to acquire quite an assemblage of titles and honors, by hook or by crook, or by service to the Crown—ah, but I become redundant, do I not?"

"And the marquessate?"

He lifted one wide shoulder. "My doing, I suppose."

"Ah," said Grace. "More service to the Crown?"

Something dark sketched across Ruthveyn's face. "Is that not the usual way?" he countered. "Yes. For service to Her Majesty."

Just then, a clock somewhere in the depths of the house tolled the hour. Grace's eyes widened in horror. "Oh!" she said. "That cannot be the time!"

Ruthveyn extracted a gold pocket watch from his waistcoat. "I fear it is," he said. "Have you another errand?"

"I don't know," said Grace pensively. "I wanted to ask Rance . . . well, if he thought I needed a barrister. But the thought horrifies me."

Ruthveyn tucked the timepiece away. "You have been accused of no crime as yet," he said calmly. "Go about your business. Behave as any innocent person would. Lazonby retained the best counsel in London—a member here, as it happens. Until I can reach Lazonby, you may rely upon his counsel to protect your interests."

To protect your interests . . .

But what were her interests? What was left to her? The quiet, inconsequential existence she had managed to carve for herself since her father's death had been drained of all hope as surely as had Ethan's. And now the outside world and all its ugliness was pressing down upon her again.

"I rather doubt, sir, that I can afford the best counsel in London," she said quietly.

"You will leave that in my hands for now," he said. It was a statement, not an offer.

She felt Lord Ruthveyn's gaze still and steady upon her, and a sudden chill crept down her spine. Grace wanted to flee from this dark, imposing man and his piercing eyes—yet in the same breath, she sensed the swirl of his darkness all around her, almost cloaking her in its protection. He was offering her his help. Moreover, he was not a man to be lied to, or trifled with. She knew it instinctively.

And he was all she had. She swallowed hard, and lifted her eyes to his. "I accept your kind offer, sir," she said. "What is his name?"

"Sir Greville St. Giles," said Ruthveyn. "He keeps chambers in the Inner Temple, but you may send word to me here should it prove necessary. If the police dare to arrest you—and I think they will not—you will tell them St. Giles represents you. Following that, you will say *not one word further.* Not under any circumstance. I shall have you released before the day is out, I do assure you."

Grace believed him. He looked like a man who might go to the ends of the earth—and perhaps even into the black pit of hell beyond—merely to prove a point.

"Thank you," she said again. Then she came swiftly to her feet. "And now I really must go. I have intruded upon your kindness too long."

Ruthveyn rose, for she'd left him with little choice. But at the door, he hesitated, blocking it with the broad width of his shoulders. "I do have one last question, if I may?"

She looked up at him. "Yes?"

Ruthveyn looked down his hawkish nose at her. "Mademoiselle Gauthier, did you by any chance *kill* Ethan Holding?"

Grace's mouth fell open. "No!" she finally managed. "I—why—how can you even think me capable of it!"

"We are all of us capable of it, *mademoiselle,*" he said coolly. "Such is the nature of man. But I accept your answer. So . . . if not you, who?"

She looked at him with unvarnished frustration. "Why, some sort of . . . of thief, of course! The house was filled with artwork and silver. No one wished Ethan dead."

"On that point I beg to differ," said Lord Ruthveyn. "I

know nothing of him, and already I can think of several people who might have done so. Who found the body?"

Grace's eyes widened. "I did."

Ruthveyn drew back a fraction. "In the middle of the night?"

Again, Grace was struck by how dangerous the man looked. How near he stood. For a moment, it was as if all the air had been sucked from the room, and she could feel the heat of his gaze running down her face to her throat and beyond.

"It wasn't the middle of the night," she managed. "It was half past twelve."

"Explain."

"Josiah Crane had lent me a book of poetry at dinner," she replied, "and I had declared my intent to stay up and finish it. Ethan slipped a note under my door, asking that if I was still awake, would I kindly come to his study."

"Indeed?" Ruthveyn's voice was a low rumble. "Did he often do that sort of thing?"

"No, never," said Grace, her brows drawing together. "And it *was* a little oddly worded."

"In what way?"

Her frown deepened. "He called me *Miss Gauthier*," she said. "And he seemed to think he owed me an apology for something."

"What did he usually call you?"

"Grace, when we were alone," she said. "After our betrothal, I mean. And when he wrote during his travels— yes, usually Grace, unless he enclosed the letter with someone else's."

"And what, pray, had Holding done to owe you an apology?"

Grace lifted her shoulders weakly. "That's just it," she said. "I cannot think. He was a little cross at dinner, for he was tired. He'd just returned from a fortnight at the Liverpool yards. He and Josiah talked mostly of business, and I . . . I, well, I did not attend, honestly."

Ruthveyn seemed to consider this. "Did you often dine with the family?"

Grace looked away. "For dinner, yes. I think Ethan was overly impressed that I was the granddaughter of an earl," she confessed. "And pleased his sister had befriended me."

"He hoped your polish might rub off?"

Grace gave a withering laugh. "Silly, isn't it, when I'd spent much of my life in military outposts? But merchant families oftentimes feel inferior to anyone with a drop of blue in their blood. And Ethan was a little"— here she smiled wistfully—"well, he used to say he would always have the air of tar and timber about him. But I think he had hoped Fenella might marry well. She had a huge marriage portion, but their social circle was not large."

"And Josiah Crane?" said Ruthveyn. "Did he dine there often?"

"Once or twice a week." She paused a moment. "When they were young, I think Ethan expected Josiah and Fenella would make a match of it, but . . . well, nothing happened."

Ruthveyn pondered it. "Very well," he said at last. "So you went at once to Holding's study when the note appeared under your door?"

Grace bit her lip, and shook her head. "No, fool that I am," she whispered. "Instead, I pinned up my hair and drew on my wrapper—I was worried about propriety, of all things!—and it was a fatal ten minutes. Oh, God! I wish now I'd not waited an instant!"

"Mademoiselle Gauthier, I am sorry," said Ruthveyn.

"But I do not think it would have mattered. Tell me, what did you do once you found Holding?"

"I screamed!" she declared. "And then I . . . I tried to help him. But there was no helping him. And then some of the servants came. Someone went to fetch a constable. After that . . . well, I do not quite recall the order of things. But there were a great many people and questions. They kept all of us apart from one another. And now I think . . . yes, I think from the very first they suspected me."

"Most regrettable," Ruthveyn remarked. "Were any locks broken? Any windows?"

Slowly, she shook her head. "No one mentioned any," she whispered. "But there *must* have been. Mustn't there? Trenton—the butler—locks everything up without fail. The house is a fortress—to keep the children safe, Ethan always said."

"And the note that was slipped under your door?"

Again, Grace shook her head. "I must have dropped it in Ethan's study," she admitted. "I daresay the police have it now."

"I daresay they do," said Ruthveyn dryly. "And you were not allowed free in the house again?"

"Almost no one was," said Grace. "Even Fenella went home with Mrs. Lester. She said she couldn't bear to stay there until the killer was caught."

"And who, pray, is Mrs. Lester?"

"Ethan's first wife's sister," said Grace. "She lives not far from Rotherhithe—which is where Eliza and Anne have gone." It was taking all her will not to burst into tears again. "And I daresay . . . well, I daresay that is where they shall stay now, isn't it? That is what Mrs. Lester has always wished."

"You do not like her?"

Grace hesitated. "I do not know her well," she confessed. "She quite dotes on the girls. But it was her late sister's wish the girls remain with Ethan, in the only home they had ever known. Mrs. Lester has five boys of her own, so perhaps it was thought they would be rambunctious? I do not know. I know only that Ethan had a good father, so he took such duties seriously."

"Miss Crane will not keep the children?"

She shook her head. "An unmarried woman with no real blood claim?" Grace mused. "No, I imagine the girls will go to their mother's side now. Mr. Lester is very rich—the family owns timber warehouses, I think—and he spoils his wife something frightful. Fenella will wish to keep the peace. And as to what I think"—here her voice broke wretchedly—"well, that no longer matters, does it?"

Ruthveyn set his head to one side in that assessing way of his. "You are thinking that Mr. Holding's death has taken the children away from you forever," he said, "when you were just growing accustomed to the notion of being a mother. Indeed, your whole life has turned upside down."

Grace managed a watery smile. "I loved the girls, you know," she said. "But Mrs. Lester does, too. She has a houseful of servants and toys, and has always yearned for daughters. Once this is over . . . well, I shall ask permission to visit. I shall hope for the best."

For the first time, his dark eyes seemed to soften. "I had a stepmother myself," he said solemnly, "though I was nearly grown. But Pamela was kind—too kind, really— and much loved. You have my sympathy."

"Thank you."

He turned, then hesitated for a moment, his hand upon the doorknob. "Where may I find you, Mademoiselle Gauthier, after today?"

"Find me?" she asked. "Find me for what?"

The softness in his eyes had vanished. "Should something come up."

For an instant, Grace hesitated. But hesitating would make matters no better. For now, she was stuck. "I am at my aunt's house in Manchester Square," she answered. "Lady Abigail Hythe."

"You look none too happy about that."

Grace's mouth twisted wryly. "One must be grateful for a roof over one's head—or so I am often told."

"Ah, like that, is it?"

She shrugged and let it go.

Lord Ruthveyn pulled open the door and offered his arm. "So you were followed here by one of Metropolitan's finest, were you?"

Grace managed a weak laugh. "Yes, and by now he must be wondering what's become of me."

Lord Ruthveyn glanced down at her. "Let's keep him wondering, shall we?" he murmured, starting down the wide, white staircase. "Do you know Spenser House? There is a narrow little passageway just round the corner from it that gives onto Green Park."

"A *secret* passageway?" Grace smiled.

Ruthveyn shrugged. "An often-overlooked passageway," he clarified. "Let me take you through the gardens and show you the back way out. Perhaps you can enjoy a leisurely stroll home in solitude."

They had reached the bottom of the wide staircase. The dark young man still stood at the tall counter, running a finely manicured finger down one page of an open ledger.

"Belkadi," said Ruthveyn.

"Yes?" The man lifted his eyes.

"Have you seen Pinkie Ringgold?"

"Across the street," he answered absently. "Playing doorman for Quartermaine's hell."

They could only mean Ned Quartermaine, thought Grace. Everyone knew of him; he ran the wickedest, most exclusive—and the most discreet—gaming salon in all London. It was so discreet, Grace had apparently walked right past it, unaware.

"Go over there," said Ruthveyn, "and start a row with Pinkie."

Belkadi shut the ledger. "Very well," he said. "Do you wish anything broken? Bleeding?"

"No, we've a constable dawdling about," said Ruthveyn. "Just put the fear of God in him and create a distraction while I show Mademoiselle Gauthier out the back."

Belkadi bowed and started for the door.

"And drag Pinkie's carcass over here when you're done," Ruthveyn added as they turned down the narrow back stairs. "I'll fetch Bessett. I should like the four of us to have a word."

Eyes wide as saucers, Grace glanced over her shoulder as Belkadi vanished out the front door.

Ruthveyn patted her hand where it lay lightly on his coat sleeve. "There, Mademoiselle Gauthier, you see? Belkadi will feign a little danger to distract the police."

Grace cut a dubious glance up at him. The only danger in St. James's, she had begun to suspect, had her fingers wrapped round his arm.

And quite possibly, her life in his hands.

CHAPTER 3

Pinkie Pays a Social Call

*W*omen, thought Lord Ruthveyn, *have ever been the bane of my existence.*

And one needed no gift of foresight to know that this one would be no different.

Try as he might to avoid the fairer sex—avoid them, that was to say, even more assiduously than he avoided the rest of the human race—he was nonetheless a man, with a man's appetites. And, apparently, a man's wish for intrigue. Perhaps there were even a few shreds of chivalry left in him.

Whatever it was that drove him, it took Ruthveyn all of three minutes to drag his friend Bessett from the coffee room and brief him regarding his curious encounter with Mademoiselle Gauthier. It took another five, however, to justify his decision.

They stood near the top of the marble staircase, Lord Bessett scrubbing a pensive hand round his chin. His eyes, as usual, were wary. "You feel strongly we should take this on, I collect," he mused. "I confess, I cannot see why the *Fraternitas* has any business in it. Even if she did know Lazonby in Algiers, the woman is not one of us."

"You don't know that."

A knowing smile tugged at Bessett's mouth. "Oh, but you do," he said. "And if she were, you would have said so already."

Ruthveyn's expression tightened. "I'm not sure of anything here."

"How much does she know about Lazonby?" Bessett dropped his voice. "Did you tell her where he was?"

"Don't be absurd," he replied. "I told her he had been called home, which, insofar as it goes, is perfectly true. Now do you mean to help me or not? Until we hear from Lazonby, this is what I mean to do."

Lord Bessett threw his arms over his chest, and appraised Ruthveyn through narrow eyes. "Now why is it, old chap, I get the feeling the lady is comely?" he murmured. "Then again, feminine pulchritude never held much sway with you, did it? You were always drawn to inner beauty."

Suddenly, there was the sound of the downstairs door crashing inward, followed by a shuddering thump, a couple of thuds, then a string of curses that colored the air blue.

"That will be old Pinkie Ring," said Ruthveyn on a sigh. He jerked open the door to the coffee room. "What's it to be, Geoff?"

Bessett inclined his head almost regally. "It is to be exactly as you wish, Lord Baphomet. Are you not our Prince of Darkness? And we your lowly Templar masons?"

Ruthveyn jerked his head at the door he held wide. "You've been reading too much medieval rubbish again," he snapped. "Get in, and try to keep those two from killing one another."

It was no easy task.

In the end, they were compelled to put a large table between Belkadi and his quarry, then send for a bottle of strong sherry, though the afternoon was but barely upon them.

"I didn't say noffik, you bleedin' savage!" Pinkie Ringgold swore, lunging across the table at Belkadi.

"Whoa!" Bessett leapt up, grabbed Pinkie, and hauled him back toward his chair.

"Fucking Moorish bastard!" Pinkie jerked against Bessett's grip, his visage swollen red with rage.

Belkadi sat, unmoved. "Terribly sorry, old boy," he said with an air of utter boredom. "I could have sworn you insulted the cut of my coat."

"The cut of your coat, eh?" Lord Bessett let his gaze drift over Pinkie's rumpled brown affair with its mismatched buttons. "A misunderstanding, I daresay. Gentlemen, we are neighbors—occasionally even business associates. Let this one go, shall we?"

"But of course," said Belkadi.

Pinkie shrugged off Bessett's grip, rolled his shoulders restlessly, then sat, snatching up the slab of raw beef one of Belkadi's minions had just set down.

Belkadi regarded him dispassionately as Pinkie slapped the beefsteak to his right eye. "Send me the bill, Ringgold, for your ruined cravat," he said.

"I shall see to that." Ruthveyn spoke for the first time. He extracted his purse and peeled off a pile of banknotes, then pushed them across the table to Pinkie. "Here. This should take care of it."

Pinkie's left eye narrowed to a squint. "Oh, aye, you rich bastards fink you can buy ol' Pinkie orf anytime yer please," he said. "That pile'd fetch threescore o' fine cambric stranglers. What d' ye really want, Ruthveyn?"

Ruthveyn smiled faintly. "Let me be blunt, then."

"Yer ain't never been known for yer pretty conversation," Pinkie returned.

Ruthveyn and Bessett exchanged glances. "There was a murder done Wednesday night in Belgravia," said Ruthveyn, tapping the tip of one finger pensively on the tabletop. "I want to know the word round Town."

Still gripping the beef, Pinkie grunted. "Cove by name o' Holding," he said, eyeing Ruthveyn warily. "And 'e's dead, ain't 'e? I'd say that's the word."

Ruthveyn peeled off another banknote. "I want to know if it was robbery," he said, tossing it onto the pile with two fingers. "I want to know if a window or door was damaged. I want to know if anything was stolen. And I want the fence's name. In short, Pinkie, I want to know *everything* the underworld knows. Do I make myself plain?"

The doorman licked his lips, hesitated, then gave half a head shake. "Don't waste the rest o' yer blunt, gov," he said, plucking a banknote from the pile. "This tenner'll do for me trouble today."

"What are you suggesting?" Ruthveyn's voice was dangerously soft.

Pinkie's squint narrowed. "That it weren't no cracksman wot done Holding. That's Johnnie Rucker's turf. 'E'd know if somefink got pinched. 'E'd make it 'is business ter know—an' 'e'd tell *me*."

"And he did not?"

"Said 'e didn't know noffink about it," Pinkie said confidently. "Besides, Johnnie don't tol'rate that sort o' violence. Rumor is one o' the servants did 'im in."

"*Which* one of the servants?" Bessett interjected.

Pinkie shrugged. "The governess, per'aps," he said. "Fancied 'erself in love wiv Holding—an' a Frog, too, for all that." Here he eyed Belkadi nastily. "Temperamental creatures, them Frogs, I always 'eard."

Belkadi merely smiled. "Pick a slur, Ringgold, and stick to it, won't you?"

Ruthveyn ignored him and pushed the pile of banknotes back at Pinkie. "Make sure of all this," he gritted. "Talk to Quartermaine, and see what he can discover. Talk to Rucker again. Spread the word to every fence in London. Whatever was stolen, I'll pay twice what it is worth, no questions asked."

"Weren't noffink stole," Pinkie warned.

"So you say."

After a moment's hesitation, Pinkie slapped the beef-steak back on the plate with a clatter, then swept up the money. "It's your blunt, gov'nor," he said, rising.

Ruthveyn extracted his pocket watch. "I'll be at Quartermaine's tonight round eleven," he said, checking it. "You'll have a report for me then." It was not a request.

"Ha!" said Pinkie dubiously. "Come have a toss wiv us, will yer? Quartermaine won't like that a bit."

Ruthveyn flicked a dark gaze up at him. "I do not gamble," he said softly. "Not with money. Tell me, Pinkie, who's been assigned this business down at the Yard?"

At this, Pinkie grinned, peeling back his lips to reveal a set of yellowing canines that would have done a wolf proud. "Now that'd be yer good friend Royden," he said. "Royden Napier. So good luck to you, Ruthveyn."

Then Pinkie stuffed the wad of banknotes into his coat pocket and waddled off toward the door.

Ruthveyn uttered a curse beneath his breath. *Napier.* He might have guessed the murder of a Crown favorite would draw attention from the top. No lowly police sergeant could possibly do justice to the corpse of Ethan Holding.

"Most interesting," murmured Bessett, watching Pinkie go.

Belkadi, too, stood. "If there is nothing else?" he enquired.

"There is something else," said Ruthveyn. "The lady who just left us—Mademoiselle Gauthier. She is the daughter of Commandant Henri Gauthier."

At last, Belkadi looked surprised, a rare occurrence. "Is she indeed?"

A wry smile twisted Ruthveyn's mouth. "So she claims," he confessed. "And she is apparently English on her mother's side."

"Le commandant did have an English wife, long dead," Belkadi acknowledged. "And a daughter, who was said to be beautiful."

"Mademoiselle Gauthier is certainly that," Ruthveyn remarked. "She claims to make her home with an aunt by the name of Hythe in Manchester Square."

"But you do not believe her," said the majordomo pointedly. "And you wish me to confirm what she has said."

"Bloody hell, Adrian!" Bessett jerked to his feet. "Do you mean to suggest that you just put us through our paces for a woman whom you do not even trust?"

Ruthveyn lifted both shoulders. "For once, gentlemen, I do not know what to believe," he answered. "It is a novel experience, to be sure. I daresay the lady is precisely what she claims, but I haven't the time to verify it—so Belkadi will."

On a soft curse, Bessett threw up his hands and walked away. Belkadi gave one of his tight, mocking bows, and followed suit.

Ruthveyn was once more alone at the table.

Just the way he liked it.

"Grace! Grace, is that you?"

The petulant voice rang out as soon as Grace cracked the front door of her aunt's modest Marylebone town house.

"Good afternoon, Aunt Abigail," Grace called.

"To you, perhaps!" came the affected cry. "Not to me!"

Grace shrugged off her cloak and wished fleetingly that she had prolonged her walk home even further and savored her freedom while she had it. But there were only so many shop windows to stroll past and too much weighing on her mind to enjoy them.

Miriam, the second housemaid, hastened in, caught Grace's gaze, and rolled her eyes.

"Police been here," she mouthed, taking Grace's cloak. "Left not ten minutes past. Then her ladyship took a spell."

A spell was servant-speak for one of Aunt Abigail's self-indulgent tirades.

"Oh, dear." Grace tucked her key into her reticule. "Has she had her draught, then?"

Miriam pursed her lips. "Aye, and I mixed it stout, too."

"Good girl." Drawing in a steadying breath, Grace checked her hair and her face in the looking glass over the console, then tucked up a wayward curl. "Here, Miriam, will I do?"

"As well as anything," said the maid evenly. "Nothing's apt to please her today."

The warning was wholly unnecessary. Grace flashed Miriam a brave smile, then hastened down the passageway into the back parlor.

Lady Abigail Hythe lay reclined in all her faded glory

upon her favorite fainting couch, a befeathered fan waving lethargically in the air, her vinaigrette and her ever-present glass of cordial on the little rosewood table beside her.

"Aunt Abigail, are you all right?" Grace hastened to her side.

"Oh, Grace, you *cannot* imagine!" cried Lady Abigail, fanning more frantically. "What a frightful morning we have had! After having murder done practically in your face! Whatever *were* you thinking, to take a place with *such people*?"

She had been thinking, Grace muttered inwardly, *that she was not wanted here.*

Indeed, she had thought to escape. She had had no wish to be a burden to a woman who so clearly preferred her fantasy of grandeur past and her dreams of what might have been over life's sadly shopworn reality. But now Grace was back again, and life with her aunt was more intolerable than ever.

She looked about the lofty chamber with its faded, almost tattered draperies, and furnishings that had been fashionable a hundred years ago. The smell of old money long spent was as heavy in the air as the moldering dust motes that rose from the sagging brocade settee by the windows, and Grace suddenly understood just why her mother had felt compelled to escape it all so long ago.

"Aunt Abigail, they really were quite nice people," she said gently. "And I am sure Mr. Holding had no inkling his murder was imminent, or he would never have inconvenienced you with even the vaguest connection to his household."

At that, Lady Abigail's head twisted toward her. "Oh, you callous, callous girl," she whispered, trembling with outrage. "Go on. Make a mockery of my distress. But you will not think it so amusing when I tell you that we have had the police here today."

Grace clutched her hands in her lap. "I am very sorry, aunt."

"Yes, *the police*!" Lady Abigail spoke over her. "And that spiteful cat Mrs. Pickling saw them from across the street! By now everyone in Manchester Square will know that we have been involved in this vile business. Oh, the indignity of it! And I blame you, Grace. I truly do. And I blame your mother for . . ."

For taking that long-ago trip to Paris. For falling in love with an impecunious Frenchman. For bringing low our entire family. For living in tents and consorting with Spaniards and Arabs and God only knows what else. For dying too young, and suffering not nearly enough . . .

Oh, this last, perhaps, Aunt Abigail never actually said aloud.

She did not need to. And Grace had no need to listen to what she *did* say, so often had she heard her aunt's tirade. So she simply shut her ears to it, stroked Aunt Abigail's withered hand, and reminded herself that her aunt was her mother's only living sibling. That she was old. That she did not really mean what she said.

Grace only hoped that was the case.

"Aunt Abigail, tell me what the police wanted," Grace suggested when the harangue faded away.

"You!" cried Lady Abigail, lifting her head from the divan. "They wanted you, Grace. They seem to imagine you can help them answer questions. Can you credit it? Questions! The vile man had a whole folio full of bits of paper—and was none too pleased to be told you were still out. Indeed, I thought him *suspicious*."

"You thought he was suspicious of me?" asked Grace. "Or you were suspicious of him?"

"Both!" cried Lady Abigail, struggling to sit up. "Oh, dear heaven! The room is still spinning! Fetch me my hartshorn."

Grace found it, then fussed and frittered over the old woman for a time, easing her back down again. Miriam came in to help, refilling Lady Abigail's restorative cordial, this time tipping the brandy bottle over it for the lightest splash.

It was time, Grace realized, to go back to Paris—whether it felt like home or not. She had been born in London, in this very house, and had lived parts of her early childhood in both France and Spain, but never had Grace felt truly settled until Algeria. And her last trip to Paris—to take her father home to die—had been an especially unhappy one.

But an unwed lady was at something of a loss in North Africa, and she had had to go *somewhere*. To belong somewhere. To be either fish or fowl—and Grace had hardly cared which. But now Ethan was dead, and the England of her childhood no longer felt so welcoming.

When the dust had settled, and her aunt's cordial was nearly finished, Grace pulled a chair nearer the chaise. "Now this policeman, Aunt Abigail," she said quietly, "do you recall his name?"

"Oh, heavens no!" She snapped her fingers repeatedly at Miriam. The girl darted off to fetch a footed silver salver still holding an ivory calling card. Which was rather odd. One would not have imagined common policemen to have calling cards.

"Are you quite sure, Aunt Abigail, that he was a policeman?"

"He might as well have been!" Abigail declared.

The wave of fatigue that Lord Ruthveyn had managed

to assuage swamped in around Grace again. Resigned, she took the card.

Royden Napier.

"I fear, Aunt Abigail, that he is not a policeman," she said quietly.

"Well, I did not mean he wore a uniform!" Lady Abigail sniffed, folding her hands together. "I told him to leave those blue-coated creatures in the street. But his attitude—well, I dared not refuse him. So I let him in, though I vow, I paid him little heed."

"I am sorry you did not," said Grace dryly. "You might take some comfort, Aunt Abigail, in knowing that your caller was just a step or two removed from the Home Secretary himself."

"The Home Secretary? Whatever can you mean?"

Grace laid the card back on the salver, facedown. "Mr. Napier," she said softly, "is the assistant commissioner at Scotland Yard."

And just possibly, she inwardly added, *my nemesis.*

CHAPTER 4

A Visit to Belgrave Square

It required no gift of prescience the following day to discover the residence of the late Ethan Holding. The morning's haze was waning a bit, and though all the massive white monoliths facing Belgrave Square looked rather alike, the black-clad mutes in sashes and weepers who materialized from the gloom at the foot of Holding's steps were the only visions the Marquess of Ruthveyn required.

He went up the stairs, his footsteps hollow and disembodied in the fog. With an air of haughty condescension, he produced his card, dropped his title, and soon found himself escorted through a soaring two-story entrance hall made mostly of white marble, and into another vast, opulently furnished chamber called—ironically, one hoped—the small parlor. Ruthveyn looked about in bemusement, finding it all a little nouveau riche for his taste, though the gilt pier glasses between the windows had been obscured by black crepe, the ormolu mantel clock lay silent, and all the draperies were drawn, in deference to the deceased.

"What a remarkable room," he commented.

Halfway out the door, the butler cut him an odd glance. "Mr. Holding himself designed it," he said neutrally, "when he bought the house three years ago."

"I see," Ruthveyn murmured, looking about. "Where, pray, did he live before?"

"At Rotherhithe," said the servant, "in a family home near the shipyards."

"Ah." He could see why a man might wish to relocate. With its dockyards, shipyards, and warehouses, Rotherhithe was, for the most part, a working-class part of town.

Ruthveyn was just in the process of pretending to admire the gilt frieze that encircled what looked like a solid gold ceiling medallion when the echo of voices in the vaulted entrance hall caught his ear. He glanced through the open double doors to see a tall, handsome woman with a pile of dark red hair coming down the lower staircase on the arm of a lanky, balding gentleman. A brace of footmen followed, bearing various portmanteaus and bandboxes between them.

"Have them set everything here, Josiah," she ordered the gentleman, "until the carriage comes back around," she ordered. "I shall be but a moment."

Miss Fenella Crane, who looked to be in her midthirties, swept into the room dressed as if for travel. She had already drawn on her gloves, Ruthveyn was relieved to see, and, as with Mademoiselle Gauthier, wore a black hat and veil. It did not, however, entirely obscure her gaze, and he could feel her curiosity burning through him like molten iron. Curiosity, and something more.

Ruthveyn opened himself quite willingly to it, and felt a certain wariness and anger thrumming through the room—understandable given the very ugly thing that had just happened here. Her eyes, he saw, were rimmed with red as if from crying. He stepped forward and bowed, praying the lady did not think to ask precisely how well he'd known the deceased Mr. Holding.

"Miss Crane, my apologies," he said smoothly. "As your butler warned, I can see you are on your way back out again."

She gave a stiff nod, but did not, thank God, extend her hand. "Yes, I'm sorry," she acknowledged. "I beg your pardon, my lord, but have we met?"

"We have not." His was the sort of face people remembered, he knew.

"I am honored, of course," she went on, sounding something less. "But I'm afraid my cousin Josiah Crane is escorting me back to the Lesters'. We're expected by teatime."

"Then permit me to promptly offer my deepest sympathy, ma'am," he returned. "Your brother was a fine gentleman, and—"

"Stepbrother," she interjected.

"I beg your pardon?"

"Ethan was my stepbrother," she corrected, something catching in her throat. "Though I loved him no less for it."

"Ah," said Ruthveyn. "My apologies."

"None are necessary," she said. "We always laughed at how the different names confused people. Now what, sir, may I do for you before I go? I am staying elsewhere, you see, until this frightful business is settled. Even poor

Ethan's"—here her voice gave—"poor Ethan's corpse cannot be laid out until tomorrow."

"I am so sorry," he said again. "Your butler did explain you'd come merely to collect some things."

"A very few things," she said a little tightly. "The police have been most unaccommodating. They seem to imagine one of us killed poor Ethan."

Ruthveyn lifted one eyebrow. "How appalling."

"Not to mention preposterous," said the lady. "No one here meant Ethan any harm. Indeed, he was beloved by all."

Ruthveyn rather doubted a man became the financial success Ethan Holding had been by being beloved by all, but he refrained from saying so. "You have excellent servants, then?" he asked. "You trust them?"

"They are like family to me," said Miss Crane.

"I am pleased to hear it," Ruthveyn remarked.

"I can't think why," said Miss Crane with a wan smile, "when we just met."

"One of your staff has been referred to me as a possible employee," he explained. "A Miss Grace Gauthier who, I believe, was in your family's employ until quite recently?"

"Grace?" Miss Crane's voice softened, her eyebrows drawing into a fretful knot. "Oh, dear. I never thought . . ."

"That she might be leaving you?" he supplied. "I have two nephews, you see—hellions, the both of them—and I need someone quite competent."

Miss Crane hesitated, the air thrumming with uncertainty. "Well, she is excellent," the lady finally said. "The girls adore her. And Ethan respected her greatly."

"One of my servants had heard that the children might be removing to the country?"

"Yes," said Miss Crane. "Their late mother's sister,

Mrs. Lester, wants them quite desperately, for she has only boys. Indeed, we are all staying there at present."

Ruthveyn did not like her use of the word *desperate*. Desperate people did desperate things. "Has Mrs. Lester a governess?" he asked.

"Oh, the very best," said Miss Crane. "A girl from Berne. I am told Swiss governesses are all the rage, if a little dear. But Mr. Lester always insists his wife have everything she desires."

Ruthveyn managed a rueful smile. "I should settle for a merely competent governess." He paused to scrub a hand pensively around his chin. "But one really does hate to use an agency. One can never be quite sure . . ."

Miss Crane took the bait. "Oh, quite so," she agreed. "One cannot know *what* one might end up with."

"So there is no question of Mademoiselle Gauthier's returning to your family's service?" Ruthveyn pressed.

Miss Crane looked sad. "I think it unlikely," she replied. "Though I shall miss them all dreadfully, Grace included."

"If it does not seem presumptuous, ma'am, would you give me Mademoiselle Gauthier's direction?"

"But of course." Miss Crane went at once to a small mahogany bureau and dropped the front. "Grace is staying with her aunt in Marylebone," she continued, extracting a sheet of letter paper and scratching something on it. "I shall just give you a note of introduction."

"How thoughtful," he said.

In a trice the note was written, fanned in the air, and folded. Deftly, Ruthveyn took it from Miss Crane's fingers with his left hand, careful not to touch her.

"Thank you," he said.

Then, recalling his true objective, he drew a deep breath and offered his right hand.

As was entirely natural, Miss Crane laid her fingers in his. Ruthveyn forced himself to hold them and to gaze into her eyes; wide, blue and unblinking behind the veil that hid nothing now. Despite the thin glove that separated them, he felt an abrupt jolt of consciousness, as if he had just been jerked from a deep and languorous sleep, to a white cold reality. It was the sudden, sickening sensation of having looked too long at something horrific. The edges of his vision darkened, then became painfully bright again, warning of what was to come.

As a young man making his way through the northern reaches of Hindustan, he had once glanced across a narrow mountain pass just as a snow leopard pounced to tear a rabbit to bits, spattering brilliant ruby drops across the snow, chilling in its beauty. The horror came to him again now. Not just the spattered blood against the blinding white but a tangled fan of dark red. Shredded black bombazine. A feminine hand splayed bloodless and limp.

Good God.

Ruthveyn dragged in a deep breath and resisted the urge to shut his eyes to the horror, for he knew it would do no good. He did not see with his eyes.

"Lord Ruthveyn?" Miss Crane's voice came from a distance. "Are you perfectly all right?"

Somehow, he found the presence of mind to bow elegantly over her hand. "Yes, and you have been too kind, ma'am," he forced himself to say. "I have intruded upon your grief too long."

He took his leave from the lady in haste, pausing only to introduce himself to Josiah Crane, who appeared to be a reserved, withdrawn sort of man. Crane muttered his thanks, but did not offer his hand, nor did Ruthveyn solicit it. He instead hastened down the front stairs and back to his waiting carriage almost numbly, the ruse of Miss Crane's note crumpled tightly in his fist.

Had the vision been real? Or merely symbolic? Good God, he was dashed glad she'd kept her gloves on.

Still, a part of him wanted to go back. To warn her.

But warn her of what? And to what end? From past experience, Ruthveyn knew the hopelessness of it. His own failings followed him through life, weighing him down even as he lifted his hand and ordered his driver to roll on.

"Whitehall Place, Brogden," he rasped. "And make haste."

The route was both short and familiar, for this was hardly Ruthveyn's first visit to the administrative offices of the Metropolitan Police. The fog had nearly lifted, but the oppressive damp had not. As his carriage rumbled slowly through Westminster, impeded by the press of traffic, Ruthveyn watched the world beyond his window; the world that went about its everyday business in blithe ignorance of all but the present.

Perhaps he would be wise to learn to emulate that greater world—or perhaps simply retire to some cliffside cottage in Cornwall and avoid it entirely. Or go home to his mother's people and disappear into the mountains to study the ancient philosophies—and in that way, his sister Anisha often suggested, perhaps learn some method of controlling the Gift.

Indeed, he sometimes found himself wondering whether the *Fraternitas*—or the St. James Society, if one preferred its public face—served any real purpose at all with all their research and reading and dabbling in world affairs. Guardians, indeed! More and more, it seemed to Ruthveyn that only the troubles of the here and now were truly within anyone's control.

He thought again of Grace Gauthier, and strangely, of Anisha, both of whom seemed outwardly so strong. Yet each possessed an air of frailty Ruthveyn was not sure everyone could see. Only Grace, however, had accepted his offer of assistance, albeit reluctantly.

But at least her needs—her *immediate* needs—were clear-cut. Something a man could understand, and perhaps even make right. Anisha's were far less definable. Worse, the pallor of widowhood still clung to his sister, damping down what had once been her youthful vivacity. It saddened him—and his inability to help her was frustrating.

The carriage lurched suddenly into Whitehall, Brogden wedging them a little tactlessly between a dray laden with lumber and an ancient hansom cab. The dray's driver shook his fist, cursing Ruthveyn's coachman to the devil. And as if his temper had willed it, the low, gray skies that hung over London began to spill rain the size of robin's eggs, sending civil servants and cabinet ministers alike hastening from the pavements into archways and alleys. Then the spill turned to a roar, hammering down upon his brougham like a score of mad cobblers.

At the Admiralty, Ruthveyn pounded the roof hard enough to be heard beyond the torrent. His driver drew up before the Pay Office, and Ruthveyn yanked an umbrella from beneath his seat. This business in Scotland Yard would be quickly settled, he vowed, and he had no wish to then find himself stuck in a side street with every man Jack and farm cart vying for space in the thoroughfares.

With London's air fleetingly relieved of its sharp, sulfurous tang, Ruthveyn set a brisk pace along the pavement. At Number Four, he shoved his umbrella into the weathered oak rack by the door, then presented his card to the duty officer, who snapped to attention. Ruthveyn's name—perhaps even his reputation—was doubtless well-known to him. He was shown up the stairs and offered the last empty seat in the antechamber of the assistant commissioner's office, where a pair of thin clerks in black frock coats perched like crows on fence posts at their tall desks, eyes glued to some mundane government task.

Impatiently, Ruthveyn sat. He could have demanded immediate attention, he considered. Indeed, he could probably have yanked open the heavy oaken door and ordered whoever was inside simply to leave. But his lordly disdain would be of little use to Mademoiselle Gauthier. While his influence, on the other hand, might be—though why he was troubling himself so thoroughly on her behalf was still unclear.

Perhaps because it seemed easier.

Easier than facing his own problems. Or Anisha's. Or even Luc's.

Good God.

Was it that simple? Was the beautiful Mademoiselle Gauthier nothing more than a distraction? With that question nagging at him, Ruthveyn settled into the stiff wooden chair, which sat squarely against the wall to the left of Napier's door. It was not the seat he would have chosen, for it was miserably designed, and Napier was not a man one wisely turned one's back on.

Ruthveyn settled in to observe the steady stream of officers, civil servants, and general human misery that tromped up and down the staircase and along the passageway. Few came to Scotland Yard of their own volition. After a time, his gaze fell upon his fellow supplicants: a ragged messenger boy with a hole in the toe of one boot who clutched an envelope as wide as his chest, and a pair of funereal-faced, blue-coated sergeants who looked as if they expected Napier to give them a proper hiding with his riding crop.

At that very moment, however, the door hinge behind him squeaked tellingly. In a flash, the messenger boy was out of his seat and halfway to the door, shooting Ruthveyn a wary but triumphant glance as he passed.

"Mr. Cook's accounts, sir," he piped, skidding around the portly gentleman who was attempting to exit. "'E said I was ter put him straight into yer 'ands meself."

Then the lad yanked his forelock and darted from the room, leaving Napier holding the envelope. Ruthveyn had no idea who Mr. Cook might be, but the thunderous look that passed over Napier's face when his gaze fell upon him was familiar.

"Lord Ruthveyn," he said stiffly. "I cannot imagine what brings you."

Ruthveyn was fairly sure he could not. Indeed, he could scarce believe it himself.

He unfolded himself from the god-awful chair. "Mr. Napier," he said without offering his hand. "Have you a moment? I should like to speak with you."

Napier lifted one eyebrow. "Am I to have any choice in the matter?"

Without waiting for an answer, Napier dismissed the waiting officers. They leapt up and hastened from the room as if fleeing the gallows. Napier thrust out an arm, as if to order Ruthveyn inside.

The moment the office door closed, however, the assistant commissioner turned on him, bitterness burning in his eyes, his spine stiffening with pride.

"You have a great deal of nerve, my lord," he said, his voice low and hard. "I won't insult you in front of my men, though I daresay you wouldn't trouble yourself to return the courtesy. But make no mistake as to your welcome in this office."

Ruthveyn threw up a forestalling hand. "Spare us both, Napier."

"Spare you? If I could, sir, I'd have you thrown into the street this instant."

The marquess flashed a muted smile. "No, you'd throw me to the wolves," he corrected, "and watch while they tore out my entrails."

Napier smiled bitterly, and Ruthveyn could see the acknowledgment flare behind his eyes. Enmity swirled like a cloud about Napier, though he was challenging to read. But Ruthveyn knew from experience that the man was angry—and ruthless.

"What do you want this time, Ruthveyn?" he demanded. "Spare me the indignity of having my decisions undermined by Buckingham Palace, and just tell me."

"I am sorry," said Ruthveyn. "I did what I had to do, Napier. You were going to hang an innocent man."

"So you say."

"So I *know,*" said Ruthveyn quietly. "I *know* it, Napier, though I know, too, you'll never believe me. But in this case, no one is headed to the gallows—not yet."

"And which case might that be?"

"The death of Ethan Holding."

"Holding?" Napier snorted derisively. "I thought your grandfather was some almighty Rajput prince, Ruthveyn—God knows you're haughty enough. I can scarce imagine you rubbing shoulders with the hoi polloi."

"You would be surprised," said Ruthveyn quietly, "what sort of men I rub shoulders with. But Holding was quite well-off, was he not?"

Napier shrugged and wandered to one of the windows

to stare down at the traffic below. He shoved a hand into his pocket, obviously measuring his words.

"Holding was not, perhaps, as wealthy as was commonly believed," he finally answered, his back turned to Ruthveyn. "We are still sorting it out. But why would you care?"

Ruthveyn hesitated, hedging his words. "One of the servants approached me," he said. "I'm not at liberty to say more."

"A servant?" Napier turned from the window, his expression incredulous. "You are here on behalf of a suspect? And you aren't going to tell me whom?"

"Not yet." Ruthveyn pretended to hold his gaze steadily, looking at a point just beyond his shoulder. "Not until I know what to make of it all."

Napier's hands curled into fists. "Damn it, Ruthveyn, whose side are you on?" he demanded. "This is our country we are talking about here! Our civilization! England has laws—and we must sometimes sacrifice our personal feelings to uphold them."

"Do not talk to me, Napier, about sacrifice for one's country," Ruthveyn snapped. "By God, I have sacrificed all I care to. And I am done with it."

Napier made a dismissive sound, his eyes all but rolling. And as quickly as it had come, Ruthveyn's temper faded.

Napier was right. Bullheaded, but right. And Ruthveyn felt suddenly weary from it all. He had suffered another sleepless night, and there hadn't been enough brandy or hashish or anything else sufficient to overcome it.

He wished to God he could speak to Lazonby, and find out what, if anything, he owed Mademoiselle Gauthier. He wished he understood why he felt so compelled to help her. Geoff had been right, perhaps, in warning him away.

Ruthveyn felt as if he were flying blind, trying to understand the fears and the motivations of a woman whom he knew nothing about. A woman he could not read—not to any degree whatsoever—a rare occurrence indeed. And one which, in this case, he found deeply frustrating.

He felt challenged by Grace somehow. And yes, drawn to her. Perhaps, despite Geoff's comment, Ruthveyn was not incapable of being deceived by a woman's beauty after all. What made Grace Gauthier any less a suspect than the next person caught up in this tragedy? People killed for all manner of hard-to-comprehend reasons. And he did not envy Royden Napier the job of sorting it all out.

He dragged a hand through his hair, a boyish gesture he'd long tried to conquer. "Look here, Napier, might I sit down?" he asked. "Must we go on like this? Always at one another's throats?"

"Ah, you want a truce now, do you?" said the assistant commissioner snidely. But he jerked his head toward a seat, then went to his desk, sitting down and drawing up his chair with a harsh scrape.

He gave something of a weary sigh. "I shall tell you what I can, Ruthveyn," he said, his voice only marginally more conciliatory. "Holding's throat was cut from behind by someone who was right-handed—and hesitant, for the job was badly done. Holding tried to crawl away, but he bled to death beside his desk. We are looking at everyone who had access to the house as a possible suspect."

"You are sure, then, that the killer came from inside?" Ruthveyn pressed. "There was no sign of burglary?"

Napier shook his head. "A robbery gone wrong is rather easier to stomach," he replied. "No, someone Holding knew killed him—and you shan't convince me otherwise." This last was said in a warning tone.

No shattered windows, then. No locks pried free.

Something inside Ruthveyn fell a little. "Whom do you suspect?"

Again, the assistant commissioner shrugged. "The business partner?" he suggested. "Or the footman who, the butler thought, might have been nicking bits of silver? And then there is the governess, a Frenchwoman. She'd managed to get herself betrothed to Holding. But we can find no motive for her—*yet.*"

His tone sent a chill down Ruthveyn's spine, no easy feat. "You have finished searching the house?"

"Almost," he said grudgingly. "But we've carted out a lot of ledgers and correspondence we've yet to review. And I've got a man down at Crane and Holding looking at the company accounts."

"What makes you think it was the governess?" Ruthveyn pressed. "I understand she found him, and that there might have been a note involved?"

Napier stiffened. "There might have been."

"Was it recovered?" he asked hopefully. "I should like to see it."

Napier's expression darkened. "You have no right to it," he replied. "You are not an officer of the court or anything remotely near it."

Ruthveyn hesitated. "I mean you no ill, Napier," he finally answered. "Murder is a sin, and whoever did it should hang. If I discover the killer—and I don't expect to—then I shall help you tie the noose, and gladly."

Napier still looked wary. "Just what is going on here, Ruthveyn? What is it you know that I do not?"

The marquess shrugged. "Nothing," he admitted. "Nonetheless, I mean to follow the case to its conclusion. It would be best for all of us if you accepted that."

At that, something like resignation sketched across Napier's hard features. He extracted a little key from his waistcoat pocket and unlocked a drawer. "You are a plague upon this house, Ruthveyn," he muttered, thumbing through a file. "I know what you mean to do. You know something, and you will hide it from me. And then you will twist and distort the facts of this case until they fit whatever theory it is you hope to prove."

"You are wrong," said Ruthveyn just as Napier extracted a folded paper and thrust it at him.

Ruthveyn took it gingerly, without touching Napier. For a time, he simply held it, rubbing the thick, cream-colored stock between two fingers. One corner had turned rusty. It was dried blood, he realized. It was just as Mademoiselle Gauthier had said, then. She had dropped it. And still he felt nothing. But nor had he expected to.

He released his grip and looked more closely. Nothing was written on the exterior. He flipped it open to find it worded just as Mademoiselle Gauthier had remembered; stiffly, and a little formally. He returned it to Napier.

"Perhaps the governess is opportunistic," he agreed. "But why would she kill him?"

Napier's expression shuttered. "Women are emotional creatures," he answered. "Though admittedly, it was a love match by no one's account—not even hers—but Holding had been keeping a high-flyer up in Soho. Perhaps she got wind of it."

Ruthveyn grunted. "Doesn't sound like a man who meant to marry."

"He broke it off a fortnight past," Napier added. "Told his mistress his betrothal was imminent—motive, perhaps. But she was not in the house."

"Not so far as you know," Ruthveyn murmured, his gaze catching Napier's.

Despite the man's dire suspicions, some tightly coiled spring inside Ruthveyn had been gradually relaxing, and at last it finally gave way. Until now, he realized, he had not even been entirely convinced of Mademoiselle Gauthier's betrothal story. Impoverished females had been known to indulge in greater fantasies. Which begged another question.

"Was there anyone else?" he asked Napier. "Any other woman scorned? Servants warming the master's bed? Anything of that sort?"

The assistant commissioner exhaled slowly. "There was a housemaid who once fancied herself Holding's favorite," he said quietly. "Like his mistress, she pretended her nose was not out of joint, but . . ."

"What about the dead wife's family?"

Napier shrugged dismissively. "Just a sister," he said, "but she and the deceased were on cordial good terms. They had occasional words, I collect, about what was best for the children—the dead wife's daughters—but it never amounted to much."

"So you still suspect the governess. Why? What is your theory?"

Napier's expression shuttered. "I have no theory. And I suspect everyone."

"Liar," said Ruthveyn softly.

The assistant commissioner's eyes glittered dangerously. "I may have to tell you what I know, Ruthveyn," he returned, "for I don't fancy being jerked up to the Home Office and run through with the blade of Sir George's tongue again. But my thoughts are my own. Even the Queen herself does not own those. Not yet, at any rate."

At that, a bitter smile twisted Ruthveyn's mouth. "Then account yourself fortunate, old chap. They used to own mine."

But Napier scarcely paused for breath. "As to what I *know*," he went on, "I know the Frenchwoman was the last to see him alive. I know she ran from the room spattered with his blood. And I know she was half-incoherent a good two hours afterward."

Ruthveyn merely lifted one brow. "Well, I daresay finding one's betrothed covered in blood and breathing his last would send any of us—"

Just then, the door squeaked again. One of the black-coated clerks slid silently into the room to drop a paper on Napier's desk, disappearing as wordlessly as he'd come. Ruthveyn glanced at the page, which appeared to be some sort of list.

Napier uttered a soft curse, then lifted his eyes from the paper to Ruthveyn. "Devil take it," he gritted. "You called upon *Holding's sister*?"

Ruthveyn simply shrugged.

"Why?" Napier demanded. "It's interference, and you bloody well know it."

Ruthveyn said nothing. He was not perfectly sure why he had done it. He knew only that he had wanted to see the place in which Mademoiselle Gauthier had lived and worked; that he had hoped something within the house might somehow speak to him. He supposed it had.

Tossing the paper aside, Napier jerked to his feet. "Do not overestimate, Ruthveyn, the power of your influence in this case," he growled, planting both hands to lean across the desk. "I know you have the Queen's ear—the tongue-lashing I got in the Welham case made that much rather plain—but do not dare to interfere with this investigation. Do you hear me? It has nothing to do with you, or with your *Fraternitas* or whatever you call your damned coven. And I bloody well will not have it. Now *get out*—before I decide to go digging around to find out precisely what it is you people are doing in St. James's and put a stop to it."

Ruthveyn jerked to his feet. "You are a fool, Napier." He, too, leaned over the desk, snatching up his hat. "I did not go to Belgrave Square to interfere with anything you are doing."

"Then why?" he demanded again.

Ruthveyn turned away and set his hand to the doorknob. "Not that it is any of your business," he said tightly, "but I went . . . to see."

"Ah, yes! Mad Ruthveyn!" Napier's voice was laced with disdain. "Then tell me, what did you spae for us this time, eh? Wee folk? Goblins? The Ghost of Christmas Past? *Fraternitas,* my arse!"

His hat still clutched in his hand, Ruthveyn turned to look at him. In all his arrogance and contempt, Napier could not even grasp his own naïveté. Could not wonder for even one infinitesimal moment if there mightn't be something greater than himself and all his power at work here.

"Napier," he snapped, "*you* are the one who's mad if you think man's every sin and secret are yours to ferret out. There are some things that are beyond man's ordinary comprehension. You have learned nothing if you have not learned that. And by God, I do not have time to educate a fool."

The assistant commissioner circled from behind his wide desk. His face had gone a little white. He watched Ruthveyn with a new intensity, his eyes burning bright— not with fear, precisely, but with something akin to dread.

"All right then," he said. "Answer the question, Ruthveyn. What did you see?"

Ah, perhaps not so contemptuous after all . . .

Ruthveyn forced his fingers to uncurl from his hat brim. "Death, Napier," he answered. "I saw death."

He turned back to the door and was shocked to feel

Napier seize his sleeve. Swiftly, he jerked free and wheeled around.

"Damn it, Ruthveyn," Napier growled, "you cannot just waltz in here with that sort of pronouncement! If you suspect something, by God, say so!"

Napier could not quite bring himself to say what he meant, thought Ruthveyn, his mouth twisting with the bitterness of it. "Unlike you, I don't suspect a damned thing," he replied. "And I know less than that."

"*Ruthveyn.*" There was a warning in his tone. "Do not leave me in the dark. This is a serious business."

"And you think I don't know that?" Ruthveyn looked at him incredulously.

"Then help me," Napier demanded. "You said that was your intent. Was it?"

Regret, followed by the all-too-familiar sense of impotence, burned through him, leaving Ruthveyn angry. What could he do? What could he say that might change anything?

But Napier was still glaring at him expectantly.

Ruthveyn refused, as always, to quite hold his gaze. "I saw blood," he rasped. "Blood glistening like rubies cast upon snow. And don't ask me what I mean by that, for I don't know. Just watch the sister. She might have . . . Christ, Napier, I don't know! Perhaps she has stumbled across something?"

At last Napier dropped his voice. "You mean she might be in danger?"

Ruthveyn jerked the door open roughly. "Oh, for pity's sake, Napier!" he snapped. "We are all of us in danger. All of us. All of the time."

And the beautiful Mademoiselle Gauthier, it now appeared, was in far more danger than most. For she was Napier's prime suspect—whether he admitted it or not.

CHAPTER 5

The Accidental Homecoming

Grace Gauthier was squirming—and for any number of reasons. Foremost was the knot of dread forming in the pit of her stomach, but a near second was the fact that she was extraordinarily uncomfortable. The plain oak chair she sat down in had a back built at an angle that seemed designed to pitch her back out again, and the curve of the seat so misshapen, she felt as if she sat upon a wad of petticoat.

The righteous indignation that had sustained Grace on her march down from Marylebone had faded in the face of these ominous, official offices that smelled of damp soot and desperation. She wriggled again to no good effect and tried not to return the surreptitious glances of the two office clerks, one of whom had very nearly tipped off his tall stool when Grace entered. No doubt few females ever entered this bastion of masculinity—certainly few of her station, low on society's ladder though she was.

She was just settling in at last when the door to Mr. Napier's office flew wide, as if blown open by some minor explosion. Then the explosion strode out, attired in a pair of glossy black boots, a gray waistcoat, and a coat of formfitting charcoal superfine. Even Lord Ruthveyn's expression resembled a thundercloud.

He paid Grace no notice whatever, thank God, but instead strode past her and out of the room, leaving her alone in the antechamber with a second man whom she vaguely recognized.

Royden Napier was looking down at her, his face choleric.

Somehow, Grace managed to rise and meet his gaze unflinchingly. "Good afternoon," she said, presenting her gloved hand. "You may recall that I am Grace Gauthier?"

"I recall it," he snapped. "What do you want?"

Grace tilted her head inquisitively. "How very odd!" she murmured. "That is precisely the question I meant to ask you."

His expression shifted uncertainly. And then, as if thinking better of his first notion, he turned and held open his door. "Then do come in, ma'am."

"Thank you." Grace swept in, chin up and shoulders back, doing her best imitation of her late mother.

Napier was a handsome man, she realized, save for the perpetual scowl that furrowed his brow and turned what might otherwise have been an amiable mouth into something far less pleasant.

"I understand you called at my aunt's house yesterday,

Mr. Napier," she said after refusing the chair he offered. "This business has left her quite distraught. I am afraid I must ask you to refrain from calling again."

Napier's expression darkened. "Your pardon, Miss Gauthier, but that is not your decision."

Grace folded her hands lightly around her reticule. "I fear it is," she returned. "If you return, I'm afraid I will not be at home to callers."

"Under the circum—"

"On the other hand," she interjected, jerking the chin a notch higher, "if you send word that you wish to see me, I will be here. In your office. Before the day is out."

Napier's entire frame had gone rigid. "You are very high-handed, madam."

"Perhaps. But my aunt is very fragile."

"Fragile!" Napier grunted. "Is that another word for haughty? I met the lady, you will recall."

"*Fragile* is another word for delicate," Grace said unwaveringly. "And she has every right to be so, whatever we might think. It is more her house than mine."

"But you are living there," said Napier.

Grace felt her face warm. "I fear my aunt suffers my presence somewhat reluctantly," she answered. "Just now she feels I have brought the most unseemly attention imaginable upon our family. I certainly did not mean to. And I certainly do not blame you for trying to do your job. Indeed, I wish Ethan's killer caught quite desperately, and I shall help you any way I can. But you mustn't call at Lady Abigail's house again."

Napier said nothing but merely crooked one eyebrow impossibly high.

Grace drew a deep breath. "You will instead send for me. And I will come at once. I promise." She extended her hand. "Have we a deal, Mr. Napier?"

He shook his head. "I do not make deals, Miss Gauthier."

Grace dropped her hand. "I did not kill Mr. Holding," she said quietly. "Indeed, I had every reason not to. He had offered me a home of my own and the chance at contentment; perhaps even happiness."

"I am aware of that," he growled.

Again, she tilted her head slightly. "You are *aware* of it, yes," she murmured, "but can you have any idea what that means to a woman like me? A woman of modest means; one who has lived all her life in far-flung army outposts, with no real home of her own? I am twenty-six years old, Mr. Napier, and I want a family quite desperately. Ethan offered me that—to be my family. To try to love me, and to share his daughters with me. Perhaps even to give me children of my own. I would have done anything to preserve that. Can you possibly understand, I wonder?"

To her shock, Napier looked away. "I understand desperation, Miss Gauthier," he said quietly. "I see it every day—in all its myriad forms. And I see what it drives people to do."

"Then you must know I would never have hurt him," Grace whispered.

But it was as if Napier no longer listened to her. His gaze was focused out the window, at a point far beyond the rain, which had ratcheted back up again, and now struck at the glass like hailstones.

"Mr. Napier, I respected Ethan Holding," she said again. "Believe me when I say that I *want* you to find out who killed him."

Napier spoke without looking at her. "I hope you mean that, Miss Gauthier. Because I *will* find out. You may depend upon it."

"Then I thank you, sir, for your diligence."

But inwardly, Grace sighed. There would be no promise extracted today. Perhaps, however, she had made her point. She turned and drew open the door, but Napier did not look back.

She left as she had come, going through the antechamber, past the gaping clerks, and down the wide flight of stairs. But as she turned the first landing, she was seized from behind, a strong hand catching her arm and spinning her half around.

"What in hell," gritted the Marquess of Ruthveyn, "do you think you are doing?"

Grace widened her eyes and opened her mouth, but he did not wait.

"Come with me," he said gruffly. He dragged her down to the next floor and into the dimly lit passageway.

"I didn't think you'd seen me," she admitted.

"Don't be a fool," he growled. "I did not need to see you."

"Stop pulling. You are hurting my hand."

He ignored her, and after counting off a number of doors, shouldered one open and dragged Grace inside. It was a storage room of sorts, lit by a bank of narrow, undraped windows and smelling of dust and old leather. It was crammed with cabinets and bookcases, the latter filled near to bursting.

"Lord Ruthveyn, kindly unhand me," she protested.

He turned and set Grace's spine to the door.

"What did I tell you?" he demanded, his face dark with rage. "What did I tell you, Grace? Did I not say you were to go home and remain there? That you were to do nothing—*say nothing*—until you had heard from me?"

Grace's stomach bottomed out oddly. "But I wanted Napier to stop—"

"Grace, listen to me!" His grip on her arms was unrelenting. "I am trying to help you. Don't interfere. Go *home*. This is a dangerous business."

She grappled for words. "I—I don't think you understand."

"What?" he barked. "What is it you think I don't understand? That a man has been murdered? Or that there is more evil yet to come? Because there will be, Grace. Napier isn't even the worst of it. Trust me."

"No, that I"—Grace swallowed hard and stiffened her spine—"that I no longer have a home to go to. Nor did I ask for your help."

If anything, the frustration on his face deepened, then just as quickly shifted to something else. His eyes glittering, Ruthveyn backed her up another inch. "Too late," he returned. "You've *got* my help."

Grace felt her pulse ratchet up. "Oh, I beg your pardon!" she managed to reply. "So you expected me merely to lie upon the sofa, weeping and waving my vinaigrette? Perhaps I might as easily demand to know what you are doing here?"

"Trying to keep you safe," he rasped. "Trying to figure out what Napier suspects. Damn it, Grace. You just . . . you shouldn't be here. For any number of reasons."

"Lord Ruthveyn," she answered, "did I give you leave to use my Christian name?"

A mocking smile lifted one corner of his mouth. "No," he whispered, still gripping her arms. "You did not, *Grace*. Shall I stop?"

She should have said yes. She should have been angry. Dash it, she *was* angry. But he wasn't just talking about the use of her name, and she knew it.

In the thick, stagnant air of the room, the temperature seemed suddenly too hot, and Lord Ruthveyn too close.

Her eyes fell to his cravat and its elaborate gold pin, its design oddly familiar. She could smell the starched linen, the scent of expensive shaving soap rising with the heat of his anger, and beneath it all, a sweet, smoky fragrance—something exotic and forbidden that made her think longingly of the press and heat of the Kasbah; of the seductive wail of music carrying over the walls, and of the secrets hidden within.

His husky voice recalled her to the present. "Is that what you want, Grace?" he murmured, his voice stirring the hair at her temple. "For me to stop all this? Because I'm not sure that's an option now."

Was it what she wanted? Grace's head was spinning just a little. He towered over her, a beautiful, untamed beast of a man, and something deep and treacherous began to twist in the pit of her belly.

But one did not tease a barely tethered tiger with impunity.

Grace tried to pull away. He softened his grip, but his gaze was still drifting over her face. "What madness," he murmured as if to himself. "A fine, rare madness, aye—but insanity all the same."

"Ruthveyn," she whispered, "what *are* you talking about?"

Wariness and something that looked like yearning warred in his eyes. Eyes which, she now realized, were not entirely black but instead rimmed with coffee brown, and flecked with bits of glittering amber. Foolishly, Grace let her gaze drift down to his mouth—that full, sinfully lush mouth—and her breath caught.

His hands tightened on her upper arms. "I think, Mademoiselle Gauthier," he said softly, "that I am about to do something for which I *will* owe you an apology. Something in the way of an experiment that—"

Grace cut him off, rising onto her tiptoes to set her lips to his.

Ruthveyn's eyes warmed with surprise, then fell half-shut. She slanted her head, and their mouths lingered, pressed pillow-soft together in the lightest of kisses.

Grace held herself to it but a minute, then drew away, the taste of him forever on her mouth. *"Et voilà,"* she said breathlessly. "Your experiment, at least, is over with."

In response, Ruthveyn cursed softly. The heat of his hands left her arms, then suddenly his lips were on hers again, her face bracketed this time between his broad, warm palms. Grace made a muffled sound of surprise, then felt something inside her melt as he urged his body against hers, pressing her back against the solid slab of wood. There was a metallic *snick,* the bolt clicking back into place as her full weight hit the door.

This time there was nothing uncertain or experimental in his kiss. It was raw, and almost alarmingly sensual. Ruthveyn opened his mouth over hers, his lips and his tongue seeking. Her shock evaporating in a surge of desire, Grace opened willingly.

Just as it had that day in the club library, she felt the heat of his touch radiating through her, seeping sensually through her skin and into her very bones, melting her to her very core. He plunged inside on a low sound of satisfaction, sliding the length of his tongue along hers again and again until he left her trembling.

Grace had been kissed before, certainly. But never like this; with a man's hands and his tongue and nearly the whole of his body enveloping hers. Good Lord; if he kept this up, she would have no free will at all; she would be held utterly captive to his touch. Already she seemed unable to push him away.

Tentatively, her hands eased up the warm wool of his

coat, then settled more firmly against his shoulder blades. Acting on instinct, she let her tongue twine with his, and to her shame, felt her belly settle firmly against the hard ridge of his trousers.

A maelstrom of loneliness and longing began to twist inside Grace. Ruthveyn's arm was banded tight about her waist, the other hand still cradling her face, and for a woman who had known no tenderness in a very long while, it was too much. She lost herself to him, begging the sensations to take her and drag her down with him into whatever dark lair such dangerous men occupied. A whimper of surrender escaped her.

It was this, perhaps, that pulled Ruthveyn back into the present.

As swiftly as it had begun, his lips were torn from hers. On a soft oath, his weight and his heat drew away, and only then did Grace realize that he had pressed her back against the door so firmly that the loss of his support was a physical thing. That absent his strength, her knees could scarce hold her weight.

As Grace sagged against the door, he stepped back, his gaze abruptly shuttering. Then Ruthveyn turned and crossed the narrow space to one of the bare, fly-specked windows. He set his hands on the sill, head slightly bowed.

Grace tried to shake off the confusion. What must he think of her? "My lord, I—"

He threw up one hand, the other almost digging into the wood of the dusty sill. "Please, just . . . don't."

Somehow Grace found her strength and started toward him. "I—"

"Stay there a moment, Grace, I beg you," he cut in, his voice still thick with emotion. "My little experiment . . . was a dangerous mistake."

Knees still trembling, Grace approached him anyway

and set a hand to his spine, making him flinch like an edgy stallion. His gaze seemed transfixed by the rivulets streaming down the glass.

"You are angry with yourself," she murmured, just loud enough to be heard over the rain. "And I am a little bit ashamed. But it was just a kiss. We must let it go, Ruthveyn. We are neither of us ourselves just now."

His eyes closed, his nostrils flared wide. He breathed in deeply and very deliberately, then let it out again on a slow exhalation. "I fear I am very much myself, Mademoiselle Gauthier," he finally said. "If you take nothing more from this little episode, I beg you will take that much."

Ah, so she was indeed Mademoiselle Gauthier again . . .

Feeling suddenly awkward, she edged back to the door. A lifetime seemed to pass as she stood, simply watching him. Even bowed forward as they were, Ruthveyn's shoulders seemed impossibly wide, his body exuding a masculine power that gave Grace pause.

He was tall, too, well over six feet, with a narrow waist, and legs well made beneath trousers that were expensively cut. But even as her gaze ran appreciatively over him, her brain was warning her that Ruthveyn was a man of secrets—a man not to be trifled with. Grace closed her eyes at the thought, and something went shivering through her, something deep and primitive. Something shameful.

Good heavens, she didn't understand any of this. Her affianced husband was not yet cold in his grave, and already she desired another, desired him in a way she had never desired Ethan, nor ever hoped to.

It was the strain, of course. Yesterday in Lord Ruthveyn's company, Grace had begun to believe that he did indeed have the power to help her. No, it was more than that. She had believed—in a few sharp, certain moments—that he was *the only* person who could help her.

Today, of course, she knew how foolish that sounded. She had gone looking for Rance and come away with some romanticized notion of a knight in shining armor. A man with a voice like warm cognac, and a touch that left her mesmerized. Except that Lord Ruthveyn—dark and hard-boned as he was—looked more like some Barbary pirate prince than anyone's idea of Sir Galahad.

"Mademoiselle Gauthier, I beg your pardon." At last he had turned around. "In my defense, I can only say that it has been a long time since . . . well, it has been a long time."

"I should rather you apologized for scolding me like a child," she said quietly, "rather than for something in which I was a willing participant."

That, he ignored. "Please go home now," he said almost wearily. "There was no reason for you to come here today."

She pressed both hands flat to the door, leaning back against it, half of her wishing she could melt and vanish into it, and the other half wishing . . . well, for something else altogether. "I had to speak with Assistant Commissioner Napier," she answered. "He came to call on me yesterday and upset my aunt. I asked him to stop."

Ruthveyn's expression was stark, his eyes almost haunted now. "Napier won't give a damn for your aunt's sensibilities," he answered. "And he won't give a damn for you, either. Not if he decides he can pin this murder on you."

"But he can't," said Grace, coming away from the door, "because I did not do it. Besides, he knows I had no motive."

At last he looked at her—really looked at her. "Nonetheless, you remain on his list of suspects," he said, pacing slowly toward her. "The police always look first to a man's wife—or his lover."

"And I was neither."

But Ruthveyn had closed the distance between them and was looking at her through eyes that were heavy-lidded and almost unnaturally calm. "I hesitate to point out, my dear," he murmured, "that you do not precisely *kiss* like a virgin."

Grace backed up a pace, and thudded against the door. "*Et alors*," she snapped. "Yes, I have been courted more than a few times. None of them suited me. What of it? And what business is it of yours?"

"I just want to know—was one of them Rance?"

The question was soft, almost as if he dreaded the answer. And yet it angered her as no stolen kiss ever could. "Was it *Rance*?" she echoed, drawing back her hand. "My God. Have we come back to that again?"

But on her next breath, she wanted to laugh—for if she did not laugh, she might well cry. She let the hand drop. *Rance, indeed!* What did any of this have to do with her dreadful predicament? Was she really so desperate for distraction as to allow herself to be . . . what? Seduced? By a madman? And then insulted, too.

"You are about to make me forget my good breeding, Lord Ruthveyn," she said sharply. "We should both be ashamed."

Indeed, she *was* ashamed. Ethan was dead. Fenella had lost her only brother. Eliza and Anne were once again fatherless. And Grace, lost in a stranger's kiss, had forgotten them.

Abruptly, Ruthveyn released her gaze. "You are right. It is none of my business." He stepped back, his mouth twisting bitterly.

She inched a little away. "I should go," she murmured. "Aunt Abigail is expecting me . . . for tea."

She had almost said *expecting me home,* but she had not lied to Ruthveyn. Her aunt's latest histrionics had brought back to her the reality that she had no home.

Perhaps when this was all over—if she found some quiet little village in France—if she sold all of her mother's jewelry, and kept only a cook or a maid; yes, perhaps then she might afford a quiet little cottage and be able to make a quiet little life to go with it. She would be far away from Aunt Abigail and Belgrave Square—and Lord Ruthveyn. The notion suddenly had great appeal.

Abruptly, Ruthveyn bent down and swept something up. It was her reticule, Grace realized. She could not recall having dropped it.

"*Merci,*" she managed, taking it.

Ruthveyn made her an almost formal bow. "May I see you safely home in my carriage, ma'am?"

Grace could imagine nothing more awkward. "Thank you, no." She managed a rueful smile. "I fancy a brisk walk might clear my head."

As if to acquiesce, Ruthveyn reached past her and drew open the door.

Lord Ruthveyn was soaked to the skin by the time he returned to his carriage, having forgotten his umbrella—having forgotten, actually, that it was raining, until he stepped immediately off the pavement and into an overflowing ditch in an attempt to evade a careening pieman.

Blinded by the empty tray held over his head, the street vendor dashed on through the torrent. Cursing, Ruthveyn plodded back into Whitehall, both boots sopping.

Upon nearing his carriage, he saw that his driver's ire, too, was barely suppressed. Brogden had been left too long at the curb, doubtless incurring the wrath—and the shaking fists—of those whose path he blocked. Seeing his master's sodden approach, the coachman leapt onto the box to glare defiantly down at him.

Ruthveyn didn't have the patience for it. "Home, damn it!" he bellowed, and was then surprised when the poor devil actually took him there.

For a few moments, Ruthveyn actually sat staring up at the grand, porticoed mansion on Upper Grosvenor Street, contemplating a hasty retreat back down to St. James's. After his utter loss of control with Grace Gauthier, he was in no mood for the clamor of his family. And then, through the waning drizzle, he saw that familiar, perfect oval peering down from the upstairs window, and the curtain of sleek, black hair that fell forward to frame it.

Anisha.

His sister smiled hugely, gave a little wave, then vanished.

Ah, well. There was nothing else for it. Ruthveyn shouldered open the door, nearly knocking aside the footman who had come round to set down the steps. Brogden, too, was already on the pavement—arms crossed over his chest and sporting what was swiftly becoming a bruised jaw.

Ruthveyn passed him a little shamefacedly. "The chap with the lumber, was it?"

"Aye," said the burly coachman. "Seems 'e took orffence at me drivin'—and then me parkin,' seeing as 'ow I hogged the curb in Whitehall 'arf an hour."

"Terribly sorry." Ruthveyn shook some of the water out of his left boot. "Tell Higgenthorpe he's to unlock the liquor cupboard and give you a bottle of the best brandy."

Brogden's arms remained crossed. "Just gin 'll do me."

Ruthveyn tried to smile benevolently, but he'd little practice, so it came out more of a grimace. "Have one of each," he insisted just before starting up the steps, "for the pain, and so on."

"Aye," grunted Brogden behind him. "And so on."

But as soon as Ruthveyn entered his house, all hell broke loose.

"Raju!" Dressed for the privacy of her suite, Anisha bounced off the last stair and hurled herself at him, the pleats of her gold silk sari crushing against his damp coat. "We did not expect you!"

"Uncle Adrian! Uncle Adrian!" Tom skidded past his mother to clasp Ruthveyn about the five. "Teddy's learning faro! And he won't let me!"

"Good afternoon, Tom." Ruthveyn looked down, praying the lad didn't clamber up his damp trouser leg.

Anisha bent at once, peeling the boy away. "Thomas," she chided, "your uncle's just got home. Do not pester him."

"But it's not fair, Mamma!" Tom's little hands fisted stubbornly.

Ruthveyn relented and knelt to look the lad almost in the eye, though he did not give in to the urge to tousle his hair. "I will teach you to play faro, Tom," he offered, "when you are old enough. I promise."

"What, that you, Adrian?" A blithe but masculine voice drifted from the front parlor. "Quick, Higgenthorpe! Kill the fatted calf!"

Ruthveyn stood to see his brother strolling out, his glass held aloft as if to toast him. Luc was wearing what looked like a new silk waistcoat, his riot of gold curls pomaded into submission.

"If it is the prodigal son to whom you refer, Lucan," said Ruthveyn quietly, "I fancy that would be you, not I. When did you get home?"

"You mean when did I escape my captors?" Luc drained

the glass, then flashed Anisha a conspiratorial grin. "That would have been yesterday, old man. Did prosy old Claytor not tell you?"

"Strangely," said Ruthveyn, "he did not."

Just then, eight-year-old Teddy peeked round the parlor door, the stitched wound on his forehead now turning a bilious shade of yellow. "Hullo, Uncle."

"Good afternoon, Teddy," said Ruthveyn before returning his gaze to Luc. "Tell me," he quietly added, "that you are not teaching that child to gamble."

Luc lifted one shoulder. "Lad's got to learn sometime, Adrian. Might as well learn from the best."

Ruthveyn clenched his teeth so hard his jaw twitched. Sometimes he wondered if he simply couldn't read Luc well, or if there was little in Luc *to* read. The boy possessed the equanimity of a shallow pond; toss in a stone, and the water might ripple for a time, but there was no depth to him, and soon enough the water would still again.

But Anisha was looking back and forth between them worriedly. "Come, Raju, you are soaked," she said, taking his arm. "You must get out of those clothes." She paused to catch the attention of a passing servant. "Find Fricke," she directed, "and tell him his master's boots want drying."

Ruthveyn went with her, for if he did not, he was going to turn Luc over his knee for a thrashing—which would have made both of them look ridiculous, given that Luc was now eighteen and apt to put up one hell of a fight.

As they went up the stairs arm in arm, his sister continued to chatter in her soothing, faintly accented voice. Unlike Ruthveyn, who had been educated at St. Andrews and brought up to be a civil servant and nabob like his father, his sister had been raised by their mother and her extended female relations. A great beauty, Anisha had been trained from birth to be noble and gracious; to epitomize traditional Anglo-Indian elegance. Indeed, she had been trained to be a wealthy Englishman's wife—even as such mixed marriages were becoming increasingly more rare.

"You are stalling, Anisha," he murmured, cutting through her chatter as they went up the stairs.

Anisha just tugged on his arm. "We are going to your room," she ordered. "I am going to draw you a hot bath."

He fell silent for only a minute. His suite of rooms commanded half the first floor, and at the entrance to his private study, he pushed wide the door, which was already cracked, and went through into his bedchamber. Silk and Satin, his cats, rose from their dimples on the bed to plop down and pad across the carpet, pausing to stretch their hinds legs as they came.

Ruthveyn took a moment to scratch their cheeks, then picked up Satin and turned to Anisha. "All right, the game is up, my girl," he warned, settling the cat on his shoulder. "Out with it."

But his sister had pushed open the door to his bathroom and gone to the tub to turn the tap. "I hope there is hot water left in the boiler," she said, kneeling to cork the drain. "I caught Tom and Teddy playing in the scullery after—"

He caught her arm and hauled her up. "Stop it, Anisha," he said firmly.

"St-Stop what?" she said, as Satin leapt down in a huff.

"I am not your husband," said Ruthveyn tightly. "He is dead. And I have a whole houseful of servants to draw my water. I do not need my sister to wait on me hand and foot."

Her face coloring furiously, Anisha dropped her gaze. "I wish only to make myself useful."

"No, you wish to avoid my questions," he answered. "Now who got Lucan out of the sponging house?"

"We are nothing but trouble to you, I know." Anisha jerked from his grasp. "If you no longer want us here, Raju, we—"

"Damn it, I sent for you, didn't I?" he interjected, following her across the bathroom. "I begged you to leave Calcutta *because* I want you here. I just didn't count on Luc's embracing the London lifestyle so quickly—or so thoroughly."

At last she turned around, the silk hems of her sari swirling brightly over the floor. "Fine, then, *I* am the one who got him out!" Anisha thrust her left hand in his face, palm down. "I went to Rundle's and sold my diamonds."

As if to emphasize the point, she gave her naked fingers a little wiggle.

"Anisha." Ruthveyn caught her hand. "You sold your *wedding ring*?"

"I sold the stones out of my wedding ring," she corrected. "I'm having the gold melted down to make a set of nose rings. So *there*."

He dropped her hand and stepped back, then, seeing the look on her face, burst into laughter. "Oh, Anisha, I should love to see that! Will you be sporting your new nose rings at St. George's on Sunday?"

Her face flushed with embarrassment. "I am teasing, and you know it," she said. "No, I shan't wear anything in public that might embarrass you."

He caught her hands, both of them this time. "Anisha, you could never embarrass me," he said gently. *"Never.* But no woman should part with her wedding ring until she is ready. Luc's comfort is not worth—"

"I was ready," she cut in, her voice firm. "I have been ready, Raju, for a long time. And it was my choice to sell the diamonds. It was my choice to spend the money on Luc. You are forever ranting about the evils of oppressing women, so do not you dare try to refuse me this!"

Already he was shaking his head. "You are a wealthy widow, sister." He dropped her hands. "You may waste your money as you please. But I ask you to think about Luc. He has never had to face the consequences of his actions. Pamela spoiled him, and now you are at risk of doing the same."

"Am I?" A soft, cynical smile curved her lips.

"You will spend your days being Luc's savior," he warned, lifting his chin to unwind his cravat. "The lad's becoming a bottomless pit of profligacy."

"You think me that naïve?" she answered. "I am making Lucan pay me back. He is to help the boys with their studies, and entertain them—*ten* hours a day until I find a new tutor, and three thereafter—for the next year."

"Surely you jest?"

She shook her head. "Luc will think the sponging house a holiday, I daresay, before all's said and done. I had Claytor draw it up properly—a promissory note, he called it."

"Did you indeed?" Ruthveyn stripped off his wet coat and tossed it aside. "That's innovative, I'll grant you."

His sister wrinkled her nose. "Ugh, your coat smells like smoke," she said, her expression chiding. "Like charas. Raju, are you not sleeping again?"

"Do not change the subject," he answered, unbuttoning his silk waistcoat. "We were discussing Luc. You can't have him teaching the boys to gamble, Nish. It won't do, I tell you." He sat down and began to tug at one boot. "Damn it, where's Fricke?"

"Oh, for pity's sake, give me the bloody boot," Anisha complained, bending down to do so.

"Anisha!" he warned. "Such language! What would Mamma say?"

"She would tell you to stop picking on me."

She was probably right, Ruthveyn acknowledged. Anisha knelt, wedged a hand behind the heel, then gave the left boot a hearty tug. But the water had swollen the leather, and nothing budged. "Blast," she grunted, "we may need the jack."

She yanked again, angrily, and this time the boot flew off. Anisha lost her balance and pitched gracelessly backward onto her derriere. Amusement danced in her eyes, and they both ended up laughing.

Then the laughter fell away, and there was only the trickle of the tap to break the silence. Hands splayed behind her back, Anisha propped herself up, her sari and petticoat snarled about her knees. Above one tiny red slipper, which was studded with semiprecious gems, he could see Anisha wore the ankle bracelet of tigers' claws and wide gold links that had once been their mother's.

Ruthveyn wore the matching pendant—beneath his shirt, but close to his heart. It was just one of the many things he and Anisha shared. Oh, he loved Luc, too—loved him just as much, and in some ways, felt more protective of him. But Luc was not just of a different generation but of a different culture. He had been born in a very different India than had his elder half siblings. Luc shared their father's Scottish blood, yes, but his mother had been an English rose of the first water. There was nothing of the *Rajputra* in him—and nothing at all of the mystic. A pity the boy did not know his own good fortune.

Ruthveyn tore his gaze from the bracelet and realized his sister was still staring deep into his eyes.

"Raju," she said quietly, "what is it?"

"Nothing," he said.

She smiled gently. "You cannot lie to me, brother," she said. "You know you cannot. I feel the uneasiness about you. And last night, your stars—you were to begin a mystical journey. What has happened?"

Ruthveyn dragged a hand through his damp hair, then sighed. "Get the other boot," he answered, "and perhaps I'll tell you after my bath."

Anisha rolled onto her knees, her gaze holding his. "Give me your hand."

"Anisha, just—"

"Give me your hand," she demanded.

Reluctantly, he did so. "You can't read me," he warned.

"I can read your palm and your stars," she said quietly, "and perhaps your heart?"

Anisha spread his hand open wide, studied it for a time, tracing the lines with the tip of her index finger. Then she stopped and set her hand over his, palm to palm, for a long moment.

"Oh, it is a woman," she said certainly, her eyes closed. "And you are much conflicted."

"One might say so," Ruthveyn muttered.

"This woman," Anisha went on, "she is the cause of your sleeplessness—your frustration. She is in your dreams, and in your dreams, she maddens you—in part, because you find her so erotically—"

"*Anisha*—!"

A sleepy smile curved his sister's lips. "Very well," she murmured, eyes still closed. "We shall say instead that you find her attractive, yes? You feel much sympathy for this woman. You fear for her. She calls out to you, and yet . . . ah, and yet you do not entirely trust her, do you?"

At that, Anisha's eyes flew wide, and she fell silent for a long moment. "Raju, you . . . you cannot see her."

"Hmm," said Ruthveyn.

Anisha squeezed his hand. "Truly, can it be?"

"It could be," he acknowledged.

Anisha appraised him slyly. "Ah, but there is only one way to be sure," she answered, grinning. "And I think we both know what *that* is. So if the lady is beautiful—"

"We are not going to have this discussion, Anisha," he warned.

But his sister merely smiled her knowing smile. "Tell me, brother, does the enigmatic lady have a husband? Or a lover? Every lady needs a lover, at the very least, does she not?"

Ruthveyn scarcely knew how to respond to that one. "I believe, little sister, that we shall leave the lady to figure that one out for herself," he said, rising and dragging her up with him. "Now let it go—before I start husband-hunting for someone to warm *your* bed."

"But I have been thinking, Raju, that I should prefer merely to take a lover." Anisha batted her eyes innocently. "Is that not what London widows do? Perhaps you might arrange that instead? I believe Lord Lazonby might suit me very well indeed."

His hand still clasping hers, Ruthveyn drew Anisha close. "Believe me, Anisha, when I say this," he growled down at her. "The minute I catch Rance Welham in your bed is the minute I'll forget all my high-minded notions about female oppression and the same minute that you, my girl, will find yourself married again—and *not* to him."

"Hmm," said his sister.

"Anisha!" He gave her a little jerk. "Do we have an understanding?"

"*Haan,* Raju!" Anisha gave a put-upon sigh, and released his fingers. "We have an understanding."

Behind them, a throat cleared sharply. Ruthveyn turned to see his valet standing in the doorway.

"Good afternoon, sir," said Fricke. "May I be of help with that last boot?"

CHAPTER 6

Tea for Two

Awaiting the black-edged invitation that never came, Grace remained at home in Marylebone for the rest of the afternoon, and the whole of the next day as well. Lord Ruthveyn, she grimly considered, would have been pleased by her compliance.

On her next breath, however, she resolved not to think of him at all. She had but limited success, for the memory of his kiss had apparently been burned into her brain. Even the warm weight of his hands roaming her body seemed to linger. And underneath all that simmering heat was the disturbing realization that Grace had been on the verge of marrying a man who would never have made her feel any of those things. Never had she felt the slightest impulse to kiss Ethan Holding—nor to slap his face, it was worth noting.

To distract herself, Grace spent Sunday afternoon pressing and airing the rest of her mourning and, in deference to English sobriety, ripping the satin ruching off her best black bombazine, a gown she'd bought in Paris for her father's funeral.

And still there was no knock at the door, so Grace fired off letters to every Parisian with whom she had a passing acquaintance—their old cook, the bachelor uncle she barely knew, her father's former batman, and a half dozen others—asking their help in finding a cottage. It made for a pitifully small pile on the hall table when she laid them out for the morning post, but it had served to keep her busy.

By Monday, however, it had become humiliatingly clear that she waited in vain. No funeral invitation had been sent to her, and Grace was reduced to reading the long and flowery obituary that appeared in the morning paper, and crying alone over her toast. Her almost-fiancé was already in his grave.

Not, of course, that she would have attended the actual services. In England, Aunt Abigail had warned, a lady should be thought too delicate for such things. But Grace had wanted very much to go home—or rather, to go to Belgrave Square—to at least sit with Fenella and the other ladies in their mourning. To offer what comfort she could to Eliza and Anne. And to dine afterward in the company of people who had loved and respected the deceased.

But it was not to be. They had forgotten her. Or perhaps—God forbid—they somehow blamed her?

For a moment, Grace considered it. She had been the one to find him, gasping his last. She had been the one who had staggered from his study with blood on her hands. Perhaps Lord Ruthveyn had been right to warn her away from Napier. It was a chilling thought.

On Tuesday, however, Grace regained her composure and simply took matters into her own hands. She returned her black gown to its muslin sleeve, then put on her dove gray walking dress and half-mourning. After counting out a few shillings of her savings, she went down to Oxford Street to buy a wreath of fresh flowers and hail a hansom. She no longer troubled herself to look around to see if anyone followed. Let them do so; she had nothing to hide.

"Fulham Road, please," she told the jarvey.

As the old, odiferous carriage clattered down Park Lane, Grace stared into the green depths of Hyde Park, and tried her best not to think of that last, awful night in Belgrave Square. Or of Lord Ruthveyn, with his harsh visage and his black eyes, sharp as shattered glass. Instead, she wanted to remember Mr. Holding's rounder, far more genial face, laughing and very much alive.

Mr. Holding.

Well. That was telling, was it not? His face, too, was something of a blur. How sad. Ethan Holding, a man who had deserved better, had died betrothed to a woman whose heart could recall from instinct neither his face nor his name.

But her rash embrace with Lord Ruthveyn notwithstanding, perhaps her failings were understandable. For better than six months, he had been Mr. Holding, her employer. He had been Ethan for less than six weeks—though in truth, Grace had never grown entirely comfortable with his Christian name. Indeed, she had never been entirely comfortable with *him*.

But many a woman, she had consoled herself, married without really knowing her husband. She had known his character. She had believed that enough. Nonetheless, if she could so quickly forget his name and face, perhaps it was no wonder his family had given up on her? Perhaps it was what she deserved.

Just past Little Chelsea, Grace ordered the driver to stop. The smell and the sway of the creaky old carriage was making her dizzy. Or perhaps it was the sharp, sudden memory of Lord Ruthveyn's hands on her face that first time—the recollection having returned to her senses with her gaze transfixed by his, utterly certain that she had somehow lost herself to him. That he had looked deep within her, and seen . . . what?

It was too much. It was ridiculous.

Why could she remember one man too acutely and the other almost not at all? Grace snatched up her wreath and stepped down.

"Thank you," she said, dropping her coins into the driver's palm. "I shall walk from here."

He tugged at his forelock and glanced again at her flowers. "You'll be wanting the West London Cemetery, miss?" He pointed a gnarled finger in the direction of Fulham. " 'Tis but a short walk thataway, then up the little lane ter the right."

Grace thanked him and made her way to the south gate to wander up one of the little paths that threaded the green expanse. She had appreciated, but scarcely needed, the jarvey's kindness. At Mr. Holding's request, she had come here at least once a fortnight during her employment, bringing the girls to lay wreaths of lush, hothouse flowers at their mother's tomb.

Holding had spared no expense in honoring his late wife, having built as her mausoleum a small Romanesque temple, its white portico supported by two pairs of Doric columns. Even from a distance, it was unmistakable. But today as she looked at it, something caught her eye.

Grace raised her hand against the sun. At the top of

the mausoleum steps, a man and a woman in a veil were coming out, both attired in unrelieved black.

"Fenella!" she cried, as loudly as she dared.

It was loud enough. The gentleman beside Fenella turned his head but an instant. Then, very deliberately, he turned the lock and set one hand at the small of Fenella's spine, urging her down the steps. Grace stepped up her pace, but they were already going up the path, leaving her no alternative save to run, or to shout after them, neither of which was appropriate in a cemetery.

Horrified, she watched as the pair hastened around the corner and between a row of tombstones, then vanished into the trees. For an instant, she could not get her breath. Grace felt not simply snubbed but vilified.

Had Fenella even spared her a glance? Given her heavy veil, there was no way to know. But it seemed Royden Napier's work had been done. Josiah Crane had most assuredly seen her, and there had been no mistaking his intent.

Grace went up the short flight of steps, only to ascertain that the iron gate beyond the columns was indeed locked. The once-mossy floor within had been trodden bare, and the signs of recent interment were plain. One hand clutching the ironwork, she bent down to lay her wreath, taking care to prop it neatly against the gate yet oddly reluctant to let go.

But he *was* dead, she reminded herself. And holding on to his flowers would not bring him back.

Grace looked down, the bouquet blurring ominously. At the flower seller's, she had chosen carefully: bright yellow roses for friendship and colorful spears of agrimony to match. Agrimony was for thankfulness—and yet she had never truly thanked Mr. Holding, she realized, for all that he had done. Oh, perhaps there had been no love between them, but gratitude there had been aplenty.

He had given her not just employment, but hope after her father's death. He had entrusted to her care the two sweetest children that Grace had ever known. And he had paid her the greatest compliment imaginable in asking for her hand.

No, she had not loved him—and today she was oddly certain she never would have done. Which made his death somehow all the more unbearable, for reasons Grace could not fathom.

The sprays of green and yellow began to swim in earnest before her eyes. One tear wobbled hotly down the side of her nose as she fell to her knees on the cold stone. And there, in the utter silence of Brompton's cemetery, Grace cried as she had never expected to cry again. She cried in great, gulping sobs. For promises unfulfilled and hope surrendered. For fatherless children, and for good men cut cruelly and coldly down, far sooner than God had intended.

And still she could not remember Ethan Holding's face. Which made her cry all the harder.

Grace returned to her aunt's house in the early afternoon more or less as she had departed, this time trudging up the last leg from Oxford Street, and bringing with her the loaf of bread and fresh rutabagas that she'd promised Mrs. Ribbings, their cook. Turning the corner at Duke Street, Grace was surprised to see a fine carriage sitting at the curb—a glossy black town coach with a red-and-gold crest upon the door, a pair of supercilious-looking footmen lounging at the rear, and a coachman with a black-and-blue jaw perched upon the box—all of it making quite a contrast, she ruefully considered, to her shabby hansom cab.

Grace passed the trio by with a chary glance, then went

up the steps to let herself in. Miriam met her in the entrance hall, her eyes wide as saucers.

"I didn't forget," Grace chided, passing the bundles over. "I even found Aunt's watercress—"

"Never mind the cress, miss," Miriam interrupted, her voice pitched low. "A gentleman's come. To see you."

"*Zut!*" she softly cursed. Grace was suddenly sure to whom the elegant carriage belonged. The Marquess of Ruthveyn had likely never seen the inside of a hired cab.

Miriam handed her the card, confirming her suspicions.

Grace laid it facedown and tried to ignore the odd fluttering in her belly. She really did not wish to see Ruthveyn again. "Is my aunt not at home?"

"Gone to her Ladies' Temperance meeting, miss," said Miriam. "But he asked for you—and I don't think he fancied waiting."

"No, no, he's not the sort who does!" said Grace dryly. "Well, fetch us a pot of strong tea, Miriam, and—"

"Your sort of tea?"

Grace considered it. "Yes, please," she said. "I shall just go and change my shoes."

Grace hastened up the stairs to exchange her dusty half boots for kid slippers, and to tidy the tendrils of hair that had slipped their pins. Then, as a last resort, she powdered the red blotches around her eyes. She wanted no one's sympathy.

There was no use asking where Miriam had put Lord Ruthveyn. The only room fit for receiving such an illustrious caller was the withdrawing room, and even there, the shabby edges showed. The door stood open.

Grace hesitated on the threshold. Ruthveyn's back was turned to her as he stood at one of the windows, his gaze seemingly fixed upon a bright yellow barouche circling Manchester Square. One hand was propped upon the gold knob of a fine ebony walking stick, while the other hand sat at his hip, brushing back his black frock coat to reveal a gray silk waistcoat and the lean turn of his waist. He looked such a vision of masculine elegance, Grace required a moment to gather her thoughts. But she was not to have it.

"Good afternoon, mademoiselle," said the marquess without turning. "I trust I have not called at an inconvenient time?"

Grace cleared her throat sharply. "You have a disconcerting way of doing that, my lord."

"Calling inconveniently?" He turned from the window, one harsh, black eyebrow raised.

"No, giving one the impression you have eyes in the back of your head," she replied, making a perfunctory curtsy. "I find it unnerving."

The marquess wafted one hand gracefully beneath his nose. "It is your scent, mademoiselle," he murmured. "It is quite unmistakable."

"But I don't wear any scent."

"That is why it is yours," he answered. "May I sit down?"

"*Mais oui.*" Grace managed a smile as she pushed the door nearly shut. "I suppose I wouldn't want a crick in my neck to go with my unnerved and disconcerted state."

Ruthveyn accepted her invitation by folding himself gracefully into a dainty chair that, given the length of his legs, should have left him looking incongruous. Instead, he looked even more dangerous, like a falcon poised upon a cliff's edge, scanning the lesser creatures below in search of something to tempt his jaded palate.

The memory of their first meeting came suddenly back to her; that vision of Lord Ruthveyn's hard face hovering over hers in the sunlit garden, his thick straight hair falling forward to shadow his eyes. In her dazed state, Grace had thought him Lucifer come to life—a beautiful, sun-bronzed Lucifer, but a devil all the same. Now, she was even less sure what to make of him.

"Mademoiselle Gauthier?" His low, silky voice jerked her back to the present.

"I beg your pardon?" Grace realized she had been staring.

"I asked if you had enjoyed a pleasant morning," he repeated.

"*Merci*, yes, I—" Her words fell away. "Actually, no. I didn't. I had a frightful morning. I went to the cemetery."

"By yourself?"

"Yes."

"I'm sorry." For the first time, Ruthveyn's sharp eyes did not hold hers. "No one should have to do that alone."

"You sound as if you speak from experience," she said quietly.

Still he did not look at her. "I lost my wife when I was a young man," he finally answered. "It was . . . unbearable."

"I'm sorry," Grace murmured. "You have my sympathy."

He said no more for a time but instead sat quietly, one hand folded over the other, the starched edges of his cuffs brilliantly white against his bronzed hands. He put Grace in mind of a grand portrait she'd once seen for sale in a village bazaar, purported to be that of Suleiman the Magnificent upon his throne—serene, self-disciplined, and utterly regal.

And yet Ruthveyn radiated restless male energy. She thought again of how he had kissed her, his mouth taking possession of hers with a skill and a hunger Grace had not imagined possible. Did he think of that moment? Did he feel the awkwardness of it between them? Was the heat of that kiss still seared upon *his* mouth?

Unwittingly, Grace touched her fingertips to her lips.

Ruthveyn betrayed himself then with a glint of some barely suppressed emotion in his eyes.

Grace dropped her hand to her lap, wondering the room didn't explode with the sudden heat. They were saved from it when Miriam came in with the tea tray. Grace busied herself by making small talk as she served, taking comfort in the fact that her hands did not shake.

Really, what *was* the matter with her? He was just a man. It was just tea. But there was no denying there was something otherworldly—and deeply sensual—about Lord Ruthveyn.

"This is a green gunpowder that we often served at home," she nattered, taking up the pot. "I recall it was Sergeant Welham's favorite. Will you take it in the traditional way? Or would you like warm milk?"

"Thank you, I shall take it as is," he said.

Grace lifted the battered old pot and poured it high, causing the tea to foam up to the top of each cup. "The sugar is already in it," she warned.

Lord Ruthveyn sipped at it pensively. "And the mint," he said, smiling faintly. "It is bitter, strong, and delicious. Mademoiselle Gauthier, I commend you. I could almost imagine myself back in the Kasbah."

"Could you?" she murmured, pouring for herself. "Did you spend much time there?"

Ruthveyn crooked one eyebrow. "With Rance Welham as my boon companion?" he asked. "I should rather not say."

"Sergeant Welham had some unfortunate habits, my lord." Grace put the pot down with a bit of a clatter. "And he lived too hard. I hope he did not corrupt you."

Ruthveyn sipped at his tea as if stalling for time. "Perhaps it was more the other way round," he finally said.

"But none of it is appropriate for a lady's ears. I called today to tell you what I've managed to learn about Scotland Yard's investigation into your fiancé's death."

"Almost-fiancé." She smiled weakly. "That is what I've decided to call Mr. Holding. It . . . makes it all somehow more bearable. I daresay that makes no sense to you."

"It makes a great deal of sense to me," he said quietly.

Grace dropped her gaze to her tea. "You once asked me, Lord Ruthveyn, if I had loved Mr. Holding," she replied. "Would it make sense to you if I now said that I wished quite desperately I had done?"

Fleetingly, his voice softened. "Actually, it would."

She could feel her lower lip tremble ominously. "I . . . I cannot seem to grieve for him," she whispered. "Not as the loss of a husband. I wish now I'd never agreed to marry him. What once seemed eminently practical now seems simply wrong."

"Grief is sometimes better expressed by helping find justice for a death, Mademoiselle Gauthier," said Ruthveyn. "Regret is useless—whilst revenge, I often find, can be rather a comfort."

Despite its ruthlessness, the remark oddly steadied her. "I would not wish to make an enemy of you, Lord Ruthveyn."

Something that might have been a smile toyed with his mouth. "Shall I bring you up to date on what I know?" he asked. "Perhaps if I do, you will be more comfortable leaving this in my hands from here out. And if there is revenge to be had, I'll see to it."

"We shall see," she replied. "Of course, I should be most grateful for anything you can tell me."

Ruthveyn's jaw twitched tellingly. "Yes, we shall see," he echoed. "Firstly, Mr. Napier has been called away—a family matter of some sort. In his absence, the Metropolitan Police have released the house. Were your things returned?"

"A van came on Saturday with my trunks. I suppose everything is there."

"Good," Ruthveyn murmured. "I understand Miss Crane has returned home, Mr. Crane has reopened the offices, and as you suspected, Mr. Holding's stepchildren are to remain with their mother's sister."

Grace's heart sank a little. "I had resigned myself to it, of course," she said softly. "At least they shall be well provided for."

"Indeed," said Ruthveyn. "The will was read yesterday. Holding left each girl a tidy trust to live on and a dowry of thirty thousand pounds."

"Good heavens," said Grace.

"Holding also left annuities to the senior servants and a few charitable bequests, with the balance of the estate going to his sister."

"That makes sense," said Grace. "It was, after all, their father's firm that created the family's wealth. Was nothing left to Josiah Crane?"

"No, but since he is already part owner, I would not have expected it," said Ruthveyn. "Might I ask, mademoiselle, if there had been any tension between Holding and his partner?"

Grace shook her head. "None I saw. Why?"

The marquess watched her quietly for a moment. "I have it on good authority that Crane was in debt," he finally said. "It seems he had developed something of a taste for gambling."

Grace's eyes widened. "*Mon Dieu*, the Crane Curse?" she murmured. "Or so Fenella called it. That's how Josiah's father lost his half of the business. Tell me, was he in deep?"

Ruthveyn lifted one shoulder. "No worse than most men of fashion," he admitted. "Nothing he could not afford to repay—in time. But his name was being bandied about by the local sharps as something of a mark."

"You mean by Mr. Quartermaine and his ilk," said Grace.

Both his dark brows lifted at that. "Have you some passing acquaintance with our neighborhood hell?" he replied. "No, I meant the cardsharps who frequent such places. Quartermaine is an honest man—more or less."

"Which means?"

Ruthveyn's mouth quirked. "Which means he is honest most of the time," he answered. "He is also full of useful information if one can pry it out of him."

"And you can?" Grace eyed him over her teacup.

"I can be persuasive," said Ruthveyn.

"Doubtless it is your charm," Grace dryly remarked. "I noticed it straightaway."

He flicked a quick, diamond-hard look at her. "Mademoiselle Gauthier, I begin to think you have a little more spine than I first suspected—and I never thought you lacking."

"Thank you," said Grace. "I do pride myself on it. What else have you learned?"

"That the competitor Holding forced out of business last month is ruined." Ruthveyn paused to sip his tea. "And that Crane was unhappy with the deal. Apparently, the maneuver left Crane and Holding overextended—not an ideal position for a gambler who has passed his vowels all over Town."

Grace stiffened. "The company is not at risk, I hope?"

"I doubt it," he said. "It will depend who comes aboard

to steer the ship in Holding's place. Perhaps Miss Crane will wish to have a voice in that. One could argue she has some right."

Grace frowned. "I can't think she would bother."

"Few women would," Ruthveyn agreed. "She showed no interest in the business?"

Grace shrugged. "Fenella merely served as Mr. Holding's social hostess," she replied. "She answered his invitations or the occasional letter, and organized dinner parties if business required it. But I think she loathed that sort of thing. She used to laugh and say their mother had often told her she had no talent for it. As to money, Mr. Holding always gave her carte blanche. She lacked for nothing material."

Ruthveyn sighed and put his cup down. "Then I daresay Josiah Crane is destined to get another visit from our friend Napier when he learns of those gaming debts," he said, "which will perhaps deflect attention from you. Tell me, are you sure Crane left the house after dinner that night?"

"Quite sure. I walked him out myself. He had the book of poetry in his carriage."

Ruthveyn pondered it. "Dare I hope he had a key to the house?"

Grace's eyes widened. "He may have done," she answered. "He occasionally brought post and papers by early in the morning—things he wished Mr. Holding to read over breakfast. They kept different hours, you see. When Mr. Holding traveled, he often sent our letters inside Mr. Crane's daily dispatch. I would find them on the hall table when I came down."

"I see." Ruthveyn set both hands on his thighs as if to rise. "Well, that is something, I suppose."

"But really, Lord Ruthveyn, I am quite sure Mr. Crane did not kill his cousin."

The marquess's face was emotionless. "That is not my concern," he answered. "My concern is you."

"Why?" Grace's voice was sharp.

He hesitated. "Because I have had a telegraph from Rance—Lord Lazonby, I should say—telling me so."

"He wishes you to help me?"

"He wishes me to take charge of this business," Ruthveyn clarified, "and to protect you from harm or scandal in whatever way necessary. If that means throwing Crane to the wolves, I'll do it."

"That shan't be necessary," she replied a little tartly.

At that, Ruthveyn's hard expression seemed to relent. His hands slid from his thighs, and he settled back into the dainty chair, and it was as if he fell into deep thought for a time.

"Mademoiselle Gauthier, might I trouble you for another cup of tea?" he finally said.

Grace was surprised. She had been sure he was on the verge of leaving. Indeed, she wished he *would* leave. Didn't she?

"I beg your pardon," she said, taking up the pot. "I should have offered."

"Your aunt is not at home today, I collect," said Ruthveyn, his gaze focused on the stream of tea. "I hope my visit here will not distress her."

Grace shrugged. "I'm not sure there's any pleasing Aunt Abigail," she answered. "Especially where I'm concerned. I am, after all, my mother's daughter. We are a disappointing lot, I fear."

"Are you indeed?" he murmured. "I would never have guessed."

She flashed a faintly bitter smile. "My mother married down, Lord Ruthveyn," she explained. "She was the daughter of an English lord, but she had the temerity to elope with an impoverished French army officer."

Ruthveyn's black eyes hardened again. "Is that marrying down?"

"That's what her family thought," Grace answered. "Doubtless it is what you think."

"With all respect, Mademoiselle Gauthier, you have no idea what I think."

Grace dropped her gaze. "I'm sorry," she said. "You are quite right. I do not."

"But all was forgiven?" Ruthveyn smoothly resumed. "Your mother was reconciled to her family?"

Lightly, she shrugged. "My mother was much loved, and much doted on," she admitted. "As a child, I visited here from time to time, and was encouraged by my grandparents to think of this house as my home. But I—" Here, her voice broke wistfully, "—I still think of Algeria as home, even though it isn't. Still, it is the place we were last happy together; Mamma, Papa, and I."

It was as if Ruthveyn read her mind. "You cannot leave London, Mademoiselle Gauthier," he said quietly. "That is what you were thinking, was it not?"

"It was, actually," she admitted.

"Your situation with Lady Abigail is intolerable?"

Grace's mouth twisted. "Few things are truly intolerable, my lord," she answered. "It is uncomfortable. My aunt lives in the past, and it is a bitter one."

"How so?"

Grace drew a deep breath. "My mother was a great beauty who was expected to marry well," she answered, "and drag the family fortunes from the brink of ruin. When she chose instead to marry selfishly—my aunt's words, not mine—she wasted her only asset."

"And that ruined your aunt's life . . . how, precisely?"

"Aunt Abigail never married," said Grace. "She claims there wasn't any money for a dowry, or even a season. That everything had been spent on Mamma, and she had embarrassed the family. So Aunt has remained here all these years, steeping in her acrimony and, since my grandfather died, living off the present earl's charity— what little of it he can afford."

Ruthveyn's lip curled with scorn. "What craven self-indulgence."

"Perhaps." Grace sighed. "But I need bear it only until Napier's work is done."

"And then?"

"And then I go back to France." Grace folded her hands carefully in her lap. "Moreover, I've made up my mind that I am going to like it. I *am*. I shall take a little cottage and make a quiet life for myself. I mean to find a measure of peace, if not happiness."

"Peace and happiness." His tone was cynical as he set down his tea, untouched. "In that, my dear, I wish you well."

Then abruptly, Ruthveyn jerked from his chair and paced back to the window where he'd been standing earlier.

"My lord?" Confused, Grace pushed from her chair and followed him. "I beg your pardon. Have I given some offence?"

"No," he said without looking at her. The cynicism had fallen from his tone. "No, of course not."

She crooked her head to look at his strong, stark profile. "Then what is it, pray?"

He dragged a hand through his mane of inky hair, a telling, almost boyish gesture. Grace wondered again at his age. Despite possessing the tall, hard-muscled physique of a virile man in his prime, Ruthveyn seemed both oddly ageless and yet old beyond his years.

But he had been married once. He had buried a wife. Perhaps he even had children?

Good heavens.

Idiot that she was, Grace had never considered such a thing. Which drove home the painful reality that she really knew nothing of him. She was still pondering it when he spoke again, in a voice so soft she scarcely recognized it.

"Do you see those shadows, Grace?" He was staring at the row of houses beyond the glass. "They come creeping relentlessly across the street, every day, without fail, ever destined to shroud us as the sun sets. That is what fate feels like to me. Like an impending shadow that cannot be evaded. And we know that it is coming. Sometimes, just before the veil falls, we can even glimpse what lies within. And sometimes what we see is but a chimera—or the reflection of our fears."

Grace saw only the Beesons' nurse from down the street, pushing a pram along the pavement. But Ruthveyn seemed to be speaking quite literally. Grace thought again of all the dark energy and strength within him and wondered, fleetingly, what it would be like were he to unleash it. She snatched back her stilled hand, which had been but an inch from settling on his arm, in what would doubtless have been a futile attempt at comfort.

He cut the merest hint of a glance in her direction. "I hope you find your peace someday, Grace," he said. "But France is still politically unstable. It simply mightn't be safe for you to leave England in the foreseeable future— nor to remain in England, come to that."

She opened her mouth to tell him how utterly absurd that was. But his words sounded so heartfelt, she could not even chide him for falling back on her Christian name again. Moreover, the sound of it on his lips had begun to feel disconcertingly *right*.

"I have no way of seeing what lurks in those shadows approaching you, Grace," he went on. "I *can't*. I feel . . . blind."

"No one can know the future, my lord." But even as she spoke the words, a chill ran down her spine. "And who would wish to? It would be a terrible curse, of that I am sure."

He set his hand to the glass, his fingers wide, as if the gesture might hold back the shadows. Not for the first time, Grace wondered if Ruthveyn knew something he was not telling her. Was his otherworldly persona something more dire? But that was utter nonsense.

"Have you forgiven me, I wonder?" His words, almost detached, cut into her thoughts. "For what happened between us in Whitehall?"

Grace knew at once what he meant. "For that kiss?" Somehow she forced a light tone. "Well, it was just a kiss, my lord. And as you pointed out, I have been kissed before—I daresay you have, too?"

Something like black humor twitched at his fine, full mouth. "Once or twice, yes."

Grace extended her hand. "Pax, then," she said. "It is forgotten."

"Pax, then," he echoed in his warm, raspy voice.

Then he turned and took her hand, but instead of shaking it, lifted it toward his lips. But at the last possible instant, he hesitated, his eyes locked with hers, his breath warm on her knuckles. Then something inside him seemed to give way. Ruthveyn closed his eyes, and drew her instead into his embrace. "Come here," he whispered.

Like a fool, Grace went willingly, yearning for the feel of his arms as they encircled her. Ruthveyn's left hand was cold on her shoulder from the window's glass, but his right felt broad and strong and warm as it gathered her to him, crushing her gown against the silk of his waistcoat. At once, his warmth surrounded her, carrying with it his subtle scent, already achingly familiar. It was as if his very strength began to seep into her; madness, she knew. And yet it felt inevitable, as if she, too, were caught up in his strange mood.

"I should like to kiss you again," he said, his eyes searching her face.

She watched him unblinkingly. "Are you asking?"

"Yes," he rasped. "And you should say *no*."

She swallowed hard. "And if I do not?"

"Then I'm going to kiss you until your toes curl," he said, "and hope, like a bloody damned fool, that you beg me for more."

And oh, how she wanted him. Against all logic, and a lifetime of hard experience, Grace longed to give herself up to him. She was so weary of being alone, and lonely. Or perhaps she was just weak. Grace no longer cared. And so, with Ruthveyn's heart thudding steadily against her right breast, she lifted her chin and let her eyes drop shut.

His lips brushed over hers in the lightest caress; once, twice, then again, as if tempting her. She answered, slanting her head in invitation, and felt his mouth come fully over hers, warm and open.

Something inside her came awake, thrumming with life and light at his touch. As his lips moved languidly over hers, Grace rose as if from a dream to urge herself fully against him, twining her arms round his neck.

Ruthveyn made a sound, something between a groan

and a sigh, then forced his tongue deep into her mouth to tangle sinuously with hers. The thing inside Grace drew taut as a bowstring, tugging from her heart to her belly and deeper still. Then the tautness became an ache, and as his mouth moved over hers—*possessing* her—Grace felt wanton and wanted and strangely free.

In an instant, she was up against the wall, his body hard against hers, his hands roaming hungrily. One palm shaped her breast, warm against her nipple, deepening the throb inside her. His opposite hand cupped the swell of her hip, lifting her to him.

Lightly thumbing her nipple to a taut, aching peak, Ruthveyn let his mouth slide down her throat, his tongue dipping lightly in the hollow above her collarbone, making Grace long to drag the fabric down and give him free rein. Her breath came short and sharp, and he returned his lips to hers, plunging inside. In Ruthveyn she sensed a desperation that matched her own, like a man long starved for the human touch. For love, perhaps.

Oh, but that was a dangerous self-deception. And she was no green girl. She felt the hard ridge of his arousal throb against her belly and knew it had gone far enough. Somehow, she controlled herself, returning his kisses with equal heat, thrilling to the pleasure of it, but holding herself a fraction from that dark edge that beckoned. The edge beyond which, she sensed, she would be entirely lost to his darkness.

Ruthveyn felt her hesitation and began to draw away; first the pressure of his thighs, then the sheltering wall of his chest, until at last only their lips remained joined. They parted with light, glancing kisses, then his mouth skimmed from hers and brushed along the turn of her jaw.

"*Grace*," he murmured, nuzzling the words behind her ear. "Ah, Grace."

One of his hands was set above her nape now, cradling the back of her head, and simply because she wanted to, she turned and laid one cheek to the fine wool of his frock coat.

"This is lunacy, you know," she murmured, her breath coming far too fast.

"Utterly," he agreed. "And what's worse, you are not going to beg me for more, are you?"

"No." She swallowed hard. "At least—*no.* I am not."

Ruthveyn buried his face in her hair, and she realized he was trembling. "Grace," he whispered. "You can't let me do this again."

"You—?" Her head came up as she said it. "*You* are a man, Lord Ruthveyn. Men are free to take what is offered them. But what am I for having offered it?"

He set her a little away from him then, and dipped his head to catch her gaze. "You are a woman, Grace, who has had her life turned cruelly upside down," he replied. "And I am a cad, perhaps, for taking advantage of that."

"What utter nonsen—"

"And in my own defense," he interjected, setting a firm finger to her lips, "I can say only that to touch a woman like you, for me, is a thing so rare—" Here, his voice hitched. "Actually, there *is* no defending me."

Grace drew away, feeling more alone than ever. "I've never known anyone quite like you, Ruthveyn," she said, wrapping her arms over her chest. "I don't know whether I like you, or if I'm half-afraid of you. But whatever it is, we seem to be flint and tinder to one another."

Again, he dragged that telling hand through his hair, this time thoroughly disordering it. "Grace, I have to ask you something."

"By all means, ask." Her smile twisted. "Shoot for the

moon, Ruthveyn. We have every reason to think I might say *yes*."

His gaze darkened ominously at that. One hand fisted at his side. "Don't be cruel, Grace," he said, "especially not to yourself. I will not kiss you again. I won't even try."

Grace gave a bark of laughter and let her arms fall. "Do you know, Ruthveyn, I actually believe you," she replied. "I'm sorry. It's just—your touch—it addles me somehow. But please, go ahead. Ask."

"My timing, of course, could not be worse," he said warningly.

"We both have a gift for that," she agreed.

"Perhaps." He relaxed his hand. "In any case, I think . . . I think that you should come to live with me."

Grace set a hand to her heart. "I—I beg your pardon?"

"As a governess," he added swiftly. "I will feel better about all this if you are beneath my roof."

"As a governess?" she echoed. "*Ça alors!* To whom?"

"My sister," he said, catching her upper arms in his hands. Then, as if burned, he dropped them and stepped back. "Not for my sister, of course, but for her children. I am entirely serious. She desperately needs a tutor of some sort. And my nephews are—well, they are a handful."

"Even if I were fool enough to do such a thing, no one would consider me qualified to tutor young men," Grace explained. "They will need mathematics and sciences and—"

"Oh, come now, Grace." Ruthveyn arched one of his black eyebrows in that gesture of disdain she was so rapidly coming to recognize. "Surely you do not believe men the only sex capable of such things? Do you mean to suggest that you know nothing of basic arithmetic? Or geography?"

Grace blushed. The truth was, she had always found such subjects fascinating and could no more teach tatting or drawing than fly to the moon. Military history and battlefield tactics were her best subjects, and she was quite skilled at geography, having seen rather a lot of it firsthand. Only her blue blood and flawless French had qualified her to be a governess.

Ruthveyn sensed her curiosity. "They are neither of them above ten, by the way," he went on, "and what little education they've seen was in Calcutta, and from a gentleman so old and so poor of sight he could scarce keep up with them. In short, they know almost nothing and are hellions of the worst sort. It's an assignment that will never give you your precious peace, but will give me, at least, a little peace of mind."

"B-But that sounds—"

"Selfish, yes," he cut in. "All men are, I am told."

"Lord Ruthveyn," she said tartly, "kindly stop interrupting me."

"There, you see?" Both brows went up this time. "You are at least willing to *try* to govern the intractable."

"Oh, I am perfectly capable of it," she responded with asperity. "Now, you will answer *my* questions."

"Very well." He stepped back another inch.

"You are doing this because of Rance Welham, and for no other reason?"

Ruthveyn hesitated a heartbeat. "For Rance, yes," he said. "For my part, I'm rarely at home. I keep a suite of rooms in St. James's."

"At the St. James Society." Her gaze fell again to his strange, yet oddly familiar cravat pin. The symbol in the middle, she realized, was a tiny gold cross.

"Grace, my servants and family are loyal to a fault," he said. "You will be safe surrounded by them."

"I never felt I was in danger," Grace said. "Certainly not from you—not in that way. And so far as Napier is concerned, the innocent should have nothing to fear. In that, at least, I am innocent."

"There is a vast chasm between *should* and *have*," he said quietly. "Grace, do you trust me to keep you safe?"

She considered it a moment. "I can imagine few men willing to cross you," she said. "Yes, I trust you."

"Do you believe me when I say you might be in danger?" he went on. "Or at least at some risk of being made a scapegoat? Or of having your good name tarnished?"

"I believe you when you say you that *you* believe those things," she conceded.

"And you cannot stay here," Ruthveyn continued. "You said as much not half an hour past."

He was offering her a way out, Grace realized. An escape from Aunt Abigail, yes, but he was also offering the broad mantle of his protection. It horrified her to think she might need it. But Mr. Holding was dead—and *someone* had murdered him.

"Perhaps not." She breathed deep and considered it. With him, she would be safe. She was certain of it. And there would be children—children who needed her. "I must be mad, of course, but these hellions—have they names?"

"When I left after dinner last night, it was Thor, Hammer of the North, and Erik the Bloodthirsty," he replied, straight-faced. "My favorite billiards table had become a Viking dragon ship, and they were rowing fiercely for Lithuania with a set of brand-new, custom-made cue sticks."

"Excellent," said Grace. "Then they have at least a passing acquaintance with Scandinavian history, and the geography of northern Europe—not to mention a proper appreciation of fine hardwoods. Their real names?"

"Tom is six, and Teddy is eight," said Ruthveyn. "They are my sister Anisha's children. She is a widow."

"Anisha?" Grace interjected. "That's unusual."

"Her name? Yes." Ruthveyn hesitated a moment. "We were brought up in India. Perhaps I never said."

"Both of you? How interesting."

"Actually, we *are* Indian—Rajputs—on our mother's side," he went on. "Perhaps that is not obvious."

Grace let her eyes drift over him. "I never thought about it."

"Does it matter to you?"

Grace blinked uncertainly. "Good Lord," she said reflexively. "In regards to what?"

One corner of his mouth lifted cynically. "You said your mother married down, Mademoiselle Gauthier," he reminded her. "Most days, I think my mother did, too."

It took Grace a heartbeat before she burst out laughing. "I think I begin to like you better and better, Lord Ruthveyn," she said. "Perhaps we shall deal famously together after all."

"Then get your things."

Her smile fell. "What? *Now?*"

"Why not now?" he asked. "What is going to change? So far as your aunt is concerned, I have offered you a position. Leave her a note. My servants will return for your trunks tonight."

"Such haste seems unnecessary."

Again, he shrugged, then propped one shoulder against the window frame. "Are you coming, Grace," he murmured, "or not?"

Grace looked beyond him to see that dusk—and Ruthveyn's shadows—were fast drawing nigh. He, too, was watching. Waiting. And soon the darkness would be upon them. But what was there, really, to fear beyond that veil?

Only herself and her own foolishness, most likely.

Nonetheless, she was going. She was going to live with Lord Ruthveyn. She was going to trust his promises and his strength. She only prayed she was making the right decision.

And for the right reason.

CHAPTER 7

A Little Family Quarrel

*A*drian, how *could* you?"

Ruthveyn knew his sister was angry when she used his Christian name.

Lady Anisha was dressed tonight in a topaz gold dinner gown, the bodice cut straight across her slender shoulders and ruched with butter-colored satin, while the wide, bell-shaped skirt was gathered up in matching rosettes on either side. The whole of it looked remarkably flattering against her warm ivory skin—save for Anisha's face, which had turned the color of overpoached salmon.

"Anisha, my dear, do sit down." Ruthveyn surveyed her from across his desk as she wore a path in his carpet. "Just tell me what you thought of her. Have you any real objection—save for my heavy-handedness?"

His sister froze, eyes blazing. "How am I to know what

my objections might be?" she retorted. "I just met the woman!"

It was in moments like this Ruthveyn realized how very much alike they were.

"At dinner, no less, where she was dropped in my lap with the dinner napkin like some freshly starched *fait accompli*!" Anisha continued. "Really, Adrian, you have put me—and your Mademoiselle Gauthier—in a most awkward position. And she knew it, too. Couldn't you see that?"

"Anisha, if you would—"

"No, I won't." Anisha spun around and resumed her pacing. "These are my *children*, Adrian. They are the fruit of my womb. How could you possibly presume to know what they need? Indeed, you have not spent above an hour with either of them since we got here!"

Ruthveyn's temper spiked at that. "Oh, don't hold back, Anisha! Ram that sword all the way home!" He jerked from his chair and went to his sideboard. "Do you want a brandy?" he snapped. "God knows I need one."

"No, I don't want a brandy!" Anisha followed him across the room. "I want respect! Aren't you the one who keeps telling me I should demand it? That I should make my own decisions?"

Ruthveyn sighed and yanked the stopper from the decanter with a discordant scrape. At three-and-thirty, he was half a dozen years her senior, but Anisha could madden him as if they were still children. He poured the liquor, then shoved all of it away in disgust to brace his hands wide on the mahogany top. In his present mood, alcohol would be nothing but fuel tossed on an already blazing fire; an inferno born of temper, raging lust, and the sickening realization that his sister just might be right.

Slowly he drew his breath deep into the pit of his belly,

then blew it out again in one long, carefully moderated exhalation. Once. Twice. Again. Until the blood stopped pounding in his temples.

He felt his sister hovering near his elbow.

"Anisha, you know I care for those boys," he finally rasped, staring out into the blackness of the rear gardens. "I would lay down my life for them. But I can't . . . I just can't play the affectionate uncle so easily. For God's sake, I can barely look them in the eyes."

"You have held yourself apart from people, Adrian, for so long, you no longer know what intimacy is," his sister whispered. "You are so afraid of what you might see that it haunts you. But they are children. They do not understand."

"Yes, Anisha, they *are* children. And for that reason, I need to see them as young, vigorous, and full of life's every promise. Don't you?"

"Even if I had the true sight, I could not see my children," she said simply. "You know that. Moreover, they are not of the Vateis, Raju, nor will they ever be Guardians. They certainly don't have your misfortune to be both. My children were born under the wrong stars and haven't a hint of the Gift. They are . . . well, like Luc, thank God."

"I'm not sure the latter is to be bragged about, my dear." His voice fell to a weary, more conciliatory tone. "But you are right about the other. I should have done this thing properly. I should have asked you about hiring a governess. I just . . ."

"Just what?" Sympathy had crept into her tone.

"I just need her to be here," he finally managed. "And I feared she wouldn't just *come*—that it would require some pretext on my part—so I thought of the boys. She worships children. One can hear it in her voice."

Anisha's delicate brow furrowed. "But why here, Raju? What is she to you?"

His mouth twisted with a bitter smile. "Not what you are thinking," he answered. "The truth is, she's a friend of Lazonby's who's run into a spot of trouble. He asked me to keep her safe."

"To keep her safe?" Anisha echoed, her hand coming out to touch his arm. "Then what is she to him? A lover?"

"Just a friend, Anisha." He straightened up and took a sip of his brandy. "The daughter of his old commanding officer. But don't let your heart wander in that direction. Promise me. Lazonby is not for you."

Anisha's jaw hardened. "And you know best?"

"In this, yes." Ruthveyn took her firmly by the upper arms. "Trust me, Nish, I have debauched my way through every whorehouse and opium den from Casablanca to Edinburgh with that man. I know his predilections and habits, and vile as they are, I still love him like a brother. But you do not want him—and even if you did, I would forbid it."

Her long, black lashes swept down. "You can't forbid it," she said softly. "But you are right. I must think of the boys. I don't want to marry again, ever. And as to the other—perhaps loneliness is the better option."

"Well, I am only warning you off Lazonby. What about Bessett? Or Curran? They are fine young men and . . . ah, but this is none of my business, is it?" Ruthveyn gave her arms a reassuring squeeze, then let go. "Look, don't fret about Mademoiselle Gauthier. I shall tell her in the morning you had already made other arrangements. I'll find another way of keeping her here—at least until her situation is settled."

Anisha cleared her throat. "That might be awkward."

"I know," he answered. "But there's nothing else to be

done. I can't take her up to one of the Scottish estates. Napier will think she's run."

Unease sketched across Anisha's delicate features. "Raju, what is it?" she asked, touching him lightly. "What do you see? What sort of danger surrounds her?"

"I don't—" Here, he stopped, and threw up his hands impotently. "I *don't know*, Anisha. I don't sense anything. I don't see anything. That is the very essence of my dilemma."

"Ah, yes, your Unknowable!" His sister's furrowed brow relented. "So *she* is the one."

Hands again braced on the sideboard, Ruthveyn dropped his head. "Yes," he said quietly. "She is the one."

"You are quite sure?"

He swiveled his head to look at her. "As sure as I likely can be," he answered, "without thoroughly compromising a lady's virtue. And pray do not suggest that again."

Anisha blushed faintly. "But she is so very beautiful with that blond hair and oval face," she murmured. "Ah, Raju, perhaps I, too, have been hasty. What did you say the lady's background was?"

He took up his brandy and motioned her toward the pair of worn leather armchairs that flanked the dying fire. "She was governess for a shipbuilder named Holding who lived in Belgravia," he said wearily. "Two girls, about the age of Tom and Teddy."

"That sounds familiar." Anisha twitched her skirts into place, then her head jerked up. "Wait, isn't he the one who was murdered?"

"Yes. He was." Ruthveyn sat and drank deep of the brandy, feeling the burn as it rolled down his throat. He needed another drink. Hell, he wanted more than a drink.

"And you fear that next this madman might come after her?"

"Not while she is under my protection," he vowed. "I think it more likely Napier will try to arrest her."

"Napier!" Anisha spat, sitting forward in her chair. "Hasn't he ruined enough lives? He persecuted Rance! He convicted an innocent man."

"Actually, that was Napier's father," Ruthveyn corrected. "Not that the son hasn't done his part since the old man died."

Anisha clutched her hands in her lap, looking a little shamefaced. "I have been too hasty in all this," she said. "I have had rather a bad day, Raju, and my temper is not at its best. If Mademoiselle Gauthier is Rance's friend, and if she has experience with children . . ."

Ruthveyn studied his sister for a moment. "What sort of a bad day, Anisha?" he said quietly. "Is your irritation about something other than Grace?"

"Hmm," said Anisha. "Already she is *Grace* to you." But she did not look at him.

"My dear, what is wrong?"

On instinct, Ruthveyn bent to catch her gaze, but it was of limited use. The Vateis could rarely read one another—and Anisha was likely one of them, whether she admitted it or not. Growing up with her had been Ruthveyn's salvation, perhaps, for it had forced him to learn to read and understand people as ordinary human beings did. And just now, he could see chagrin and unhappiness in her face.

"Is Luc in trouble again?" he pressed. "You'd best fess up, old thing."

Her eyes fell to the Turkish carpet, and she shook her head. "No, it's just that I had another message from Dr. von Althausen," she confessed. "The man is going to bedevil me until I run back to Calcutta to get away from him."

"Anisha." He flashed an encouraging smile. "You might just consider . . ."

Her eyes flashed. "But I am not a Guardian, Raju."

"No, because you are a woman," he conceded. "People such as you are the very reason the Guardians exist."

"I do not want your protection," she bit out. "Or Rance's or Curran's! And I don't want to spend one minute in that drafty old cellar of his being poked or electrified or whatever it is he does. Besides, I don't even have the Gift. The wisdom of *Jyotish* guides me. I have studied hard to hone my skills. Do not demean them."

Ruthveyn picked up his empty glass and began to turn it round to reflect the firelight. "So you think all you do is read stars and palms, hmm?" he mused, watching the cut crystal spark with light. "You are a lot like Lazonby, Nish. Always trying to deny the obvious. Von Althausen can learn from you, and help you hone your abilities."

"One does not hone one's executioner's blade for him!" she hotly replied, coming halfway out of her chair. "I just want to study the stars, Raju. They are not subject to interpretation."

"Actually, my dear, they are," he answered. "They just don't look that way to you."

"But you will not work with von Althausen," she challenged. "Why should I?"

Slowly, Ruthveyn exhaled. She was perfectly correct. Ruthveyn was devoted to the Guardians and their greater purpose, yes. But unlike some, he had no wish to strengthen or even to understand his abilities. He wanted them to *go away*—and would literally have sold his soul to the devil to make it happen.

But he could not. His soul had been sold long ago, for the visions had plagued him since his earliest memory. As a child, he had been called freakish. Unnatural. No one save his mother could hold him, or even hold his gaze beyond a passing glance. Not until Anisha had come along. Even his father, in whose blood the Gift ran strong, had thought him beyond strange.

There had been a reason Ruthveyn's mother had remained unmarried until the age of thirty, Ruthveyn's father had belatedly learned. She had been a *rishika*— a mystic of such power her own people had feared her. Her wealthy family had thought it a coup to marry their beautiful princess to a titled Englishman, and to ally themselves politically with England. But the union had produced a potent mixing of the blood, and Ruthveyn— the freakish, introspective, unloving child—had been the result.

It had taken all of his willpower and all of his courage to learn to hide what he was behind a façade of unwavering formality and distance. Only in Hindustan, land of distance and formality, could he have succeeded in the guise of a diplomat. But his father's ruthlessness and his mother's grace had combined to stand him in good stead. He had survived.

And now he wanted his sister to do what he was unwilling to do?

Ruthveyn set his empty glass down with a heavy *clunk*. "Fair enough, Anisha," he said. "I will tell von Althausen you will not be coming. I will tell him to stop asking."

"Dhanyavaad, Raju." Her hands relaxed on the chair arms.

He looked at her appraisingly. "And you will consider giving Grace a chance?" he asked. "You will at least try, I hope, to be her friend? If not for me, then perhaps for dear old Rance?"

Her eyes flashed for an instant, then Anisha relented. "Very well, brother," she conceded. "As usual, you know just the right words to strike your bargain—but first, *you* will do something for *me*."

He did not like the resolve in her tone. "Go on."

She settled back into her chair. "You will tell me everything," she said. "Everything you suspect—and everything you've *seen*—regarding Mademoiselle Gauthier's involvement in this murder business."

"Now *that*," he said quietly, picking up his empty glass, "is going to require another brandy."

Grace settled into Lord Ruthveyn's vast Mayfair mansion with a measure of unease. The house itself was quietly elegant without the ostentation Grace had grown accustomed to in Belgravia, with touches of Eastern influence in the fabrics and objets d'art that made the house feel welcoming.

The two boys, Teddy and Tom, were filled with devilry, but after three days spent sequestered with them in the schoolroom, Grace did not wholly despair. The little imps were intelligent—almost too much so—and eager to learn so long as the teaching was creative and allowed some outlet for their monkeylike energy.

The children had brought with them from India a huge, raucous parakeet named Milo, and latched slavishly onto Silk and Satin, Ruthveyn's haughty housecats, both of whom were solid silver and disdained most everyone else's advances. It took all Grace's resolve to ban the trio from the schoolroom.

What the boys lacked in formal education, they more than made up for in the areas of applied physics and chemistry; slingshots capable of shattering glass at fifty paces, and an imaginative experiment with homemade glue that left Teddy's stockings bonded to his shoes. On her third day, Grace caught them under the schoolroom tea table after elevenses shaking a little jar of something that roiled and hissed threateningly, but turned out to be nothing more than baking soda and vinegar, and provided a quick tutorial in exothermic reactions, followed by a long lesson on how to properly clean a soiled carpet— which they did, on hands and knees.

Of Lord Ruthveyn's sister, Grace was less certain. Lady Anisha Stafford was a quiet, exotic beauty who possessed her brother's quick black eyes and his proclivity for staring straight through to one's soul. Though her skin was pale as cream, Anisha's face possessed a far more foreign cast than did Ruthveyn's. Or perhaps it was her penchant for floating through the private rooms of the house swathed in ells of brilliantly hued silk, one end thrown over her shoulder, and dripping in opulent embroidery. Once Grace even spotted her sporting a pair of baggy pantaloons and looking for all the world like a princess plucked from some mughal's harem.

For the most part, however, Lady Anisha was the perfect English hostess, and indeed, she treated Grace like a guest. She was given a bedchamber twice the size of her old room, its walls hung with paisley silk in brilliant shades of gold and green, and green velvet draperies tasseled with gold. The room was adjacent to a modern marvel; a water closet with a delft-tiled fireplace and an iron tub that could occasionally be coaxed to produce hot water from its tap. Grace had never seen the like.

She was also asked to dine with the family each evening—an ensemble that did not include Lord Ruthveyn, save for the first night. It did, however, include Ruthveyn's brother, an angelically handsome young scoundrel whose existence came as something of a surprise to Grace. As did his hand on her knee one night during the fish course. But a fish fork, Grace had learned during her army days, made for a fine defensive weapon. Lord Lucan Forsythe took his punishment like a man— one sharp grunt, then silence—and the wound, Grace was pleased to see, did not even fester.

And that, she was quite certain, was the end of her troubles with Lord Lucan. The young man was as perceptible—and about as predictable—as ever a rogue could be. Grace set about making a friend of him, and it was easily done.

One afternoon a few days later, Grace went in search of Teddy's lost grammar book and came upon Lady Anisha stitching in the sunlit conservatory. As they did every afternoon at four, the boys had gone out for a romp with their uncle.

"*Pawwwkk!*" Milo, the parakeet, swung from his perch. "*British prisoner! Let-me-out!*"

At the sound, Lady Anisha looked up from her work with a vague smile. "Milo, hush," she said. "Good afternoon, Mademoiselle Gauthier. Has Luc taken the boys to the park?"

"Yes, ma'am." Grace straightened up from the palms where Teddy had last been hiding. "I must say, he is most diligent. Not many dashing young blades would have time for their nephews."

Anisha's smile turned inward. "Oh, trust me, I have encouraged Luc to make time."

"*Help-help-help!*" Milo chortled. "*British prisoner! Let-me-out!*"

With a wry, exasperated smile, Anisha laid aside her needlework and rose. "All right, you tyrant," she said, going to the wicker cage. "Will you join us, Mademoiselle Gauthier? I just sent for tea."

"Of course, thank you."

With another loud squawk, the bird sailed onto the back

of Anisha's chair. A little ill at ease, Grace crossed the flagstone floor and took the seat Lady Anisha indicated. She wished she did not feel quite so uncomfortable with Ruthveyn's sister. So often, Grace found, men were easy to comprehend—as with Ruthveyn and his brother, one knew whom to trust—but women were far less discernible. Not that she distrusted Lady Anisha. She just wasn't sure of her welcome.

"Milo is beautiful," she remarked. "And he certainly gets on with the cats."

"*British prisoner!*" said Milo, who was indeed magnificent, with apple green plumage and a huge, hooked beak of fuchsia. "*Help-help-help!*" He toddled behind Anisha and began to nibble at her dangling earrings.

"Silk and Satin were rather taken aback when we first arrived," Anisha admitted. "My brother treats them like pampered princesses, of course. Milo learned to bow down to them early on."

Grace's attention, however, had wandered. "Oh, my, what are you stitching? Is that *silk*?"

"It is, yes." Anisha laid the cloth on the tea table and smoothed the wrinkles from the dark blue fabric. "It's to be a Christmas gift for Adrian."

"Adrian?"

At her puzzled look, Anisha laughed. "My brother," she clarified. "Did he not tell you his name?"

Grace considered it. "I don't know," she admitted. "He may have done. I . . . I was rather distraught when I first met him in St. James's. Did he tell you about it?"

Anisha shook her head. "No, but he told me of your situation," she said. "I hope you do not mind?"

"*Mais non,* I am caring for your children! You must know everything about me." Absently, Grace touched the embroidery. "Oh, but this needlework! Lady Anisha, it is stunning."

Again, she laughed. Her voice, Grace thought, was like the tinkling of bells, her words tinged with the faintest hint of an accent. "My needlework is a strange muddle of East and West," Anisha confessed. "Rajput women, you know, pride themselves on their embroidery, especially *Zari,* with this fine, metallic thread. But my wording— alas, it looks more like a schoolgirl's sampler."

"Oh, no one could mistake this for a child's work."

"*Pretty-pretty,*" said Milo, cocking one orange eyeball. "*Pretty-pretty.*"

Milo was right. Using silver thread, Lady Anisha had stitched onto the dark blue silk something that looked like a glimmering night sky, though Grace could identify but one or two groupings of stars. Still, they were precisely done, with a wide decorative border round the whole of it, and in the middle of the sparkling array, a verse.

"These are constellations, aren't they?" said Grace. "It is a night sky."

"Yes, as it would have appeared on the night of Adrian's birth."

"How remarkable," Grace murmured. "When was he born?"

"Shortly after midnight, April 19," said Lady Anisha. "In English, he is Aries, the Ram."

"As in astrology?" said Grace. "I don't know much about it."

Lady Anisha shrugged. "Ah, well, most think it nonsense anyway."

Grace looked more closely at the lettering. It was a poem, all of it done in the fine, metallic thread, the individual stitches so delicate and tiny she could barely make them out. Lightly, her finger traced the words:

> *And my good genius truly doth it know:*
> *For what we do presage is not in grosse,*
> *For we be brethren of the rosie cross;*
> *We have the mason-word and second sight,*
> *Things for to come we can foretell aright,*
> *And shall we show what misterie we mean,*
> *In fair acrosticks Carolus Rex is seen.*

"What, exactly, is it?" Grace asked.

"A verse from a poem," she answered. "By Adamson."

"Yes, *The Muses Threnodie!*" Grace murmured. "I tried to read it once, but it was beyond me. Thank heaven you needn't embroider the whole thing."

Again, Anisha laughed. "That might take the rest of my days."

Grace crooked her head to better see it. "What does it mean?"

Anisha's expression faded. "It's a sort of ode to a departed friend." She hesitated a heartbeat. "It's believed they were Rosicrucians—there, you see?—*the rosie cross* reference. Are you familiar?"

"They were a secret society of mystics, weren't they?" said Grace musingly. "Or still are, for all I know."

Lady Anisha flicked a strange glance at her. "Like so many, I believe they have splintered," she said vaguely.

"What sort of people belonged?"

Anisha lifted one delicate shoulder. "Men of science, I believe—or at least the science of their day," she explained. "Alchemy, astrology, natural philosophy. They also studied the great Greek and Druidic mysteries, and had some connection, perhaps, to Masonry."

"Druids?" Grace was still staring at the lettering. "Didn't they sacrifice people?"

Lady Anisha snatched up the needlework. "Ah, here is Begley with the tray!" she said. "Begley, set it here, then be so good as to fetch us another cup."

"I shall get it." Grace moved as if to rise.

"No." Anisha's hand forestalled her. "Stay. I wish to talk to you. Tell me how my children go on. Are they hopelessly recalcitrant?"

Grace gave her view that the boys were bright but resisted structure. When that went over well enough, she told the tale about the baking soda.

Anisha's lips pursed. "Imps!" she said. "They did not get it from me. Like Adrian, I was a good, solemn child."

That raised a question Grace wished to ask, for Lord Ruthveyn had deposited her in such haste, she knew next to nothing of the boys' history. Still, she hesitated. The extra cup came, and she watched Anisha pour.

"Is that an Indian tea?" she asked.

Anisha set the pot down. "Just Chinese from Oxford Street," she said. "Parts of India have begun to grow tea as an export crop, but rarely to drink. Occasionally it is boiled strong and spiced—*chai masala,* we call it—but you would not sleep for a week, I daresay, were you to drink it. By the way, did you meet Dr. von Althausen?"

"No," she said, taking the cup Anisha passed.

"He is a scientist of sorts at the St. James Society." Anisha shuddered. "A mad scientist, like in that frightful novel."

"What is the St. James Society, anyway?" asked Grace. "I know it isn't quite like a gentleman's club."

"Oh, mostly just a group of adventurers and mercenaries, to be honest." Anisha gave a sheepish smile. "Men who have a natural curiosity about the world—like von Althausen and the tea."

"The tea?"

"He was a friend of my father's," Anisha went on. "Now he and my brother have hy—hybreed—what is the word?"

"Hybridized?" Grace suggested.

"Yes, that—von Althausen went to India and made some special teas for Adrian to grow, but I know nothing of them. Still, Lucan says they are going to make us rich—that is to say, *richer.* But there—! In England, I am told, one never talks of money."

Faintly, Grace smiled. "Not unless one has some to talk about," she said. "Otherwise, everyone would rather pretend it's too vulgar."

Lady Anisha laughed her delightful laugh again, and it was as if the wall between them shattered. "Adrian said you were half-English," she said, "but you sound like a practical Scot to me. Many of the Company men are, you know—like my father."

Grace was surprised. "I hardly know enough of names to tell the difference," she confessed. "But I *did* have a Scottish ancestor somewhere in the family tree— strangely, though, on my French side."

"I do not know much of France," said Anisha. "Is it lovely?"

Grace smiled. "I've seen little of it myself," she confessed. "I grew up in North Africa. My father was a soldier."

Anisha's gaze fell to the teacup she now balanced on her knee. "Ah, like my husband."

Grace seized the moment. "Might I ask, Lady Anisha, how long Tom and Teddy have been without their father?"

She looked up and sighed. "All their lives."

"I beg your pardon," said Grace softly. "I must have misunderstood."

"Oh, I am not long widowed, but my husband was never home," Anisha went on. "John was a captain in the Bengal Horse Artillery. He was cut down at Sobraon."

"Against the Sikhs in the Punjab?" Grace murmured. "That was a controversial war, was it not?"

Lady Anisha shrugged. "Not to the East India Company."

"Well, I am sorry for your loss, Lady Anisha," said Grace. "I am sure it has been hard, too, on your children."

She smiled wanly. "They do run a bit wild," she conceded, "but I believe they are not quite so bad as Raju believes."

"Raju?"

"Yes, another name!" Lady Anisha laughed. "Adrian is his Christian name. But in his youth, we called him by his pet name, Raju."

"Raju," Grace echoed, trying to mimic Lady Anisha. "What does it mean?"

"Pampered little prince, more or less," said Anisha on another laugh.

"And was he?"

Lady Anisha rolled her eyes. "Oh, yes! My mother doted on him."

"Your parents—was it a love match?" Grace immediately felt her face turn red. "I'm sorry. I beg your pardon. I ought not have asked such a thing."

"It is perfectly all right," she replied. "No, it was a political marriage. My grandfather actually *was* a prince, or something like it, in the Rajputana. But such mixed marriages are frowned upon nowadays—and unnecessary, too, for there are a great many Englishwomen in India now."

"Oh," said Grace softly. "I hope it was a happy union."

Again, Lady Anisha shrugged. "It was not, I think,

the marriage either would have chosen. But my mother was a great beauty, and my father very rich. There were worse lives to be lived, I daresay. My father's second marriage—to Lucan's mother, Pamela—ah, now *that* was a love match."

They continued on for a time, talking of Lady Anisha's childhood in India. If the comparison between her mother and her stepmother left her bitter, one could not discern it from her manner. Indeed, she was at all times gracious, with an elegance few highborn Englishwomen could have mimicked.

Still, life in London could not have been all roses for her, Grace conceded. The old tabbies of the *ton*—like Aunt Abigail—would have been hard-pressed to acknowledge Lady Anisha Stafford as "one of us."

Grace could certainly sympathize. She had come to England with every intention of making a new life and allowing her grief to heal. But she had found instead another tragedy; one that was still to play out, and, if Ruthveyn were to be believed, fraught with danger. Worse, she was beginning to fear she was falling a little in love with her rescuer, and that would never do.

Yes, some days she wished, quite desperately, to flee England altogether.

Milo, apparently, understood.

"*Help, help!*" said the bird. "*Let-me-out, let-me-out!*"

CHAPTER 8

The Damning Evidence

Cheroot in hand, Lord Ruthveyn descended the old stone staircase into the cellars, his path weakly lit by the hissing flame of a wall sconce. This was a journey made a score of times each day by the Society's members and staff, for it was in these dark, dungeonlike rooms that Belkadi stored bin upon bin of Europe's finest wines, and Dr. von Althausen kept his laboratories.

There were other rooms farther along the vaulted stone passageway, tucked beneath the houses that were connected like rabbit warrens to make up the headquarters of the F.A.C. but those chambers were used rarely, and mostly for ceremonial occasions, or for prayer and meditation. Ruthveyn entered the first room on the right, a long space lit by high, grated windows that ran beneath the ground-floor balconet.

Seated at the worktable, Lord Bessett was rolling down his sleeve, his face drawn, his eyes shadowed beneath with dark circles. Beside him, von Althausen was bent over his electricity generator with one of his silvery tools, making some sort of adjustment.

"Any luck?" asked Ruthveyn, sliding into one of the empty chairs.

Lord Bessett winced and shook his head. "I'm no good at it," he said, casting a rueful glance at the doctor. "After two weeks, the visions cannot be electrically produced."

"Patience, patience, my friend." Von Althausen glanced up from his machine, then scowled at Ruthveyn's cheroot. "Ruthveyn, would you blow us all to Kingdom Come?" he barked. "Not all of us are bent on suicide."

"What?" Ruthveyn lifted his hand, the cheroot dangling. "It's merely smoldering."

"This is a laboratory, *um Gottes willen*!" snapped the doctor. "Put it out!"

Bessett turned his bleary gaze on Ruthveyn. "I love when he curses you. No one else dares."

Ruthveyn lifted one eyebrow and stabbed out his cheroot. "Was he cursing?" said the marquess blandly. "You look accursed already, my friend."

"Rough night." Bessett secured his cuff, then stood to draw on his jacket. "You know what it's like, old chap."

"The brain! The brain!" von Althausen muttered, throwing an old Holland cloth over his contraption. "It's all in the brain! It is nothing but electricity. It *must* be. Galvani proved as much."

"But Bessett is not a dead frog," Ruthveyn calmly pointed out. "You cannot teach his brain to control itself if you—"

"Do I tell you how to do *your* job, Ruthveyn?" Von Althausen turned around, glaring. "Do I?"

"I do not have a job," he said blithely.

"You are a Guardian," snapped the doctor, stooping down to look for something, "and one of the Vateis. Those are solemn duties—"

"Yes, but not jobs," Ruthveyn interjected. "I am a retired diplomat, you will recall."

"You're a retired *spy,* if you ask me," Bessett countered, flinging himself back into his chair. "But Her Majesty can call you what she wishes, of course." He turned to the doctor. "Dieter, have you a bottle down here?"

"Yes, of course." The doctor's voice came from a set of tool bins beneath the table. "In the cupboard."

It was scarcely four in the afternoon, but Ruthveyn took pity. "Sit, old chap, before you collapse," he said. "I'll fetch it."

Ruthveyn rose to rummage through the cluttered cupboard until he found a dusty bottle of armagnac, and three almost clean glasses. No servants were allowed in this room to tidy up, for the laboratory was filled with things both dangerous and private, a few of which even Ruthveyn did not comprehend.

There was all manner of optical equipment: microscopes, lenses, and in one corner on a wooden frame, one of those newfangled photographic cameras. There was an assortment of glass flasks, and cups—all handblown to von Althausen's specifications—as well as calipers and other assorted measuring devices, and piles of thick, leather-bound tomes on subjects from alchemy to zoology that had been pulled from the main library's shelves and carried down into the doctor's lair, never to be seen above-stairs again.

Ruthveyn gave it all a passing glance, then returned to the battered wooden table, watching his younger friend from the corner of one eye as he poured. Geoff had been

Lord Bessett but a short while, and the mantle of the earl-dom did not lie easy on his shoulders. The reasons, Ruth-veyn knew, were complicated, but primary amongst them was the fact that Geoff had never expected to inherit.

Unlike Ruthveyn, who had been brought up expecting his father's title and duties to fall to him, Geoff had not. Not until his much-older half brother had died suddenly. The grief had merely added to Geoff's already challenging life. Even before his inheritance, the young man had made quite a name—and a fortune—for himself as a partner in MacGregor & Company, his stepfather's firm. In addition to his many metaphysical gifts, the old boy was one hell of an architect and artist.

Ruthveyn finished pouring and pushed the glasses round as von Althausen finally settled into one of the chairs. "To the *Fraternitas Aureae Crucis,*" Ruthveyn said, lifting his glass with a twisted smile.

"*Auf uns!*" the doctor replied.

They drank in companionable silence for a time, Ruthveyn surreptitiously studying the shadows beneath Geoff's eyes. Despite their occasional clash, he was fond of the young man. Though he had known of Geoff's existence within the *Fraternitas*, they had met quite by chance in North Africa, where Geoff had been engaged in overseeing a construction project for the French colonial government.

Toward the end of his assignment, Ruthveyn and Lazonby had come upon Geoff a little worse for wear in the parlor of a Moroccan brothel, his pockets being picked by a pair of dubious-looking Frenchmen.

It was a bit reminiscent, in fact, of Ruthveyn's first meeting with Lazonby—though on that occasion, they had both been something worse than glassy-eyed. They had also been naked—and stretched out on a pair of red silk banquettes, a smoldering four-hosed hookah on the floor between them, and two willing lovelies curled round it like cats, all of them lethargic and sated in the aftermath of what could only be described as an orgy—in more ways than one. Then, at some point in the evening's finale, Ruthveyn had looked across the roiling haze at his new partner in debauchery as the sergeant rolled over to find his shirt.

And there it was.

The unmistakable mark on his flesh. The mark of the Guardian.

Geoff's voice cut through the reverie. "We've been asked to take an acolyte," he said to no one in particular. "From Tuscany."

Ruthveyn looked up from his drink with a frown. "Under what circumstances?"

"The lad has been brought along by one of the Advocati," said Geoff. "Signor Vittorio. But now the doctors tell him he is dying."

Ruthveyn cast a glance at von Althausen. "The doctors are forever saying that," he remarked, "and it's very rarely true."

"This is a cancer," Geoff countered, "and these are uncertain times in Tuscany."

"*Ja,* there is much clamor for war against Austria," said von Althausen. "And talk of deposing Grand Duke Leopold."

"Precisely," said Geoff. "Vittorio thought it best the lad come here."

"Does he have the Gift himself? Is that Vittorio's concern?"

Geoff winced. "There is potential, I gather—enough to worry Vittorio that the boy might be ill used—but he is not, I collect, a strong Vates."

Ruthveyn did not like idea. Too often, he knew, very young men were like Lazonby in his youth, not quite ready to commit themselves to the *Fraternitas*. Or like himself, tormented and angry. Few came to this life as Geoff had done, resigned to his fate and already under the tutelage of his grandmother, a powerful Scottish seer. To give oneself wholly to the life of a Guardian was an almost monastic conversion, and sometimes the first real acceptance of one's fate. Better never to come to it at all, Ruthveyn believed, than to come but half-committed.

But von Althausen and Geoff were still staring at him. "We need a majority vote," said Geoff quietly. "I have three, including Alexander. Lazonby and Manders are away. Will you use one of your vetoes?"

Ruthveyn considered it. There were but twelve vetoes allotted a Founder in his lifetime. It was what they had all agreed upon setting up the St. James Society. They had been fortunate in recruiting some of the *Fraternitas's* most senior Savants—learned, well-honed men like von Althausen—and their priests, or Preosts, like the Reverend Mr. Sutherland, to aid in their objectives. But the voting, and the responsibility of it, was left to the Founders.

"Has the lad been initiated?" he demanded. "Is he marked?"

"I cannot say," said Geoff. "But he can travel here in a few months' time with all the proper documentation from Vittorio."

"Belkadi won't like it," Ruthveyn warned. "He dislikes Italians."

"Belkadi dislikes half of humanity, including you," said Geoff evenly. "Besides, he isn't a Founder."

"And Italians hate London," Ruthveyn went on. "It's cold, it's damp, and the air is foul. Did anyone tell the lad?"

Von Althausen grunted. "Who pissed in your porridge this morning, Ruthveyn?" he muttered. "You'd be well advised to take him. Who knows when one of you might be needed elsewhere? Already Lazonby is stuck in Scotland, and Manders is tending his political fires."

The doctor was right. And Vittorio was an honorable man who had been doing yeoman's duty for the *Fraternitas* long before Ruthveyn's birth. This was more about his strange, black mood, he acknowledged, than an acolyte.

"What is his birth date?" he asked.

"The fourteenth of April," said Geoff.

Ruthveyn shoved his empty glass away. "Very well," he said. "But send word to Lazonby."

"Consider it done." Geoff drained his brandy and moved as if to rise.

At the last instant, Ruthveyn caught Geoff's arm. "I'm in a foul mood today. I should be horsewhipped, no doubt."

Geoff's smile was wan. "Well, I would call you out for being an ass, but I haven't had above three hours' sleep in an age."

It was a torment he and Geoff shared—one that Lazonby never felt. He slept like a baby and snored after a drunk like one of those monstrous locomotives. Ruthveyn jerked his head toward the ceiling. "I have the cure for sleeplessness upstairs."

Geoff's expression went blank. "I am afraid I had to leave that habit back in Morocco, old chap."

Ruthveyn shrugged one shoulder. "It's hardly opium."

"Opium. Charas. It all rots the brain, Ruthveyn."

"Perhaps," Ruthveyn said quietly, "but a man must survive."

Von Althausen set his brandy down. "Once again, my boy, they are mind-altering chemicals," he said, casting a warning glance at Ruthveyn. "They are to be used only ceremonially—and only then if they elicit information rather than quell it—which has never been the case for you. You would be well advised to give them up."

"What, and merely drink myself into a stupor like half the gentlemen in London?" Ruthveyn jerked from his chair. "I see little difference."

"Suit yourself," replied the doctor. "But oftentimes 'tis better to deal with your devils firsthand."

"Spoken like a man who doesn't have any," Ruthveyn complained.

But the truth was, he was beginning to fear his friends might be right. For the first time in a long while, Ruthveyn wondered if the discomfort he was staving off wasn't more than sleeplessness and visions.

It had grown worse since Anisha and Luc arrived with the boys, for, inexplicably, he felt more alone than ever when his house was full of people he cared about. Perhaps it was because he felt compelled to hold them at a distance. It had become second nature to him now, that need to set an emotional pane of glass between himself and those he loved.

And now Mademoiselle Gauthier was living in his house. Beautiful, elegant Grace, who made him wish, foolishly, to shatter that glass. Grace, who elicited in him his every protective instinct yet gave up to him nothing of herself—in part because he had never really learned how to ask. And in part because he dared not.

It had been challenging at first, separating the raw lust from the fascination. Save for one of the Vateis, he had never met a woman he could not eventually read, though admittedly, some were less transparent than others. And there were a few—women like Angela Timmonds, or Melanie, his wife—whom he could shut out for a time by

sheer force of will. Until a deep and genuine affection—
or even love—began to set in.

In his youth, Ruthveyn had not understood this. He had
not grasped until too late the awful truth that the more
one cared, the wider Hades' door would swing; that he
and the object of his desire became like a pair of mirrors
hung opposite one another across a corridor, allowing
him to see deeper and deeper, and into infinity.

Oh, he certainly had not married Melanie for love; at
twenty-three he had been too callow, too caught up in
wrestling his own demons. But Melanie, with her soft,
honey-colored curls and wide blue eyes, had been beautiful, and even then, something in her feminine frailty
had stirred him. Worse, her father's position as one of the
most powerful men within the East India Company had
tempted his father to strike a bargain almost before Ruthveyn had known he'd *wanted* a bargain.

At first, he had been relieved at the ease with which he
could shut her out—until he realized, too late, that it was
as much the other way round. Caught up in his career, it
had been weeks before he'd realized Melanie emotionally
shut herself off to him, choosing instead to quietly mourn
the young army captain her father had denied her. She
had not welcomed his touch; she had tolerated it.

But by then, they were married. And the army captain
had not mourned Melanie at all. The social circle in Calcutta being a small one, he had managed to console himself with another well-dowered beauty.

He had married Ruthveyn's sister.

But Ruthveyn had kept heaving away at his sinking
rowboat of a marriage, seeing hope where there was
none. Melanie with her pink, pouting mouth and shimmering eyes had drawn on his sympathy until—fool that
he was—he'd begun to wish he *could* fall in love with her.

Before his marriage, Ruthveyn had been much in demand. The lonely wives of the Company men and the army officers had apparently found his dark eyes faintly exotic, and even when suppressed, the Gift sometimes gave an extraordinary, almost mesmerizing energy to his touch. With little effort, he could lull women into a strange sensual lethargy that even now he scarcely understood.

As to his own desire, Ruthveyn had learned early on that if he chose his partners carefully, cared little, and shut his mind tight, his body could find release before his brain exploded. Eventually, he learned that charas, and later opium, would inexplicably still his brain without damping down the raging sexual desire that seemed always to burn inside him.

But with Melanie, perversely, the more she distanced herself, the more he wanted to *see* her.

And then one night the veil lifted.

Atop her in bed on a near-moonless evening, the lamp doused just as she always insisted, Ruthveyn had gazed down at his wife with what felt like the nascent fluttering of love, and his mind had lit up like lightning in a night sky. In one horrific, glaring instant, he had seen. Seen not just her dashed dreams, but what was to come of them, too.

Too late, he tore his body from hers, spilling his accursed seed across the sheets.

Far, far too late.

"Ruthveyn?"

He was jerked to the present by a harsh rapping at the door.

Ruthveyn looked around to realize Geoff had gone, and von Althausen was staring at him from across the table. "Answer that, for pity's sake," he grumbled.

Ruthveyn strode to the door and threw it open. Belkadi stood in the passageway, his black suit and white linen as immaculate as if he'd just put in on. "There's a lad upstairs with a rather terse message," he said in a low voice, "from Scotland Yard."

"Damn it all," Ruthveyn cursed. "What now?"

"Assistant Commissioner Napier is on his way, and requests a moment of your time." The majordomo hesitated a heartbeat. "I bribed the boy. He says it's about the Frenchwoman who's staying with you. Gauthier's daughter."

Ruthveyn cursed again, more vehemently. Napier was about the last thing he needed in his present mood. And, of course, he'd not said a word to anyone within the Society about Grace's having moved into his house. But a man with Belkadi's skills did not need the Gift to know two-thirds of what went on in London. After all, there was a reason—other than sheer affection—why Lazonby brought him into the *Fraternitas*. Belkadi was Machiavelli reincarnated.

Ruthveyn felt his hand tighten on the doorknob, his mind racing, his every instinct to protect Grace surging. "Where was Napier this past week?"

"A deathbed vigil," said Belkadi. "A wealthy uncle up in Birmingham."

"Ah, those always bring the relatives out of the woodwork." Ruthveyn jerked his head toward the stone staircase and drew the door shut behind them. "Have someone escort him to the private study. I'll await him there."

Upstairs, much of the club lay in silence. Ruthveyn strode past the genealogical library to see Mr. Sutherland, one of the Preosts, poring over what looked like a massive Bible, no doubt borrowed from some unsuspecting family, and under what pretext, heaven only knew. Sutherland believed God would forgive him his little fibs.

Outside the smoking room, he hesitated. Within, Lieutenant Lord Curran Alexander was sitting by the windows, his cane hooked over his chair arm. One of Ruthveyn's father's protégés, Alexander was another casualty of war; in this case, the disastrous retreat of the British from Kabul.

Ruthveyn had been there, too, carrying diplomatic dispatches, and trying to sense which way the wind blew with Akbar Khan. It had not taken long. Within a day of his arrival, the Afghan prince—or his minions—had driven a knife, quite literally, through the heart of the Army of the Indus. Even a fool could have seen what was to come. Ruthveyn had seen it in stark, horrific detail.

But alas, such visions never came with a calendar attached. Having made no headway with the paralyzed British leadership, and sick with despair, Ruthveyn had reprovisioned and headed east into the worsening Afghan winter for Jalalabad to make one last plea for help, with no one save Alexander and a small contingent of his men for support. But they had known, the both of them, it was likely futile.

In the end, it had been Ruthveyn's greatest failure in what felt like a string of failures. They had been but five days ahead of the general retreat through Jagdalak Pass. There had been no hope.

But he and Alexander had lived through their journey, which was more than could have been said of those who came after. Sixteen thousand British—most of them women, children, and camp followers—had frozen to death or been cut down.

He wondered why he thought of it now. It had something to do with Grace, but he couldn't quite grasp what. He let his hand slip from the doorframe and strode on. He had an uneasy feeling about Royden Napier. It was unlike him to call here at the St. James Society.

It had been a rare, clear day, and inside the library, both windows still stood open despite the growing chill. Ruthveyn toyed with shutting them, then thought better of it. There was no need to make Napier comfortable; the sooner he was gone, the better.

Instead, he poured himself another brandy and went to the open window to stare down at the entrance to Quartermaine's pernicious hell. Pinkie Ringgold stood lounging to one side, laughing with Maggie Sloane, one of London's high-flyers, and Ned Quartermaine's occasional bedmate.

But nothing beyond the window could long hold his attention. Instead, he hitched one hip onto the sill and let his gaze run across the study. Although the intimate chamber was his favorite at the St. James Society—and one of six given over to study or reading—Ruthveyn had not returned here since meeting Grace Gauthier.

Perhaps that had been intentional. In his mind, this place would ever be associated with her. Even now, if he shut his eyes, he could smell her scent in the room. He remembered precisely how she had looked that day, sitting on the sofa opposite the windows, her hands folded elegantly in her lap. This, despite the panic in her eyes and the flashes of grief he saw sketched across her face.

He had not known quite what to make of her. Whether to believe her or—when she'd collapsed into his arms—whether he ought simply to kiss her and have done with it.

But he did know one thing. He knew she had not loved Holding. He knew this because he'd asked her, and rather heartlessly. Even then, he had been fascinated by Grace.

It had required every inch of his restraint to stay away from her these past few days, to simply trust that his well-trained staff was keeping her safe. Instead, he had limited himself to sending her one or two notes, merely to tell her what little he had learned, and had otherwise continued to live his monastic existence in his upstairs suite. Not that anyone had ever accused him of being a monk, precisely.

Just then the door opened, and one of the footmen came in, Royden Napier behind him. The servant bowed wordlessly to Ruthveyn and went out again, leaving the assistant commissioner alone on the Turkish carpet.

Ruthveyn lifted his glass. "Afternoon, Napier," he said evenly. "Will you join me?"

Napier's head swiveled toward the windows. "Ruthveyn," he gritted, "you interfering blackguard. Don't you dare pretend this is a social call."

"With all respect, Napier, I can imagine no circumstance in which you and I might socialize," he replied, coming away from the window. "Still, you're welcome to a drink."

It was a subtle dig, and both men knew it. Ruthveyn couldn't have cared less for the concept of nobility, but he'd learned early on that the combination of his lofty title and mixed ancestry stuck in the craw of many Englishmen. He did not hesitate to use it.

"Go to hell, Ruthveyn," Napier spat, stalking across the carpet. "You have gone too far this time."

"Have I?" Ruthveyn smiled. "Whatever I've done, old chap, I should rather take my scold sitting down. Feel free to join me. Or not."

With that he brushed past Napier, just close enough to make his point. And although he could barely read the assistant commissioner, Ruthveyn felt the heat in the room ratchet up a notch.

Napier followed him to a pair of nearby chairs, fists clenched. "You, sir, are no gentleman," he choked. "You are a manipulative bastard who has used Scotland Yard, who has lied to my face, and who means to try and cheat the hangman one more—"

Ruthveyn held up a forestalling hand. "The bastard part I'll give you," he said, sitting. "But I take exception to the lying part. What, precisely, did I lie about?"

"You have been scheming on behalf of that French-woman from the very first—I knew it the moment I heard about that damned prayer book—thick as thieves, the whole bloody lot of you, and now you have—"

"But what did I lie about?" Ruthveyn again interposed. "And what prayer book?"

This brought Napier up short for a moment. "You claimed—you came to my office, and you said—"

"That one of the household staff had approached me," Ruthveyn interjected.

"You implied it was a servant!" Napier bellowed. "Not the dead man's bloody fiancée!"

"A governess is, technically, a servant," said Ruthveyn calmly. "She was in Holding's employ for months."

"A technicality, Ruthveyn, and you know it!" shouted Napier, whose right eye was starting to twitch ominously. "And now you are harboring a fugitive."

Ruthveyn lifted both eyebrows. "A fugitive?" he said lightly. "That's a dangerous charge, old chap. I take it you've obtained an arrest warrant for Mademoiselle Gauthier."

Napier's choleric expression flushed a brighter shade of red. "No, but I can bloody well get one."

Ruthveyn sipped pensively at his brandy. "Do you imagine so?" he finally murmured. "Well, why don't you just go give that a try."

"By God, I should give my right arm to know what it is you hold over the Crown's head," Napier gritted.

But the truth was, he held very little. Ruthveyn enjoyed the thanks of a grateful Queen—one who never knew just when she might need him. And when her ministers called, he would likely go, and do what he could for whom he could, so long as none of his vows as a Guardian were broken. For the reality was—however bad *he* might feel about it—not all his "diplomatic missions" had been the utter failure Jagdalak had been. Occasionally—more than occasionally, perhaps—he had done something right. He had helped save lives—both British and Indian—and averted disasters. It was his cold comfort during the long, dark nights.

Ruthveyn flashed a faint smile. "If you can prove Mademoiselle Gauthier a murderess, Napier, you won't need to know," he said, opening one hand, palm up. "I shall serve her up to you on a silver platter."

"Then I hope you have a large platter," Napier snarled, reaching inside his jacket. He jerked out a fold of paper, the red wax seal broken, and thrust it at Ruthveyn.

Ruthveyn took it carefully, without looking directly into Napier's eyes, or so much as brushing his hand. And still, his stomach sank.

This was bad. He knew it before his eyes alit on the stiff, meticulous copperplate. He knew it the way Lazonby knew things; on a visceral level, without comprehending how or why, no visions required.

Ruthveyn read it through once, then jerked to his feet. He went to the window, turned it to the light, and read it a second time. He did not look at Napier until he had regained himself.

Napier, of course, had followed on his heels. Ruthveyn turned his gaze to him, focusing his eyes somewhere near Napier's left ear. "When was this written?"

"It's dated, for God's sake!" Napier stabbed a finger

at it. "Holding wrote the bloody thing a week before his death. Obviously, the man had come to his senses."

"And you found it where?"

"When I returned, I was told one of my men found it tucked under a false panel in the bottom of her letter box," said Napier. "It had been hidden, and quite deliberately. That's why we overlooked it the first six times."

"She never saw this." Ruthveyn snapped it back into its folds and flicked it toward Napier.

"What do you mean, she never saw it?" Napier looked incredulous. "It was *in her things.*"

"Then someone else put it there."

"Are you daft, man?" Napier's eyes rounded.

"Holding was away." Ruthveyn inhaled slowly, forcing down the swell of panic. "He was in Liverpool the fortnight before his death. You have nothing but a letter with no envelope, no address, and no stamp, Napier. It is worse than worthless. It smacks of entrapment."

"You think the police utter fools?" Napier glowered at him. "Besides, we asked the business partner, Crane, about it. He said Holding wrote the woman every bloody day he was gone. Always sent his personal letters inside the business ones, to save money. Everyone does it."

"And does Crane attest to having seen this particular letter?"

"No, for he—"

"Ah, I thought not."

"—for he dropped the sealed letters on the foyer table each morning and moved on," Napier snapped. "He hadn't time or inclination to read a load of female drivel. That woman is dangerous, Ruthveyn, and clearly she is vindictive. My only indecision is whether to leave her in your house in the faint hope that, left long enough, she'll eventually run *you* through with a kitchen knife."

Numbly, Ruthveyn glared at Napier. "You will not arrest her," he said flatly. "If you try, I will have your job. If I fail in that, I will have your head—"

"You—why—you cannot threaten an officer of the Crown!"

"I just did," said Ruthveyn. "You will not arrest her. You will leave this to me to be dealt with. Or you will rue the day you were born. Do you understand me, Napier?"

"Go bugger yourself!" Napier stalked toward the door, then threw it open.

Ruthveyn followed him out. "Find St. Giles," he snapped at a passing footman. "And fetch my carriage."

Oblivious to the craning heads that peered from the clubrooms, they argued all the way down the sweeping staircase. "You need to reexamine this case, Napier," he said grimly. "There's something we've missed."

"*'We'?*" Napier bellowed. "Oh, and by the way, Ruthveyn, are you aware your paragon of virtue is toting around a brace of pistols?"

That did surprise him. "Still, that's hardly against the law, is it?"

"Neither is arsenic, but innocent women don't keep a tin of it tucked beneath their underdrawers." The assistant commissioner paused long enough to snatch his greatcoat from the first-floor attendant and went out into the bracing air.

"Napier, don't be a fool," Ruthveyn continued. "By your own admission, the man wrote her every day for a fortnight. Does that sound like a man who had come to his senses?"

The wind caught the door, slamming it shut behind them.

"Oh, you think you see this one clear, eh?" Napier glanced back, his lip curled with disdain. "What with your special gifts and your superior attitude? Do you think I haven't heard the rumors about this place, Ruthveyn? By God, give me half a chance, and when I finish with this case, I'll put a period to you and your so-called St. James Society."

People had been trying to do that for over fourteen hundred years, thought Ruthveyn. The *Fraternitas Aureae Crucis* might be bloodied, but it was not broken, and Napier would have no more luck than the others.

He reached for Napier's arm, but accidentally seized his bare wrist. "Damn it, Napier, I—"

At once, light stabbed into Ruthveyn's head, a shaft of pure pain. Napier's every emotion exploded to life like flame to dry kindling—rage and disdain, and a seething hatred that coiled like a serpent inside his brain. He tried to think, to focus. To tell himself it would be worth the agony. But nothing came. With Napier, it rarely did.

"What in hell is the matter with you?" Napier's voice came from far away.

Ruthveyn jerked back his hand and drew a deep breath, forcing down the rush of emotion. At once, the brilliance relented.

"Christ, Ruthveyn, your pupils are the size of ha'pennies," Napier muttered. "You really do look half-mad."

"Just *listen to me,* for God's sake!" His gaze locked with Napier's. "I have seen this danger. And you ignore it at your peril."

Napier tore his eyes away and threw up a hand at an approaching hansom. "Do you know, Ruthveyn, they used to burn people like you at the stake?" he said, but there was a tremor in his voice. "Go muster your *Fraternitas* forces. You're bloody well going to need them."

Ruthveyn watched, enraged and still reeling, as Napier

climbed into the carriage and rolled on. But the hansom passed from his view to reveal a tableau beyond it almost as unwelcome.

Jack Coldwater loitered on the opposite pavement, one heel set back against the Quartermaine Club, Pinkie Ringgold beside him, grinning and picking at his teeth.

"Ah, the curse of an open window!" Coldwater chortled. "Sounds like you and old Roughshod Roy had another mill."

Ruthveyn stalked across St. James's Place. "Coldwater," he said grimly. "It's about time you learned to respect your elders and betters."

Coldwater feinted left. "My, you're about to let your infamous dispassion slip yet again, Ruthveyn," he said. "Something to do with Lazonby? I hear you've sent him off to Edinburgh on some sort of Society skullduggery."

"What in God's name is your problem, Coldwater?" he growled. "Did Lazonby fuck your mother in prison?"

At that, something like pure hatred chased over the young man's face. He lunged with a right hook. In an instant, Ruthveyn had Coldwater up against the wall again—this time a solid brick one—careful not to hold his gaze.

"Settle down," he gritted.

Pinkie dropped his toothpick and thrust himself between them. "You need ter bugger off, Jack," he said, planting a hand on each of their chests. "Now let 'im loose, my lord. Think 'ow this looks."

It was humbling to be chided by Pinkie Ringgold, of all people. Ruthveyn relented. "One day, Coldwater"—he paused to give his shirt collar a good twist—"one day, I *am* going to throttle you."

"Only if Lazonby doesn't get to me first," said the reporter.

Pinkie elbowed Ruthveyn sharply. On one last oath, he let the fellow loose. Jack Coldwater darted down the street after Napier's hired hansom.

Ruthveyn turned to give a terse nod to Pinkie. "Thank you," he managed, "I suppose."

Pinkie spat onto the pavement at Ruthveyn's feet. "Don't thank me," said the doorman. "'E's a right annoyin' little bastard, but I like 'im. In stark contrast ter some, oo's a mite too high in the instep, considering wot they are."

Ruthveyn merely smiled. "Insulting my ancestry now, Pinkie? Or just Belkadi's?"

"Take yer pick," said Pinkie, going back inside the hell, and slamming shut the door.

Fifteen minutes later, Ruthveyn's carriage drew up before his town house. He stepped down to give terse orders to Brogden, then went inside.

"Mademoiselle Gauthier?" he snapped at Higgenthorpe.

The butler took his hat and stick. "In the conservatory, my lord."

Ruthveyn strode from the entrance hall through the house until he reached the passageway that led to the glass-walled room. Anisha sat in her favorite rattan chair, her parakeet perched behind, and in a seat adjacent was Ruthveyn's new governess.

"*Awwk!*" said the bird, arching his green wings. "*British prisoner! Help! Help!*"

"Raju!" Anisha laid aside her stitchery and hastened to meet him. "What a surprise."

Grace rose to bob a curtsy.

"Anisha. Mademoiselle." He bowed stiffly to each.

But Anisha was looking at the thing tucked under his arm. "Raju, what have you there?"

"Ah, this." He had almost forgotten the jar of lemon drops. "For Tom and Teddy," he said, thrusting it at her. "It's been rattling round in my carriage since we last spoke."

Anisha's eyes widened. "You bought the whole *jar*? For two little boys?"

Ruthveyn set it on the tea table, feeling vaguely annoyed. He was *trying,* damn it all. "Don't children like sweets?"

His sister smiled dotingly. "Next time just ask the shop-keeper to give you a little bagful," she suggested. "Here, I'll tuck it away, and you may give it to them later, with the understanding that I shall dole them out at my discretion."

She was right, of course. He knew nothing at all of children. "As you wish, then," he said tightly. He turned his attention to Grace. "Mademoiselle Gauthier, do you ride?"

"*Moi?*" Her chin jerked up, something like panic sketching over her face. "Why, yes . . . yes, I do."

"I wish you to ride with me," he said.

"Ride with you?"

"In the park," he said curtly. "Will a quarter hour be sufficient time to change?"

She laid aside the book she'd been carrying, shot an uncertain look at Anisha, and bobbed again. "Yes, my lord. Fifteen minutes."

"Thank you," he said.

He turned and strode out again, feeling the heat of Anisha's eyes burning into his back.

Grace was better than her word. Ten minutes later, Ruthveyn stormed back down the stairs clad in knee boots and breeches, his whip tucked under his arm, to find her dressed in the feminine equivalent, a plain black habit paired with a white shirt that was pleated across the bodice. Her hat was a dainty affair, with a bow of black ribbon knotted to one side of her chin and plumed with three black feathers.

Despite the storm that raged within, Ruthveyn was still a man, with a man's appreciation of feminine beauty, and Grace was surely a feast for the eyes. Moreover, she possessed that eternal French flair for simple elegance, a look that could outshine the most elaborate silks and satins.

As ordered, Brogden had sent round Ruthveyn's horse and a small bay mare from the stables. Grace seemed entirely comfortable, and vaulted smoothly into the saddle with minimal assistance. She wheeled the bay around, her eyes catching his, and set off beside him in the direction of Hyde Park.

As soon as they were out of earshot of his grooms, she leaned nearer, her eyes looking worriedly toward him. "What's wrong?"

"I wish to speak with you," he said tersely. "Away from the house."

Within minutes, they reached the park and Rotten Row. Ruthveyn set a brisk pace, and they were soon well beyond the carriages and riders who had come merely to see and be seen.

As they crossed the bridge, he cut another surreptitious look in Grace's direction to see that her jaw was set hard, her face pale as milk against the black silk of her hat ribbons, as if she steeled herself. But against what? A reckoning? Or simply bad news? For the first time in his life, he wished desperately that he *could* see another's innermost thoughts.

But why did he need to read Grace when he had only to ask her the truth? He knew her character. He had made a choice in deciding to help her.

And yet, in the face of Napier's letter, Ruthveyn's analytical brain told him he must at least consider the possibility that his desire—and yes, the almost overwhelming tenderness he felt for Grace—was clouding his brain. Was it possible that, beyond his gifts, he had learned nothing of ordinary character judgment? For the first time since his marriage, Ruthveyn was not entirely certain.

Devil take it, he did not suffer self-doubt well. He didn't believe Grace a killer, but wasn't it just *possible* she was hiding something? Or that there was more to the story than she'd shared? Ruthveyn was a little troubled by how desperately he wished to know, by how much of himself he'd invested in Grace. He felt blind, just as he'd said to Anisha.

How in heaven's name did ordinary people forge relationships? How did a man trust a woman in the way he needed to trust Grace? The thought of never reading her as he did other people was as exhilarating as it was daunting. And the thought of never seeing himself through her was just . . . daunting.

The simple act of tempting Grace to kiss him had been a new, wildly erotic experience. In the past, with very few exceptions, whenever he'd begun pursuit of a woman, he'd known from the start that she wanted him. But Grace wakened in him the thrill of the chase—the lion claiming his lioness—and when she trembled to his touch, it sent the blood of victory thrumming, and not just to his heart.

Good Lord.

Was that what he was doing? Was he *pursuing* Grace Gauthier?

It would not do. It simply would not. This was no longer an experiment, no mere taste of temptation. If not an outright virgin, Grace was certainly inexperienced by his standards. Moreover, Ruthveyn had no intention of repeating his mistake of marriage again. Once their intimacy deepened, that window to the soul would almost certainly come crashing open. And Grace would find herself bound to an aberration. A *freak,* Melanie had called him.

But the truth was, logic was rapidly ceasing to matter. Ruthveyn had been unable to think clearly since that ill-fated kiss in Whitehall. His already sleepless nights had become a torment of tangled sheets and pathetic self-gratification the likes of which he had not succumbed to since boyhood. He burned for Grace all the way down to his soul, or what was left of it. And while a score of willing women could have been his for the taking—or just for the night—he had not so much as considered it. He had grown tired of rutting like an animal with half his mind engaged.

There was a knot of trees up ahead, and within, a small, grassy clearing. When they reached it, Ruthveyn guided his mount off the bridle path. Grace followed, then reined her horse near.

"Ruthveyn, what is wrong?" she asked.

Ruthveyn forced his eyes from the delicate pulse point of her throat, and shut away his private thoughts. "Grace," he said quietly, "do you own a weapon?"

She gave an almost imperceptible flinch. "What? No!" Then she hesitated. "Actually, *yes*—I have Papa's side-arms."

"Your *father's*?"

"A brace of Mr. Colt's five-shot revolvers; an anniversary gift from *Maman*. But I haven't any ammunition, so the boys could not possibly—" Here, her brow furrowed. "Oh, dear! What has happened?"

Ruthveyn closed his eyes a moment and let the relief flow through him. *Her dead father's pistols.* And of course she was carrying them. Everything she owned was likely kept in those three old trunks his staff had brought down from Marylebone. She was, just as she'd once claimed, a daughter of the army.

Ruthveyn swung himself out of the saddle, the leather creaking against his weight. After securing his mount, he lifted Grace down, his hands set round her waist. It felt trim—almost too trim—and he wondered mechanically if she were eating enough.

"*Merci*," she said.

Ruthveyn did not release her waist, but instead held her near, drawing in her scent, his eyes drifting over her face. Grace's palms lingered but a moment on his shoulders, then slid away. It was a sign—one from God, most likely. He forced his hands to relax, releasing her.

"Grace," he said quietly, "did you know Ethan Holding meant to break off your betrothal?"

She went absolutely still. "I . . . I beg your pardon?"

"The week before he returned from Liverpool." Ruthveyn held her gaze steadily. "Holding wrote you a letter. He had changed his mind about betrothing himself to you."

She blinked her eyes slowly. "Is this some sort of joke?" she whispered. "Who told you this?"

"Napier," he answered.

"Well, he is mistaken. There was no letter. And Mr. Holding seemed quite the same toward me."

"Grace, remember the note someone slid under your door that night?" Ruthveyn pressed. "The one that made no sense?"

"I shall never forget it." She set her gloved fingertips to her mouth, her hand shaking a little. "He said he wanted to explain—no, to *apologize*."

"And he called you Miss Gauthier," Ruthveyn reminded her. "You said that was unusual."

"When we were writing to one another, yes," she said.

"But mightn't it make sense if he had broken the engagement?" Ruthveyn pressed. "Or thought he had?"

"Well, I daresay." She dropped her hand, looking bewildered. "But Ruthveyn, he *didn't*. I would have known. And there would have been a—a sort of strain at dinner. *Wouldn't* there?"

Ruthveyn could make no sense of any of it. "You said he quarreled with Mr. Crane?"

Her brow creased. "Did I?" she murmured. "Yes, there were words. But not a quarrel. I would not have called it that."

Ruthveyn began to pace the little patch of grass, pensively tapping his crop against his boot cuff, the opposite hand set at the small of his back. "Grace, Napier showed me the letter breaking the engagement," he finally said. "But perhaps someone failed to give it to you? Or hid it? The only other option is outright forgery, which would suggest someone targeted you."

But Grace was already shaking her head. "Ruthveyn, I am entirely sure a man *could* betroth himself to me and later think the better of it," she said. "I am just telling you Holding *didn't*."

"How can you be sure?"

She shrugged. "I just know," she said. "I'm an extraordinarily good judge of men. But if you want an example, *très bien*. After we agreed to marry, he always came straight up to the schoolroom upon arriving home. He would kiss the girls, and then . . ." The words withered.

"And then what?" he urged.

"And . . . And then he'd make a great pretense of bending over my hand," she said, her voice going thready. "He would kiss it, and declare that I was his queen. That the girls were his princesses. And that we were all going to live happily ever after in a palace. All nonsense, of course, but they thought it a great joke, and we'd all fall into giggles. And that's just what he did on . . . on that day. The day he died."

Ruthveyn suppressed an irrational flash of jealousy at the thought of Holding laying claim to Grace. And though he could not feel it, he could certainly hear the grief in Grace's voice. She had said she did not love him, and she'd no reason to lie, but for the first time since Melanie's death, he found himself compelled to watch every nuance of a woman's expression for some hint of what she felt.

His friend Lazonby believed that a person's every emotion showed on his face and in his gestures, that one need not *read* people so much as *observe* them. Moreover, he maintained that it was more a talent than a gift. Whatever it was, Ruthveyn suddenly wished he had it.

"Christ, this is all so hard to believe," he muttered.

Emotions passed like scuttling clouds over her face, pain, quickly followed by anger, her entire posture stiffening. "And you do not," she said flatly. "Believe me, I mean."

"Grace, I didn't say that," he answered.

Her voice was sharp. "I think you did."

"No, I just . . . I don't understand."

"It's rather simple, actually," she replied. "You either trust someone, or you don't. There is no guarantee."

She was right, he realized. In her world, it really was just that simple.

Ruthveyn searched for the words to explain how he felt, but Grace forged ahead, speaking more sharply than ever he'd heard. "So let me understand this," she said. "The police have found Papa's sidearms in my trunks, ergo I must harbor violent tendencies. And someone has forged a letter in Mr. Holding's hand to give me motive for killing him."

"Grace, I didn't say—"

"But if all this is true," she cut in, more loudly, "why did I not simply shoot the poor man, pistol-packing murderess that I am? Why bother with a knife? Or a note under the door?" Grace's voice took on a faintly hysterical edge. "I think, frankly, that it is a very good thing I left Papa's dress sword with his brother. God only knows what they might have accused me of."

Ruthveyn grabbed her upper arms. "Grace, they found the letter in your things," he said. "*Hidden* in your things."

She froze. Her eyes searched his face. "Oh God. That's . . . not possible."

"It was in what Napier called a letter box," he said. "Beneath a false bottom of some sort."

"A false bottom?" Her voice was hollow. "What nonsense. My letter box is lined in velvet. And yes, the bottom panel came unglued—it's been loose for years—but to call it *hidden* . . . ?"

"Grace, I—"

Her eyes caught his, wide and frightened, like those of some wild thing snared in a trap. "Oh, God," she whispered. "Someone really wishes me blamed for this, don't they? Someone means for me to . . ."

She backed away, her arms wrapped round her body as if she might retch.

He followed her. "Grace, calm down," he said softly. "We shall think this through."

"You already have," she answered. "And I have, too. I can see how this looks. You don't know me. You cannot know what to believe."

He held out his hands. "Grace, I think I do know you," he said quietly.

"You think. But you don't know." Abruptly, she snatched

the bay's reins. "I want to go back. Take me back, Ruthveyn, please. I shall get my things."

That was not going to happen. "Grace, don't be a fool." He grabbed her arm and spun her around, causing the bay to shy. "I have not asked you to go."

"Then you are a fool, too," she whispered. "Oh, I rue the day I came back to England! And I rue the day, Ruthveyn, that I laid eyes on you."

"Grace," he said, catching both her arms and pulling her nearer. "What are you saying?"

"I was not ready to meet someone like you," she said on a hitching sob. "I was not ready to believe that I might . . . oh, I don't know! I just want to go back to Aunt Abigail's. *Please.*"

He had hurt her. He had meant . . . *something* to her.

And for the first time in his life, Ruthveyn realized he had to take a chance, that two very distinct paths lay open to him, and he had to choose one. He had to *trust* Grace—blindly, and using nothing but his heart. For whatever reason, no other faculty lay within his grasp when it came to understanding her. Even now, as he held her close—close enough to kiss, with all their emotions rubbed raw—he felt nothing beyond the here and now.

"Grace." He gripped her arms hard. "I *do* trust you. I do not think for one moment you are capable of hurting anyone. And if you tell me Holding did not break the betrothal, then I believe that, too."

"No. You don't," she whispered. "You want to. But you don't."

He wanted, suddenly, to kiss her senseless again. To drug her with his touch and show her how he felt for her in ways both emotional and earthly. But he had sworn he would not touch her—not like that. He wanted—no, he *needed*—Grace to believe he spoke the truth when he said he trusted her, and to believe with her heart, not with a mind befogged by some potent, poisonous mix of grief and lust. So he drew her firmly into his arms—dragged her, really. But in the end, she came against him with a shudder.

A little roughly, he pushed the bonnet from her head, and allowed himself the comfort of setting his lips to the top of her head. "Damn it, Grace, don't tell me what I know," he said into her hair. "Just . . . don't, all right? I trust you. And I will discover who is behind this treachery, I promise you. Do you understand?"

"But you . . . you cannot stop Napier."

He threaded a hand through the loose hair at her temple. "I already have," he said, something heavy and certain bottoming out in his stomach. "You'll have to write him out a bloody confession before he dares darken our door with a warrant."

Our door.

Yes, Grace was his now—at least in as much as she lived beneath his roof and under his protection. He set one hand to the back of her head and cradled her against his riding coat as he banded the other arm tight about her. She was his in the only way that mattered to a gentleman; be she saint or sinner, he was sworn to defend her. And for the first time in his life, he was no longer certain whether right or wrong would matter if it came to it.

A long silence fell across the clearing, broken only by the cry of distant birdsong and the soft flutter of leaves just beginning to shimmer with autumn color.

"Grace?" He set a finger beneath her chin.

"Thank you, Ruthveyn." Her watery gaze flicked up at him. "Just . . . thank you."

But she was still shaking.

He released her and stepped away, remembering what

he had promised her. And himself. He snatched his mount's reins from the branch where he'd knotted them. "Come on," he rasped. "Let's walk, Grace, before I forget myself again. Walk with me, and tell me everything you know about every person who lived in Belgrave Square. Can you do that?"

"Yes, all right." She managed a tremulous smile, then caught the bay's reins.

They fell into step alongside one another, the horses clopping along behind. "Now let us begin," said Ruthveyn, "with the butler. Isn't it always the butler who did it?"

Finally, she laughed. "Not poor Trenton! I adore him."

"Seriously, Grace, we are going to make a list," he said. "I shall have Belkadi turn their lives inside out and shake loose the dust. I'll meet with each one of them if I must."

"But to what purpose?" she asked. "What will they tell you that they won't tell Mr. Napier?"

A vast deal, perhaps, thought Ruthveyn. And already, he dreaded it.

They walked, their heads bent in conversation, almost the length of the park, dipping south to follow the turn of the Serpentine Pond as Grace went one by one through the staff, none of whom sounded the least bit remarkable— or, regrettably, the least bit homicidal.

Nearer Park Lane, the crowd began to thicken. A few riders and carriages were still tooling toward Rotten Row, but in the grassy areas and along the paths, the nannies and their perambulators reigned supreme. Mr. Holding's unremarkable staff aside, by the time they had nearly reached the Grosvenor Gate, Grace was feeling perhaps a little better, he thought.

It was not, however, to last.

Near the end of the Serpentine, a short, blond lady was watching two little girls toss bread into the grass in an attempt to entice a trio of ducks from the water. Behind them lay a blanket and a basket, and what looked like the remains of a small picnic.

Just then, one of the ducks darted between the girls. Both turned, shrieking with delight, the taller of the two chasing it across the blanket. The duck flapped its wings, honked disapprovingly, and circled back to the water.

But the young girl was no longer watching the duck. "Mademoiselle!" she cried, running toward Grace. "Oh, Mademoiselle! Wait!"

"Anne!" Eyes suddenly alight, Grace dropped her reins and knelt to sweep the girl into her arms. "Oh, Anne! How very pretty you look. Oh, how I've missed you!"

The child drew back, quivering with excitement. "Mademoiselle, I have a pony now!" she said on a rush. "And a little cart, too. Aunt lets me drive it."

Grace's expression faltered but an instant before breaking into a smile. "Have you indeed?" she said as the smaller girl drew up. "And Eliza! Come, let me see those marvelous braids. How elegant!"

The girl beamed up to reveal a missing tooth. "Miss Effinger made them."

"Can you come to see us?" Anne's words spilled out. "*Please?* I could show you the pony. I could let you drive him."

"And he's brown," Eliza squeaked. "We named him Cocoa."

But the blond lady was sweeping across the grass toward them, her face fixed with consternation. "Anne! Eliza!" she said. "Calm yourselves." Her accent was crisp, and faintly Continental.

Grace set the child away and rose. "I do beg your pardon," she said at once. "I am—or *was*—their governess, Grace Gauthier." She extended a hand.

The blond lady took the hand and smiled, but there was little warmth in it. "Good afternoon," she said. "I am Miss Effinger."

"I am so pleased to meet you," said Grace. "Mrs. Lester sings your praises."

"She is too kind."

Ruthveyn stepped nearer, his crop hand tucked behind his back. "Lord Ruthveyn, at your service, ma'am," he said, bowing. "I am a friend of Mademoiselle Gauthier's."

Grace blushed profusely. "Yes, how rude of me."

Miss Effinger could scarcely conceal her surprise, but she made a perfunctory curtsy. "A pleasure, my lord," she murmured. "But if you will excuse us, we have a carriage waiting near the corner."

"Allow me to fold your blanket, then." Ruthveyn passed both reins to Grace.

He doubted Miss Effinger missed the ache in Grace's voice as she went on. "And the girls are well?" she asked. "They are sleeping? And back at their studies?"

"They are very well indeed," said Miss Effinger. "I believe the country air has done them good."

"That's where the pony is!" Anne piped. "We have a big courtyard, mademoiselle! And our very own fountain! And we drive round it in the cart—but Eliza is not allowed the reins. Only I am."

"So you are just visiting in Belgrave Square?" Grace asked, stroking Anne's hair.

"Yes, to see how Miss Crane goes on," said Miss Effinger coolly, "and to pack up a few things from the schoolroom. Mrs. Lester thought it best to take the girls out whilst that was done."

"Very wise," said Grace. She smiled again at the girls and stepped back, but Ruthveyn could see what it cost her. "I am sure you will come to adore Anne and Eliza as I have done."

"I already have." Then, with a tight smile, Miss Effinger took the basket from Ruthveyn, the blanket now tucked inside it. "Thank you, my lord. I am much obliged."

The trio turned to go, the two girls looking back almost forlornly. The taller girl threw up her hand to wave, her face wistful. "Good-bye, Mademoiselle Gauthier!"

For an instant, he could feel Grace hesitating. "Miss Effinger?" she finally called after them.

She turned. "Yes?"

"Might I write?" Grace asked. "To the girls, I mean?"

The woman bobbed faintly. "How very kind of you," she said. "But perhaps be so good as to write to Mrs. Lester first?"

It was as gentle a rebuke as could have been made, but Ruthveyn cringed for Grace nonetheless.

They stood on the slight rise above the water's edge, watching as the three circled round the wide end of the Serpentine, then down toward Hyde Park Corner. Below, a large town coach waited, two well-dressed ladies standing to one side.

"Look, it's Fenella!" Grace whispered. "And Mrs. Lester."

The younger lady's red hair was indeed unmistakable. Grace lifted a hand as if to wave. But the pair looked quite deliberately away, one of them opening the door as if to climb back in. Ruthveyn edged nearer and slipped his hand around Grace's to squeeze her fingers.

It was a tender, reflexive gesture, one that, with almost any other person, he would have avoided as unconsciously as another man might blink. But with Grace, physical contact—any sort of physical contact—came naturally to him. It would have been a deeply disconcerting realization had he allowed himself to ponder it.

But he did not, for in that moment, his only concern was for Grace, and for the heart he could all but hear breaking. Oftentimes, he well knew, the worst sort of pain was the silent kind, the kind inflicted not by a slash of an assailant's knife but by a thousand little cuts made up of thoughtless comments, cold restraint, and condescending eyes. And Ruthveyn wished to God he could have spared her.

Grace had not harmed Ethan Holding, he realized. It simply was not possible—if for no other reason than she would not have done such a thing to his children, children whom she looked at with such love. He was ashamed he had ever doubted her.

They stood thus in the first edge of dusk, watching until the girls were halfway down the hill. Then Eliza slipped one hand into Anne's, and the other into Miss Effinger's, and skipped the rest of the way down.

He heard the faint sob catch in the back of Grace's throat. "They do look happy," she said. "They are, aren't they? I want above all things that they should be happy."

"I think the girls are fine," he said quietly. "And perhaps the family will come round. Just give it a little time."

"It isn't going to matter, Ruthveyn, and you know it. They are gone from my life." Grace had frozen to the grass with something that looked like fear, and perhaps even horror. "*Mon Dieu,* do you think they will hear anything?" Her voice was a hollow whisper. "Children will listen to gossip, you know. They cannot help themselves."

Ruthveyn did not pretend to misunderstand her. "I am sure no one has laid any open accusations against you, Grace," he said, praying he spoke the truth. "They would not dare. And certainly not in front of children. Come, let's go home. The air grows cold."

A moment later, the coach rattled away. Grace turned to him with a watery smile. "Was that what the English call the cut direct?"

"It is possible the ladies could not make you out," he suggested.

"I think we both know that is unlikely," she murmured. "But I thank you."

Ruthveyn helped Grace mount, and they continued from the park in silence. Grace looked, for the first time, as if she had lost hope. As if her heart had been ripped from her breast. She had loved the children very much, he realized. It had quite likely been the whole of her reason for marrying Holding. And how sad that would have been for her.

And yet, what did he have to offer? What did he even *wish* to offer?

Nothing. And all of his reasons for that decision came flooding back tenfold as they rode home through Mayfair in silence.

But upon their arrival, they soon discovered yet another surprise lay in store.

CHAPTER 9

A Soldier of Fortune

*S*ergeant Welham?"

Grace froze in disbelief just beyond the conservatory doors.

"Gracie?" Rance Welham unfolded himself from the rattan chair beside Lady Anisha. "Grace Gauthier, as I live and breathe! And ever more beautiful!"

He strode through the conservatory, his bootheels ringing on the flagstone. To Grace's shock, he caught her at the waist and lifted her to twirl her madly about. "My God, girl, you've wasted away to nothing."

Grace felt her face flame. "Sergeant, I am fine. Set me down, if you please."

With a laugh, he did so, then turned to Ruthveyn. "And you, old man—" Here, he paused to embrace Ruthveyn, but it came out as more of a hearty, double-handed back-slap. "Grace, this dog is not fit to shine your shoes, and I hear you are his governess?"

"And very pleased to be," she said.

Lady Anisha had wandered from the conservatory. "A marvel, is it not?" she said to her brother. "He turned up an hour past, skulking round the windows like Satin when she's been caught filching tidbits from the kitchen."

"Oh, ho, *skulking,* was I, Nish?" Rance turned round and laid a smacking kiss on Lady Anisha's cheek. "I thought I was just taking the lay of things. Old soldiers never die, you know."

"And I thought you would be away for weeks." Ruthveyn's voice was cool. "Mademoiselle Gauthier will imagine I've lied to her."

Rance winked at Grace. "Looking for me, were you?" he said. "Of course I hurried back. I needed to be sure my girl was being looked after properly."

"I can assure you," said Ruthveyn, "your haste was unwarranted."

At that, Rance threw back his head and laughed again. "Yes, as usual, Adrian, you've stolen a march on me," he said. "Isn't it just my luck to be off on some adventure when the prettiest girl in all North Africa comes by?"

Lady Anisha rolled her eyes. "I must go down and see Mrs. Henshaw about dinner," she said. "Rance, will you stay?"

"No, no, I thank you," he answered. "Bessett and I have laid some plans for the evening."

"Ah," said Anisha knowingly as she started for the stairs. "I wonder if they involve a certain set of leggy young dancers from—"

"Anisha!" Ruthveyn chided. He returned his attention to his visitor. "If I may ask, Lazonby, what *are* you here for, if not a free meal?"

Rance scratched his stubbled jaw pensively. "I'd like a word with Grace, to be honest," he said. "Do you mind?"

For an instant, Ruthveyn hesitated. Then, "Not in the least," he said smoothly. He turned to her with a tight half bow. "Thank you, mademoiselle, for the pleasure of your company. Lazonby, I trust you can let yourself out?"

"Grace," said Rance when they were settled in the conservatory chairs, "why didn't you tell me you were living in London?"

"I meant to, as soon as I heard you had got out of prison again," she said, her gaze falling to her lap. "But Aunt Abigail said such things weren't done. That unmarried ladies mustn't seek out the company of gentlemen to whom they are not related."

"But they do seek out the company of their friends," Rance said.

"It was awkward," she said honestly. "I did not want to go to your club unless . . . well, unless it was an emergency."

Rance smiled, his brilliant blue eyes lighting up. "Well, I am oddly certain that you do not need me now," he said. "You could not be in better hands than Ruthveyn's."

Grace was very much afraid that was precisely where she was—in Ruthveyn's hands, and in more ways than one. Moreover, she had forgotten just how charming Rance could be—and how handsome he was, if so rugged a man could indeed be called handsome.

"*I believe,*" Ruthveyn had once said, "*I can safely claim to be his best friend in all the world.*"

How odd that it should be so. Lord Ruthveyn was all lean, predatory grace clothed in elegance and civility, and handsome as sin. Rance was like some charming highwayman—filled with restless energy, always smelling of leather, with a few fine lines about his merry, ice blue eyes.

Suddenly, he slapped both hands on his thighs. "Well, Grace, my girl," he said, those merry eyes twinkling now. "We've seen a lot of water flow under the bridge since we left El-Bahdja, haven't we?"

"Yes, you have lost your father," she murmured. "I was so sorry to hear it."

"And you have lost yours, Grace." His expressive face fell. "I owed him my life, three times over. Henri Gauthier was a brave man."

"And a good father," said Grace. "And yours—oh, Rance, he fought the good fight for you. Never did he falter. How sad that he is gone."

"I think he lived for that fight," Rance admitted, falling back into the deep rattan chair. "I think it kept him breathing, that determination to see me avenged and out of prison."

"And now you are."

Rance shrugged. "Well, I am out of prison, thanks to Father's tenacity, and Ruthveyn's influence," he said darkly. "But the vengeance—now *that*, it appears, will take some time."

He sounded so very like Ruthveyn when he spoke of revenge. Coldly certain. Ruthlessly determined. And suddenly Grace began to understand just what it was they shared.

"Tell me," she said quietly, "did Papa know from the first you were a wanted man?"

Rance laughed and set his broad hands on his thighs again. "Gracie, love, every soldier in the legion is a wanted man," he said, leaning toward her. "You know that. It's nothing but a place for rascals on the run. We are a rough bunch, us legionnaires. That's why your father so rarely befriended his men—to keep the riffraff away from you."

"Oh, Papa trusted my judgment when it came to rogues

and rascals." Grace flashed a muted smile. "After all, he befriended you."

"And some things last beyond the grave," said Rance solemnly. "I swore I would always look after you—and I will, should Ruthveyn fail. Which he won't, trust me. And yes, Grace, I told Henri precisely who and what I was. He always knew. "

"But why do the papers keep hounding you?" she asked. "And asking questions about your father? There's been a reporter around. A man by the name of Coldwater."

A dark expression passed over Rance's face. "Coldwater, eh?" he said. "I'll have to deal with the bounder eventually, I suppose. He and half of London are obsessed with my release."

"Because the witness against you made a suspicious deathbed recantation?" said Grace. "I read about it in the *Chronicle*. Who was this man they say you killed?"

Rance's expression had sobered. "Oh, I've killed many men, love," he said quietly. "That's a soldier's burden to bear. But the one I didn't kill—Lord Percy Peveril—was heir apparent to an earldom. His uncle was a member of the Privy Council, and had the old King's ear. Alas, I chose my enemies poorly."

"And was he your enemy?"

Rance's smile twisted. "Peveril was just an overbred fop who cheated me at cards," he answered. "Back when I was young and rash, and didn't understand I'd no business at the table. A dozen people watched him cheat, too. But like El-Bahdja, Gracie, that's water gone by. Tell me, what do you think of my friend Ruthveyn?"

Grace hesitated. "I think he is very kind."

At that, Rance laughed uproariously. "Oh, damn him with faint praise, Grace! No one thinks Ruthveyn *kind*.

Now, be honest with me. You always knew how to sum up a man's character better than any woman I knew."

It was true. Her father had often remarked upon her good sense, especially where men were concerned. But with Lord Ruthveyn, she was oddly uncertain. What she felt for him seemed to come only from her foolish heart—and when he kissed her, from a few other places as well. And then there was that extraordinary, mesmerizing heat in his touch . . .

"Grace?" Rance prompted.

Grace let her gaze wander to the window. "All right," she said, staring blindly out. "I think he is a little frightening. His eyes—they look right through me. They make me feel—"

Safe. Breathless. Frightened. Of myself, and of him.

But those words she would not say aloud. Grace closed her eyes. "—I don't know how he makes me feel," she finally finished.

Rance leaned forward and caught her hand. "Grace, he is a good man." His voice was low and, for once, serious. "He's enigmatic, yes. Even a little . . . otherworldly, perhaps. But just *trust* him. Trust him to take care of you. And what you feel for him—well, trust yourself, my girl. Your father was right. You have uncommon good sense about men. And good taste, too."

Grace's eyes opened wide with embarrassment. She opened her mouth to speak, to rebuke him, perhaps. But to what end? Rance had always spoken his mind—and possessed an almost uncanny knack for knowing everyone else's.

She exhaled sharply. "I just buried my fiancé, Rance," she said, "or would have done, had I been able to go to the funeral."

Rance gave a bemused smile. "Is that meant to chide me for my blunt tongue?" he asked. "Or yourself for falling in love? Either would be a waste of time, Grace. It is what it is."

"Rance, *arrête*!" Abruptly, she jerked to her feet. "What it is is *quite enough,* thank you."

He laughed again and caught her hand. "By God, you are Henri's girl through and through," he said, tugging her back down. "All right. I overstepped. Now listen, and let me be serious a moment."

She glowered at him warningly. "*Oui,*" she said. "Please do."

Rance dropped her hand. "Whatever you do, Grace, do not tell Royden Napier we are friends," he warned. "He harbors a great hatred of me."

"Why? Have you given *him* advice for the lovelorn?" When Rance scowled back at her, she relented. "All right. I'm sorry. Why would he hate you?"

"Seeing me convicted and sentenced to the gallows was his father's last great gasp of bureaucratic glory," said Rance. "His final and finest effort at social justice, or so he pretended. But in truth, I was just a bone to be tossed to the madding throng of radicals and Chartists—a sop meant to show even a highborn gentleman could be called to account for breaking the law."

Grace's eyes widened in horror. "You were made an example of?" she whispered. "And it cost you *eight years* in the legion? That is a long time, Rance, to walk in the desert."

They both knew she was not referring to the geography of Algeria. He shrugged. "Royden Napier took no pleasure in seeing my conviction overturned and his father's motivations impugned after the old man was dead." He paused, flashed a bemused smile, then jerked to his feet. "Ah, well! More of that water—"

"—under the bridge," Grace finished, rising.

Swiftly, he snatched her hand and planted a kiss on the back of her glove. "I will not see you again, Grace, until your situation is resolved," he said. "Not unless you need me. If you do, you have only to send word to the St. James Society. I've been staying there until I find a place to settle down."

"Rance," she said quietly, "you will never settle down."

He laughed as they strolled to the door. "Ah, you are likely right, Gracie girl! And you—well, you will not need me. You are in the best possible hands—and they are far more influential than mine."

"Am I?" she asked softly.

Rance's smile fell. "Oh, Napier will not touch him," he said certainly. "Not without a mighty long sword—and a sure one, too, for he'll get but one pass at Ruthveyn's throat. And he *knows* it."

Just then, heavy, measured steps sounded down the stairs. Lord Ruthveyn appeared, freshly dressed in a severely formal coat of jet black, his impossibly thick hair drawn back off his face, damp as if from the bath. With his waistcoat of cream brocade silk and the large cabochon ruby glittering on the last finger of his right hand, he looked every inch a Rajput prince—or at least what Grace imagined one might look like.

"Ah, Adrian, there you are!" said Rance amiably. "I forgot to say—I have some bad news for you."

Lord Ruthveyn lifted both of his slashing black eyebrows in that condescending way of his. "Do go on, Lazonby."

"Belkadi has evicted you from the guest suite," he said.

"We've a village padre visiting from Lincolnshire—one of Sutherland's old cronies. And I—well, alas, old friend—I have taken the other."

Ruthveyn's gaze flitted from Rance to Grace and back again. "Remarkable timing," he said tightly. "Simply . . . remarkable."

That evening, Ruthveyn joined his family for dinner for the first time since the night of Grace's arrival in Upper Grosvenor Street. Save for Lord Lucan, who spoke excitedly of a boxing match he meant to attend in Southwark the following day, they made for a quiet table. Lord Lazonby's arrival seemed to have cast some sort of pall over Anisha and her brother, and Grace could not make it out.

That evening she retired to her room to write Fenella in some faint hope that whatever breach had opened between them might be mended. She said how happy she was to have seen Anne and Eliza in Hyde Park, and of her hope for their happiness in their new home. Then, on second thought, she tore the letter to bits and tossed it onto the smoldering coal. Her friendship with Fenella was obviously over unless Ethan's killer was caught—and in part, she blamed Royden Napier. He had obviously spread his poison far and wide.

The awful truth was, not one person from Belgrave Square—not even the cook or the housekeeper—had written her so much as a note of sympathy, or even good-bye, and she had been exceedingly fond of them all. Perhaps everyone had leapt to the same conclusion without Napier's help. She had been betrothed—*almost* betrothed—to Holding, and he had been murdered. Now there was a letter indicating he had jilted her. The police had likely warned the entire staff against her—which was understandable, since someone had clearly gone to great lengths to lay the blame at her door.

The fear was stealing over her again. Grace sank onto her bed, remembering her last meeting with Royden Napier.

"I wanted a family quite desperately," she had said to him. *"Ethan offered me that—to be my family. To try to love me, and to share his daughters with me. I would have done anything to preserve that."*

Even to her ears, those words now sounded vaguely damning. Napier had undoubtedly written them down in his black leather folio so he might quote them against her at will. No wonder Ruthveyn had ordered her to *say nothing.* Sometimes it felt as if the only thing that was keeping Grace from falling into a swamp of grief was his faith and strength. And today, when she had feared for one instant she might lose that faith, she had—for the very first time—felt like giving up.

But his strength did sustain her. Indeed, it sometimes seemed as if everything that had happened between them really had been fated. Ruthveyn had even suggested as much on the day they met. Perhaps Grace was beginning to believe it, simply to have someone and something *to* believe in. Or perhaps she imagined that it somehow excused the deep and undeniable desire she felt for him. Rance, as usual, had not been wrong.

On a sigh, she rose and gathered her things, then went down the passageway to the marvelous bathtub for a long, hot soak. Afterward, she tried to read, having taken from Ruthveyn's library a worn copy of *The Muses Threnodie.* But soon gave it up again as too deep and too philosophical for her comprehension.

At ten, she went to bed, only to toss sleeplessly between the night constable's cries. At "twelve o'clock and all is well!" she came bolt upright in bed, suddenly certain that all was *not* well—and it had nothing to do with Royden Napier.

"*Pssst, Miss Gauthier?*"

This time the small, disembodied voice cut through her mental fog.

"Tom?" She whipped back the covers. "Tom, what's wrong?"

"Ma'am, Teddy's sick," he whispered from somewhere near her footboard. "I think you'd better come."

But Grace had already slid from the bed to feel about for her slippers. "Sick how?" she pressed, snatching up her wrapper. "Sick to his stomach? Or feverish?"

"He's retching. Can you come? Please? And not tell Mamma?"

Grace felt for his hand and headed toward the door. "Tom, you know I can't promise that," she said quietly. "Has Teddy eaten something he oughtn't? Please don't hide anything from me."

But Tom would say no more.

In the boys' bedchamber two doors down, Teddy had managed to light a lamp, and now lay curled in a ball upon his sheets. At her entrance, he looked at her a little plaintively and managed to sit up.

"I puked again," he said as if to reassure her. "I'm all better now."

"Teddy, what's happened?" Grace hastened toward him, and sat down on the edge of his bed. "Are you feverish?"

Teddy looked away, the scar on his forehead angrily red against his chalky skin. "I just puked," he said. "It's nothing. I'm fine now. Truly."

"Let's say you vomited," Grace gently corrected—and indeed, the front of his nightshirt was soiled with the proof of it.

But there was a good deal more wheedling in the boy's voice than she liked to hear from a child. Suspicious, and still gravely concerned, she stroked the hair back from his face to better feel his forehead, and it was then she realized the hair was matted with something disgustingly sticky.

"Teddy, dear, what have you got into?" she said. "I think you'd best tell me."

"He ate Uncle's sweets."

Grace looked around to see that Tom had perched himself on the adjacent bed and pulled his knees up to his chin.

"Sweets?" she echoed.

Tom just shrugged his narrow shoulders, then pointed at the floor.

Grace glanced down to see an old chamber pot had been pulled from beneath the bed—kept to hand, no doubt, for just such a contingency. On an inward groan, she got up and lifted the lamp over it. The pot was a third filled with a disgusting, pale yellow sludge bobbing with lumps of something that looked suspiciously like melting sugar.

Like lemon drops.

Lots and lots of lemon drops.

Grace set a hand to her forehead. "Teddy, you didn't."

"Yes he did," said Tom's small voice.

"Tattletale," said Teddy nastily. "You ate some, too."

"I ate twelve," Tom piped. "And I didn't pu—er, *vomit*."

Grace turned to face him, still holding the lamp aloft. "And how many did your brother eat?"

Tom shrugged again, and pointed at the empty jar on their night table. "The rest," he said simply.

Grace set the lamp down and seized the jar. "Oh, Teddy!" she whispered. "Not the *whole jar?*"

Teddy set a hand to his stomach, which was beginning

to look distended. "I guess," he said morosely. "And it all came up, too."

Grace sat back down on the bed. "Tom, fetch your brother a fresh nightshirt," she said, turning to Teddy. "Come here. I want to see your hair."

The boy bent forward. Two yellow lumps were caught in his dark blond hair, matting great knots of it together. "Oh, Teddy!" said Grace on a sigh. "Do you feel well enough to get up and let me change your sheets?"

As if resigned to his fate, Teddy slid from the bed.

Fortunately, the yellow goo was limited to the pillow slip, Grace soon discovered. The boy had obviously fallen asleep with his mouth stuffed full. Grace tried not to laugh, remembering Lady Anisha's horror at Ruthveyn's having bought a whole jar. She had sensed, correctly, the potential for disaster.

Teddy seemed to read her mind. "Are you going to tell Mamma?" he asked miserably.

"My dear, I have to," said Grace. "She is your mother, and you are very sick."

"Not anymore," he said on a heaving sigh. "But I will be when you tell her."

Grace set a hand to his forehead again and found just what she expected: nothing. The boy did indeed seem himself. But the room was cold, and the fire banked.

In a trice, she had exchanged the pillow slip for a fresh one from the linen press, and wiped the worst from Teddy's face. "Come along with me to the scullery," she said, holding out her hand. "We are going to have to work those wads of goo from your hair and get you out of that nightshirt."

Together, they went along the passageway and down the first flight of stairs. Near the landing, lamplight leached from a cracked doorway. It was Lord Ruthveyn's private study, a room she'd never entered. Curious, Grace slowed just as one of the silvery cats nosed the door open a few inches wider and went slinking through.

Within, Lord Ruthveyn sat reclined upon a long leather sofa in a roiling cloud of smoke, his head propped in one hand, the other holding a cigarette. His eyes were closed. On a tufted ottoman before him sat a tray with a decanter and an empty glass. Attired in a sort of loose-fitting banyan, and a pair of baggy white trousers, he appeared unaware of their presence. Indeed, he looked the very picture of wanton repose.

Grace swiftly tugged Teddy past, at last recognizing the sweet, smoky smell that sometimes clung to Ruthveyn's coat. Someone else, it would appear, had overindulged tonight—and on something a little less benign than lemon drops.

"Uncle Adrian looks scary again," whispered Teddy, as they went down the stairs.

"*Shh,*" said Grace. "He's tired. He has a lot of responsibilities." And he also, according to his sister, never slept—which perhaps explained that incessant look of world-weariness etched upon his face.

Once inside the kitchens, she set Teddy up on the edge of the kitchen table and deftly stripped off his nightshirt. Unlike the upstairs rooms, here the old stone floor still radiated with warmth.

"You mustn't be scared of your uncle," she chided, tossing the shirt and the sticky pillow slip into the basket kept for kitchen laundry. "He just hasn't slept."

"He never sleeps," said the boy. "And I didn't say I *was* scared, silly. I was just explaining. 'Cause you're new. And I thought *you* might be frightened."

Grace seized the poker. "Good heavens, Teddy. I am not"—here she knelt to poke up the fire a little too vigorously—"*frightened* of Lord Ruthveyn."

The boy lifted his bony shoulders. "Everyone else is," he said evenly. "Well, not me. And not Tom. But all the servants are—except Higgenthorpe."

"What nonsense." Grace went into the scullery to fill a pan with warm water. "Why should anyone be afraid of your uncle?"

"Because he has the Gift."

Temporary distracted by positioning the pan, Grace glanced over her shoulder. "What gift, Teddy? Who gave it to him?"

Teddy was clutching both hands between his knees. "I don't who gave it to him," he muttered. "I just know he's got it. I heard Mamma say she didn't know why the Scots called it a Gift when it was nothing but a curse."

"A curse? What sort of gift could be a curse?"

"I don't know that either," said the boy. "I just know the servants aren't allowed to touch him on account of it. And Mrs. Henshaw told the tweeny never to look Uncle square in the eyes, or he'd know when she was going to die."

"That's just servants' nonsense, Teddy." Still, Grace mulled it over as she set the pan on the table, then rummaged about for a tub of lard.

"What's that for?" asked Teddy suspiciously.

Grace set it beside the pan. "I'm going to work a little into the goo," she explained, "so we don't hurt you combing it out. Afterward, we'll use soap, and dip warm water over your hair. Then we'll dry you by the fire before putting you back to bed. Having braved a whole hogshead of lemon drops, it seems pointless you should expire of a chill."

"It wasn't a whole hogshead," Teddy corrected. "That's *a lot*."

The kitchen fire was catching now, bathing the room in a warm golden light. Grace reached over to rub a little lard into his gummy hair. It was then that she noticed the strange markings on the boy's shoulder. She caught his upper arm and turned him.

"Teddy, what is this?"

"Nothing."

Grace studied it. Rough, smudged, and crookedly done though it was, it suddenly jogged a scrap of memory. She'd seen it before, and not on the pediment of the St. James Society. No, it had been far longer ago than that.

"Teddy, this isn't nothing," she murmured. "Did you draw it?"

The lad's shoulders fell. "It's just ink," he said. "It'll wash off."

Grace turned him a little to the right. It looked vaguely like a family crest, but instead of a shield, it was a sort of thistle-shaped cartouche bearing a cross within, and something that—with a generous stretch of the imagination—might have been a crossed quill and sword. It was undeniably the same strange symbol engraved on Ruthveyn's gold cravat pin. The only thing missing were the letters below.

"Why did you draw it on your arm, Teddy?"

Again, he gave his childlike shrug. "Sometimes people have it."

"Like who?"

"Grandpapa," he said. "But he died. Besides, it's just a mark."

And he was right. It was just a mark. Moreover, the room was as warm as it was going to get. "All right, Teddy," she said. "Let's lean over this pan, shall we?"

Thirty minutes later, Grace was seated in Mrs. Henshaw's favorite chair, which she'd pulled closer to the kitchen hearth. Teddy sat in her lap half-asleep, tucked into his clean nightshirt with his short hair nearly dry. Grace had not needed to cut any of it away, thank heaven. Now she gave it one last ruffle, then stood and carried the boy from the kitchens.

"I can walk," he muttered in protest. Then he tucked his head beneath her chin and went promptly back to sleep.

Upstairs, the light still spilled from Ruthveyn's study. Grace glanced in to see he still sat upon the leather sofa in his cloud of smoke, but this time, his legs were drawn up and crossed, his arms at repose, and his eyes closed. The brandy glass on the ottoman was half-full, and the silver cat—Ruthveyn's familiar, perhaps—had vanished.

Little Tom was sound asleep by the time Grace tucked his brother back into bed. After pulling up the covers, she put out the lamp and went down the passageway, telling herself that Ruthveyn was none of her concern. She knew, too, that going back downstairs was just asking for trouble. Something more than trouble, perhaps.

And yet, at the entrance to her bedchamber, her hand already on the doorknob, Grace turned around. She told herself that the least she could do was throw open a window and order the man up to bed. She told herself that it was fate.

Inside the study, a lamp burned on the desk, the wick turned down to a mere glow. His hands relaxed on his knees, Ruthveyn still sat in his strange pose, seeming unaware of her presence.

Tentatively, Grace stepped a foot inside. It was a beautiful, intimate chamber, clearly the most exotic in the house, lined with books and dotted with exotic pieces of art. A lethal-looking jezail was mounted to the wall above the hearth, its long barrel stretching the width of the mantel, and what looked like a solid gold statue of some four-armed Hindu deity with the head of an elephant sat on one corner of a carved mahogany desk. On the opposite corner sat a pierced brass bowl of potpourri; beautiful, but useless in the face of Ruthveyn's smoke.

Gathering her courage, Grace closed the door and tip-toed across a carpet as luxurious as soft spring grass. "My lord?" she whispered.

His eyes opened at once, though they looked heavy-lidded and dreamlike. "Grace," he said quietly.

"It is nearly one in the morning," she said, easing the stopper back into the brandy decanter. "What are you doing up?"

"Meditating," he answered.

"Meditating?"

"Thinking about . . . not thinking," he mumbled. "That is the goal, is it not?"

He made no sense. "I think you'd best go to bed," she said gently.

"No." His gaze seemed to grow more distant. "I cannot sleep."

Grace bent down to better see him. "Nor can you stay up all night drinking and smoking," she said, plucking a still-smoldering stub from the silver tray. "It's no wonder you look hagged. Precisely what is this, by the way?" She held it before his eyes.

A sideways smile lifted one corner of his mouth, and Grace could see the dark stubble that shadowed his lip and cheeks. Absent the civilizing influence of fine tailoring, he looked a good deal more disreputable, too.

"That, my Grace, is a cigarette," he said.

"I know what a cigarette is," she said. "I believe we French invented the term. What I wish to know is what you have *in* it."

"Turkish tobacco," he said calmly.

"And?"

"Herbs."

"And—?"

He lifted one broad shoulder. "And charas."

"You mean *kif*," she gently chided. "Or hashish. Perhaps you forget that I have seen something of the world."

"Perhaps." The word dared her to challenge him.

But she did not. Instead, she moved the entire tray to the desk and sat down on the ottoman opposite him, their knees but inches apart. The intensity that seemed to almost thrum through Ruthveyn had somehow been stilled, and it was as if Grace saw him for the first time as an ordinary man—a very handsome, very dangerous-looking man—but ordinary in a way she couldn't quite describe.

He still sat perfectly relaxed, his legs crossed such that his bare feet were tucked atop his thighs. His toes, she noticed, were long, his feet narrow and beautiful like his hands. The robe he wore was made of gold silk shot with silver, brilliant against the loose white fabric of his trousers, and wrapped round the waist with a wide black scarf. He would not have looked entirely out of place, she thought, on a corsair's ship with a scimitar tucked in his sash—or standing over a harem, surveying his possessions.

"Why?" she said quietly, trying not to stare at the expanse of masculine chest that his gown exposed. "Why do you smoke it?"

"It calms me."

"You never look otherwise to me," she argued. "In fact, it is a little disconcerting just how calm you *do* look. Do you mean it soothes a physical pain?"

"I do not suffer physical pain." He smiled a little drowsily and waved his hand toward a carved wooden box on the corner of his desk. "The night is still young, my dear. Try it."

"I don't have to," she said. "There is enough of it floating in the air, I daresay, to knock me senseless."

He crooked one black eyebrow. "Afraid, my Grace?"

"I am not your Grace," she answered. "And no, I am not afraid. But you should think of the boys. One cannot count upon their sleeping through the night, Ruthveyn, or assume they won't go pilfering where they ought not."

This clearly had not occurred to him, for he looked at the box and frowned. But she was indeed feeling lightheaded. "Really, this just won't do," she said, moving as if to rise. "I am going to open a window, and air the—"

In an instant, Ruthveyn's hand lashed out, snaring her round the wrist, and dragging her half over him. Another tug, and she was almost atop him. "Why are you here, Grace?" His voice was low and a little threatening.

"Ruthveyn, let me go."

"*No.*" The brandy and the drug were sweet on his breath. "You came down here of your own volition. You know I'm not going to bed. Not alone. And you know I'm not entirely sober. So *why?*"

She jerked back, but he held her fast by both her wrist and her eyes, which were locked with his. "I just came to help—"

"Liar," he softly interjected. "Lie to me if it makes you feel better, Grace. But don't lie to yourself."

He was right, she realized, her gaze drifting down his face. When he looked through her with those ageless, all-seeing eyes, he saw straight to the heart of her, saw what she had wanted from the very first. Now her body was arched over his, one hand splayed against the sofa behind his head, the other caught fast in his grip, their faces but inches apart, and the ache was like a hunger in her belly.

How in heaven's name had it come to this?

She licked her lips uncertainly. "Perhaps it's just . . . *fate*," she whispered.

And then she kissed him.

CHAPTER 10

A Taste of Temptation

$\mathcal{R}$uthveyn turned his face into hers and kissed her back, his sensuously full lips sliding languidly over her own. At once something hot and breathtakingly sweet melted through her, and Grace opened her mouth over his. His lips parted on a soft groan—an aching sound of male surrender—then he drew her tongue deep into his mouth. Rhythmically, he began to suck it, sending that sweet, hot heat spiraling lower and lower, from her nipples to her womb, all the way to the apex of her thighs.

Then, with a move that was not in the least languid, he twisted sideways on the sofa, dragging her fully astraddle him, hitching her nightclothes up to her knees as he plunged both hands into hair. He lay almost reclined beneath her now, propped up by the sofa's arm, his black gaze locked with hers, and for an instant, the world stopped spinning.

"If this is fate, Grace," he said quietly, "then let it take us."

In answer, she set a hand to his cheek and closed her eyes. He drew in a deep, shuddering breath, and it was as if she could feel his darkness leaching into her, pulling through her like a magnet finding true north, then flowing away like a river into the night.

It wasn't just the cloud of *kif* that lingered, and it wasn't the madness of desire too long suppressed. It felt as though a metaphysical force surged between them, purifying and clean. It had been thus the first time he'd touched her face that long-ago morning in St. James's, when she had come out of herself somehow, only to return to a self free, at least for a time, of grief and fear.

His hands still tangled in her hair, Ruthveyn pulled her down to him and kissed her again—long, drugging kisses that left her trembling.

There comes a time in every woman's life, perhaps, when she realizes that whatever it is she's been clinging to—her pride, her virtue, or perhaps just her sanity—really isn't worth hanging on to anymore. Or perhaps she just meets the one thing that's well worth throwing it away on.

Ruthveyn—with one warm hand cupping her hip and his tongue thrusting slowly into her mouth—felt like that one thing. Tonight, the darkness in him didn't frighten her; it was what he was, and he was what she wanted. So when his mouth slid from hers to trail fire down her throat, then along the neck of her nightgown, she arched back and let his teeth catch in the flannel.

He tore at it, and the first ribbon slipped free, the neckline gaping. On a low sound of approval, he cupped one breast through the cotton of her nightclothes.

"*Grace.*" Ruthveyn spoke her name like a prayer. "*Shouldn't . . . be here.*"

"I understand this," she whispered. "I understand *you*. You think I don't, but I am not naïve."

He didn't argue but instead set his open mouth against the vee of her throat and placed a row of kisses up her collarbone. "So beautiful," he murmured. Then his hands came up, shaking ever so slightly, to slide the wrapper from her shoulders.

She wriggled it free, and it slithered down her back and onto the floor. He rolled his hips beneath her, and she felt the hard, hot weight of his manhood against her pubic bone. Grace closed her eyes and thought of how long she had wanted this. Of how long she had waited for the man who could make her ache this way. And never could it have been any man save this one.

She understood now the dreadful mistake she had almost made in marrying where she did not love and the life of emptiness she had almost surrendered to. Perhaps this was all there would ever be—this one night—but it would sustain her far longer than a lifetime of inadequacy. And perhaps, had he been sober, Ruthveyn would have refused her even this. And had her life not gone so thoroughly to hell, she likely wouldn't have asked. But that she would not think about. Not tonight.

On a soft sigh, she rode back on him, the compelling, unfamiliar ache overwhelming whatever shame she should have felt. Beneath her, Ruthveyn was all sleek, hard male, the silk of his clothing sensuously slick against her inner thighs. His hands roamed boldly over her body, warm and demanding.

On impulse, her hands went to his black sash. "What is this?" she whispered, unfurling one end.

"A *kamarband*," he rasped. "Untie it."

Grace's shaking hands made poor work of it, but the silk knot soon slid free. The gold fabric slid open across Ruthveyn's chest, which was layered with muscle and lightly dusted with black hair. A deeply puckered scar, now white with age, slashed across the turn of his shoulder. She traced her finger along it.

"What happened?" she murmured.

He flicked a quick glance at the chimneypiece. "A Ghilzai rifleman took exception to my looks."

"Ah." She bent to kiss it. "The jezail over the mantel?"

"It was him or me," Ruthveyn muttered, preoccupied with weighing her breasts in his hands.

Grace's fingers raked the fabric of his robe open. Round his neck he wore a pendant on a gold chain, something that looked like a piece of polished ivory mounted in gold. It was, she realized dimly, some sort of claw.

She moved as if to slide the robe from his shoulders, but instead, he set his hand behind her head and drew her down to kiss her again. She came against him chest to chest, so close she imagined she could feel his heart thud slow and steady, every beat matched to the thrust of his tongue. She felt his warmth—that pure, almost sensual energy—melting through her once again. She wanted to tear off her own clothes, to lie with him skin to skin, as only a lover could.

Again, his fingers speared into the hair at the back of her head, lightly threading through it. Ruthveyn's other hand spread wide and warm across her upper back, clasping her body to his. For long moments, Grace lost herself in his kiss, then lifted a little away to look at him.

Seen in such sensual repose, the care stripped from

his face, Ruthveyn looked fleetingly like the boy he'd doubtless once been—a dark, beautiful Apollo, with his long, inky lashes fanned above his cheeks, and perhaps even the gift of Delphic inspiration, too. Grace cradled his face with one hand and kissed him again, more tenderly, something inside her heart soaring almost dangerously high.

Ruthveyn pressed his lips along her cheek, to the tender spot just below her ear. "Grace," he said, his hands going to her nightdress. Without asking, he dispensed with the remaining ribbons, then slowly pushed the fabric off her shoulders. The cotton slid away, cool air breezing down her arms, then her bare breasts, as it fell.

"Grace," he whispered again. "I have longed for this."

She closed her eyes, faintly embarrassed. Ruthveyn's warm hands skated up her ribs to cup both breasts. Lightly, as if she were the most delicate thing on earth, he circled his thumbs over her nipples, making them peak with pleasure.

"*Oh.*" Grace tipped back her head, her breasts filling his hands with each breath.

Somehow, he pulled himself to a sitting position, the muscles of his belly and groin going impossibly taut beneath her. Then he turned until he was seated on the sofa, Grace straddling him, her knees set to either side of his hips.

His eyes, dreamlike and melting, flew to hers, then he pulled her against him, his lashes falling shut again as his lips went to her breast. For long moments he suckled her, his tongue circling, then teasing, his mouth pulling and drawing her nipple into the tantalizing heat of his mouth until Grace thought she might die of the pleasure, and of the yearning that coiled tighter and tighter, deep in her belly, to leave her gasping.

"Please," she whimpered, her nails digging into his broad shoulders. "Please, Ruthveyn, just . . ."

Just what? Grace hardly knew what she begged for.

Ruthveyn's tongue circled once more, then his mouth drew away. *"Adrian,"* he whispered, his breath cool against her wet nipple. "Say it, Grace."

"Adrian." It came out more of a sigh. "Adrian, please."

"Please what, my Grace?" He nuzzled one side of his face against her breast, the rough bristle of his cheek lightly scraping her. "If this is fate, then I am yours."

Grace drew back an inch, caught the hems of her nightdress, then drew it up and shimmied it off. His eyes warmed appreciatively, but he set his hands to either side of her ribs as if to lift her away.

"No," she pleaded, her fingers going to the draw cord of his loose trousers. But he lifted her and stood. On instinct, Grace twined her legs round his waist and her arms round her neck as they rose. "Ruthveyn, no, *wait.*"

"Not like this, love," he murmured into her hair.

And then, as if she were weightless, Adrian spun her about and carried her into the shadowy depths of the room. He elbowed his way through a door built into the oak wainscoting, then carried her through a narrow passageway into a chamber lit by lamps that flanked a wide, canopied bed. Satin leapt up, gave a tremulous stretch, then bounded away.

Adrian laid Grace in the middle of the mattress, letting her sink into a fluff of wool and down. From beneath half-closed eyes, she watched him. Somewhere along the way, the gold robe had been lost. Adrian wore nothing save his odd trousers—a pair of long, silk drawers that hung low on his hips and tied under his navel, and beneath which, she was oddly certain, he wore nothing.

A trail of dark hair began at his breastbone and ran

down a belly flat as a slab of tawny marble, to vanish somewhere beneath the draw cord. And suddenly, Grace wanted to stroke her hands down that belly. To feel those warm layers of muscle above, so lightly furred. To skim her palms beneath the silk and feel his flesh quiver to her touch.

She rolled up onto her elbows, one knee slightly lifted, and surveyed him across the mattress.

"If you are my fate, Adrian, come here."

For an instant, he hesitated as if he might refuse her. Then surrender sketched over his face, and he set one knee to the mattress. On hands and knees, he crawled over her like some lean jungle cat, the silk almost dragging off his hip bones, the ivory pendant swinging from his neck as he came.

Grace set her palms to his belly and felt him shiver. His straight, heavy hair fell forward to shadow his face as he bent his head and kissed her hard without preamble, his tongue plunging deep, in and out, again and again, the rhythm of his intent unmistakable, even to Grace.

She slid her hands lower, hooking her thumbs in the silk, dragging it down until she felt it slither over the swell of his buttocks. She felt the hard weight of his erection spring free, long and silky-warm against the flesh of her inner thigh.

As if to distract her, Adrian deepened the kiss, cradling her face in his hands. But the weight of his manhood was unmistakable and a little daunting. Experimentally, Grace eased one hand along his belly. Adrian caught it and pulled it lower, inviting her to touch. Grace brushed her fingers over the tip, watching, mesmerized, as Adrian sucked in his breath on a hiss.

"Do you want this?" he rasped, his eyes still dreamy in the lamplight. "Tell me you want it."

Tentatively, her hand crept lower to stroke the length of it. She thrilled to the sensation of warm silk beneath her fingertips and the tangle of curls at the base. Never could she have imagined lovemaking would be like this: so much pleasure in touching; so much warmth and bare skin and aching need. It all came together in an incredibly complicated mélange of emotion that left her drowning yet craving more.

Adrian's body hovered over hers, warm and sheltering, his weight still on his knees. She drew in his scent of soap and smoke and male sweat and felt that strange sensation writhing in the pit of her belly again. He nuzzled beneath her ear, then sucked lightly at her earlobe.

"Grace?" he whispered.

She knew what he asked. Since that first day in the library, she had wanted him, even amidst all the pain and fear and confusion, she had been drawn to him on a level that went beyond mere attraction. Yet now she felt oddly foolish and inadequate. A man such as Adrian would likely have had dozens of lovers, all more experienced than she.

But this was the here and now, and for now, he wanted her, this dark man who was beautiful and desirable beyond words. On an unsteady breath, she drew up her knees and let his weight cradle between her legs. Guiding himself with one hand, Adrian probed lightly between her thighs, the smooth head of his manhood sliding effortlessly between her folds.

"Do you want this, Grace?" he rasped, his voice thick. "Say it."

"*Yes.*" She was wet and slick with need, and he entered her with a firm, sure push, stretching her tight—almost beyond bearing.

"Oh!" Grace bit her lip as Adrian held perfectly still.

"Oh, my." She exhaled deeply. "That is . . . are we . . . ?"

He made a sound, something between a laugh and a groan, then lowered his forehead to touch hers. "Not even close, my Grace."

"Oh," she said again, feeling foolish.

He lifted his head, a hint of contrition in his eyes. "Ah, Grace," he whispered, "you are ever an enigma."

"Am I?" Her voice came out high and thready.

To her relief, he drew out a little and hesitated. She could see a fine sheen of perspiration forming on his forehead.

"If it were done," he muttered as if to himself, "'twere well it were done quickly."

"I don't think," Grace whispered, "that Shakespeare meant—"

But Adrian chose that instant to be done. He impaled her on a deep, certain thrust, leaving nothing but a cry of pure male satisfaction in his wake, and leaving Grace unerringly certain she would never walk again.

"Oh!" she cried, her eyes flaring wide.

Again he held himself perfectly motionless, his damp forehead dipping down to touch hers, his lips brushing over the tip of her nose. "'Tis over, love," he crooned. "Be still, and know that it will pass."

"Adrian?" Grace swallowed hard. "Could it be we don't—"

"No." He kissed her lightly. "Fate is never wrong."

Then, as if to prove it, he drew out just an inch, then slid gently back inside her again.

"*Ahh*," she said softly.

The pain was exquisite. Sweet. A pain yet not a pain at all, but instead the promise of pleasure to come. Grace forced herself to relax, to hold herself open and welcoming to him. The weight and the pressure still felt impossible, but to stop—even to slow—was not possible, either. And what she felt for him—the almost breathtaking need to give him joy—was beyond her own imagining.

She watched, mesmerized, as Adrian's eyes fell shut, and he slowly sheathed himself all the way inside her. Then he set a rhythm, thrusting in and out, their one flesh joined together in a delicate, age-old dance.

Grace closed her eyes, focusing on the incredible sensation of being one with him. She slid her right leg up higher still, reveling in the feel of his well-muscled calf and thigh and the hair that lightly dusted them. There was a pressure building inside her, an urgency that Adrian did not seem to feel. His face was beautiful, almost youthful and carefree as he hung over her, his arms planted wide above her shoulders, his black hair shimmering in the lamplight with his every thrust.

"Adrian," she whispered. "Oh, I want . . ."

"Grace," he said. "I know."

She had thought, foolishly, that lovemaking would be fast and frantic. That passion would overwhelm, and that the end—whatever the end was—would be swift. But Adrian's every move seemed deliberate, and slowly calculated to ratchet up the need burning inside her. She felt afire with a ravening, building hunger for him—for that *thing* she needed. The thing only Adrian could give her.

She opened her mouth to plead for it—to surrender herself completely—but he came fully down atop her to cover her body with his. Banding one strong arm about her, Adrian cradled Grace against him as his tongue delved into her mouth again, tasting thoroughly on a sound of pleasure.

Slowly he thrust inside her mouth as his manhood thrust deep inside her, setting a perfect, sensual pace. Sensation drugged her. The scent of damp skin and fresh linen and sex swirled round her in a dizzying, sensual heat as Adrian loved her for what felt like an eternity. She writhed beneath him, arching and pleading for release, and when at last Grace thought she would go mad with the wanting, Adrian lifted himself away, his face twisted as if with agony.

"*Come to me, my Grace,*" he whispered. "*Oh, God. So sweet . . .*"

Yes, this was what she had longed for. She had come here wanting to give herself up to him. And in this moment of passion and pleasure, Grace did not care what that made her. Caution, like her virtue, had flown to the four winds. She lifted her hips to him, and he thrust and thrust again until something bright and blinding exploded in her head and ran through her like a bolt of lightning, setting her every nerve aquiver. Pleasure surged in wave after wave, until she fleetingly lost connection with time and place. Until her body and her heart flew to him.

When she came back to herself, she again felt that otherworldly sensation of having left her body, but this time magnified by a thousand, and channeled into pure and perfect bliss. She opened her eyes to see Adrian staring down at her, his eyes soft now, yet still intense in the lamplight. He had withdrawn from her and now lay a little to one side.

"Grace—" He dipped his head and brushed his cheek over hers like a cat seeking warmth. "Grace, you cannot know—"

To her shock, some nameless emotion choked his voice; something that went beyond ordinary satisfaction, or even joy.

"What?" she pressed.

His smile was sleepy. "'Tis nothing."

Then he bent and rummaged in the floor to find his trousers, and it was only then that she realized he had spilled his seed upon the counterpane. He made short work of it, then collapsed half atop her with a grunt of satisfaction.

For an instant, Grace felt oddly bereft. But how foolish when he had, in fact, done her a great kindness. "Come," she said quietly, urging his head onto her shoulder. "Come, sleep now."

He tucked his bristled cheek against her neck. "Too heavy," he murmured.

"No," she whispered. "It's perfect."

But it did not matter. She could already feel Morpheus's arms surrounding them, and the utter letting go that was happening inside Adrian.

Ruthveyn stirred to the sound of a clock somewhere deep in the house. Snuggled against Grace's warmth, he counted the chimes—three in all, unless he'd drowsed through the first. Grace lay on her side, spooned against him. On the other side, he could feel Silk tucked into the small of his back, rumbling away as she always did.

Careful not to disturb either, Ruthveyn reached round to absently scratch the cat's ears, then rolled up on his elbow to see that one lamp had sputtered out, but the other still burned. The light cast a warm, golden glow over Grace's face and the long blond hair that fanned across his pillow, and looking at her, Ruthveyn felt something deep in the pit of his belly give an ominous flip-flop.

Grace. *His lover.*

Feeling rueful—but not entirely regretful—he stroked a finger over one of her lightly arched eyebrows. Hers was a classic English-rose sort of beauty, and now that her expressive face was at rest, he could savor the pleasure of simply studying the soft curve of her mouth and the high swell of her cheekbone.

At some point in the night she had grown cold, and he had tucked her beneath the covers. He hardly remembered it now, so dead to the world had he been. Indeed, he could not remember the last time he'd slept so dreamlessly, and for the first time in a long while, he felt refreshed.

And sober. Painfully, acutely sober.

The evening came starkly back to him. The driving need to claim her. The carnal satisfaction that went beyond the sensual and into a realm of contentment he had not known existed—with no otherworldly communication between them whatever. Nothing beyond the erotic flow of shared energy and the bond of two lovers giving of themselves to each other, with all the sweet, sensual uncertainty that entailed. Grace's mind had been completely, blessedly, closed to him.

In part, it had likely been the charas. Or perhaps, as she suggested, it was simply fate. In the gloom, his mouth twisted. Assuredly that was what he'd like to believe—but he wasn't fool enough.

And then there was that other small, niggling problem.

He had known, of course, Grace was likely a virgin. There was no use to pretend now that taking her innocence had been anything less than a mistake born of intoxication and suppressed desire. Now, his mind more clear, Ruthveyn bent to kiss her cheek and prayed she would forgive him, that she would have no regrets.

In sleep, she had none. Grace snuggled back against him with a drowsy sigh of pleasure, the swell of her bottom dangerously inviting. Ruthveyn wriggled onto his back between Grace and the cat, then dragged an arm over his eyes. He was not a man much given to regret; he had meant what he'd said about fate. Nonetheless, the wiser part of him wished he had not risked it—not her virginity, or her heart. Or even his. But that sort of dazed, drugged lethargy made a man all too willing to give in to his baser impulses.

In the past, it had been opium and whores for him—not that he was proud of it. But at least his partners had known where they stood, and the euphoria had been enough to keep the demons at bay. But that was his old life. Or his *in-between* life. Those long, lost years after abandoning his diplomatic post and wandering aimlessly through the desert—sometimes quite literally.

But eventually those hedonistic wanderings had taken him to Algiers, and to that whorehouse where he had stumbled upon Lazonby, then in Tangier, Geoff. They had brought back to him the vow he'd made his father, and his grandmother. And he had begun to accept all over again that what he was would never change, and that if he chose to play out his days lotus eating, those days would be short indeed.

So he and Geoff had followed Lazonby to London— albeit not under armed guard—to carry through with their grand plan of formalizing the *Fraternitas*, and to see Lazonby freed of the accusations against him. And in helping Lazonby, Ruthveyn had reacquainted himself briefly with his Queen, and accepted, with all the grace he could muster, the thanks of a grateful nation. He had already been quietly created Marquess of Ruthveyn, the reward for his so-called diplomatic efforts abroad. Some- times, even now, he still felt a little like Judas with his thirty pieces of silver.

But that did not bear thinking about just now. Lazonby was free, the Society was slowly reconstituting itself, and Ruthveyn was rarely called upon by the Crown for anything. He was *retired*—and his foremost concern was Grace. He rolled back to embrace her, only to realize she'd been watching him.

She smiled drowsily and cuddled against his chest. "I wonder," she said quietly, "what you are thinking."

He tucked his chin to look down at her. "Nothing of consequence," he said, brushing his lips over her forehead. "But Grace, we do need to talk."

She rolled her blue eyes back up at him. "Actually we don't," she said. "I know, Adrian, how things stand. May we not simply enjoy our short time together?"

Did she understand? He bloody well hoped so. Save for his wife, he'd never deflowered a virgin. He had no idea what might be expected of him. Still, something inside him fell a little at the ease with which she dismissed it all.

"Why don't you tell me, Grace, just how you think things stand?"

She gave a soft laugh. "I think I shouldn't have come downstairs tonight," she said. "I think I tempted you into something you would not otherwise—"

"Just stop, Grace," he interjected. "I take responsibility for—"

Her hand came up, palm out. "May I finish, please?" she asked. "No, I do not take all the blame upon myself. You had the bad judgment to smoke yourself up into the clouds, and for that, *oui,* you are to blame. Between the two of us, there was bad judgment all the way around last night—though I'm not complaining of the result, mind."

He curled tighter around her then and set his lips to the top of her head. "What are you saying, exactly?"

For a heartbeat, she hesitated. "I'm saying that I do not make a habit of enticing my wealthy employers into marriage," she answered. "It is, in fact, quite out of the question."

For a long moment, he said nothing, a little surprised at the strange mix of relief and disappointment he felt. He did not wish to marry again. No, not even to Grace. And the fact that he was already half in love with her only strengthened that resolve. Because he knew how it would end; that the more he loved her, the worse it would be. *That* was his fate. At some awful, inopportune moment, probably when he was thrusting inside her, right on the edge of release, that portal to hell would fly off its hinges. He could not live that way again, waiting for the inevitable to happen. Waiting to know the worst.

Oh, perhaps Grace was destined to give him a dozen healthy children, then outlive him by a decade—but that might be worse, in some ways, than the other. He would likely crawl out of her bed every morning the sun rose knowing not just that his days with her were numbered but how many they numbered, and perhaps even how they would end.

At that thought, he held Grace a little tighter. Good God, he would never be able to leave her as he had left Melanie, to go haring off on a series of ill-conceived attempts at portending the fate of the British Empire. Already he knew career and country would never supersede his need to be with her. He would not even try to use it as an excuse.

And there was no way to explain himself to her.

Just then, Satin bounded over the footboard and onto the bed. Grateful for the distraction, he sat up to scratch the cat beneath her chin. It would have been better, of course, had he not. He realized it the moment Grace's fingertip stroked over the top of his hip.

"Hmm, this is interesting . . ."

He turned, and lay back down, propped on one elbow. "What, that mark?" he said. "It's a tattoo."

"I know that much," she said. "The Berbers sometimes wear them."

"Do you find it unappealing? Some people do."

She laughed, her eyes dancing. "Some *women* do, you mean to say."

He managed to smile. "It's been mentioned, yes."

"Very few, I daresay, given what the rest of you looks like," she murmured appreciatively. "May I see it again?"

"Why?"

She shrugged one shoulder against the sheets. "It just looks familiar."

Reluctantly, he sat up again. The mark was customarily placed high on the left hip, though Ruthveyn had often seen it elsewhere. His father's, in fact, had been on his shoulder.

"What is it?" Grace asked, her fingertip cool against his skin. "I've seen it before—on the pediment of the Society's front door, yes—but somewhere else, too."

He crooked his head to look back at her. "It's a common symbol," he said. "I've seen variants of it all over Europe—on doorways, in frescoes, incorporated into family crests—rather like the fleur de lis."

"Oh, not *that* common," she murmured, still tracing, "These letters at the bottom—FAC—and the quill crossed with a sword—it's all very odd. And above is a Latin cross inside some sort of cartouche."

"It's the Scottish thistle," he said. "My father's people hail from Scotland, so they use it. Now, may I crawl back under the covers with you? You look desperately warm and inviting."

She smiled and scooted to one side.

"Strangely, Teddy drew one of those on his arm," she said when he was just beginning to get comfortable again. "Have you any idea why?"

Again, he shrugged. "My father had one, so perhaps, when he lay ill, Teddy saw it? But as I say, they are not uncom—"

"Uncommon, yes, you did say that," she interjected. "Now yours—as you say, it is a tattoo. But the one on Rance Welham's derriere is more of a scar, is it not? Like . . . Like a brand?"

He turned to look at her incredulously.

She threw up a hand as if to forestall him. "Do not even *think* of changing the subject by accusing me of anything to do with Rance's arse," she said. "I have not seen it. I do not wish to see it. Though I do have it on quite good authority that it is magnificent."

"Have you indeed?" he growled.

"Indeed," she said. "A young lieutenant's wife once explained it to me in great detail over a bit too much champagne. She had somehow got—one hates to speculate how—a rather good peek at it."

Ruthveyn could only stare. All rational thought had flown from his mind—a circumstance further compounded by the fact that his sheets had slipped down to reveal one of Grace's rosy nipples, which was hardening in the chill of the room.

Grace let her hand fall back against the pillow. "But I have actually *seen* that mark somewhere," she said more to herself than to him. "I just cannot put a time or place to it. Do you mean to tell me what it really is? And why you have it?"

Ruthveyn lay quietly beside her for a moment, wondering what he ought to say. But the truth was, none of it was precisely a secret. If one dug through the ancient texts long enough—as several of the Society's researchers were in the process of doing—one would eventually find parts of it. And put together, the whole of it was so incredible, no one would believe it anyway.

He sighed into the stillness of the room. "It is called the mark of the Guardian," he finally said. "It's just an old symbol that's been around in the north for centuries—like a Celtic cross. In some of the noble houses of Scotland—the older ones—it's passed down sometimes in families. A strange tradition. That's all."

"Ah," she said quietly. "So Luc has one, too?"

He hesitated. "No," he finally said.

"I see." She crooked her head to look up at him. "So why do they call it the mark of the Guardian?"

He managed to laugh. "It's all to do with an old legend," he answered. "And it has a little to do with the St. James Society, and how we came together."

Grace smiled. "Is this going to sound a bit like the Hellfire Club?" she mused. "Rich, dissolute gentlemen playing with secret rites and ceremonies? Perhaps even debauching virgins?—oh, wait—that was tonight."

Incredulous, Ruthveyn turned to see Grace barely restraining her laughter. For a man so somber, it was a bit much. Abruptly, he rolled half atop her just as she burst into peals of laughter.

"Witch!" he said, just before he kissed her. "*Be quiet!*"

But the playfulness swiftly ratcheted up to something far more serious. Ruthveyn dragged himself fully over her, flattening her round, high breasts against the width of his chest and thrusting his tongue deep. Slowly and sinuously, he plumbed the sweet recesses of her mouth, until she was sighing beneath him. Until his cock began to twitch demandingly, and his brain began to toy with the notion of having her again.

But that would not be wise. Slowly, he drew away, gazing down at Grace's soft, exquisite face and wondering what the future held for them. The irony of it struck him hard. Had he not just decided that knowing their future was his greatest fear?

He had assumed instead they would not have one. But

already they were like playful lovers together. Already they behaved together as if . . . well, as if there *was* a together. It came to them naturally. Spontaneously. Like the passion that had sprung to life so quickly between them.

Beneath him she sighed affectedly and began to twine one strand of hair around her finger. "I suppose you mean never to tell me?"

His mind blanked. "About what?"

"About the Guardians," she said on another sigh.

"It's just an old legend," he said again. "No one believes it anymore."

Grace watched him as he shoved up his pillow and shifted higher in bed. She scooted up, too, and laid her head on his shoulder. "Just tell me," she said. "I shall keep it a secret."

"As you wish," he answered, "though I can't think why you'd want to hear it." He hesitated, but when she said nothing, he dropped his voice and carried on. "So, the story has to do with old rumors about a people who were descended from the ancient Celtic priests—"

"You mean the Druids?"

"Actually, there were three kinds of Celtic priests," he answered softly. "The Druids, yes. They were the philosophers. But also the Bards, who were the poets, and the Vateis—as they are sometimes called—who were the prophets. Or so they say."

"And I'm guessing the people in your legend were not the philosophers or poets, but the prophets?" Grace murmured. "They had the gift of second sight?"

"Something like that," Adrian answered. "The Celtic priests came to England after Gaul was overrun by the Romans, then fled farther north as the legions invaded here. Eventually, the race was Christianized and absorbed, but it was believed the Gift still carried in the blood of some for centuries, especially in the north."

"Well, much of what you say is more truth than legend," Grace commented.

"Yes, some," Adrian hedged. "In any case, the legend says that the Gift began to die out, and by the Middle Ages, the Vateis—the prophets—were all but unknown. Those who were born were often persecuted. In Spain, they were caught up in the Inquisition. In other places, they were burnt, like Joan of Arc. Later, in America, some were drowned as witches. Women with the Gift were always especially vulnerable."

"Ever the same story, *n'est-ce pas?*" Grace mused. "Women with great abilities are soon made small—one way or another. But go on, do."

Adrian slipped down a little lower in the bed and hitched her closer. "So the legend goes on to say that despite the persecution and the rarity of the Gift, eventually a Scottish noblewoman conceived a special child through some rare confluence of blood," he went on. "A sibylla, the child was called, a great prophetess descended from those Celtic priests driven northward. She was not, however, the lady's husband's child, but that of her lover, an emissary of the French king."

"Oh, dear," said Grace. "We know where this is going."

"Indeed," Adrian murmured. "When her adultery was discovered, her husband killed the Frenchman. Eventually, however, the child was born hale, and in time became known simply as the Gift, or Sibylla, for she possessed powers of divination such as no one had seen before or since. But her mother, sadly, faded slowly away and eventually died of a broken heart."

"Oh, dear," Grace repeated. "The child was orphaned?"

Adrian nodded. "The mother's brother, a powerful Jesuit priest, took the child, and at the behest of the Church, undertook to escort the Gift to France, to be presented to the Archbishop of Paris. He took with him a cadre of his kinsmen—knights, monks, and noblemen— and he called them simply the Guardians, and supposedly he marked them one and all, so that they might remember their solemn duty and be known to one another ever after.

"But in France, all did not go well. The child was snatched away by a madman. A friar, who believed her the devil incarnate. Or perhaps he meant to use her for nefarious purposes. In any case, the Guardians followed him across the Seine onto the Île Saint-Louis. Trapped, he first made as if to return the child, then attempted to set himself afire, still clutching the child."

"Oh!" Grace jumped. "Was she killed?"

"No." Adrian shook his head, his black hair scrubbing the pillow. "Her uncle managed to snatch her from the flames, and in great haste the Guardians rode for the bridge—the Pont Marie—the only way back to Paris. But just as the riders started across it, a bolt of lightning shattered the sky. Amidst the thunder, the bridge collapsed into turbulent water, sending most of the Guardians to their deaths. The collapse was said by some to be a sign of God's wrath."

"A bridge collapse?" said Grace sharply. "You are quite sure?"

"Yes, but amidst it all, the uncle escaped with the child and hastened back to Scotland. Now wary of the world, he supposedly hid the girl away in the Highlands, where she lived a somewhat normal life. Eventually, she took a husband, and bore twelve children, all of whom carried the Gift strong in their blood. Guardians were appointed to the small children, and to the women."

"And to the men?"

"Once grown, a man was expected to guard himself— his honor, his powers—and often, if born at a particular time, to guard anyone who shared them."

"A double burden, then?"

His gaze focused somewhere in the depths of the room, he smiled faintly. "Perhaps."

"And so you . . . you are given these marks at birth?"

"No, as young men," he said. "But the history of the thing—it is lost now. Save for the old legend I just told you, no one really remembers much."

"Are you and Rance related?"

"Most likely." He lifted one shoulder. "He had the mark. I had the mark."

"How did you see his?"

Adrian turned to her with a twisted smile. "Like Anisha, my dear, you just won't quit," he remarked. "It was in a brothel of sorts—an opium-induced orgy, writhing with men and women and a few things in between. Yes, I *have* seen Lazonby in the altogether. May we not discuss it again?"

Grace felt her face flame, but forged on, burning with curiosity now. "And so the mark is burnt or tattooed onto your flesh," she said, "carved into your pediments, and engraved onto your tea services and your cravat pins. Does no one notice?"

Again, he lifted one shoulder. "The same symbol is etched upon lintels and coats of arms and tapestries all over France and Scotland, and a few places farther afield," he said. "What does that mean? We do not know. We know only that we were marked as young men and told some version of the story I just told you. We were told to hail any man so marked as a brother and to guard his back as we would our own."

"And . . . do you all possess the Gift?"

Again, the faint smile twisted. "My dear, did I not just tell you? The Gift is but a legend."

She gave a slow, sly grin and stretched like Satin after her nap. "I see we have reached an impasse," she replied. "Very well, Adrian, keep your secrets if you do not trust me."

He sat up at once, carrying her with him. "Grace, it's not that."

"All right. It's not that. But if it was, I would respect it." She set one hand to the muscled wall of his chest and kissed him on the mouth. "Let us talk of something else."

"Such as?"

She kissed him again, slowly and more intently. "Let us talk," she murmured, lifting her lips but a fraction, "of us."

"Of . . . us?"

"I want to know, Adrian, if you will be my lover," she whispered against one corner of his mouth. "Until things here are settled for me—with Napier, I mean—and I can go back to Paris. Will you do that? If we are very careful—very discreet—will you do that?"

"Grace, that would be most unwise," he said. "There are . . . risks."

"Which you can mitigate," she said, kissing him again. "As you did tonight."

He looked at her warily. "Grace, is this about feeling that you owe me something?"

"I owe you a great deal," she acknowledged. "But this is about your being a skilled and wonderful lover. You . . . enchant me somehow with your touch. And, frankly, I rather doubt, once I'm gone from England, I will ever meet anyone like you again. I would like to go with no regrets."

Ruthveyn listened carefully to the words she spoke,

words as honest as a newly stropped blade, and laced with no subtle entreaties or twists of the heartstrings. Grace, he was beginning to understand, was that rarest of women, one whose honestly left him breathless.

He caught her to him then and kissed her fiercely. "No regrets, then," he whispered. "Not a one."

Then he turned her on her back, his heart suddenly breaking, and made love to her once again, this time with his mouth and with his hands, and with the whole of his heart. And in the doing of it, he did not once think about that portal to hell, or about *coulds* or *mights* or even *shoulds*.

And when he was finished—when Grace had cried out softly beneath him and drifted back to sleep, still shuddering—he got up from the bed and went into his study to do what he should have done eons ago. He carried his wooden box into his bathroom, dumped the contents down his fancy porcelain privy, reached up, and yanked the chain.

Perhaps he had not yet answered Grace's question. But he had assuredly answered one of his own.

CHAPTER 11

The Guessing Game

*A*nd this is it?" Lord Lazonby refolded the piece of foolscap and tapped its edge impatiently on the club's breakfast table. "Besides the note under her door, this is the sole evidence Napier has against Grace?"

"It's not the original, of course." Ruthveyn reached for the teapot and found it empty. "But I had Claytor copy it down word for word."

Lazonby gave a low whistle. "I'll bet that galled old Roughshod Roy no end, having your man come round demanding to see Crown evidence." He grinned ear to ear. "I wish to the devil I could have seen him."

"You will stay out of his way," said Ruthveyn grimly. "It will go far worse for Grace if you do not."

"Precisely what I told her in your conservatory some days ago," Lazonby agreed, his expression turning pensive. "What we need, perhaps, is someone more intuitive. Someone like Bessett, who might elicit an emotion from this document."

"That might work," Ruthveyn pointed out, "if that were the killer's original hand."

"Aye, and if Bessett hadn't just left for the harvest in Yorkshire," Lazonby muttered. "Even then, it's a long shot. Which reminds me—where have you been all week, old chap? You're looking remarkably well rested. I believe London is beginning to agree with you."

"Let us stick to the topic at hand," Ruthveyn suggested, snapping his fingers at one of the club's footmen. Without asking, the servant hastened away for more tea.

"And I haven't seen you up at seven in the morning since . . . well, never in my life," Lazonby went on. "Unless, that is to say, you had not yet gone to bed."

But Ruthveyn had opened the letter and was rereading it again. "May we worry about Grace instead of my lack of a social life?" he murmured. "It has been recently brought home to me that I have two children under my roof now—and you have taken my suite of rooms upstairs."

"Actually, the padre took yours," Lazonby clarified. "By the way, have you seen the prize that chap brought Sutherland? The most amazing illuminated manuscript! He found it in some abbey ruins on the Isle of Man, where the Druid priestesses were last believed to reside. It takes some of Strabo's writings in *Geographica,* and expounds—"

Ruthveyn held up one hand. "Since when do you give a damn about ancient texts?" he said. "If he'd brought us the Holy Grail, it wouldn't excuse your giving up my suite."

Lazonby grinned. "Actually, I should have thought you'd be thanking me for that by now."

Ruthveyn exhaled slowly. He did not know whether to thank Lazonby or curse him, for the hell he'd been living in after having made love to Grace was worse than the hell he'd been living in when he'd merely lusted after her. At least he was sleeping again.

But he had not touched her since, nor exchanged anything beyond the most mundane of dinner conversation. Instead, he had drifted through his own home like a wraith, barely inhabiting it, never settling long, watching her surreptitiously every chance he got. He felt eaten up inside with a restlessness and a yearning that went beyond the sexual and into something far more deep and disconcerting.

Lazonby apparently realized he'd pushed too far. "As to Grace's predicament," he went on, "what can I do to help?"

Ruthveyn exchanged a poignant glance with his friend. They had few secrets, he and Lazonby, and there were some things they did not even need to speak aloud.

"Find Pinkie Ringgold for me," he said grimly. "Belkadi asked him three days ago to run down all the local forgers capable of faking Holding's hand, but we haven't heard back, and he's vanished from Quartermaine's."

"Oh, I'll run him to ground." Lazonby smiled predatorily. "I'm always at my best with thugs and criminals. What did the original hand look like, anyway?"

"Ordinary schoolboy copperplate." Ruthveyn's shoulders fell. "The truth is, Rance, anyone could have written the bloody thing—but there again, Josiah Crane springs most readily to mind. He saw Holding's penmanship on a daily basis and had an office full of samples."

"But why would he kill Holding? He didn't inherit."

"Not unless," said Ruthveyn quietly, "he persuades Fenella Crane to marry him. Then he will own the entire company."

Again, Lazonby whistled. "Good Lord! And if we accept that letter as a forgery, then we accept that there was great premeditation."

"What do you mean, *if*?" asked Ruthveyn darkly.

"Jesus, Adrian, I know it's forged! You needn't worry about my loyalty—to you or to Grace." Lazonby tapped his finger pensively on the tabletop. "Any chance Napier will try to arrest her?"

"He doesn't dare. He knows she is under my protection." Ruthveyn pinched the top of his nose between his fingers, warding off a headache. "But just in case, I sent St. Giles round to call upon a couple of magistrates we know, to make sure no warrant is issued. And I can go far higher if I must. Also, Belkadi managed to compromise one of Holding's footmen in an attempt to ferret out any secrets Holding's staff might be keeping, so—"

"And you thought Belkadi was more trouble than he was worth," Lazonby cut in.

"He continues to prove resourceful," Ruthveyn admitted, just as a fresh pot of tea was set down. "And now, old chap, I need you to follow Pinkie's good example and take yourself off."

"Was it something I said?" Lazonby pushed back his chair.

"No, I am having some special guests to breakfast in a quarter hour," said Ruthveyn. "Napier and Ned Quartermaine."

"Napier and Quartermaine?" Lazonby echoed. "Have you quite lost your mind?"

"Yes, they will both be surprised, I daresay." Ruthveyn

calmly poured a fresh cup of tea. "But I think it's time the two got to know one another, don't you?"

Lazonby shrugged and strolled from the dining room.

Ruthveyn snapped his copy of the *Chronicle* back open and laid it flat upon the table. The cause of his nascent headache—the morning headline—still stared back up at him, taunting and ominous: *No Arrest in Belgrave Square Murder.*

The article painted an ugly picture of Belgravia's rich up in arms and the Metropolitan Police as dawdling and disinterested. It was not the sort of criticism that Sir George Grey, the Home Secretary, would long be able to tolerate politically. More articles like this, and there would be demands for an arrest from the highest levels in the land. And Ruthveyn could not but wonder if he had Jack Coldwater to thank for yet another piece of journalistic butchery.

On that thought, he got up and tossed the paper in the rubbish bin, then rammed it home with his foot.

Her coffee nearly finished, Grace was alone in the dining room when Lord Lucan Forsythe came in, attired in a dashing striped waistcoat, his mop of gold curls perfectly styled—just the sort of curls, thought Grace sourly, that enterprising young misses dreamt of running their hands through.

His gait hitched on the threshold. "Mademoiselle Gauthier!" he said, as if she did not, in fact, breakfast every day at seven. "Good morning. Am I to have the pleasure of your company over my coffee and kedgeree?"

"So it seems, Lord Lucan." Grace looked at him over her cup and inwardly sighed. She was feeling sorry for herself and really not in the mood for company. "You are up bright and early," she managed to say. "You are preparing, I daresay, for this morning's nature walk?"

"Yes, yes, the nature walk!"

Lord Lucan flashed a tight smile, then went at once to the sideboard and began to fill a plate. Grace watched a little grudgingly from her chair. The young man looked as much like an angel as his elder brother resembled Satan incarnate, and yet she had the most overwhelming suspicion that Lord Lucan was the one who was up to no good. Then, feeling slightly ashamed, she relented.

So he was up at an early hour. What of it? He had been kind to her—and nothing more than lightly flirtatious, particularly since the fork wounds on the back of his hand had healed. He was also quite good with the boys and spent a great deal of time with them—though Grace had recently discovered the reason for the latter. He was in debt to his sister.

He turned from the sideboard and set down his plate with a heavy thunk. "Mademoiselle, may I warm your coffee?"

"Coffee?" Grace lifted her gaze from his towering heap of food. "Oh. *Merci.*"

"Sugar?" he asked, tipping the pot.

"Just black, thank you."

"May I refill your plate?"

"No, but you're very kind."

He smiled again, but it looked a little strained round the edges. Grace was certain of it now. He was up to something. Her intuition in such matters was unfailing.

Lord Lucan sat down and fluffed out his napkin. "Have you any special plans for the day?" he politely inquired.

Grace lifted her eyebrows. "Beyond being a governess?" she said lightly. "No, as usual, that will take up the bulk of my day."

"Oh, dear." He made a sympathetic face. "It does sound onerous when you put it that way."

"Then I would advise you, Lord Lucan, never to put yourself in such straits that gainful employment becomes a necessity," she remarked. "It cuts into one's social life something frightful."

He laughed as if she were the cleverest creature in the universe. "My brother will thank you for that advice, mademoiselle," he said. "And I was wondering, too, about that nature walk?"

"*Oui?*" Grace felt her smile fade.

"I was wondering," he said slowly, "if I might prevail upon you to take the boys instead? You see, my chum Frankie—Francis Fitzwater—is in rather a bad way, and a friend asked if I might call upon him, just to see—"

"*Frankie Fitzwater,*" said an acerbic voice from the doorway, "is a charming, out-and-out rotter. A blighter. A bounder. Even, occasionally, a cad. And if he's in a bad way, it's something to do with a horse. Or a horse race. Or a game of cards. If not something worse."

Grace looked up to see Lady Anisha standing in the door, her arms crossed over her chest.

"Good morning, Nish." The young man leapt up to draw out her chair. "You are looking lovely this morning."

"Balderdash, Luc." Anisha strolled into the room. "And Friday, by the way, is Michaelmas. So if you wish to escape indentured servitude, you may repay your loan in cash rather than blood once you get your allowance. Until then, if you want out of your two hours with the boys, it is I to whom you should be speaking, not Grace."

Luc hung his head. "Very well," he said. "I'll take the lads. I gave you my word as a gentleman, and I shall honor it."

"*Good,*" said his sister.

"But Frankie really has been brought low, Nish, I swear it." Lord Lucan's eyes took on the cast of a starving Bassett hound. "His mistress threw him off, and he's been on a three-day binge. Drunk as a lord from Friday until Monday, and now Morrison says they can't get 'im out of bed. I thought . . . well, I thought if I asked him to take me down to Tattersall's this morning to buy those matched grays, it might perk us both up?"

Anisha said no more but merely poured her coffee, filled her plate, and sat down at one end of the table. She took one bite of her kedgeree, then stabbed her fork into it on a curse. "Dash it, Luc, don't look at me like that! Do you think me the veriest idiot?"

"No, of course not." Luc hung his head again. "I think you are kind. And compassionate. Like . . . why, like Mademoiselle Gauthier."

Anisha flung down her fork. "Oh, the devil!" she said under her breath. "Go on, then. But the next time I hear Frankie Fitzwater's name, it had better be because his obituary is in the newspaper!"

His pile of food forgotten, Lord Lucan leapt up, kissed his sister soundly, and fled.

Anisha propped her elbow on the table and let her head fall into her hand. "God, I'm such an fool."

Grace cleared her throat. "I knew he was up to something the minute he came into the room," she remarked. "I shall be happy to take the boys. It is my job, and the lesson plan was mine, after all."

Anisha rose and went to one of the deep windows that looked out over the rear gardens. "The truth is," she said, pulling back the underdrapes with one finger, "this fog is not going to clear for another hour. There is no rush."

"As you wish," said Grace. But she had the oddest notion that Lady Anisha was up to something, too. She pushed back her chair as if to go.

"Oh, do not leave just yet," said Lady Anisha. "Here, have more coffee."

Grace relented and wondered vaguely if one could drown in coffee. Lady Anisha had been giving her odd, sidelong looks for the last three days, though there was nothing she could possibly know. But it wasn't *nothing* that now danced in Anisha's eyes. It was burning speculation.

But two could play at Anisha's game.

Anisha set the pot back down. "Isn't it odd," she said musingly, "how much time Adrian is spending at home? And how frightfully restless he is? What do you think is going on?"

Grace hesitated before she answered. She wished she did know what was going on. Ruthveyn had been walking wide circles around her all week, and yet so often she could feel the heat of his eyes upon her. And at night, she could still feel the heat of his hands and his mouth as they roamed restlessly over her—even the weight of his body bearing down into the softness of his mattress—but these were only memories. Vivid, yes, and kept perilously close to her heart, but Ruthveyn had not invited her to his bed again, and Grace was wretchedly certain that he never would. Absent the haze of euphoria, perhaps she did not seem worth the risk.

"I'm sure I couldn't speculate about Lord Ruthveyn," said Grace, "but speaking of odd behavior, I have been meaning to mention something a little peculiar that Teddy did. When he was ill Sunday night, I noticed he had drawn something strange on his arm."

"Did he?" Anisha had resumed eating her breakfast. "Well, most everything Teddy does is strange. What did he draw? Not parts of the female anatomy, I hope? Because he and I already discussed that."

Grace had to laugh; it sounded just like Teddy to do such a thing. "No, it was that strange symbol on Lord Ruthveyn's cravat pin," she said. "The one with the gold cross? When I asked Teddy about it, he said his grandfather had such a mark."

For an instant, Lady Anisha blanched. Then, "Oh, that!" she said, making a dismissive gesture with her fork. "It is just a family tradition. A tattoo. Ignore it."

"A family tradition," Grace echoed.

"Why?" Anisha cut a strange glance at her. "You have not, by chance, seen one elsewhere, have you? I mean, if you *have*, perhaps we might discuss it. As the mature, adult ladies we are."

"I just thought it looked vaguely familiar," she said quietly. "Do your brothers have them?"

Lady Anisha appraised her carefully across the dining-room table. "Why, I am not perfectly sure," she finally said. "It is a matter of personal choice, I suppose. What do you think? If you were to hazard a guess, I mean?"

"If I were to hazard a guess," said Grace slowly, "I would say that Ruthveyn does and that Lord Lucan does not."

"Hmm," said Anisha. "Interesting."

"And if you wish to know," Grace went on, "whether or not your brother is bedding the help, you should probably just ask him."

At that, Lady Anisha gasped so hard she inhaled a little coffee and was compelled to hack violently into her napkin. "My, but that is plain speaking, Grace!" she said when she had recovered herself. "But to be honest, I already asked. And as usual, he'll tell me nothing."

"Well," said Grace calmly, "your brother is not a fool. I daresay he can tell the difference between a female who wishes merely to sink her claws into him as opposed to one who simply appreciates him for what he is and hopes to move on with her life. At least, that would be my guess."

"*If* you were to hazard a guess," Anisha added. "You must be quite a good guesser, Grace."

"Yes, and a good cardplayer, too," she said. "Unless I make the mistake of playing with Rance Welham—excuse me, Lord Lazonby—which I stopped doing years ago."

A sly smile curved Anisha's mouth. "No, and you must on no account play charades with that rogue," she added. "He is so good, everyone thinks he cheats. In fact, that's more or less how he got convicted of murder, I believe."

"I'm sorry," said Grace. "I do not follow."

"I believe he was so good, someone decided he *was* a cheat," said Anisha. "But since they couldn't catch him at it, they decided to simply cheat back."

"You mean Lord Percy Peveril?" said Grace.

Anisha lifted one of her narrow shoulders and took up her coffee cup. "From all accounts, he was an idiot," she said pensively. "No, it was someone else. Or that would be my guess, were I to hazard one."

"We are doing a lot of guessing today," remarked Grace. "What do you think—does Lord Lazonby have one of those marks? And if so, where?"

Anisha lifted her eyebrows at that. "Why, I suspect he does," she went on. "As to where, I could not say."

Grace hesitated a moment. "I could," she said.

Then she got up, shut the door, and told the story of the lieutenant's wife.

"I was all of twenty-one, mind, and brought up in the army, which is not the most genteel of environments," she added when Anisha's eyes nearly popped from her head. "But the lady's description was most marvelously detailed, and even then, it jogged my memory."

"Yes?" Anisha was all ears now. "About what?"

"About that symbol," Grace said. "When she described it, I was quite certain I had seen it somewhere."

"But that's not very likely, is it? In North Africa?"

"Well, that depends, I think," said Grace, "on precisely what it means."

Lady Anisha pushed back her chair and stood. "And *I* think that I had best go get ready for our nature walk," she said. "We may have *lots* to talk about—regarding nature, I mean."

But at the last instant, Grace caught her arm. "Teddy told me something else, too," she said quietly. "He told me that the servants believe Lord Ruthveyn can look into a person's eyes and tell him the time of his death."

All the color drained from Anisha's face, and a stillness fell across the room. "Good Lord," she finally whispered. "We have not been here above six months. They are quick with their black tales, are they not?"

"Servants will talk," said Grace consolingly, "but Teddy seemed more amused than anything else. As to me, I do not mean to make trouble for anyone. Certainly I shan't spread gossip—well, save for the tale about Rance's arse."

"That *was* a good one," Anisha admitted, grinning.

"Too good, really, not to share." Grace grinned back. "But as to your brother, Anisha, please know that I mean him no harm. Indeed, I owe him more than I can ever repay. But I do worry about him. And if ever there was . . . anything that I might do—or *not* do—that you think would benefit him, I hope you will let me know? And then I could . . . well, not do those things."

"Or not," said Lady Anisha. "Not *not* do them, I mean. Because my brother knows his own mind, Grace."

"Lovely." Grace smiled, and drew open the door. "It seems we have struck a gentleman's agreement, then."

* * *

"Is this your idea of a joke, Ruthveyn?" Royden Napier flung a piece of paper onto the breakfast table.

"Not in the least," said Ruthveyn, waving at an empty chair as he sat back down. "This is my idea of breakfast. Try the kippers. They are very good indeed."

Across the table, Ned Quartermaine merely stretched out his legs and steepled his long, thin fingers.

"Your gall knows no bounds, does it?" Napier snatched up the paper again. "You have dragged me down here on the pretext of—here, let me see—*breaking developments in the Holding case?*" He motioned at Quartermaine. "What 'breaking developments'? As if you are not thought trouble enough down at Number Four already! Have you any notion what Sir George would say to my hobnobbing with a bookmaker and a turfite?"

"The mind boggles, does it not?" said Quartermaine quietly. "Perhaps next time he's by my club, I shall ask him."

Napier went rigid, his lips whitening.

"Oh, sit down, for God's sake," said Ruthveyn, waving an expansive hand. "We Scots must simply accept, Napier, that half of London is in hock to men like my esteemed associate here."

"I'm a man of business, Napier," said Quartermaine, "but I haven't all day, what with all the gentry waiting to be fleeced and Her Majesty's laws to subvert. Now, Lord Ruthveyn has somehow persuaded me it would be in my best interest to share some information with you. You may have five minutes of my inordinately valuable time. Do you wish to hear what I have to say? Or shall I hand my information to Sir George myself? And yes, I do occasionally see him." With that, he extracted yet another fold of paper and laid it on the table.

Napier jerked out a chair and sat down. "I apologize," he said stiffly. "But Ruthveyn here seems to think the laws of the land are his to subvert as well."

Ruthveyn merely raised his hand, and a warm plate was brought and set down before them. "Do have one," he suggested. "It will improve your mood."

Napier simply glowered, but Quartermaine leaned over the plate with interest. "What the devil are they?"

"*Makrouts,*" said Ruthveyn. "A sort of a fried biscuit stuffed with fruit and dipped in honey. Belkadi had the chef specifically trained to make it—amongst other delicacies."

"Don't mind if I do," said Quartermaine, whose taste for fine dining was no secret.

But they reached across the table at once, their hands brushing. Ruthveyn's eyes caught Quartermaine's just an instant. He felt a blade of light cut close to his temple, then the flash of an image; a passing vignette, like something glimpsed from a carriage window.

He jerked back his hand. "Please, after you."

Quartermaine took one, turned it this way and that, then bit in, chewing with relish. "Oh, bloody good," he said, his eyes widening.

"Magnificent, is it not?" said Ruthveyn quietly. "Which reminds me, Quartermaine—do you know what the Berbers do to a man who tries to steal from them?"

"Haven't a clue," said Quartermaine, biting into the pastry again.

"They chop off his hand. The one he eats with, generally."

Quartermaine seemed to choke on the pastry.

"Are you right-handed, Quartermaine?" Ruthveyn murmured. "Ah, yes, I feared as much. I advise you to rethink your strategy."

Quartermaine got the food down at last. "And what is it, precisely, you think I'm scheming to steal?" he demanded.

"Belkadi's chef," said Ruthveyn. "He will take it very ill. I suggest you stop meeting with the man and put an advertisement in the *Times*."

For a moment, Quartermaine looked vaguely apoplectic. He set down the rest of his pastry and shoved the note at Royden Napier. "I'm wanted across the street," he said. "This is what you need. Send word if you have questions."

Napier opened it and let his eyes run down its length. "Lists? Of what?"

"Josiah Crane's unsecured gaming debts," snapped Quartermaine. "With the name of the establishment or individual, the date of indebtedness, and whether or not they have been repaid. You will see, alas for Mr. Crane, that the vast majority are outstanding."

"*Christ Jesus,*" whispered Napier under his breath.

Quartermaine pushed away what was left of his pastry. "And *you,*" he said, turning a dark look on Ruthveyn, "you will remember, I hope, our little understanding? You are never, ever permitted at my tables."

Ruthveyn merely smiled. "About that hand-chopping business, old chap," he murmured. "Now that I think on it, I maybe have confused the Berbers with the Arabs. The Berbers, I believe, go straight for the throat."

Quartermaine sneered, proposed to Ruthveyn a rather vulgar—and anatomically impossible suggestion—then stalked from the dining room. But his color had faded just a trifle. Quartermaine was far from a coward, but only a fool backstabbed Belkadi. It would have made, Ruthveyn thought, for an interesting fight.

He shrugged and picked up the last bite of Quartermaine's *makrout.* "Now a good Scot, Napier, would not let this go to waste, would he?" he said, then popped it in his mouth.

But Napier was still staring at the list of debts. "How long have you known about this?" he asked, his voice a little hollow.

"The specifics?" said Ruthveyn, chewing round the pastry. "About three minutes." He swallowed the last and stood. "And now I think it's time for a little jaunt across the river."

Napier rose and followed. "What?" he said vaguely. "To where?"

"Rotherhithe," said Ruthveyn, heading for the stairs. "To the Surrey Commercial Docks. I should very much like to make a closer acquaintance of Josiah Crane."

Napier caught his arm on the landing. "Damn it, Ruthveyn! You are interfering in a police investigation again. I won't have it."

Ruthveyn bit back his temper. "With all respect, Napier, you would not have an investigation—not this part of it, at any rate—were it not for me. A man like Quartermaine wouldn't talk to the police if he were hanging by his nails from Blackfriars Bridge, and you were the last chap walking past."

"Damn you, that is not—"

"Now, I'm going down to Rotherhithe," said Ruthveyn, speaking over him. "I am a private citizen, and I have every right. You cannot stop me. I would advise you do not try. I suggest, in fact, you come along."

Napier's jaw hardened. "You will do anything, won't you?" he gritted. "Anything to protect and deflect attention from that woman."

"Yes," said Ruthveyn tightly. "Anything. Are you coming? Or not?"

"Is that an order, my lord?" Napier snapped. "If it is,

simply say so. I do not need another visit from Sir Greville Steele to tell me how to do my job—particularly when I'm already standing in the middle of the magistrate's court with my papers in order."

"Took it that far, did you?" Ruthveyn fought down his sudden shaft of fear. "In any case, you waste your time, Napier. Mademoiselle Gauthier is innocent."

"If you think that, Ruthveyn, then you are being a fool for a woman," he said. "Never would I have believed it of you. I've always heard you were heartless."

"I've heard that, too." Ruthveyn smiled thinly. "Now, shall we go by river? Or my carriage? You will find it far better sprung than a hansom, if I do say so myself."

Napier snatched his coat from the waiting footman. "I daresay I'd better go," he snapped. "Lest you bollix this up beyond saving."

Ruthveyn motioned Napier toward the door. "After you."

They went out into the peculiar London air—a dense, yellow-white fog that reeked of burned coal, horse manure, and the effluent of the nearby river. He would never, Ruthveyn thought, grow used to this oppressive haze, which could all but burn the hair from a man's nose. And yet it was a part of London's inscrutability, the veil that cloaked a thousand sins, and gave up her secrets but reluctantly. How ironic that they were going to call upon Josiah Crane to lift the veil on a few of his.

"The river, I think, would be most unwise," he remarked, peering across the street in a futile attempt to see Quartermaine's front door.

Napier grunted his agreement, and Ruthveyn waved for his carriage. They waited patiently on the curb, the silence between them deepening even as they climbed into the conveyance.

"I just want to know one thing," said Napier, as they swung round the corner into St. James's Street.

Ruthveyn lifted both eyebrows.

"How did you know?" Napier turned to glower out the window. "How did you know Quartermaine was trying to steal Belkadi's chef?"

But Ruthveyn merely settled back against the banquette and said no more.

In the Surrey Commercial Docks, maritime London surged and shouted with life, from the deal porters who darted from the fog with their towering shoulder-loads of lumber, to the lightermen plying back and forth from ship to shore. Brogden deftly edged Ruthveyn's carriage along busy Rotherhithe Street, squeezing past a dray laden with sacks of grain and a pile of staves that had spilled out into the cobbles.

According to Grace, the offices of Crane and Holding were located at Thirty-five Swan Lane, just above Albion Yard and the main dock, but in the wretched brume, Brogden very nearly drove past, then turned at the last instant, tossing Napier against the side of the carriage. He cursed beneath his breath, then shot Ruthveyn another black look as if holding him personally responsible.

So far as Ruthveyn could make out in the fog, the offices looked like every other establishment in this part of London, which was to say weathered and practical in construction.

Inside the small antechamber, several callers waited, one carrying a roll of drawings under his arm, the other two in warm work clothes—yard foremen, Ruthveyn guessed.

Beyond a narrow counter, a pimpled young man sat at a tall desk, ticking off what looked like receipts in a green baize ledger. Ruthveyn stepped up and cleared his throat, but he was soon to learn his journey was in vain.

"M-May I h-help you?" The lad slid off his perch, his face reddening.

Ruthveyn smiled and extended his thick ivory calling card across the counter. "I should like to speak with Josiah Crane," he said. "This is my associate, Mr. Napier."

To Ruthveyn's exasperation, however, the lad would not lift his gaze nor even take the card from Ruthveyn's hand. "V-Very s-sorry, milord, but Mr. Crane is out, and n-not expected back today."

The little speech had the ring of recitation about it, and Ruthveyn wondered vaguely if the lad was compelled to give it often. Just then, a door behind the counter opened, and a lady in black swished her skirts through sideways. She carried a basket over one arm and a light cloak tossed over her shoulders.

"I believe I shall take the ledger up, Jim," she asked before turning, "and the post."

It was Fenella Crane, dressed for the out of doors in a light cloak and her usual black veil.

"Good morning, Miss Crane," said Ruthveyn.

Her head turned toward the counter. "I beg your pardon. I did not see you there. Lord Ruthveyn, is it?"

Ruthveyn tucked his hat beneath his arm and bowed. "It is indeed. How lovely to see you again." He stepped to one side. "Have you met my acquaintance, Mr. Napier?"

"Who? Oh, yes. How do you do, sir?" She seemed to wither a little, and Ruthveyn felt instantly like a cad. Of course she'd met Napier—on the night of her brother's death and probably many times since.

The shy lad with the stutter closed the ledger and handed it off as she passed. Her color, Ruthveyn noted, was high, and she looked vaguely unwell. It was the strain, no doubt.

"Is there a place we might speak privately, Miss Crane?" Ruthveyn asked quietly, when she approached.

"Why, certainly." She tucked the ledger under one arm and shot a little bolt under the counter. "Just lift that, if you please, and do come through."

They followed her into what looked like a small, unused office, the few furnishings layered with dust and the shades drawn.

Ruthveyn opened himself to the emotion of the room, fleetingly closing his eyes, but he felt nothing save that thrumming urgency he'd felt before. There was not, thank God, any flash of dead rabbits or bloody snow. He wondered again if his vision had been an anomaly of some sort. *Was* Miss Crane in danger? And if so, from whom?

Miss Crane did not sit, nor offer them chairs, but her face turned to Napier's as soon as the door was shut. "Has something happened?" Her voice was low and breathless. "Has Ethan's killer been caught?"

Napier shook his head. "Not yet, but—"

"But we had hoped, actually, to speak to Mr. Crane about it," Ruthveyn interjected. "We had a question about the business finances. I collect he is out?"

As Napier glowered at him, Miss Crane turned to Ruthveyn. "Yes, he is ill," she said, turning to set her basket down on the desk. "My poor cousin suffers from— *eeekk!*"

On a shriek, she leapt away from the desk, just as something darted from beneath it and ran over Napier's shoe.

"What the devil?" Napier leapt back.

"Oh!" Miss Crane set a hand to her heart.

"Merely a rat, I believe," said Ruthveyn, kneeling down

to see where the creature had gone, but there was nothing.

"I shall never get used to that," said Miss Crane. "The hazards of working in the dockyards, I daresay." She dropped her hand from her chest and kicked a rectangular white tin under the desk. "Josiah tells Jim he *must* keep the poison put out, and have the rat catcher in once a month, but I wonder if he listens?"

"Perhaps a cat?" Ruthveyn suggested. "I find them indispensable, myself. In any case, you were saying?"

"Oh, yes, about Josiah," said Miss Crane. "He suffers terribly with a bilious liver, but really, he has not been himself since . . . well, since so much additional responsibility fell upon his shoulders. Perhaps you might call again in a day or two? I shall tell him to expect you."

Ruthveyn glanced at the basket. A glass jar of what looked like beef tea was nestled between a rolled newspaper and a great lump wrapped in cheesecloth—fresh bread, from the smell of it.

"You are going to visit him?" said Ruthveyn.

"He asked if I would," she said, "so I thought I might take up his post, and perhaps the monthly ledger, in case he felt up to . . . to whatever it is he does with it." Here, she made an airy gesture with her hand.

"Is that safe, ma'am?" asked Napier.

She turned to look at him. "I beg your pardon?"

Napier exchanged a wary glance with Ruthveyn. "Perhaps, until this is all settled . . ."

"Surely, sir, you do not suggest my cousin had anything to do with this dreadful business?"

"We have eliminated no one from suspicion," said Napier.

"What nonsense!" Miss Crane seemed to quiver with outrage. "My cousin doesn't have it in him, sir. Really, did you come all this way with such preposterous drivel?"

"We understand he disapproved of Ethan Holding driving a competitor out of business by underbidding contracts," Ruthveyn suggested. "Perhaps that was the cause of their quarrel on the night of Holding's death?"

"A *quarrel*?" said Miss Crane with asperity. "They had words, perhaps, but no more. What, precisely, are you two suggesting?"

Ruthveyn and Napier exchanged glances.

"Oh, wait, I see the way of things." Miss Crane's voice arched. "You have hired *that woman*, haven't you? I suppose she has turned your head, too. Really, I cannot think this is any of your business!" Then she wheeled on Napier. "And *you*—you are the one who suggested to Mrs. Lester and to me that she was the killer! My God, have you seen the article in today's *Chronicle*? Perhaps Ethan did a foolish thing, but you are doing *nothing*. At least our losses will be made up eventually."

But not, perhaps, before Crane suffers a personal bankruptcy, thought Ruthveyn.

"We understand Mr. Crane has some outstanding gambling debts," Napier snapped, apparently having given up all efforts at diplomacy. "That suggests, ma'am, a certain amount of financial desperation."

At that, she fell fleetingly silent. "Josiah has weaknesses," she finally agreed. "What man does not? But he will be fine now. I shall take care of him. Ethan never quite knew how to manage such things."

"The business could simply be sold," Napier suggested, "and Crane's creditors paid off."

Ruthveyn did not need an unobscured view of Miss Crane's face to feel her bristle. "Josiah would never agree to that!" she said. "Our grandfather died building this business. It is a family treasure."

But the truth was, Josiah Crane would have had little

say in the matter. Fenella Crane now owned the controlling interest. Was she so naïve, Ruthveyn wondered, that she did not realize that?

But the lady had picked up her basket and was sweeping toward the door. "Now, I bid you both good day," she said over one shoulder. "Kindly do not come back, Mr. Napier, until you can talk sense to me."

It was on the tip of Ruthveyn's tongue to insist they would take her up in his carriage and call upon Crane with her, but she would obviously have refused. They went back out into the sharp autumn air, both of them a little deflated.

As soon as the door was closed, Napier turned to him. "*Really,*" he said, cleverly mimicking Miss Crane's voice, "*I cannot think this is any of your business!*"

"You could not resist, could you, Napier?" In the thinning fog, Ruthveyn lifted a hand to signal Brogden. "Yes, I have fallen under the sway of a regular she-devil, I collect. Perhaps Mademoiselle Gauthier will stab me in my sleep after all and make your dreams come true."

"It really is too much to be hoped for," said Napier. But his voice was morose, and for the first time, Ruthveyn sensed that he was rethinking his position with regard to Grace.

"Perhaps Miss Crane could be persuaded to do the job for you instead?" Ruthveyn suggested, opening the carriage door. "She seems to have taken a strong dislike to me."

"Awfully fond of her cousin, though, isn't she?" Napier remarked, as they climbed back in.

"Perhaps he has taken pains lately to make himself agreeable," Ruthveyn murmured. Then he told Napier the story of how Holding had once hoped for a marriage between the pair.

Napier's gaze had narrowed considerably by the time Ruthveyn was done. "Rum!" he said pensively. "Never thought of that. And if they were to wed, ownership of the company would be . . ."

"You begin to see my point, I collect," said Ruthveyn.

"But there's no proof Josiah Crane was in the house," Napier mused, as the carriage lurched into motion. "And your notion about his having a key came to naught, according to Holding's butler. Still, one does get the feeling Crane was simply avoiding us today. After all, she took us into an empty office—and she seems naïve enough to protect him."

"I think it far more likely the man is avoiding his creditors," said Ruthveyn. "And a sickbed is the best place for that."

Napier slumped against the seat as Brogden lurched the carriage forward. "You are likely right, of course," he said on a sigh.

"Ah," said Ruthveyn softly. "Music to my ears!"

CHAPTER 12

The Enchantment

Just a few nights after his strange trip to Rotherhithe, Ruthveyn dreamed again of the Jagdalak
Pass, and of the brutal slaughter in the snow. Then the
snow became the endless sand of the desert, and somehow it was all tangled up with rabbits, and with the corpse
of Fenella Crane lying in a field of white poppies. The
poppies undulated as if caught by the wind, and it was no
longer Miss Crane, but Grace. She lay deathly still among
the flowers, a bloody knife in her hand, her eyes open but
unseeing.

He awoke in a sweat, flailing across the mattress in an
attempt to find her.

Nothing.

He jerked upright in bed, gasping for breath.

She was not there. She was not there because he had

convinced himself it was unwise—for both of them. But what if by not being with her, he had doomed her to a worse fate? Was that what the dream meant? He could still hear his heart thundering in his ears. He could taste the fear in his throat.

Bloody hell. This was insane.

He dragged a hand down his face, and then, by sheer force of will, stilled his breathing, drawing it deep and slow until his body relaxed, and his fist let go the wad of counterpane he'd been clutching. Then he drew up his knees and breathed some more, until his mind cleared and became one with the air flowing in and out of his lungs, and all the rational reasons why Grace was not in his bed came back to him.

Still, in that dark and uncertain moment of awakening, her absence had felt intuitively wrong, and the fear had been real. But it had been a *dream,* he reminded himself, not a vision, and unlike his friend Alexander, never had his dreams been prophetic. Horrific, yes, but portending nothing save a miserable night.

At least he had slept for a time—had been sleeping, really, for the last several nights. It likely would not last. Always the sleeplessness returned, and with it the scraps of horrors remembered, edging round his memory like assassins in the night. Before, he had stilled them by any means at his disposal—opium, alcohol, gratuitous sex. His list of sins was long.

Absently, Ruthveyn picked up Satin, who slept curled at his feet with her sister, and set her fur to his cheek. She began to hum happily. He was oddly glad to be in his own home, in his own bed, with his own cats. And yet he felt incomplete.

As if to soothe him, Satin rumbled drowsily for a time, but after a while, her feline patience was exhausted.

"Leaving me, old girl?" he murmured, just as she slipped free and slunk round him to snuggle in the warm hollow on his pillow.

It was a sign, perhaps. Or perhaps his infamous self-discipline was failing him. *Heartless,* Napier had called him. But now, in the gloom, he slipped from the sheets, then padded naked across the floor to snatch his robe from the chair. Drawing it on as he went, he strode out through his study into the corridor.

He missed Grace, missed her with an ache that was unfathomable given how short a time they had known one another. He had made love to her twice—in the same night, no less—and already he knew the rhythm of her breathing when she slept. The scent of her skin. The way she wriggled into the middle of the bed to tuck herself against him.

Upstairs, he did not hesitate, but instead, driven by a force he did not understand, opened the door to Grace's room. The light underdrapes were closed, but the velvet curtains were drawn wide, allowing a nearly full moon to cast the room with a faint sheen. Grace lay in the middle of her bed, one fist thrown back into the pillow, her face turned toward the milky light.

He locked the door behind and settled himself on the edge of the bed. Apprehension drained away the moment he set his hand to her cheek. All was well. His dream had been just a dream, such as any man might have.

She stirred and rolled fully onto her back, turning her face against his hand to nuzzle his palm.

"Grace?" he whispered.

Her eyes flared wide. "*Adrian?*" Grace rolled up onto her elbows, her heavy blond hair spilling over one shoulder. "Adrian, what—? The boys?"

"No, I just . . . I had a strange dream." He felt suddenly foolish.

The eyes relented, softened, and a drowsy smile curved her mouth. "Was it a good dream?"

"No, a bad dream," he said.

She waited, still propped on her elbows, but her gaze had drifted down to his mouth.

"I have been thinking, Grace," he said, feeling awkward as a schoolboy.

"Well, you *are* in my bedchamber," she remarked, her eyes trailing up again. "I should hope you gave that some thought."

"Dashed little," he muttered. But beyond that, he had no words.

"*Hmm*," she said. "Have you been thinking, I wonder, about that question I asked you?"

He set his hand round the turn of her cheek. He knew what she meant. "Grace, where are you going when all this is over?"

"To Paris," she said quietly. "I had a letter from my uncle yesterday. He thinks he has found a cottage for me."

"To Paris," he echoed, dropping his hand. It was what he had expected, of course.

She struggled up to a sitting position, her cotton night-gown tied at the throat, her eyes wide and a little anguished in the gloom. "Adrian, I have been thinking," she whispered. "I think perhaps I should go soon. I can't bear just waiting here in England with Napier's sword hanging over my head. If he has grounds, let him arrest me at the ferry."

"Grace, why go?"

She looked away. "The boys need a proper tutor, and I . . . well, I do not have a life here."

But you could have, he wanted to say.

He could marry her, of course. If he were honest, however, about who and what he was, she would likely think him insane, or—if she believed it—she would not want him. But driven by something—he told himself it was the urge to protect her—he opened his mouth.

"Grace, don't go," he whispered. "I could give you a life here. I could m—"

Her hand came up, her fingertips going to his lips. "Don't," she whispered. "Oh, *don't,* Adrian. Please."

He lifted her hand away. "Why?" he said. "Grace, the protection of my name would—"

"No." She cut him off, her voice low and hollow. "If nothing else, think how that would look to the police. My second wealthy employer, my second betrothal? And the truth is—" Here, she looked at him plaintively, "—the truth is, Adrian, I do not know you. You hold a part of yourself away from me. Will you deny it?"

It was his turn to look away. "No."

"And perhaps you do not know me," she softly added. She laid a hand on his thigh, but there was nothing save comfort in her touch. "In a different time, and a different place, perhaps things could have been otherwise between us. But the *here* is all we have now. And I do desire you. I do admire you, and I am grateful to you. I believe we must content ourselves with that."

"That part about desire does soothe the sting." He managed a sideways smile.

But more and more he realized that he was falling in love with her, with her quiet grace and her kindness.

So often when she was not looking, he watched her with the boys, sometimes as she read to them in the late afternoons, or as they romped in the gardens after luncheon. But as with most of life, he watched through that ever-present pane of glass—sometimes literally. And it was in those moments, with his hand pressed almost longingly to the window, that he realized what a lucky man Ethan Holding had been to have had even a hope of a happy marriage with her.

He did not have that hope. But he did have tonight.

"I want you so much, Grace," he whispered. "Even now, stone-cold sober, I still want you. Whatever I am, whatever I was in the past, in that little piece of *here* that we have *now,* I burn for you."

Grace tossed back one corner of the covers and slid over. She was asking him, Ruthveyn knew, to make love to her—in the here and now, with no expectation of a tomorrow. Because she admired him, and desired him, and because he needed, with her, to step beyond that pane of glass. He was going to accept her offer and be grateful. So he slipped into bed beside her and eased one arm beneath her, drawing her fully against him.

She set her cheek against his shoulder and brushed a light kiss over the turn of his jaw. "Did you lock the door?" she whispered.

"Yes. Might the boys come in?"

"Tom did once," she said.

He threaded one hand through her hair. "Ah, then it will be the wardrobe for me, will it not, my Grace?"

She gave a quiet laugh. "With those shoulders? I think you'd best try the draperies."

Burning with sudden impatience, he sat up against the pillows, scooped her into his arms, and dragged her across his lap. He kissed her once, lightly, then drew away, sliding his hand into the loose, warm hair at her temple, turning her face to the moonlight. Grace looked back at him, her expression honest, her eyes warm with the stirring of desire.

Ruthveyn lowered his mouth to take her lips and felt her tremble. He kissed her slowly, gradually stoking the passion in her as he plumbed and thrust and tasted her thoroughly. It was the greatest of luxuries to him, this ability to open his mind, and even a part of his heart, as normal men did.

Yes, he was going to make love to Grace one more time and take what was not his. With his mind clear, he was going to kiss her and thrust himself inside her until he was blinded by the sweet rush of his release, and the blessed letting go that only Grace could give him. He was going to leave himself with something—heartbreak, most likely—to remember her by when all this was over, and she was gone. And he was going to give to her a part of him to take away. He would give her what was left of his heart.

He had spent the last three days trying to convince himself that never to touch her again was the wisest course for both of them. But fate, again unseen, had played him false. Fate had led him here, and now he wanted Grace with a fire and a desperation that shut away all logic. Like a starving man, he kissed her, driving her head back against the crook of his elbow as his other arm bound her tight.

Grace returned his kisses with equal fervor, the girlish uncertainty of her touch gone. She entwined her tongue with his, her hand skimming lightly down his ribs. Ruthveyn wanted to touch her until he drowned in the wanting, thrilling to her body, which was obviously naked beneath the cotton nightgown.

So often as he had watched her, he had imagined touching her like this, peeling away the somber half-mourning, the crinolines and petticoats. Unfastening the stays that bound her breasts. His fantasies were endless. Yet now he held her all but undressed in his arms, and she was returning his kisses stroke for stroke.

He lifted his lips and looked down. Grace's chest was rising visibly, her breath already fast and shallow, her nipples hard beneath the fabric. Lust coursing through him, Ruthveyn bent his head and captured one sweet nub between his lips, making her gasp into the night. Through the nightgown he suckled heedlessly until the wet fabric clung.

He ran his tongue round her dark areola one last time, then turned his attention to the other breast. Grace's hand speared into his hair. "*Mon dieu,*" she whispered, the words catching in her throat.

Impatience ratcheting up, he swiftly unfastened the ties, catching one nearly into a knot.

"Here," she said, her clever fingers making short work of it.

The nightgown sagged off her shoulder, and Ruthveyn returned his mouth to her breast, laving and suckling until she writhed a little in his embrace. Her derriere rubbed against his cock, now swollen hard, and lust shot through him like a living thing, seizing at his bollocks. A little roughly, he drew her left nipple into his mouth and bit until she gasped. Then he soothed it lightly with the tip of his tongue until she began to beg him with soft whispers to lay her down and take her.

Too much, too fast, his conscience warned. She was all but a virgin. And yet Grace seemed as caught up in the passion as he. He eased her onto the bed, her nightgown gaping open. Unable to resist, he leaned across the night table and lit the lamp, turning the wick low, then he sat back and willed himself to slow.

In the flickering lamplight, he let his hungry gaze sweep over her, taking in her swollen lips, her taut, pink nipples still wet from his mouth, and her just-tumbled hair. Good Lord he wanted to spend himself inside her this instant—wasn't even sure, truth be told, he'd last that long. It was a humbling thought.

But lighting the lamp had been, perhaps, a mistake. Grace's face was warming with embarrassment. Leaning over her, he kissed her again. "Don't be uneasy, Grace," he murmured, lightly lifting his lips. "You are a passionate creature."

Her laugh was thready. "I feel . . . so naked," she whispered. "So hungry for you, and yet . . . so wicked, I suppose, is the word."

He let his hand slide down to cup her feminine heat through the nightgown. "I should have said you're not nearly naked enough."

Impatiently, he stood, unfastened the tie of his robe, and let the silk slither to the floor. His manhood sprang free, and he watched her eyes widen. "It's all right, love," he crooned, setting one knee to the bed.

Tentatively, she touched him, stroking her warm fingers down his length, causing his breath to catch. Her gaze flicked up at him. "Adrian?"

"Enough of that, perhaps," he rasped, drawing back. His eyes went to the hem of her nightgown, which was now gathered about her knees to reveal a pair of perfect calves and dainty feet. "Take it off, Grace," he whispered. "Let me see you."

Obediently, she rose onto her knees, caught the hem, and drew the garment slowly up and over her narrow shoulders. The lamplight bathed her in warm light as her breasts rose with the effort, her nipples still hard and sheened with damp.

His mouth going dry, Ruthveyn willed himself to slow. To savor her. To take in her every delight before he lost himself in the rush. Grace's belly was softly rounded, with a navel that turned inward. Her hips were slender, her last ribs lightly visible above the turn of her waist. Her small, perfectly formed breasts were high and tempting.

He wondered, fleetingly, what she would look like with those small breasts growing round and her belly swelling with his child. Then the sadness of it almost unmanned him.

That he could never ask—nor suffer through again.

The pain made him gruff. "Lie down, Grace."

Her eyes wide, she did so, her golden hair dragging over her pillow as she scooted lower.

Again, he set one knee to the bed and eased a hand down his erection. He wanted, suddenly, to shove her legs wide and push himself at once inside her. To rut with her like a beast. The feminine in her seemed to stir something deep and animalistic in him.

It was the strain of wanting, perhaps—or better put, the conflict of wanting too much, for unlike Angela Timmonds and all the other women in recent memory, he could not see a time when throwing her off would come easy to him.

But it would not matter. Grace would be the one to leave him.

"Do you want me, Grace?" he whispered.

"Yes." Her voice was small.

He lay down beside her, desperate to feel her bare flesh against his, and took Grace into his arms. He kissed her again—never, he thought, would he tire of it—then kissed his way down her breasts, her belly, slowly dragging lower. Setting his hands against the soft flesh of her inner thighs, he pressed gently, then kissed her there, too.

Grace gasped again, a sweet, uncertain sound. "Adrian?"

"Lie still, sweet," he said, "and let me please you."

He watched the muscles of her throat work up and down, then he dipped his head and stroked his tongue lightly through her feminine heat as she quivered instinctively beneath him. He teased her with short, sweet strokes until her breath came fast, and her hands twisted at the sheets to either side of her hips.

"Oh!" she sighed. "Oh, I can't—I can't—"

But she could. She did. And the vision was sweet to him. Her thighs went rigid, and her breathing ratcheted up to sweet gasps of need. And then he felt the pleasure coursing through her—his own moment of triumph.

While she was still sated and languid, Ruthveyn drew himself up and eased his cock into the warm, wet valley of her thighs. He couldn't wait. Couldn't find the words to ask. Her hands came round his neck, but her eyes were still closed, her breathing still audible in the quiet of the room. The scent of feminine arousal and the faint heat of lovemaking was erotic beyond anything he'd ever experienced, and when he pushed himself inside her, it was without hesitation.

She cried out softly at the intrusion, her hands going to his shoulders again as if to hold him back. Ruthveyn could feel the sheen of sweat on his upper lip as he stilled himself.

"*Adrian*—?" His name was a thin, breathless whisper.

"You'll grow accustomed, love," he rasped. "Hold . . . ah, yes, hold still."

Sliding his hands beneath her hips, he lifted and tilted her slightly. He felt her breathing ease, and yet it took all of his self-control not to drive deep and spend himself inside her.

But good God, he was a better, more skilled lover than that, surely? In recent memory, never had he left a bedmate disappointed. Grace was inexperienced, yes, but she was passion personified, and if he tutored her—if he took his time and let her learn the siren's song of her own body—he might bring her to that height yet again.

A part of it was purely selfish; he wanted to enslave her to him if it was humanly possible. But a part of it was knowing what real lovemaking was, and it had been a long time since he had joined his body with a beautiful woman for the slow and graceful thing the sexual act should be.

Perhaps it was time he steeled himself and found the discipline he knew he possessed. Perhaps it was time he sought something other than a quick release and instead opened himself and took what came. Bracing himself, he pushed deeper, causing Grace's eyes to widen. Good God, he didn't want to hurt her. He was a generously made man, in almost every physical way, but for an instant, he felt almost brutish. And then he moved back and forth inside her, his cock tugging sweetly at her feminine core, and he felt Grace sigh and relax beneath him.

Slowly—oh, so slowly—he stoked the passion inside her, thrusting all the way in, then drawing out with exquisite slowness at what he hoped was the perfect angle. Again. And again. Holding himself ruthlessly in check, he moved inside her, bringing his body fully against hers and lifting her hips against him.

"Adrian—?" she said again, with an edge of urgency in her voice.

That was good. Torment was very good.

"Be still, sweet," he cautioned, never flagging in his exquisitely slow, painstaking rhythm.

"Adrian . . ." Her breath was soft against his cheek. "I want . . ."

"Patience, love." Opening his mouth against the turn

of her throat, he drank in their mingled scents and raked his teeth lightly down her neck. "Lovemaking can be slow, Grace. It can be a prolonged, worshipful act. We could find divine ecstasy together, perhaps. We have all night."

But they did not, in fact, have all night. These were stolen moments, and in another few hours, the servants would stir. And yet Ruthveyn yearned to share something deeper with Grace, ill tutored as he was in the old ways of lovemaking.

Her breathing, however, had begun to roughen again. "Adrian," she whispered, shifting restlessly beneath him.

"Will you trust me, love?" He kissed the turn of her jaw. "Will you let the journey be your pleasure?"

"But I—" She gasped, her nails digging into his shoulders. "I want . . ."

He knew what she wanted. And eventually, he meant her to have it. But this was what he had been born for—for her, and for this slow, exquisite bliss—and now, with his body fully under his command at last, he yearned to draw out their pleasure as long as he could. He wanted to drink her in, wanted to become her, and feel the life force surge between them. He rode her slowly, focusing on her every sigh and on every breath that they drew.

He took her mouth and kissed her again, slowly and deeply, thrusting his tongue in rhythm with his cock. He let himself absorb her passion and returned it to her tenfold, until she moved beneath him, arching up hard against his body. Never had he felt such power over a woman. Never had he felt such need. And yet he savored every moment of self-control.

"*Just . . . don't stop,*" she begged. "*Don't stop.*"

"I won't, but . . ." Then, spreading one hand wide between her shoulder blades, he sat up, rocking back onto his heels and carrying her with up him, until he knelt with Grace astraddle him.

"Oh!" she cried, grabbing on to him.

"Grace," he whispered, holding her perfectly steady. "Grace, open your eyes."

She did so only gradually, her eyes wide in the lamplight as she clutched him by the shoulders. "*Adrian*—?"

"Relax, love, I have you." He somehow managed to straighten his legs as he held her against him. He kept one arm banded about her waist, his shaft buried deep. "Keep your eyes open and wrap your legs round my waist. We are heart to heart now, Grace. Relax, and let the tension inside you go."

Steadier now, she nodded. Ruthveyn smiled into her eyes even as he felt his heart break. "You are going to leave me, Grace." It was not a question. "Let us experience lovemaking in its purest form. Let us try to be one breath and one flesh tonight."

"Yes." She said the word slowly.

"Do you trust me?" It was not the first time he'd asked her such a question, though this time, the context was quite different.

Her answer was the same, and it was certain. "Yes."

"Take my breath," he whispered. "Draw me deep inside you."

Then he covered her mouth with his, his eyes open. She did so, breathing him deep, melting into him. "How . . . extraordinary," she whispered.

Her touch on his shoulders was lighter now. "Look at me, Grace," he commanded. "Look deep into my eyes. Let me breathe through you."

She did so, and Ruthveyn opened himself to it. The rush toward ordinary orgasm had slowed, and been transcended, and the force within Grace—and himself—

began gradually to spiral up and up. He drew the breath from her body again and again, Grace following suit. The pleasure denied was exquisite.

His cock was fully inside her, rock hard, but the urgency had passed, and after a time felt himself slipping into a deep, almost ethereal state of relaxation. And yet all around them was a sense of total sensual awareness, as if their every nerve was as alive to sensation—as alive as the very point at which his shaft entered her. He moved within her so slowly it was as if they were the moon and the sun traversing the sky. They were Shiva and Shakti, the supreme power and the celestial energy.

For so long he had wished to experience this, and for so long he had resisted it, this complete opening of himself to another. He had not the training, nor even the patience the tantra required, but even so, he could glimpse paradise.

"Look at me, Grace," he whispered. "Open yourself to me."

She gazed deep into his eyes now, her body perfectly, exquisitely still. She surrounded him—not just her warm, feminine passage, but her arms and her legs and at least a part of her mind, or so he wished to believe. This sort of intimacy—the giving and receiving, the awareness of the moment, and the elevation beyond the mere physicality of sex—could lead to the deepest opening of the mind possible. To the thing he most feared. Yet with Grace—at least for tonight—he did not fear it.

They moved together thus for what might have been an hour, perhaps longer, slowly and erotically, breathing and sharing of themselves. When she neared orgasm, Ruthveyn would stop, or change position ever so slightly, until he could feel the energy around them heightening and strengthening again. He felt grounded to Grace, rooted to her with an intimacy that went beyond the physical.

Oh, it would not last. He had little enough practice at this, and if he let his mind slip so much as a fraction, he could feel the earthly lust begin to gnaw at him like a raw, fierce hunger. He shut it away and opened himself to the divine play, but eventually Grace sighed as she drew his breath deep, and at last something inside him seemed to snap.

"Grace," he whispered, "come with me."

Then he tumbled her forward into the softness of the bed again, his shaft buried deep, her body fisting around him greedily. He hitched her knees over his shoulders and bent her back until her eyes widened with delight. She said something in French, breathless and thready. Then the orgasm took them as one, surging through him and into Grace like an avalanche too long repressed.

For one glorious moment, it was as if he left his physical body. As if his entire mind was a core of pleasure, radiating and pouring into Grace like a liquid sun. He felt her shudder and rock beneath him, heard her keening wail of pleasure and swallowed it, drawing it inside him like breath and energy, and breathing it back to her again in pure, unadulterated joy.

When he left that place beyond himself and returned to the bed, he rolled to one side until they lay entwined in one another, her head tucked on his shoulder.

"Good heavens," she whispered, long moments later. "What *was* that?"

He bent to kiss the top of her head. "That was lovemaking, I think, as it was meant to be," he murmured. "Or as it is meant to be at least some of the time."

She said nothing more for a while, but he could hear her

breathing slow and steady. "Is that really how it is done?" she finally asked.

"In some cultures," he agreed. "But that sort of oneness of energy is not something easily achieved."

"Did we . . . achieve it?"

He drew a deep breath. "On some level, yes." He kissed her again. "But to reach a plane of true harmony and shared energy takes hours oftentimes—and practice. Lots and lots of practice. One must cultivate self-discipline, and a capacity to delay pleasure in favor of the journey. We are, I fear, mere neophytes."

"Hours and hours, *hmm*?"

She was twining that finger in her hair again, a little-girl gesture of pensiveness he had come to find endearing. Then she planted that hand in the center of his chest and rolled over him, her eyes pure seduction.

"I do not think there are enough hours in the day for that," she whispered. "Adrian, that was . . . I felt . . . I cannot even find the words to tell you what that felt like. It was nothing, then everything all at once. It was like . . . experiencing the divine." Then she bent her head and kissed him.

And that was it. He fell. Whatever little scrap of himself he'd managed to hold back from her went slithering over the edge and into the abyss.

CHAPTER 13

The Mystic's Tale

Ruthveyn drowsed for a time with Grace in his embrace, her head curled upon his shoulder. He could not remember a time when he had felt such bliss. Such comfort—though that seemed the wrong word for what he felt when he was with her. But whatever one called it—rest, ease, or pure emotional sustenance—anything like it had been sadly lacking from his life for . . . well, nearly forever. Perhaps to find that comfort in another was the greatest compliment one could pay one's lover.

Tonight he had given in to the manifestation of the eternal energy between man and woman in a way he had never dared, nor even dreamed possible. He had opened to Grace his mind and his heart, and there had been nothing beyond it: no sudden, blinding flash of impending doom; no insight into her darkest recesses; no visions of a fate as yet unfulfilled. With Grace, he was normal—with a normal man's needs, and with a woman who caused him to lose himself inside her in the way God had surely intended.

Was it possible? Was it just remotely possible that this was how it would ever after be between them? Was Grace the lover who had been meant for him all along? Or had the tantra merely blinded him to what was to come?

It should have been just the opposite. Edging into that state of universal awareness—even as superficially and inexpertly as they had done—should have opened every path of communication between them. Instead, he had felt the *prana*—the vital life force—coursing through him unimpeded, perhaps for the first time ever. He had been able to reach the divine, or at least glimpse it, by sharing of himself so deeply with Grace. Had he ever believed such a thing within his grasp, he would have listened more carefully to the old wisdom.

He wished he understood more fully, wished he had not, on some level, rejected the part of himself that was his mother. There was always Anisha, of course, could he but bring himself to talk of it with her. Unlike him, Anisha had been encouraged—or at least not actively discouraged—in her study of the tantras. She had been female, and her Gift—if she had one—had been carefully cloaked in the veil of Hindu tradition; first by their mother, and later by their servants.

But Ruthveyn had been brought up by the rod in the Company schools of Calcutta, and later, at university in Scotland, where they had not taught much in the way of esoteric Hindu philosophies. Certainly they had taught nothing of sexual enlightenment. Most of his fellow students had believed lovemaking was a drunken pump-and-tickle up an alley wall behind some village tavern.

Ruthveyn had known better—but he had behaved no better.

Beside him, he felt Grace stir. She nuzzled against him, her lips warm on her throat. "*Umm*," she said. "So serious, that face. What can you be thinking?"

He turned to her and managed a smile. "Oddly enough, I was thinking of my mother."

Grace set a small, warm hand against his chest. "Anisha told me a little," she said, looking up at him. "What was her name?"

"Sarah," he answered. "Sarah Forsythe."

"Sarah," Grace echoed. "It sounds so . . . English."

He laughed, but there was little amusement in it. "She was called Sarah after her marriage," Ruthveyn clarified. "Her name was Saraswati, but my father wished it anglicized—he wished *her* anglicized—though that didn't happen. But Sarah she became."

Grace winced a little. "How did she feel about that?"

"Do you know, Grace, I daresay you are the first to ask or care," he said quietly. "A wife's wishes—especially an Indian wife's wishes—were rarely consulted. She made her own peace with it, I think, whatever my father's disappointments were."

"Disappointments?" said Grace, curling more tightly about him. "I thought she was a great beauty."

For a long moment Ruthveyn hesitated, weighing how much to say. "My mother was . . . unusual," he finally said. "Ordinarily, a Rajput woman would never have been given in marriage to an outsider, but her family had had difficulty finding a husband for her."

"A great beauty?" said Grace. "And the daughter of a wealthy prince? How odd."

Ruthveyn slicked a hand down Grace's hair. The gesture oddly soothed him. "My mother's people were a little intimidated by her," he said quietly. "They believed her a powerful *rishika*—a seer or a mystic—and no man wished to marry such a woman. It was a gift, you see, and yet a curse. So a political marriage was arranged for her."

Grace was silent for a moment. "There it is again, that 'gift' business," she murmured. "We seem to keep talking circles round it. Your father, was he afraid of her?"

Ruthveyn had crooked his head to look down at her. "Merely surprised, I think," he said, wondering what she was getting at. "He was not told the truth before their marriage. But it little mattered. He had no wish to move in her society, and the English . . . well, mixed marriages were more common then, but rarely at so high a level. Mamma just never really fit in anywhere."

"But she loved you?" said Grace hopefully. "You and Anisha were her happiness, I imagine."

"Yes," he said simply. "We were her life and her breath." *And leave it to Grace,* he thought, *to understand something so fundamental.*

Just then, she stretched and threw one leg across his, the nest of curls between her legs brushing his thigh. And suddenly—and a little sickly—he realized. He must have made a sound of dismay.

"What?" Grace lifted her head to look at him.

Ruthveyn turned to face her, easing a hand between them and settling it lightly over her abdomen. That was the problem with attempting to become one with the cosmos, he supposed. One tended to forget the world's problems and practicalities.

"Grace," he said softly, "when did you last bleed?"

She colored furiously.

"Grace." There was gentle admonishment in his voice.

"We are lovers now. There should be no embarrassment between us. Not in this."

She rolled onto her back, reality dawning on her face. "A fortnight past?" she whispered up at the ceiling. "A little less, perhaps."

Inwardly, he cursed himself to the devil. But outwardly, he made a light circle over her belly with the palm of his hand and forced a smile. "Well, my Grace," he said quietly. "It is possible you will not see Paris at all—not unless it is on your honeymoon."

She rolled up onto her elbow and looked him in the eyes. "It will not happen," she declared. "It will *not*."

"It might," he answered. "I forgot myself, Grace. I'm sorry. I pray you do not pay an unbearable price for my error."

"Unbearable—?" She looked at him poignantly and shook her head. "Is that what you think it would be to me? Because . . . why? Because you are different? Is that it?"

"Different?" he murmured. "How?"

Grace looked away. "Different in that way we don't talk about," she answered. "You do not trust me—indeed, we will not likely be together long enough for you to learn to trust me. But Adrian, I am not stupid. And yes, I want a child—not like this, when we have not committed to one another out of choice—but it is the sum total of my hopes and dreams, to have a child. Can you say that? I somehow doubt it."

She was distraught, he realized, looking across the pillow at her. But what was he to say? There was much truth in her accusation. And he was not a man to run from the truth. He had tried, and found it did no good at all.

"Grace, you would make a good mother—a *wonderful*

mother," he answered. "But no, I do not want a child. I had a child once, when I was a younger man, and wanted so desperately for life to be full of hope and promise. And to lose her—to see her, and to know that no matter what I did . . ." He let his words trail away and was compelled to pinch hard at the bridge of his nose.

"I am sorry," she whispered, her gaze piercing him. "I did not know."

He regained himself, for the years had taught him well. "Her name was Hannah," he said. "She was born a few weeks after the withdrawal from Kabul, but I was delayed. I could not get home in time."

She cupped a warm hand round his cheek. "Your sister said you traveled widely," she said. "Were you there as a diplomat?"

"More or less," he answered. "I was dispatched by the Government to try to figure what was happening, and I went knowing that . . ."

"Knowing what?" she asked softly.

He shrugged, but did not look at her. "Knowing that my wife was with child," he said. "That . . . all was not well at home. But I had to choose, Grace. I had to choose. If there was any hope of stopping that death and slaughter, I had to go. And so I left her. Melanie died in childbed, but Hannah lived long enough that I did at least get to hold her."

"I am sorry," she said again. "I cannot imagine a worse pain than to lose one's wife and child in practically the same stroke."

"But it is an everyday tragedy," he said quietly. "We men are expected to cope, and so . . . we do. I did. No, I have never wished for another child, or another wife. But if it came to it, Grace, that is what we would do. We would marry, and we would do what legions before us have done—we would make the best of it. And in all like-lihood, we would be fine. Perhaps even happy."

But Grace no longer looked at him. "It will not happen," she said numbly. "And I will not marry a man who thinks he *might* manage to be happy with me."

"Grace, it's not—" He lifted his hand, then let it fall again. "It's not you, it's me."

She turned her head, her hair scrubbing on her pillow. "It will not happen," she said again. "But the hour grows late, Adrian. It would be best for you to go."

Yes, it would be that, he decided.

With a sadness he had never expected, Ruthveyn kissed her cheek, then felt about on the floor for his dressing gown. The evening that had begun with such promise now seemed a hollow joy. She was hurt, justifiably. And there was little he could do to explain.

His hand was already on the doorknob when she spoke again.

"Adrian," she said, her voice like a bell in the gloom, "how did you know?"

He turned to see that she had thrown on her nightdress and now sat up in the moonlight, her knees pulled tight to her chest.

"How did I know what?" he asked.

"That there would be death and slaughter," she said quietly.

For an instant, he hesitated. Then, "It was Afghani-stan," he said. "There is always death and slaughter. It is a hellhole."

And since his words were near enough the truth, he left it at that and hoped she did not know her history. But Grace set her chin on her knees and sighed.

"Come back to my bed, Adrian, when you have a better lie than that one," she said.

He dropped his hand. "What?"

"Come back to my bed and make love to me again," she said, "and perhaps—just perhaps—you will be good enough, and I will want you desperately enough, that I can be persuaded to believe that pathetic taradiddle. But tonight, I somehow doubt it."

He stalked back to her bed, the silk dressing gown lashing about his ankles. "What do you want me to tell you, Grace?" he demanded, planting both hands on the mattress and leaning over it. "*What?* Do I bare my soul? You are leaving anyway."

"Oh, I see!" She let her knees slide down. "*I* am leaving. But were I not, then you would confess everything about your murky past, would you? And we would ride happily ever after into the sunset? You, me, and this child you fear I might conceive?"

"What do you want, Grace?" His voice was hollow now. "Do you want me to tell you I was once little more than a common spy? That I lied and manipulated and pulled any string that the East India Company or Her Majesty's government wanted pulled? That I even backstabbed my own people once or twice? I did those things, yes, because sometimes a man can do nothing but choose the lesser of two evils. I did them because my father told me it was my duty. That I had been born to it. But I don't do those things anymore, Grace. Not for anyone. I prefer to drink and smoke myself into the clouds, as you say, rather than think about it anymore. Or dream about it anymore. So now you've heard it. Is that what you wanted?"

She slowly shook her head. "What I want, I think," she whispered, "is just not to love you so much."

"Grace." He caught her face in his hands. "Grace, don't love me. *Don't.*"

She held his gaze steadily, even as one tear wobbled down the side of her nose. "I wish I did not," she said. "I have tried to pretend, even to myself that it wasn't coming to this. I wish I could just stay here until this awful business is finished, enjoying a friendship with your sister, and the pleasure of teaching those children, and yes, perhaps even enjoying your bed from time to time. But I wish I did not love you because you are so dark inside. You speak, Adrian, of this cosmic sharing of sensual and spiritual things. But you don't really share anything. That's how it seems to me."

He sat down on the side of the bed and drew a shuddering breath. "What, then?" he rasped. "What in God's name do you want to know? What can I tell you, Grace, that will make you feel better?"

"Just . . . everything." Grace dragged the hair back from her face in a gesture that spoke of weariness. "I want to know if you are one of the Vateis, or whatever they are rightly called," she went on. "I want to know why, when you touch me, I sometimes feel as if you cast a spell over me, and why your eyes look as if they are a thousand years old and have seen a thousand terrible things. And I want to know why you brought me here. I want to know what you *saw*."

"Grace, it isn't—"

"No," she said, speaking over him. "I know it isn't Napier you fear—in fact, I don't think you fear him at all—or anyone else. So I want to know what it is you have seen—or sensed or divined or whatever the word is—that makes you concerned for me. I think I have that right."

He was quiet a long while, turning over in his mind all that she had said, and even the ease with which she could ask such questions. He felt suddenly as if his entire life was balanced on the blade of a sword. As if fate were waiting for him to tip this way or that before slicing him to ribbons.

"I *have* seen a thousand terrible things, Grace," he finally said. "Like my Scots grandmother before me, and her father before that, and a hundred generations before that, perhaps. Yes, we carry it in our blood like a curse. Are we the Vateis? I don't know. It's as good a name as any."

"So that mark on your hip is not just a mark," she said. "And the legend of the Guardians is not just a legend. You and Rance and the people like you are the descendants of Sibylla, the Gift."

He looked away. "We are that," he said, "beyond any doubt. There are enough family Bibles to prove it."

"So your mother was a mystic," said Grace slowly. "A Hindu prophet, or something like it, and she married a man who carried in his blood the Scottish Gift. A man who bore the mark of the Guardian, whose job it was to guard you as a child, I daresay. With bloodlines like that, Adrian, you could not have escaped your fate had you tried."

He was shocked by how easily she accepted it—his sister's doing, no doubt. He turned on the bed to face her and took her hand in his. "You speak of all this as if it's red hair or rheumatism passing through the blood. I wish I could be so blasé."

"Oh, I am certainly not that," she said, her voice low and a little tremulous. "I had a poor aunt who had the most terrible dreams—dreams that could come true, or so the villagers whispered. Papa said she was treated like a pariah, and eventually she threw herself off a cliff. It broke my father's heart. No, Adrian, of all the things I am, blasé is not one of them."

That quieted him for a time. Oh, it was a story he'd heard time and again—old village suspicions died hard. But to hear it from Grace saddened him.

"Why did you bring me here, Adrian, to this house?" she whispered. "I *know* it wasn't to seduce me—for that was my doing, not yours. But the man I first met in St. James's was very different from that angry, troubled man who stalked me down the stairs in Whitehall and kissed me nearly senseless."

Ruthveyn considered what she asked. She thought she had a right to know. And perhaps she did. Initially, he'd not wished to frighten her, had not even been sure himself what he'd seen. He still wasn't. But perhaps it was time to be open with Grace.

Sitting opposite her on the bed, he drew his legs up into *siddhasana* and exhaled fully, trying to let go of the frustration warring inside him.

"I went to Holding's house in Belgrave Square that morning," he said after a time. "And there I saw . . . something. The evil that is yet to come, I think. I do not believe Holding's was the last death in this terrible business. I just feel it strongly. And now I have dreamt . . ."

I dreamt of it, and I saw you dead, he thought, closing his eyes. *Oh, Grace. My love. I saw the knife and I saw the blood and I felt my life draining away with it . . .*

But Grace had set her hand over his where it lay relaxed upon his knee. "Who, Adrian?" she whispered. "Who did you see?"

He opened his eyes, and realized she was talking about his vision, not the dream. And his dreams were not prophetic, he reminded himself. *They were not.* Even a vision could be misinterpreted. And they could sometimes be altered by intervention, divine or otherwise. That much had been proven throughout history, and was in part the reason Guardians existed. To keep the Gift from being ill-used by those who would maliciously tinker with the course of human events.

He swallowed hard and looked away, lest she see more than he wished in his eyes. "I cannot be sure," he hedged, for that was true.

"But you saw *someone*," she said.

He turned to her, his eyes bleak, and surrendered. "I saw Fenella Crane," he said. "I saw her dead on a field of snow—dead by violent means. Hatred and fear swirled in the air around her, but . . . I could not quite make it out."

"Fenella," Grace whispered, her hand going to her throat. "Dear God! Is she going to die?"

He shook his head. "I cannot know, but I fear it. The vision, it might have been metaphorical. Or just wrong in a way I cannot yet interpret. But I warned Napier some time ago."

"And did he believe you?" Her voice was urgent. "My God, does he know you have the Gift?"

This time he did not even bother to deny anything; he felt suddenly beyond it. "Someone told Napier about me," he rasped. "Months ago, when Lazonby was still imprisoned. Someone placed high within the Government. It had to be, for only three or four people know. Everyone else is dead now, and no one in the Society would betray me. But most days, Napier still thinks it's all balderdash."

"Mon Dieu," Grace murmured.

"But you may take comfort in the fact that Napier is having the house watched," he said quietly. "I dragged him to Rotherhithe yesterday, and we saw Miss Crane. She seemed unsettled, mistrustful, and caught up in fretting over Josiah Crane. I could not see what it was that threatened her."

"And when these things come to you," she pressed, "what form do they take? Dreams? Visions?"

"Visions. Or, if I open myself, just . . . impressions. Like an emotion that manifests itself in a sort of energy around me." He looked away and stared at a point deep inside the room. "Good God, that sounds insane."

"No, it doesn't." Her voice was firm. "Tell me how it happens. Tell me exactly."

"I don't know how it happens," he said, opening his hands, palms up, on his knees. "I know only that if I am not on my guard when I am with others—if I do not deliberately shut my mind—it just comes. When I touch people—bare skin, usually. Or sometimes when I simply look into their eyes, even accidentally. It's as if God just throws up a window sash and lets me see into their souls."

"Everyone's?" Grace's voice went up a notch, as if she was envisioning what that would be like. But no one could understand, he thought, unless he had lived it.

"Not everyone, thank God," he whispered, his shoulders slumping. "Some people are what the Vateis have always called *Unknowables*. We are blind to them."

"What makes someone unknowable?"

He laughed, but it was bitter. "That, too, is unknown," he confessed. "And some people are more open than others. Some people can be read by one Vates more easily than another. The Vateis generally cannot read one another—but there can be nuances. Anisha can read my palm and my stars, for example, skills she was taught in the traditional way of our mother's people, so it is possible her gift is one she inherited maternally, and she is not of the Vateis at all."

"Remarkable," Grace whispered. "There must be some rhyme or reason to it."

He shrugged. "I have given up looking for any," he said. "In Mr. Sutherland's genealogical research, he has found none."

"Mr. Sutherland?"

"Our Preost—it's something like a priest," said Ruthveyn. "Indeed, he has found people who have a Gift so vague they think it is just ordinary intuition, as if it has been all but bred out of the blood. Some, like Lazonby, have powers of keen perception—clairvoyance, perhaps, but not precognition. Some Vateis can read the opposite sex only. The Gift tends to skip a generation, but even so, we cannot read our own children or grandchildren at all, nor our siblings very well, if at all—my grandmother always said that was God's small mercy. Yet von Althausen swears it has nothing to do with God. That visions are merely uncontrolled electrical pulses in the brain; but I'll be damned, Grace, if I understand any of it."

"Von Althausen," Grace murmured. "The one Anisha calls the mad scientist."

"*Anisha,*" he said grimly. "I could throttle her. She is the one who told you all this, isn't she?"

"She did not have to." Grace shook her head, the confusion suddenly clearing from her visage. "*That* is what the St. James Society is, isn't it? You are studying the metaphysical."

"I am funding the studies, yes, along with Lord Bessett," he said. "The organization, however, has numbered natural philosophers amongst its membership for centuries. Now we are trying merely to foster a haven for research. To formalize initiation rites and make members known to one another. And to identify, if we can, any unknown family lines. The Society has lost its structure over the centuries—and that could be dangerous."

"For centuries this has gone on?" Grace was staring at him. "So . . . it isn't even the St. James Society, really."

For a moment, he considered how best to answer her, but he was in so deep, honesty seemed the only avenue left. "Not exactly," he finally answered. "It is called the *Fraternitas Aureae Crucis*—the Brotherhood of the Golden Cross. In its oldest known form, the symbol had no thistle, and the ancient writings suggest the *Fraternitas* was once more a religious order than anything else."

"Like the Knights Templar?"

He shrugged. "We think the Guardians sprang in part from the Jesuits, but even that is no more than legend," he answered. "It must have something to do with the old Celtic civilizations of Europe, for some of the terms used by the *Fraternitas* are Celtic in origin. But the name is Latin, which suggests it was clearly Christianized under Roman influence. I think, frankly, we'll never know the truth, no matter how hard Sutherland works at it."

Grace's eyes widened. "And all these people in this organization . . . they have the Gift?"

"No, no." He dragged both hands through his hair. "All manner of scientific men belonged to the *Fraternitas*—the Savants, they were traditionally called. And then we have our men of law or of letters—the Advocati. Our men of God, the Preosts. But all of them protect, in one way or another, the Gift."

"The Savants. The Advocati. The Preosts." Grace's tone was musing. "It begins to sound like the Rosicrucians, or even something Masonic."

He shook his head. "It predates Masonry," he answered, "though many believe the *Fraternitas* was once a sept of the former—thus the cross emblem. But no one knows with certainty."

Grace dipped her head to catch his gaze. "Adrian,"

she said tentatively, "can you read me? Can you see my future? Is that what's wrong?"

Ruthveyn fell silent for a time. He did not know what to say, and so he decided to be honest again, and this time he took both her hands in his. "I can feel your presence, Grace, when you are near me. I don't even need to look. When I said it was your scent, I lied. And when I touch you, yes, I feel we almost seep *into* one another. There are moments when we share an energy and a life force, much as the tantras teach. But to see beyond that? No, I cannot. Not yet." He stopped, and bowed his head. "But we cannot hold out hope, Grace. For me, intimacy deepens the mind connection. Given what I feel for you . . . well, in the long run, I think we dare not hope."

"I see." After a moment's hesitation, Grace gently drew her hands from his, and stared into the gloom. "Well, I am touched. But it would be awful for you. I can understand that. One would have no secrets from one's lover."

"And one would see, quite likely, the time—and even the means by which—that love would end," he added, "which would be the hardest part of all."

But Grace turned to him, her eyes suddenly shimmering in the lamplight. "Oh, Adrian, there is where you are wrong," she said huskily. "True love does not end. It simply does not."

At that, Ruthveyn felt something catch in the back of his throat, and he found himself compelled to look away. She had a point, he realized, for what he felt for her would never fade. Of that, he was increasingly, almost painfully, certain. He searched for the words to tell her, then thought better of it.

Just then, somewhere in the bowels of the house, there was a clanking sound. A bucket—or a coal shuttle—being set down. Ruthveyn's gaze flew to the window. No hint of dawn yet lit the window, but the moon was waning. And most certainly, his servants were stirring.

Hastily, he caught Grace's face in both hands and kissed her. "I must go," he said when at last he lifted his mouth from hers. "I do not know, Grace, how much more I could feel for you than I already do. I look at you, and it just takes my breath. But I shut off so much of myself so long ago—"

The *clank*! came again, ominously near now.

There really was nothing more to be said, and already he had said too much. Ruthveyn rose from the bed and left her, as he should have done long before.

But the catch in his throat was still with him, and the bittersweet taste of her was still on his lips, even as he slipped out the door.

CHAPTER 14

The Bréviaire's Secret

Sunday was, technically speaking, Grace's half day. But because of Lord Lucan's indebtedness to his sister—and his sister's perverse pleasure in extracting her pound of flesh—the boys generally spent the time after morning church services with their uncle. In this way it came about that Grace, having the afternoon to herself, asked Higgenthorpe's assistance in fetching down from the attic her father's army trunk, which had accompanied her from pillar to post since his death.

The butler snapped his fingers, and in a trice, two of Ruthveyn's burly footmen had hauled the old beast down the stairs and into her bedchamber. Grace was on her knees and up to her elbows in memories—quite literally—when Lady Anisha wandered into her room in a pair of her silk pantaloons and plopped down in the chair by the hearth. Today she even wore a gold ring in her left nostril and looked altogether different from the elegant young Englishwoman Grace had accompanied to church.

"What are you doing?" she asked, propping her chin on her fist.

Grace laughed and dusted a blob of smut from her cuff. "Woolgathering, mostly," she said. "Or perhaps *dustgathering* is the better term. Do you need me? This can wait."

"No, I'm just bored." Anisha studied her for a time. "So, my dear, Raju tells me he has explained the *Fraternitas* to you."

Grace flicked an appraising glance up at her. "*Oui,*" she said swiftly. "Have you any objection?"

Anisha's eyes widened. "*Me?* I have nothing to do with it."

"You are not . . . one of them?"

Anisha rolled her eyes in that expressive way of hers. "My dear girl, the *Fraternitas* is for men only—very stubborn, arrogant, hotheaded men, too, for all their fine talk of intellect and science. They may speak loftily of protecting women, but admit one? *Never.*"

"Ah," said Grace. "I did not perfectly understand."

As if the topic bored her, Anisha prodded the battered wooden trunk with the toe of her slipper. "Is that monstrous thing yours? It looks twice your age."

Laughing, Grace sat back on her heels and lifted out a wide leather case. "Actually, it was Papa's, from his school days at the *École Spéciale Militaire,*" she said. "Our family treasures—pitiful lot that they are—have been packed in here an age. Here, have a look at Scotland Yard's incriminating evidence against me."

With that, she snapped loose the lid and lifted it back.

Her father's Colt revolvers gleamed up from their blue velvet beds, brilliant as the day they were made.

"My, a brace of pistols!" said Anisha. "Will those be your weapons of choice on your next murderous rampage? Is that Napier's theory?"

But the mere mention of Napier's name brought back to Grace the shadow hanging over her—and the reason for it. Something in her expression must have withered.

Eyes widening with dismay, Anisha set her fingertips to her mouth. "Oh, Grace, how wicked of me! It is not funny, is it? Mr. Holding was to have been your husband."

When Grace burst inexplicably into a full flood of tears, Anisha slid onto the floor. "Oh, Grace, forgive me," she said, gathering her into her arms. "I am the most thoughtless person on earth."

"No, I st-st-started it," Grace managed. "I keep t-trying to make a joke of Napier, but—"

And for a moment, the grief swamped her anew. She sobbed into Anisha's shoulder as if the world were ending, yet not entirely sure just what it was she cried about. She did not precisely miss Ethan Holding, but she was deeply sorry he was gone.

Still, her grief seemed somehow more profound than that. It was the sadness of wanting and being afraid to want. The grief of fearing one might never feel normal again. The sorrow of missing her father, and of being so damnably weary of fearing Scotland Yard might skulk up behind her and drop a noose round her neck.

Worse, she had not seen Adrian in days, and she could feel the distance between them. He had not been at dinner, and last night Luc had remarked that his old suite in St. James's had come empty again. Adrian was avoiding her, Grace sensed, and in her darker moments, she began to fear she had stirred up in him something he did not want to face—and but for her, would not have needed to.

"There, there," said Anisha, patting her lightly on the back. "It cannot be as bad as all that, Grace. Have heart, my dear. It will all work out eventually, I do promise you."

Confused, she lifted her face from Anisha's shoulder. "*B-B-But he's dead!*" she said through her hitching sobs. "How can it work out?"

Anisha's face fell. "No, no, it will not," she agreed squeezing both her hands. "You are quite right about poor Mr. Holding."

At last Grace sat back on her heels again, dabbing away at her eyes with her pocket handkerchief. "Oh, Anisha, do forgive me," she said. "I am not quite myself."

"Of course, how could you be?" Anisha smiled gently, then smoothed her hands over the leather gun case. "Tell me about these," she went on. "Your father must have loved them very much."

"Yes, he did." Grace flashed a watery smile. "When I was perhaps fourteen, Mamma had someone bring them back from America as an anniversary gift. He loved them so much, I could not bear to part with them."

Anisha crossed her legs on the carpet in that odd way her brother had, then lifted a small wooden box Grace had left perched on the ledge in the trunk. "And what is this?"

"Some of Mamma's jewelry," said Grace. "Small things mostly, but all Papa could afford. They were given, though, with great love. Let me show you."

And bit by bit, Anisha coaxed her from her gloom by turning Grace's attention to the trunk and allowing her to let go some of the grief. Save for her tears at Mr. Holding's grave, Grace realized, she had not cried since leaving France and her father's funeral mass.

Eventually, when half the contents of the trunk lay spread about the carpet around them, and a dozen little stories had been told, Anisha caught her hand and squeezed it again. "You need to simply accept, Grace, that you have had a couple of very hard years," she said. "You should, perhaps, cry more often. Not less."

"I don't know what you mean."

But Anisha had opened Grace's hand on her knee and was lightly tracing her finger over Grace's palm, her expression pensive. "You have had to leave your beloved Algeria to take your ailing father home to die," she said. "But you faced it, and you went on to face a new job in a new place, then you faced the prospect of a new but uncertain future with Mr. Holding. And when you thought that settled, fate dashed it all to pieces again. And now you are here, with Adrian and all his darkness to deal with."

"Oh, Anisha, it's not—"

But Anisha raised a forestalling hand. "Believe me, Grace, when I say I know something of tragedy and sudden change," she said. "It wears one's emotions to a bloody nub, no matter how brave we may appear on the outside."

She returned her gaze to Grace's hand, drawing her finger down the deep line that hooked down the center of her palm, then made a *tch-tching* sound. "See all these little lines crisscrossing everywhere?" she said. "This is just what I am talking about. They come from the strain in your life. Your sorrows, if you will."

Grace leaned over to look, then sighed. "Well, Anisha, at least they are still on my hand, not my face," she managed. "*Yet.*"

At last, they both laughed again.

Anisha's finger ran over one of the fleshy mounds of the palm. "And this—this is Venus. It represents Shakti, the great, divine mother." She looked up slyly. "My dear Grace, your passion is impressive—a little too impressive. Have a care that your sensual appetites do not bring you to grief."

Grace felt her face flame with heat. "I fear it may already be too late," she muttered.

At that, Anisha gently closed Grace's hand. "This is too much for one day," she said. "If you will permit me, I will do this at greater length after I have charted your stars."

"Why not?" Grace knew nothing of astrology, or whatever it was called, but according to Adrian, it clearly mattered to his sister. "I will put myself in your hands, Anisha. Perhaps I shall learn something."

Anisha smiled faintly. "Then write down the date and precise place of your birth," she said, "and the time, please, as near as you know it."

Grace cast a glance at the trunk. "It is written in there somewhere."

"Excellent," said Anisha. "Find it, then I will be able to consult the stars with great exactitude. And in this way, I will be able to tell you precisely when you should next go to my brother's bed."

"*Ça alors!*" Grace uttered. "Anisha!"

"What?" Anisha blinked innocently. "You have not, I hope, given him up? Raju will not take it gracefully. No, you must go to his bed at the time when his mind is most clear and his *prana* is abundant. Go, and show him that overdeveloped Venus, and ask him what is to be done for it."

Grace imagined her face was cherry red. "Really,

Anisha," she said. "Here, if you are so full of mischief and energy, help me finish going through this trunk."

"Of course." Anisha uncrossed her legs and leapt up with ease. "What are you looking for?"

Grace knelt and peered down into it. Mostly books and bundles of papers remained. "I'm not absolutely certain," she admitted. "Something I saw as a child—a book or perhaps a drawing? I think I shall know it when I see it. Let's just unload everything bit by bit."

"Loose papers first," declared Anisha. "I shall get them out, and you sit down and sort. This thing—was it a certain color?"

"Not that I can recall." Grace began to go through the first pile of detritus passed down to her. "But do you remember, Anisha, that old legend about the Guardians?"

Anisha looked over her shoulder and flipped her long, silk scarf back into place. "About the little girl being kidnapped? And how they rode onto the Île Saint-Louis after her?"

"*Oui,* and then the bridge collapsed." Grace scowled at her papers. "I didn't mention it to your brother, but something has been nagging at me. And it's the oddest thing."

Apparently catching something in Grace's tone, Anisha turned slowly around. "Yes?"

"I had an ancestor who almost died in a bridge collapse—a *Scottish* ancestor—and according to family lore, he was left for dead in Paris."

Anisha froze, eyes wide. "Truly?"

"Eventually he recovered, and may even have returned home for a time. But I believe he died in Paris—Papa once said something about his tomb. I cannot quite recall."

"It makes one wonder how many bridges there are in Paris," said Anisha.

"More than half a dozen," said Grace pensively. "But how many, over the centuries, could have collapsed?"

"Good question." Anisha set the next pile of papers down. "And this thing we are looking for, has it something to do with that ancestor?"

Here, Grace was compelled to lift both hands. "I do not know," she said, "but that symbol—the golden cross—I *know* I've seen it somewhere. Somewhere in childhood. And since I was raised mostly in North Africa, isn't it more likely what I saw was something my father already had?"

"Very likely," said Anisha, hefting out another load. "Let's sort the books first, for they shall go much faster."

The sixth book Anisha handed out—a slender, crumbling volume of faded red leather—instantly struck a chord with Grace.

"This looks familiar," she murmured, turning it over. The book had once been deeply embossed in gold, but much of it had worn away, and the cover was all but rent from the spine. Still, it looked beautiful—and costly.

Anisha knelt beside her. "What is it?"

"A *bréviaire*," she said. "Or a sort of prayer book. It is in Latin, of course."

Gently, Grace flipped it open, and there it was, emblazoned upon the frontispiece, hand-colored in brilliant shades of red and blue. In this version, there was no thistle. The Latin cross was illuminated in shimmering gold, positioned above a crossed quill and sword, the letters F.A.C below.

"Good Lord, the *Fraternitas Aureae Crucis!*" Anisha whispered, brushing her finger over it. "And look! What does this say?"

Excited, Grace turned the book to show her. On the top right corner of the title page, in a spidery, cramped hand, someone had written his name and address. "*Sir Angus Muirhead*," she murmured, "*Rue de la Verrerie*."

Beyond that, however, there was nothing to indicate who Muirhead had been or how he had come to own the book, though the pages looked well thumbed. The publication date was given as 1670, and within, the book was beautifully illustrated in brilliant hues of red, blue, and gold.

"Muirhead," Anisha repeated. "Is that a Scots name? Could he be your ancestor?"

Grace sighed. "Angus is a Scots name, I believe," she said. "I suppose he is a relation, or Papa would not have had the book, but oh, I do so wish I had listened more as a child!"

"Is there a family Bible, perhaps?"

Grace laid the prayer book down. "It's possible my uncle has one. And that address is near the Place de Vosges, just round the corner from his house. The house where my father and many generations before him were born. Is that not odd?"

"Grace," said Anisha excitedly, "what if you are descended from the Gift? From Sibylla?"

"Well, it couldn't quite be that," said Grace. "Even if we stretch probability, and say this *is* my ancestor, and that he *did* come to Paris with her, it would mean only that he was, at best, her kinsman."

"In whose blood the Gift was carried," Anisha reminded her. Rance did say what a sensible young woman you were—and that when he flirted with you, you would never give him the time of day. Perhaps you have some hint of the Gift?"

Grace smiled up at her faintly. "Oh, Anisha, I am sure I do not!" she answered. "And Rance never flirted with me at all."

"But Grace," Anisha said thoughtfully, "do you never find that you know things others don't—know them instinctively, I mean, in the pit of your belly?"

Grace considered it. "*Mais oui,* doesn't everyone?" she answered. "Though I did have an aunt . . ."

"Yes?"

Grace shook her head. "She had odd dreams, that is all," she said. "Certainly I have never known the future, Anisha."

"That's not what I mean," Anisha pressed. "Mr. Sutherland and Dr. von Althausen have come to believe the Gift in some families has been watered down to nothing more than perspicacity. Not second sight so much as a sort of muted clairvoyance. They theorize, however, that with training, the sight can be—I don't know—restored, perhaps? *If* one has the propensity for it—the right blood, if you will."

"Well, I don't know . . ." Grace answered. "I cannot see myself being trained for any such thing—nor would I wish to be. But Mamma did always say . . ."

"What?" Anisha prodded, leaning forward. "What did she say?"

Grace gave a chagrined smile. "She always said I had a gift," she answered. "A gift for knowing people—well, men, at least. She called it uncanny, and said that Papa was the very same. That we could sum up a man in one look; that we always knew who meant us well and who was dishonest."

"Is it true?"

Grace shrugged. "I've never been swindled, if that's what you mean. And I've turned down a few marriage proposals over the years because . . . well, because I just felt something was a bit off."

"Off in what way?"

"That . . . they were not right for me," she said musingly. "Or that they were not the faithful type. And then there was this one in particular . . . oh, but that does not bear mentioning."

"I can bear it," Anisha assured her. "This is fascinating."

"Well, there once was a handsome young army major detailed to the legion," said Grace reluctantly. "I adored him desperately from afar. Oh, Anisha, if you could have seen his shoulders! But later, when Papa brought him home to dinner . . ."

"Yes? Go on."

Grace dropped her gaze to the carpet. "Well, it's just that when I looked in his eyes, chills ran down my spine," she said quietly. "I told Papa that I had changed my mind, and he would not do—which Papa was not at all displeased to hear. Just before his return to France, he met and married the niece of the *maréchal-de-camp.* But apparently, he had a frightful temper, and within the year, he had beaten the poor girl to death in a rage."

"Good God," said Anisha. She pulled her knees to her chest, hugging them. "That's horrific."

"Oh, Anisha, I just felt . . . so terribly *guilty.*"

"The guilt of a survivor?"

Grace's brow furrowed. "No, it was worse than that," she murmured. "I felt as if I . . . I should have stopped it somehow. As if I knew what he was capable of and should have done something."

"This evil you saw," said Anisha intently, "did it come to you in a dream? Or in a wakeful moment?"

Grace looked at her and laughed. "Oh, Anisha, you sound so dramatic!" she said. "As I said, it was just the proverbial chill down the spine."

Anisha relaxed into her chair. "Of course," she answered, "and there is nothing to be done about that, is there?"

Again, Grace shrugged. "I don't know what I could have done, really," she said softly. "As to me, Papa just said I was waiting for the right man, as he had waited for Mamma, and that I would know it when I found him."

Anisha was quiet for a moment. "Grace," she finally said, "Raju said you were an Unknowable—at least to him. Is that still the case?"

"For now," she said carefully, "but he is much tormented."

Anisha sighed. "His Gift is strong," she said, "and unlike some, not easily governed. Yet he is a ruthlessly disciplined man in all other ways, so this is most difficult for him to accept. He is angry in his heart—mostly at himself."

"I think I understand."

Anisha hugged her knees tighter. "When Raju was a child," she said quietly, "Mamma feared this. Before she died, she tried to teach him to control his mind through *dhâranâ* and *dhyâna,* but these are not skills one can teach a boy, as they require much discipline and long years of training. And Papa—well, he disapproved. He feared the Gift might be weakened. I don't think he ever understood the burden it was."

Grace was confused. "And what are these skills?"

Anisha's perfectly arched eyebrows drew together. "It is hard to put in English words," she said. "It is like disciplined thinking, but in an inward way, using *pranayama*— the retention of breath. And then *Samâdhi*—the control of the mind—the ability to mentally block unwanted distractions. One can achieve inner unity, thus gaining a better control over one's thoughts. Raju tries, but he has not been trained—and when he fails, he turns to *charas* instead, but this brings only a false silence. A temporary peace. I could help him a little perhaps, but despite all his broad-minded words, he still sees me as his responsibility, not the other way round."

Grace sighed. "I still don't understand. Are you saying, Anisha, that with practice, he could turn the Gift off and on at will?"

"It might take years of work and study, but yes," she said. "That is my theory. In India, I have heard, the great holy men can cut themselves with a sharp blade and still the blood with their minds. But von Althausen, the stubborn man of science, thinks everything must be explained in a book." Suddenly, Anisha's smile brightened. "Oh, enough of that," she said, bounding up from the floor. "Come on, get up, Grace. Let's take that *bréviaire* or whatever one calls it down to the St. James Society."

"Whatever for?" asked Grace, rising.

But Anisha had that mischievous look on her face again. "I should like to see if Sir Angus rings any bells with the Reverend Mr. Sutherland," she said. "And then I mean to poke about in their rare book holdings to see if I can determine just how many bridges have collapsed in Paris."

Anisha's question was to be easily answered little more than an hour later as they sat in the shadowy depths of the main library at the St. James Society.

"Precisely three that I know of," said the Reverend Mr. Sutherland.

He presented a thick, musty tome bound in black morocco and laid it open to one of the middle pages, beaming at it through his silver reading glasses with the pride of possession that only a bibliophile can project.

"*Three* bridges collapsed?" Grace glanced down at the miniscule print.

"Four, if one counts the Pont Royal," the gentleman corrected. "That one burned, flooded, then collapsed—all within a span of a few years."

"Sounds like my luck," Grace muttered, turning the book so that she might better read it.

"What is it?" asked Lady Anisha, leaning forward in her chair. "And what does it say? My French is frightful."

"It is an architectural history of the city of Paris." Mr. Sutherland was still gazing at it almost lovingly. "One of Lord Bessett's favorites."

"So the Pont Saint-Michel and the Pont Notre-Dame have also collapsed," Grace murmured, skimming the words. "Both in the fifteenth century, rather too early for Sir Angus, given the date of his prayer book."

"Quite so, quite so!" said Mr. Sutherland, peering down his nose. "Which leaves either the Pont Royal or—"

"—the Pont Marie," finished Anisha triumphantly. "Just like the legend of the Guardians."

"Indeed, Lady Anisha," said Sutherland. "Now, let us turn our attention to this beautifully illuminated prayer book—a remarkable thing, and a costly one, in its day. Sir Angus was a wealthy man, of that we can be sure."

"Can we?" Grace returned her attention to the book, which Sutherland had carefully laid open with two leather-cased weights so that he might better study the symbol.

He had laid aside his spectacles and was now studying it through a silver loupe. "Quite fine work. All done by hand, of course. And gold leaf on the cross, too, not gold paint." He removed the loupe and straightened up with a pensive expression. "A presentation piece, I think. Or possibly a gift. And the absence of the thistle is telling."

"But you've never heard of him?" asked Anisha for the second time.

Mr. Sutherland gave a sort of wince. "Let me review my genealogical charts, my lady," he said, rising. "Perhaps I have forgotten a name?"

Grace watched him go with mild interest. A strikingly handsome man, he was graying at the temples and wore a salt-and-pepper beard. Nonetheless, he possessed the carriage of a soldier, a ready laugh, and a mischievous twinkle in his eye.

It made her think, strangely, of Adrian, of the man he could have been, perhaps, had life not burdened him with great gifts and great responsibilities.

"Anisha," she said quietly, "tell me again what the Guardians do."

Anisha looked up from the prayer book. "They guard the Gift, in a universal sense," she replied. "Anyone possessing the Gift is believed a treasure—and a weapon."

"A weapon?"

"Throughout history, prophets have been exploited by evil," Anisha went on, "so the Vateis must be kept safe from those who crave power—especially the women and children. Indeed, no child who possesses the Gift is ever left without a Guardian or his delegate—a blood relation, almost always. That, you see, is where Rance went. His father was a Guardian to a grandchild who is believed to have the Gift, but she is young. Now that his father is gone, the duty passes to Rance."

Grace wrapped her arms over her chest. "And does one simply volunteer?"

Anisha shook her head. "No, it must fall to you by

birth," she said. "The ancient manuscripts say that a Guardian must be born between the thirteenth and the twentieth of April."

"Why so specific?"

"Who knows?" Anisha lifted one slender shoulder. "But the dates coincide, interestingly enough, very near the sign of the Ram in both *Jyotish* and Western astrology."

"The Ram?"

"The sign of fire and war," Anisha explained. "In *Jyotish* astrology, it is called *Mesha,* and in the west, Aries."

"Like the constellation," murmured Grace.

"Just so," said Anisha. "The Ram possesses great stamina, both mentally *and* physically—a fine skill to have, I think you will discover."

"Anisha—!"

"Oh, very well." Anisha grinned. "But you should also remember that the Ram is capable of bending others to his will. Rams are born leaders, aggressive and clear of thought, but also stubborn and tactless. Does that sound like anyone you know?"

Grace gave a withering laugh.

Anisha smiled her serene, knowing smile, and returned to the *bréviaire*. While she studied the colorful drawings, Grace got up to roam restlessly about the room. It was long and narrow, rather like a gallery, spanning the width of the building, with a row of deep windows overlooking St. James's Place. The room boasted a thick Turkish carpet that ran its length and heavy bottle green draperies that swept the polished floors. As with the rest of the St. James Society, no expense had been spared here.

This was but one of four libraries, Anisha had explained, that the Society maintained, and one of two that could be opened to the public. The other two were the small private study that Grace had seen upon her first visit, and the Artifacts Room, which contained rare manuscripts of religious and historical significance, many of them illuminated, and none less than two hundred years old.

They had arrived at the Society shortly after tea and found the library only after having passed by the dining room, the coffee room, the smoking room, and, at the end of one corridor, the ubiquitous card room, with its massive, six-decanter mahogany tantalus open on the sideboard—the Society's members might have been templar knights after a fashion, but not a one of them was a saint, so far as Grace could see. Indeed, Ruthveyn was about as far from sainthood as a man could get—in any number of ways.

Smiling inwardly at the thought, Grace roamed to the windows and looked down at the quiet street below. There, however, her gaze fell upon someone familiar. Near the small portico across the street, a young man lounged upon the pavement, one hand thrust in the pocket of a dull-colored mackintosh, chatting idly with a fellow who appeared to be manning Quartermaine's door.

It was the newspaper reporter, Jack Coldwater. And turning the corner from St. James's Street was Rance. She would have recognized his confident, loose-limbed gait anywhere. Her hand went to the window as if to warn him, but it was an impotent gesture. The glass shimmered coldly between them, and already the hound and the hunted had espied one another.

Coldwater sauntered into the middle of St. James's Place, his ever-present folio shoved under one arm. Grace watched as they exchanged words. The reporter's stance was cocky, his chin up. Rance held himself loosely, unconcerned, then threw back his head and laughed. Coldwater returned with something, and in a flash, Rance had him by the arm and was dragging him toward the steps. Coldwater hadn't a chance.

"Anisha," she said sharply, "where is your brother? Is he here?"

Anisha's eyes widened. "Why, I believe he may be," she said almost teasingly. "Have you some sudden urge to see him?"

"I—yes, actually, I do," said Grace.

"Out the door, and take the left-hand corridor all the way to the end," said Anisha. "His private sitting room will be the last door on your right. If he's not there, stop a servant and ask that he be found."

Scarcely considering the consequences, Grace hurried from the room. She could have told Anisha, but she wasn't sure precisely what, if anything, lay between Anisha and Rance. And what could Anisha do, anyway? No, this business wanted Adrian.

The passageway was empty. At the last door, Grace pecked lightly with the back of her knuckles, a tiny part of her hoping he was not in.

"Come!" he barked.

Grace cracked the door to see a small, comfortably furnished gentleman's sitting room that included a leather sofa and a desk. Adrian stood at the window, his back to the door, a glass of red wine held lightly by the stem. He wore, strangely, a flowing robe of coarse brown wool, the hood thrown back. Clearly, he had expected a servant.

"I beg your pardon," she said awkwardly.

He turned at once, his black eyes sharp as shattered ice. "Grace." The word was low and a little raw. "Grace, what in God's name—?"

"I had to see you."

She shut the door, and came farther into the room. To the left, she could see a set of double doors that were closed, and she knew unerringly they were the doors to his bedchamber.

Adrian set his wine aside, the hem of the robe dragging the carpet as he did so. "Grace, why have you come down here?"

"I came with Anisha," she said. "To use the library. But never mind that. Adrian, I saw that young man—the one who's been hounding Rance?"

"Coldwater." Adrian's eyes flashed again as he closed the distance between them.

"Yes, he was lying in wait across the street," Grace said. "I was looking down from the library windows and saw Rance haul him up the steps. After that, I could not see, but I think he dragged him inside."

"Rance can deal with Coldwater," said Adrian, his gaze running down her length.

Grace felt as if she suddenly stood too near a blazing hearth. "B-But mightn't he simply throttle the lad?" she managed. "Rance can ill afford more trouble with the law—or the newspapers."

Adrian stepped a little nearer. "He knows how to handle a jumped-up jackanapes like Coldwater," he said tightly. "Trust me."

The air in the room seemed suddenly close. Adrian clearly disapproved of her being here. His eyes were grim with a strange mix of temper and thwarted lust—the latter an odd relief to Grace. She had come to help Rance, but he was fast becoming the furthest thing from her mind.

"I . . . yes, you are right, I daresay," she murmured, stepping back a pace. "W-What is that you're wearing?"

He looked down at the open garment as if just now remembering it. "A ceremonial robe," he answered. "To be worn in the chapel."

"You actually have a chapel?" she said, strolling toward the window.

"In the cellars," he said behind her, the words clipped.

Grace feigned nonchalance, but she could hear the pounding of her own heart in her chest. She was oddly reluctant to leave, and yet half-afraid to stay. He seemed more tightly drawn than ever, like the barely held blade of a guillotine just waiting to slice someone's head off.

But eventually, they had to get beyond this impasse, this thing that had driven him from the house—and from her bed.

She spun around to find him nearing. "And this chapel—what do you do there?" she asked, her voice artificially light. "Still no sacrificing of virgins, I hope?"

"We use it for rites and initiations," he said, his face hardening. "Prayer, if we wish."

"But the Reverend Mr. Sutherland was not there," Grace pointed out. "He was with us—Anisha and me. And the coffee room was full of people."

"I was alone," he gritted. "I spend a lot of time alone. Grace, why did you come here? *In here,* I mean. Is this really about Lazonby?"

She swallowed hard. "It was," she managed. "But now . . . I'm not sure. I suppose I would like to know where you've been these last few days."

"In and out," he said quietly. His dark, crystalline gaze moved over her face, then down her throat, spreading heat as it traveled. "Last night I came here. I thought it best."

"Why, Adrian?" Grace lifted her chin. "Are you done with me?"

A bitter smile lifted one corner of his mouth. "You know why," he said, his hand coming up to toy with a strand of her hair. "Because I cannot stay away from you.

Because I'll never be done with you, Grace—not until we've at least a continent between us."

"Then why stay away?" she said a little angrily. "This is nonsense, Adrian. Why waste what little—"

Her back struck the wall before Grace could draw breath. He hitched her up against it, trapping her with his weight. He kissed her almost savagely, his mouth coming down over hers in a way that was raw and visceral. His tongue thrust deep, and Grace could feel a sudden craving for him burning through her like a red-hot shaft.

She gave as good as she got, tangling her tongue with his until Adrian groaned into her mouth. Heat and frustration rolled off his skin in waves, and she drew in his scent as if she were drowning for the want of it. Heedless of who might enter, she kissed him back, twining one arm round his neck as if to draw him fully against her.

With one broad, warm hand cupping her derriere, Adrian lifted her firmly against the ridge of his arousal, urging her hard against him. Lust came alive inside Grace, catching her breath and sending her blood rushing from her brain to places aching and needy.

Madness. *It was madness.*

And yet she let one hand skate beneath the rough wool robe and round the waist of his trousers. When that did not yield, she eased her fingers between them, caressing the weight of him where it strained against the taut fabric of his trousers.

Dear God, she had missed him. Already he was like an addiction. She drew away to plead with him mindlessly, but his mouth skimmed over her temple, his breath hot, his lips feverish.

"I'll never be done with you, Grace," he whispered. "*Never.* You will have to leave me. I only hope you'll have sense enough—"

She kissed him hard, stopping the words.

A long, heated moment later, his mouth again left hers, this time wordlessly, his lips caressing their way down the length of her throat as one hand unfastened a button at the back of her dress. In moments, the front of her gown sagged free. A little roughly, he dragged down her chemise until her breasts were bare where they thrust above the boning of her corset.

Lightly, he circled one nipple with his tongue until it hardened with need, and Grace stabbed her fingers into his hair on a breathless gasp.

"*Your bedchamber,*" she choked. "Please. We'll be quick."

Her opposite hand slid back to the close of his trousers, caressing the hard, heavy length of him, but when her fingers went to his buttons, he stilled her hand.

"*No,*" he rasped. "Not that."

Then his mouth was on her again, sucking and laving her areola until Grace's brain turned to mush. Until she would have done anything he said with scarcely a thought. Until, amidst all the surging heat and rushing blood, she felt cool air breeze up her leg and realized his hand was fisting up her skirts.

Then he knelt, the voluminous robe pooling round their feet, and untied her drawers. When his tongue touched her intimately, the mush in her brain turned to something hot and throbbing. Absent Adrian's wide shoulders, the room swam before her like a dream. Dimly, she realized she stood opposite the door through which she'd entered. *Had he locked it?*

But her fingers were entwined with Adrian's hair, and his tongue—his wicked, wicked tongue—was doing something so wanton and so decadent, Grace could scarce catch her breath.

"The door," she gasped softly. "Is it . . . ?"

"Naughty girl," he murmured, his lips brushing her thigh. "Don't come tempt me if you aren't willing to pay the price."

"The price?" she rasped. "No, I—"

But his tongue stroked deep, Grace lost all coherent thought, and forgot what it was she was so determined not to do. She came apart on a keening sound, splintering into shards of pure, white light as pleasure rolled over her, wave after wave.

She must have slid down the wall, boneless and shattered, for she came back to find herself cradled in Adrian's embrace, his shoulder propped against the wainscoting, his breath rough with need.

"*Mon Dieu!*" she murmured. "That was just . . . *oh.* I haven't the words." Her fingers went to the top button of his trousers, but there was little will in the gesture.

"No," he said, gently lifting her hand away. Then he kissed her cheek and whispered her name like a prayer.

After a long moment, she inhaled raggedly. "I won't do it, you know," she managed.

"Won't do what, my Grace?"

"Should someone burst through that door this minute, Adrian, I still would not marry you," she said quietly. "That's what you meant, wasn't it? But I've no more wish to be wed for that reason than for the other—for that child we are not having."

But Adrian's lips were hovering warmly over her temple, and his fingers were stroking through her silky-wet folds again. "For this, then, love?" he murmured as she shuddered in his embrace. "Would you do it for this?"

"*No.*" She said the word as firmly as a wanton, thoroughly disheveled woman possibly could—especially one whose bodice was half-down, and whose skirts were rucked up to her hips. "No. Not even for that."

"A wise woman," he murmured, tucking his head against her. "You would soon regret it. Besides, why marry the bull when you can get the . . . what is that English saying? About getting milk for free?"

But Grace was looking at him, appalled. "It's *marry the cow,* Adrian," she corrected. "And how dare you, anyway? This isn't about my not wanting you."

"There is a part of me," he said quietly, "that would be happy to hear it was."

"I think you're a liar." Grace managed to sit up from his embrace. "In any case, this is about your living in dread of what you might see or know," she said, yanking down her hems almost violently. "Right now you are intrigued by me because you cannot read me. If you could, I daresay you'd not be half so charmed."

"Grace, that is not—"

"And while you're being charmed," she barged on, "you're waiting for the other shoe to drop. If we were wed, you would wake up every day wondering if that was going to be the day the dreadful window flew up between our minds and made us one in that way we could never wish for. Can you deny it?" She looked at him in hollow triumph.

But Adrian clearly did not mean to gainsay her. Wordlessly, he began to restore her clothing to order

She watched him for a long while, her heart half-breaking. "I will wed you, Adrian," she finally whispered, "if ever you beg me to. When you say you love me and cannot live without me, and when you tell me that we can face down together whatever hardships the future brings. If ever that day comes, yes, I will marry you, and account myself the most fortunate of women. But I will never wed you because we have thrown up our hands and left it to bad luck. Fate may be inevitable, Adrian, but it will not be my master. It *will not*."

Without another word, he urged her round and began to do up her buttons, pausing between each to set his lips to the back of her neck.

And just like that, the longing began to spiral up again. Grace closed her eyes, drew a steadying breath, then shook out her skirts and rose, angry with herself, and with him. Yet she knew on her next breath that should he come to her bed that night, she would welcome him, knew that she would surrender easily to the temptation of that lush mouth. Those dark, glittering eyes and clever hands. Not to mention his—

Ruthlessly, Grace severed that thought and spun around to see Adrian heading toward the double doors. Moments later he returned from the bedroom in shirtsleeves, his cuffs rolled up to reveal his sculpted forearms, the robe gone. He held her gaze watchfully as he rolled the cuffs back down but said nothing.

It seemed such an oddly intimate thing, to be alone with a less-than-fully-dressed gentleman in his sitting room—which was bizarre considering the state of dishabille she'd just been in.

"I still think," she said stubbornly, "you should go find Rance. I have an uneasy feeling."

Engaged in fastening one cuff, Adrian looked up at her from beneath a shock of thick black hair, his eyes heavy-lidded and seductive. "And I still think," he said softly, "that I should show you back to the library and the shelter of my sister's side, where we can both pretend I didn't just finish satisfying you in a way that would raise eyebrows from here to Hampstead Heath had anyone caught us."

"*Adrian—!*"

"Otherwise," he said, speaking over her, "I'm apt to haul you through those doors to my bed and do to you what I so desperately long to do—turn you over my knee, then have *my* way—but that sort of racket would almost certainly be heard downstairs in the coffee room."

Grace felt her knees weaken, and along with it half her resolve. But she managed instead to go to the chair where his clothing lay and hold up his waistcoat for him.

With an acknowledging twist of his mouth, Adrian slipped it on and buttoned it, his every gesture annoyingly calm. On an inward sigh, Grace picked up his coat. But almost at once, the door flew open.

"Your carriage is ready, sir, and Brogden says—" Fricke froze on the threshold. "Oh. I do beg your pardon, sir."

"It's quite all right, Fricke." Adrian shrugged into his coat. "Mademoiselle Gauthier was just conveying a message from Lady Anisha. I am required in the main library. Tell Brogden to wait on the curb."

"Certainly, sir." Fricke stepped inside and held the door open.

Adrian paused long enough to take up his walking stick and hat from the side table

"*Mademoiselle?*" Very formally, he presented his arm.

She took it and went with him down the corridor and back to the library without exchanging another word. At the last instant, however, Grace jerked to a halt and turned to face him. "Come home tonight, Adrian," she said, her voice husky. "Just . . . come home. Come to my bed. Let the rest of it sort out as it will. *Please.*"

He opened his mouth to speak, but at that moment, the library door flew open, and his sister burst out like a whirlwind. Her eyes lit up when she saw him.

"Raju, thank goodness!" she said, sounding exasperated. "I need that book of sketches Curran did for you. The one with the various forms the mark has taken over the years? Mr. Sutherland is trying to date the one in Grace's prayer book."

"In Grace's prayer book?" Adrian's brow furrowed.

Anisha looked at Grace, exasperation deepening. "Good Lord, isn't that what you went to tell him?" she said. "Oh, never mind!" She returned her gaze to her brother. "Adrian, that sketchbook—can you find it?"

"Downstairs in the private study," he said. "I'm late for a meeting at Number Four. Come quickly, and I shall get it for you."

"Thank you," said Anisha. "Grace, Mr. Sutherland wishes to show you some names to see if any ring a bell."

Ruthveyn went down the steps, his sister on his arm, resisting the urge to look back over his shoulder at Grace. He could still feel the heat of her gaze boring into him. Even to himself, he could not quite explain why he was so frustrated. Perhaps because she was making it difficult to keep the distance between them. That glass wall he so desperately needed between himself and the rest of the world seemed to fall so easily before her.

And those last words!—That husky, come-take-me voice, and the way her gaze caught on his mouth—it sent shivers of unslaked desire down his spine. The truth was, he was in love with Grace Gauthier—completely, hopelessly in love—and had been almost from the day they'd met. But worse than the love was the aching need. Not the physical lust, or even the head-over-heels yearning of a new romance, but the deep and abiding cry of one soul for another, as if their roots had already entwined inexorably, like a couple wed twenty years rather than lovers for less than a fortnight. And still he did not understand how he had fallen so fast and so hard.

Beside him, however, his sister was all but vibrating with suppressed emotion. He flicked a quick look down at her. "Anisha, what is going on?" he asked quietly.

His sister cast an assessing look at him. "This moment?" she asked. "I'm wondering what you and Grace have been up to."

"Anisha, you will kindly answer my question," he said in a tone that brooked no opposition.

His sister sighed. "Very well. Grace found an old prayer book in her father's army trunk," she said, hastening her pace to his. "It dates from the seventeenth century, and it has a copy of the mark of the Guardians on the frontispiece."

He stopped on the landing and turned to face her. "*What?*"

"Raju," Anisha said quietly, "Grace is not an Unknowable."

He searched her face, trying to make sense of her words. "I hope to God you are wrong."

"No, you don't understand," Anisha whispered. "She is not an Unknowable because . . . well, because I think she's one of the Vateis."

Ruthveyn went utterly still inside. Then, "You must be mad," he said.

Anisha shook her head so hard her earbobs jangled. "I do not think so," she went on. "She has commented to both you and to me that the mark looked familiar. Well, we found one. In her father's trunk, Raju. Inside a prayer book that belonged to her ancestor. Guess what sort of name he had?"

"I . . . obviously have no notion."

"A Scots name," said Anisha. "Sir Angus . . . something. And while she was out—doing whatever it was the two of you were doing—Mr. Sutherland found his name referenced in one of the ancient manuscripts regarding initiation ceremonies. I tell you, Raju, this is the truth. She is of the Vateis. I feel this strongly. Remember, I have seen her palm."

"But Anisha . . . this would mean—"

"Yes," said his sister meaningfully. "It would."

Ruthveyn shook his head, wishing something would clear the cobwebs from his brain. This was too much and warranted a great deal of thought—not to mention a long conversation with Grace. "I can't think about this just now," he said, almost to himself.

"What do you mean?" said his sister indignantly. "What could be more important?"

He hitched her by the arm and set off down the stairs again, keeping his voice low. "Napier sent a missive an hour past," he said, scarcely aware he was all but dragging Anisha. "There's been bad news."

"Of what sort?"

"The Home Secretary is under fire," said Ruthveyn. "Holding's wealthy neighbors have met with him to demand the Metropolitan Police do something—they seem not to care what. So Sir George has decided that arresting Grace will be the surest way to convince them they do not have a murderous cracksman running amok in Belgravia—a crime of passion, he means to play it."

"But that's absurd!" she hissed. "They haven't enough evidence."

"I don't think Sir George is worried about a conviction so much as a speedy trial for Grace, followed by the first mail packet to Paris," said Ruthveyn quietly. "Just something to hush up the well-heeled populace. But good God, Anisha, a trial? Imprisonment? Even temporarily, it doesn't bear thinking of. No. I won't have Grace subjected to such horrors."

Anisha shot him a dubious, sidelong glance as they turned down the corridor. "And Napier is warning you about this arrest?"

"Oh, not out of altruism," said Ruthveyn grimly "The man just cannot abide the thought of a trial without a conviction. But I think, too, that a part of him is beginning to believe me when I say Grace is innocent."

"And you believe that matters to him?" Anisha snorted. "It did not matter with Rance."

"In this case, it seems to," said Ruthveyn tightly. "He has written to warn me, and to tell me that if I have means at my disposal to override Sir George Grey, now is the time to do it."

"He wants you to ask the Queen to intervene."

"I think he may," said Ruthveyn.

"And will you?"

"If I must, yes," said Ruthveyn swiftly. "But she is at Balmoral just now, which will slow matters a bit. Besides, even the mere suspicion of a crime will haunt Grace all of her days. What I should rather do is offer up a better suspect to Sir George."

"What do you mean to do?"

"Geoff can sometimes elicit information from inanimate objects," said Ruthveyn, thinking aloud. "There are two letters—well, a note and a letter—almost certainly forged by the killer's hand."

"But Lord Bessett is in Yorkshire," Anisha protested. "And Napier isn't going to release Crown evidence to you."

"No, but we could go—" Ruthveyn paused, suddenly aware of angry voices echoing farther along the passageway. "What the devil?"

Apprehension sketched over Anisha's face. "That's Rance's voice," she said, picking up her skirts to run. "He sounds murderous."

It was then that Ruthveyn remembered Grace's warning. "Hell and damnation," he muttered, setting off after his sister.

Outside the study door, the tirade rose to a crescendo, though the words were unintelligible through the slab of oak. Seizing hold of the doorknob, Ruthveyn reluctantly weighed his choices. Good God, didn't he have trouble enough without Rance adding to it?

"Mamma always said it was rude to listen at doors," Anisha urged. "So open it."

Just then there was a heavy thud, a thump, followed by the crashing of porcelain.

On a muttered oath, Ruthveyn pushed open the door.

He wished at once he had not.

Beside him, Anisha gasped, both hands going to her mouth.

Lazonby had Jack Coldwater wedged against the back of the sofa, caught in what looked like a passionate embrace, one booted leg thrust between his quarry's legs. A porcelain bust of Aristotle lay in pieces, the marble pedestal overturned.

Ruthveyn closed the door as swiftly as he'd opened it. But there was no blocking out the image.

"*Oh, God.*" His sister's voice was a tremulous whisper.

Ruthveyn caught her arm again, more gently. "Come, Nish," he said. "This is none of our concern."

But a few feet along the corridor, Anisha balked. "Raju," she whispered, jerking to a halt. "It looked as if—do you think Rance was—"

"Damn it, I don't know," he bit out.

Behind them, a door flew open, crashing inward. In an instant, Jack Coldwater pushed past, then dashed down the stairs into the reception foyer as if the hounds of hell were at his heels.

Ruthveyn turned back to his sister and softened his tone. "I don't think either of them saw us," he said. "Anisha, I think we must tell ourselves that it wasn't quite what it looked like."

But his sister's eyes were still wide as saucers, her skin deathly pale. "W-What do you think it looked like?" she asked, her voice tremulous. "Tell me, Raju."

Ruthveyn shut his eyes and cursed beneath his breath. Anisha was not naïve. Despite his words to her, there was no mistaking such a compromising position. *Was there?*

Oh, Lazonby had not been precisely kissing the young man. Lust and rage had been thick in the air. But Lazonby, of all people?

It made no sense. Oh, he was as dissolute as they came, certainly, and Ruthveyn little better. They had both of them done things in the heat of lust and intoxicants that they'd as soon as not be reminded of in the harsh light of day. But this—stone-cold sober, and in a moderately respectable house—went beyond the pale.

"I'm going to talk to him," he said abruptly, releasing Anisha's arm. "I want you to go back upstairs to Grace. Tell her you wish to go home. All right?"

Anisha was staring at the floor.

"All right, Nish?" He tipped up her chin with one finger.

"Yes." She managed a smile. "All right."

He kissed her lightly on the forehead. "I'll take the book up to Sutherland," he said. "Now go, before Lazonby comes out."

Anisha nodded and dashed up the steps. Ruthveyn watched her go, his emotions torn. Grace was still in the forefront of his mind. Grace, and the implications of Anisha's strange story about the prayer book. How unfair it seemed that he might harbor some faint hope of having all he'd ever dreamt of, while his sister had just had her dreams dashed to pieces.

Oh, never would he have permitted Anisha to marry Lazonby. But he had hoped her infatuation might die a natural death. This was not natural. Indeed, some would say it was most *unnatural*—not to mention depraved. Ruthveyn wouldn't have gone that far, but he meant to have some hard words with Lazonby.

The door to the private library still stood open. Lazonby had gone to the windows and was looking down at the street, his arms ramrod stiff, his hands fisted. Even without the Gift, Ruthveyn could have felt the rage inside the room.

"Well," he said, softly closing the door. "Sometimes, old friend, you can still surprise me."

Lazonby turned from the window, his color draining. "I beg your pardon?"

Ruthveyn made a vague gesture toward the sofa, and the broken bust. "It's not my place to judge a man's taste in such matters," he said. "But you should know that when I cracked the door three minutes ago, Anisha was with me. Next time, for God's sake, lock it."

As Lazonby gaped at him, guilt struck Ruthveyn hard. Not a quarter hour past, he, too, had been fool enough to leave a door unlocked and a reputation at risk—not that he hadn't had a solution in mind, or perhaps even harbored an unconscious wish to *be* caught. But Grace was right; a man ought never leave such decisions to chance. He ought never risk hurting—or ruining—another.

"You . . . saw?" Lazonby finally rasped.

"I fear so," he said quietly.

Lazonby's face reddened furiously. "Damn it, it's not what it looked like."

"Then what was it?"

"It's none of your damned business what it was."

Ruthveyn strolled farther into the room, his hands clasped behind his back as he resisted the urge to plant Lazonby a facer. "Quite so. It is not," he finally said. "But I have my sister's tender feelings to worry about. She fancies herself half in love with you, you know."

"Anisha?" Lazonby looked at him incredulously. "Surely you jest?"

"Surely," said Ruthveyn quietly, "I do not."

This seemed to pain Lazonby. "I'm more than fond of your sister, Adrian," he said, wincing, "but she . . . well, she's not quite my type."

So it would appear, thought Ruthveyn. But what he said was, "Just have a care for your reputation, my friend—and a care for the good name of this Society, and the important work we must do. Beyond that, regardless of what you do in private, you *are* my friend."

"B-But it wasn't . . . it wasn't anything," Lazonby protested.

Ruthveyn cocked one eyebrow. "Oh, it most assuredly was something," he replied. "And I think you need to decide *what*—then get a choke hold on it. I'll stand by you, Rance. You should know that by now."

Lazonby drew an unsteady breath, then dragged a hand down his face as if he might wipe away the last few minutes. "I do know it," he said. "If ever there was a man who came handy in a hard spot, Adrian, it's you. The little bastard just rattled me, that's all. He just won't quit. He just *won't*. And I'm so bloody sick of having my past dragged through the papers. Tired of the questions. The innuendoes. Tired of him being in my face, so goddamned holier than thou. So this time I . . . I just snapped, I guess. I just wanted to teach him a lesson."

"But what you have done," said Ruthveyn quietly, "is given him grist for his mill. *If* he chooses to grind it."

"Christ, Adrian." Lazonby's voice was hoarse. "What am I to do? I . . . I'm not like that. I'm not."

"The longer I live," said Ruthveyn, "the more I think that we are none of us entirely one way or another—not all of the time, and not in every circumstance."

But Lazonby seemed not to hear him. He had paced back to the window and was staring down at Quarter-maine's club again, hands braced wide on the frame, as if he restrained himself from jumping.

Ruthveyn wished—suddenly and acutely—that he had listened to Grace. She had sensed something was amiss.

"*You should go find Rance,*" she had said. "*I have a bad feeling.*"

Oh, one Vates could not read another, it was true. But all of them had a certain intuition, could draw in un-leashed emotion as easily as others drew in air. Was it possible Anisha's theory was right?

Lazonby fisted one hand and pounded it upon the window frame. "How the devil did I let matters get so out of hand?" he whispered. "I mean—oh, hell, I don't know what I mean! Just tell me—what am I to do if Coldwater suggests . . . suggests that I . . ."

Ruthveyn followed and placed a hand between Lazon-by's shoulder blades. "I do not think he will," he said quietly. "He looked as shaken as you. No, I think he will keep silent."

"But if he doesn't?" Lazonby demanded. "What then?"

"Then I was there," said Ruthveyn. "Standing in the doorway the whole time. And my sister was *not.*"

Lazonby turned around. "You mean you'd lie."

"I mean I would do what was necessary to protect someone I care for," said Ruthveyn calmly. "And to protect the *Fraternitas*. We have work to do here, Rance, that outweighs both of us—and all our petty little lives, should it come to it."

But Lazonby merely turned back around, his gaze focused out the window again.

"Look, I'm keeping Brogden waiting at the curb," said Ruthveyn, patting him on the back again. "He's become testy about such things. Shall I see you across the way for dinner?"

Lazonby sighed, and at last let his shoulders relax. "Going somewhere in a rush, are you?"

"Yes, to Number Four," he said. "Scotland Yard is on the verge of having Grace arrested."

CHAPTER 15

The Rogue's Return

*H*e went to her that night. He went because she
had asked. And because he longed to lie with
her—not just to make love to her, but simply to exist in
the same sphere as she, and to draw the same breath into
his lungs. To rest his head on her shoulder and seek solace
in the warmth of her gaze.

Just a few weeks earlier, the depth of his need for Grace
would have given him pause. But as his sister often reminded him, the *Upanishads*—the ancient Vedantic
scriptures—taught that the fate of a man's soul was written, and to struggle against it was in vain. He wished now
he had actually studied them, for he felt as if he had surrendered his soul to Grace, and in this act he had begun
to feel peace.

All his fears, and all his sister's far-flung theories about Grace and the Gift, were rapidly ceasing to matter. He knew only that fate was taking him on a journey—just as Anisha had predicted weeks ago—and that he had yielded to it.

He slipped into her room just after midnight, without knocking, certain in the knowledge that Grace would know it was he. She rolled up onto one elbow, drowsily dragging the heavy blond hair from her eyes.

"Adrian," she whispered, her voice flowing over him like warm honey.

He let his silk robe slip to the floor and made love to her wordlessly and slowly, telling her with his body and his sighs that what he felt for her would never end. And when at last she lay sated beneath him, he drew her fast to his side and buried his face against her throat, his lips set to the tiny heartbeat beneath her ear. He hadn't even bothered to withdraw but had filled her with his seed exultantly, and perhaps with a measure of hope.

"I have to go away tomorrow, Grace," he finally said, whispering the words against her skin.

She stiffened in his embrace. "For how long?"

"Three days." He brushed his lips over the turn of her jaw. "And when I come back, we need to have a long talk, you and I."

"Hmm," she said. Even in the gloom, he could feel her gaze roaming over him. "Can I ask where you go?"

Inwardly, he sighed. He really did not want to distress her with Napier's fears. "To Yorkshire," he said. "To Lord Bessett's country estate. We have some unfinished business."

"*Fraternitas* business?"

"Yes, of a sort."

She rolled onto her back and made an exasperated sound. "Why is it, Adrian, that I suspect you're being faintly disingenuous again?"

He dragged an arm over his eyes and considered his words. "Because I am," he finally said. "And because Anisha is right—you're too perceptive by half. But Grace, do you still trust me?"

"Yes." As always, her answer was swift.

"Then may we leave it at that for now?" he asked gently. "Will you just simply put your faith in me and trust that I'm doing what is right?"

She acquiesced with surprising ease, rolling back against him and curling one leg over his. "Done," she murmured, kissing him lightly on the temple. "There, you see? I actually do trust you. But something else is troubling you, isn't it? Something besides us, I mean."

He gave a harsh laugh. "Aye, too perceptive by half," he said again. "I wish, Grace, I had listened to you this afternoon. About Rance, I mean."

"There was trouble, wasn't there?"

"I—" His words broke off, and he felt frustration sketch across his face. "I saw Rance with Coldwater. In a compromising position."

"I don't understand," Grace murmured.

He let his head fall fully back against the pillow. "I saw Rance almost kissing Jack Coldwater—or that's what it looked like."

"*Ça alors!*" Grace sat up straight in bed. "Surely you were mistaken."

Again, he shook his head, his hair scrubbing the pillow. "I hope so," he whispered. "But *something* was going on."

"But not that, surely," she muttered.

"Afterward, Coldwater bolted like a startled hare," he

went on. "But I had Anisha with me and had to drag her away."

Grace seemed to ponder it for a moment. "Long years in the legion sometimes do strange things to men," she finally whispered. "It is a hard life. But *Rance*? He was the worst sort of womanizer imaginable. Now I see why Anisha wanted to leave in such a rush."

"I was struck sideways by it, I can tell you," said Adrian. "I have lived like a brother with the man, and never knew that he . . . well, that he could feel . . . oh, hell, I don't know."

Grace rolled over him and laid her bare breasts against his chest, settling her cheek on his shoulder. "I hear a hesitation in your voice."

"No, not . . . a hesitation."

But the truth was, he *had* occasionally wondered at Lazonby's attachment to Belkadi. Belkadi and his sister Safiyah had spent their youth as ragtag camp orphans, as best Ruthveyn could gather, and Belkadi had ended up a sort of batman to Lazonby. After his capture, Lazonby had given strict instructions they be brought out of Algeria, and Ruthveyn had done it. Not that Belkadi felt an ounce of gratitude, mind. It was all very odd.

"What are you thinking?" Grace murmured, tucking a lock of hair behind his ear.

He rolled with her to one side. "That I wish I wasn't leaving you," he answered, his eyes searching her face. "Grace, do you think it's possible? Is there any chance? This mad notion of Anisha's, I mean?"

She knew at once what he meant. "I didn't at first," she confessed. "But I do believe I'm descended from Sir Angus Muirhead, and that he went to France and nearly died in a bridge collapse. It would certainly appear he had an association with the *Fraternitas Aureae Crucis.*"

"Sutherland is convinced," Ruthveyn replied.

Grace sighed and flopped onto her back to stare up at the ceiling. "But do I believe I have some sort of gift?" she went on. "No. I am what I've always been."

Propped on one elbow, Ruthveyn laid the flat of his hand against the faint swell of her belly. "Grace," he said, "I put my seed in you tonight. And I did it . . . I did it half-hoping. Because I love you, Grace, and I think we—"

"Stop," she said gently, covering his hand with her smaller, warmer one. "Just . . . stop, Adrian. You *want* to love me, perhaps. But right now, it's just possible you're in love with hope, and nothing more."

"Damn it, Grace, don't tell me—"

"No, let me speak," she gently insisted. "Right now, Adrian, you hope I am—oh, I don't know—one of the Vaties, I suppose? It sounds mad even to say it. I'm just *not.* And what you feel is predicated on my being something I'm not. That is my fear. Can't you see how I might think that?"

Ruthveyn cupped his hand round her face, holding her gaze to his. "I love you, Grace," he said firmly. "Don't tell me what I feel. I love you. I need you, and sometimes I ache for you so badly I feel as if my heart will be torn from my chest if I lose you. *That* is my fear, Grace. So don't tell me what I feel. Tell me you love me. Tell me you'll marry me."

"You cannot be serious," she whispered. "Not now."

"Very serious," he rasped. "I have never been more serious."

When she shifted her gaze away, he turned her face back to his. "All right," he continued, his voice softer still. "Tell me *you* don't love *me.* Look me in the eyes, Grace, and say it."

In the gloom, she made the faintest little sound. A sort of mewling, as if she might burst into tears. "Of course I love you," she said on half a sob.

He felt instantly like a cad. "Oh, Grace," he whispered, gathering her to him. "Oh, Grace, don't. I'm sorry. Just . . . don't."

"Of *course* I love you," she said again. "But I don't want you to want me just because you think you can't read me, or because you think I might be carrying your child. I meant what I said today, Adrian. Love that is love only when things are right and easy, and everything tumbles into place is just not enough for me. And when you think on it, you'll know it isn't enough for you, either."

"So you think I've decided I love you merely because of my sister's wild theory," he said.

"I think that a few hours ago you were dreading our future," she whispered. "You wouldn't even bed me properly—and I begged you."

"Grace, in the club?" he choked. "I was expecting Fricke, for God's sake. He practically walked in on us as it was. And I told you then that I would never leave you."

"And that you hoped I had sense enough to leave you," she finished.

He cursed under his breath—and using a word no gentleman used in a lady's presence, let alone in her bed.

A long moment of silence followed as they lay together, the weight of his body over hers, her arm wrapped round his waist. She was partly right, he realized. He had let Anisha's wild notions propel him toward something that, though inevitable so far as he was concerned, had not been well thought out.

Oh, he loved Grace—and he was determined to marry her. He needed to spend whatever days fate allotted him by her side, even if those days were no more than a fortnight, and even if he knew them numbered to the very hour. For even a fleeting moment in her presence brought him a joy and a peace he had never imagined possible, and a moment without her was . . . well, not worth living, perhaps.

Eventually, he would convince her of all this. But it was, perhaps, unreasonable to expect her to suddenly fall into raptures just now.

"Very well," he said softly. "Have it your way, Grace. Just . . . stay with me. Don't give up. Don't run back to France. Give me time to convince you of the rightness of *us*."

She turned her face into his and kissed him. "Make love to me again," she whispered. "Slowly, as we did once before. Share my breath and my soul, Adrian, with our bodies joined as one. And just for a few hours, live only in the present. With me. Don't think about the future."

And as he stared, losing himself in the deep blue infinity of her gaze, Adrian decided it was the best suggestion he'd heard in days.

Grace awoke the following morning to a house that felt empty and soulless. Adrian had left her bed before dawn—and left her frightfully short of sleep after two hours of his slow, exquisitely torturous lovemaking. He had kissed her hard, then whispered something about the first train out of Euston Station. Already she felt his absence like an ache in her bones.

Throwing back the drapes, she saw that the haze of fog and smoke had lifted to reveal the remnants of a fine drizzle running down the windows, the cobbles beyond yellow and glassy in the muted gaslight. A milk cart rumbled past in the gloom, the driver hunched forward, his hat brim sagging.

Oddly restive, Grace breakfasted alone, the food like ashes in her mouth, then spent the following two hours drilling multiplication tables into Teddy while his brother tried to set his trouser hems on fire and Milo flapped and squawked, "*Help, help! British prisoner!*"

"I think I'm the British prisoner," Teddy finally declared, shoving his slate away. "This stuff's worse than the Black Hole of Calcutta."

Grace sighed. "Over a hundred of England's bravest were suffocated in the Black Hole," she reminded him.

"Well, the old *nawab* should have made 'em do multiplications," he returned, "and the rest would have died of boredom."

Perched on the punishment stool in the corner, Tom turned round. "Can I get down?" he asked hopefully. "I think I've learnt my lesson now."

"Yes," Grace snapped. "Get down and go ask Higgenthorpe if the maids have finished cleaning the conservatory. Milo must go back, else Cook will be serving parakeet for dinner."

"*Awwkk!*" Milo protested, flapping his wings. "*Pretty-pretty! Pretty-pretty!*"

"It's far too late for flattery, old boy," said Grace grimly.

"What, ho!" said a silky voice from the doorway. "Sounds as if I'm just in the nick!"

Grace turned to see Lord Lucan saunter into the room. "*Alors,* one rascal after another," she said with a muted smile. "Here to defend poor Milo, are you?"

"No, no, to recommend a madeira sauce," said Lord Lucan. "Or a velouté, perhaps, and a chilled Viognier, if you mean to sauté him?"

"Aww, she ain't really going to eat him, Uncle Luc," said Tom. "She's just worn to a frizzle because Teddy don't know times-nine from times-eight, and because I struck a match to his trouser leg."

"*Isn't, doesn't,* and I believe I said I was worn to a *frazzle,*" Grace corrected.

"Frizzle, frazzle," said Lord Lucan, beaming a mouthful of white teeth at Grace. "My dear girl, you're going to crease that lovely brow. Look, the sun has finally peeped out. What say I grab a cricket bat and take the lads to the park to burn off a little mischief?"

Grace tossed a knowing look at the young man. "And would that be your sort of mischief, Lord Lucan," she asked sotto voce, "or theirs?"

The teeth shone brighter, if such a thing were possible. "Oh, just theirs, ma'am," he replied. "My sort is resilient—and shameless."

"Just the word I was thinking of." Grace snapped shut Teddy's arithmetic primer. "Thank you, nonetheless. I accept your kind offer, and will debit your sister's account accordingly."

"Ah, there it is again!" Lucan's smile broadened as she rose. "The razor's edge of a most tempting tongue."

"Better than a fork, I daresay," murmured Grace, shoving the primer back onto the shelf.

"Aye, but with either implement, ma'am, you are going to keep some poor devil on the straight and narrow." Lord Lucan snatched the bat and ball from its basket by the door. "Come, lads! Fetch your coats."

"Hurrah!" said the boys, bounding from the room.

Just her side of the threshold, however, Lord Lucan hesitated. "But just so I'm clear, Miss Gauthier—are you quite, *quite* settled on my elder?" He dangled the bat gracefully from two fingers. "I mean, prophets can be so portentous and gloomy, don't you think? And then there is that whole Vedantic philosophy thing—dashed hard to get your noggin round *that* business, I always say. And some women, let's face it, just prefer the golden Greek god look to dark and myst—"

"*Lord Lucan.*" Grace thrust out a hand. "Give me the bat."

His brows shot aloft. "Thank you, no. I've seen your swing." He beamed one last wolfish smile. "Anyway, looks like the better man won. Usual thing, eh? Mustn't keep the lads waiting!" Hastily, he turned, and slammed at once into his sister.

"What was he up to?" Lady Anisha cut a suspicious glance over her shoulder as her brother hastened away.

"Just taking the boys to the park," said Grace evenly. "How do you do this morning?"

Anisha sighed and fell into one of the chairs. "Well, I had hoped to see my children," she complained, propping one elbow on the worktable. "It seems to me Luc has taken to indentured servitude a little too cheerfully, and now the boys would rather play ball than be read to."

"Don't despair," said Grace, sitting down opposite her. "Luc's heart is good—if not pure—and the children are of an age when boys long for a fatherly influence."

"Now there's a frightening bit of syntax," she said. "The words *Luc* and *fatherly* in the same sentence. By the way, where did Raju hare off to at the crack of dawn?"

Grace lifted both brows. "*I* should know?"

"Yes," Anisha returned. "And you do."

It was Grace's turn to sigh. Were there no secrets? Not, apparently, in a houseful of psychics. Then why didn't Anisha know the answer to her own question?

"To Lord Bessett's," she finally said.

"All the way to *Yorkshire*?"

"So I gather," said Grace. "He left from Euston Station."

"Do trains go to Yorkshire?" Anisha's dark brows snapped together. "I don't even know where it is."

"North, I think?" Grace suggested. "My French governess believed the geography of England a waste."

"Did she indeed?"

"Oh, yes. She lived secure in the belief that one day the French would triumph and simply rename all the towns and counties, so there was no point troubling to learn them."

"Ah, the hazards of a foreign education!" said Anisha, grinning. "We've doubtless learnt all manner of heresy, you and I."

Then at once they burst into peels of laughter, but the laughter fell away, leaving only a heavy silence.

"Seriously," said Grace. "Are you all right?"

Anisha cut her an odd look from beneath a fringe of inky lashes. "Raju told you?"

Grace looked away. "Anisha, I am sorry," she said. "You harbored a certain fondness for him, did you not?"

She gave a sharp, bitter laugh. "And you think you don't have the sight."

Grace reached out and covered Anisha's hand with her own. "Rance Welham is a *good* man," she said fervently. "A good man and a brave soldier, and whatever else he may be is quite beside the point. But that does you no good at all, I know."

Anisha shrugged and sat up straight on a sigh. "Oh, I'm over it, I daresay," she said evenly. "But it would have been . . . pleasurable, perhaps. And it would have driven Raju wild."

"You . . . aren't in love with Rance?"

Anisha lifted one slender shoulder. "Oh, not hopelessly," she admitted. "A little taken, perhaps. All right, a great deal taken. But what woman wouldn't be?—No, wait. Don't answer that. *Not you*, that's who—but only because fate has been saving you for my brother."

"Anisha—!" Grace said warningly.

Anisha broke her gaze and leapt up to ring the bell. "I fancy a cup of tea," she said abruptly. "And while we wait, I shall finish your palm."

"And my stars?" Grace asked teasingly.

"I can tell you a little, perhaps," said Anisha. "But I have not completed my charts."

A footman came in, and went out again to do Anisha's bidding. Anisha sat back down, extended her hand across the narrow table, and waggled her fingers at Grace.

With a bemused smile, Grace thrust out her hand, palm up. Anisha swept her fingers down it, as if clearing away cobwebs, then began to work her way around the palm, rubbing her finger lightly over the bumps and swells of flesh, her brow creased.

"These are your mounds," she finally said. "Each tells us something different."

"My future, do you mean?"

Anisha cast up a scowl. "*Jyotish* and Vedic palmistry are sciences," she said with mock censure. "Not tent tricks at a country fair. They can help you understand your true nature, and your tendencies—both good and bad—and teach you to manage your life with grace."

I have a tendency, thought Grace, *to fall in love with dark, incomprehensible men.*

Could Anisha help her cope with that, she wondered?

But Anisha was tapping the tip of her finger lower on

the hand now. "This is Saturn." Her voice had taken on a soothing, almost singsong quality. "Saturn tells me that you possess good judgment. That you are a woman of judicious restraint in most things."

"Am I?" Grace laughed. "Well, that is a comfort, I daresay."

"This," said Anisha pensively, "now *this* is your Sun line. It is . . . merely average."

"Oh," said Grace. "What does that symbolize?"

"It is . . . what is the word? Something more than charm. Your *magnetism*. How you draw people into your orbit. Adrian's is much the same, though he can charm when he wishes—which is almost never. And you . . . well, you have a quiet grace, not a magnetism. You are well named, which is a good omen. Now Rance's Sun line—oh, it is like a deep groove cleaving apart his hand."

Grace laughed again. "Why am I not surprised?"

But Anisha's face had taken on a serious cast. "Your head line tells me you are an optimistic person, and that you know yourself to be capable. All things I would agree with, by the way. And I see here that you have clear thinking. Whatever fears you possess, they are rational. You must never dismiss them outright. I beg you will remember this."

"Oh, dear," said Grace. "That sounds dire."

Anisha did not answer but instead set her hand flat over Grace's, her fingertips touching Grace's pulse point. "Grace, you are a woman of strong emotion and energy," said Anisha quietly. "Now tell me, what specifically would you wish to know?"

"What *I* would wish?" she murmured. "Why, just the usual, I daresay."

"*Jyotish* and the hand together tell us many things," said Anisha. "Who we are, and who we will be. Who we will love. How we will live, and how we will die. All these things are written. *Karma* is the summation of our words, thoughts, and deeds. One reaps what one sows, either in this life, or the next. *Prarabdha* is the karma in this life, and *sanchita* is past—"

"But I know my past."

"Sometimes, my dear, we *know* the past, but we do not *see* the past." Anisha's lilting, musical voice had dropped to a near whisper. "Moreover, *sanchita karma* is the accumulation of all your actions through all your past lives, not just this one. Now, shall I tell you what I see? And be certain when you answer."

"*Mon Dieu.*" Grace swallowed hard. "Anisha, are you *trying* to alarm me?"

"Only ignorance is alarming," she replied.

Grace felt suddenly foolish. "Yes, go ahead."

"Very well." Anisha flashed a muted smile. "Now, I see that the death of Mr. Holding has brought you much sadness. And guilt. Yes, you feel in some way to blame for his death."

"Do I?" Grace's unease returned.

"Yes, I feel it strongly," she murmured, and Grace had the oddest impression they weren't really talking about palms or stars any longer. "In your unconscious mind," Anisha continued, "you feel that but for you, or your actions, this death might not have occurred."

A heavy warmth was seeping up her arm now, bringing with it a strange and certain clarity. She *did* feel guilty. All along she had blamed herself. But why?

"Grace," said Anisha sharply, "what does number thirty-five mean to you?"

"N-Nothing, why?"

Anisha gave a little shake of her head, her eyes still closed. "I cannot say," she answered. "It is a bad number for you. You must avoid it at all costs."

"Avoid it?" Grace was beginning to feel oddly lethargic, much as she had the first time Adrian touched her. "As in . . . roulette, for example? Or some sort of cards? I never gamble."

Anisha sighed. "I cannot say," she said again, sounding frustrated. "And the sign of the swan?"

"The swan?" Grace frowned, and tried to think. "Like a public house?"

"Perhaps." Anisha's inky eyebrows were almost drawn together now. "Were you born there? Have you ever stayed in such a place? Sailed on a ship so named, perhaps?"

"Non," said Grace slowly. "And you know, I was born in London—Manchester Square, to be precise."

"Yes, it must be nothing." Anisha sounded suddenly awkward. "Very strange. Let us turn to your present and future, and to your propensity for love, health, and happiness."

"Why not?" Those sounded far more pleasant, and her arm was growing wonderfully warm and heavy.

"Grace, you are ruled by the plant Mercury," Anisha said. "You are *Mithuna,* the pairing of male and female. Your match with *Mesha* will bring you many challenges and difficulties."

"Who would have dreamt?" said Grace dryly.

Without opening her eyes, Anisha smiled. "You will bring *Mesha* into the light with your energy, but you must not push too hard or he will . . . what is the term?—buck up? Yes. But you can temper his stubbornness and give to him much joy if you are careful. You will help *Mesha* find his direction and reenergize his wish to learn and grow."

"But what does that mean?"

"Specifically? That Raju has much to learn about himself." Her voice took on a lulling, decidedly singsong quality. "He has shut away the half of him that is spiritual and truth-seeking."

"His *Rajputra* half, you mean?"

"We hold no claim over spirituality," she answered. "But yes, perhaps. His life force—his *prana*—has suffered because he has not nurtured this half of his soul. This neglect, in turn, is the cause of much inner pain."

"*Oui.*" Grace murmured, giving in to the relaxation. And Anisha's explanation actually did make sense, at least in her lethargic state.

Anisha's words continued to flow around her. "And I warn you, Grace, that though you are very attracted to *Mesha*," she went on, "a fire sign can burn badly. Be serious in this relationship or back away. If you choose, however, to go down this path, *Mesha* will wish to lead the way, and you must let him—or let him think you do."

Grace laughed, but even to her own ears, the sound seemed far away. "*Alors,* is that my future?"

"In part." Anisha's voice was low and fraught with frustration. "But there is something else. What, though? What is it . . ."

"What do you mean, something else?" Grace murmured drowsily.

"Something frustrating. Just beyond my reach. Like a sneeze that will not come."

For a time, Anisha said no more, but merely began to breathe deeply, in that way Adrian sometimes did when they made love with slow, exquisite lassitude. The pressure of her hand against Grace's seemed unrelenting. Grace still felt as if she were held in thrall in some way she could not quite give words to.

"Damn it all," Anisha finally uttered, most uncharacteristically. "Grace, give me your other hand."

Grace opened her eyes and did so. Anisha held both her hands across the table, her head slightly bowed, no longer even pretending to look at Grace's palm. She held the position quietly, and for so long Grace wondered vaguely if Anisha had fallen asleep.

But after a few quiet moments had passed, the strange lethargy began to drain from Grace, the heat flowing down her left arm, like a river of cleansing warmth flushing all the way through her, only to return to the mother sea.

When the warmth was gone, Anisha lifted her chin, opened her eyes, and spoke. "Someone, Grace, bears you much ill will," she said, her voice clear as a bell and no longer rhythmic. "You are the tool of another's vengeance."

"*Mon Dieu!*" Grace's breath seized an instant. "Someone does want me blamed for Mr. Holding's death."

"It feels likely," she said. "It is what Raju has long believed."

"I think it is why he has gone to Yorkshire." Grace's voice went up sharply. "But Anisha, who could hate me that much?"

Anisha shook her head. "This is about envy," she said. "Not hate."

"But I have nothing *to* envy," she stridently protested. "Nothing. Not unless . . . Mr. Holding had a scorned lover?"

Again, the shake of the head. "I think the envy is not directed at you, but at others," she said. "I feel, as I said, that you are a tool of vengeance. Sometimes animals symbolize emotions. I think that is what the swan means. Tell me, Grace—think very hard—what does the swan mean to you?"

"The swan again?" Grace felt her eyes widen with

horror. "Anisha, th-this doesn't have anything to do with *jyotish* now, does it?"

"Never mind that," said Anisha impatiently. "The swan, Grace. What might it mean?"

"It means nothing, Anisha, I swear it! They are big, white birds with nasty tempers. I know nothing else about them."

"The evil manifests itself in the sign of the swan, and in the number thirty-five." Anisha frowned intently. "These are very bad omens, and much associated with the enmity directed toward you, Grace. I beg you will give it careful thought."

Then Anisha released her hands, her mind still obviously turned inward. Grace blinked and straightened up in her chair. To her shock, a galleried silver tray sat at her elbow, the teapot and service laid out upon it.

On impulse, she touched the pot. It was merely warm. Good Lord.

She looked at Anisha, who appeared wan and pale. "You look tired," she said. "Shall I pour?"

Anisha bestirred herself to glance at the pot. "Oh. Yes, thank you."

"Anisha," she said as she tipped the cup full, "may I ask you a question?"

"Yes. Yes, of course."

"A moment ago you said *others*," she replied, passing the cup across the table. "That envy was directed *at others*. Whom did you mean?"

Anisha looked at her with that dark, steady stare, putting Grace very much in mind of her elder brother. "There is evil all around you, Grace," she said quietly. "Raju's fear is well-founded."

"But Anisha, mightn't you be mistaken?" Grace protested. "After all, if I had even a hint of the Gift, you could not read me?"

"I do not read," said Anisha almost hollowly. "My skills are not those of the Gift. They are . . . different. But even the Vateis can feel emotion—sometimes even emotion directed *in* as well as radiated out."

Grace felt suddenly uneasy. For so long she had allowed herself to discount Adrian's fears for her safety because it seemed the only way to go on. But in doing so, had she unwittingly brought danger into his home?

"Anisha, could any of this be a threat to you?" she asked. "To the *children*? Tell me, for God's sake."

"The evil is not here." Anisha spoke as if her life's blood had drained away. "I can say to you only what I have seen, Grace. Never have I seen such a seemingly pointless thing so clearly. It must mean something."

Grace just shook her head. "I can think of nothing."

As if frustrated, Anisha snatched up Teddy's slate. "*Thirty-five,*" she said determinedly, "and *Swan.*" She wrote it out with swift, hard clacks of the chalk, then flipped the board around. "*Think*, Grace, for God's sake."

Grace couldn't get her breath. Her eyes widened, her hands clutching at the table.

"What?" Anisha demanded.

Grace inhaled raggedly. "Anisha, it's Thirty-Five Swan *Lane,*" she whispered. "It's Crane and Holding. It's the address of *Josiah Crane's office.*"

Anisha's eyes widened. "Good Lord!" she uttered, letting the slate clatter onto the table. "The disinherited cousin?"

"Yes, yes." Grace set a hand to her mouth. "*Mon Dieu!* It's just as Adrian said—and I refused to believe him! Josiah was deeply in debt. He needed money, and Ethan beggared him by tying up their cash reserves."

Again, Anisha's perfect eyebrows snapped together. "But this helps him how?" she asked. "He inherits nothing. This was no killing done out of rage. He planned it. Why?"

The sick feeling in Grace's stomach swamped her. She remembered again Adrian's horrific vision of Fenella's death.

"*Mon Dieu!*" she whispered again. "I think Josiah Crane means to marry Fenella—or try to. Aunt Abigail says that in England, a woman's property conveys straight to her husband unless her father sets it aside. And if that should happen, Josiah will own everything."

"Will she have him?" asked Anisha. "Surely she would not be fool enough?"

Grace shook her head. "No, she *won't* have him," she whispered. "I'm sure of it. But how will he react, Anisha, if she says as much? What then might he do?"

"God only knows," said Anisha.

"We should send word to Scotland Yard."

"And tell them what?" said Anisha, her voice unsteady. "That Mad Ruthveyn's half-caste sister is having visions, too? No, Grace, we've no proof. I think we'd best send for Rance. He'll know what to do about this murderous devil until Raju returns."

"Yes, yes, that's it." Grace shoved back her chair. "Rance will know, won't he? As to me, Anisha, I think it is time I did what I should have done days ago. Indeed, I am ashamed of myself for being such a coward."

Anisha's chin came up. "What are you going to do?"

"I am going to Fenella's," she said. "And I am going to convince her of my innocence. Moreover, I will make her see—in some roundabout way—that she must step carefully around Josiah."

"Can you?"

"I have to try," Grace whispered. "If he has proposed marriage under the guise of protecting her or taking care of her, or any such nonsense, I shall suggest she delay, but under no condition to refuse him."

"No, no," Anisha whispered. "She mustn't. If he's mad enough to do murder, her refusal might send him into a rage."

"And I could not bear another woman hurt under such circumstances," said Grace, her face crumpling a little. "Not when I could have spoken a few words, perhaps, and stopped it."

Anisha winced. "You are thinking, are you not, of that poor girl the major killed," she murmured, reaching for her hand. "But Grace, that was not your fault. Nor is this. Josiah Crane merely used you to take the blame for his deed."

"Whatever happened, I can think only of Fenella now. I should have done so sooner." Grace took both Anisha's hands and squeezed them hard. "You go run Rance to ground. I shall call upon Fenella, and I will not let her turn me away. Wish me luck."

"I do." Anisha smiled wanly, then kissed Grace on the cheek. "Good luck."

CHAPTER 16

Rubies in the Snow

$\mathcal{T}$he rhythmic *clack-clack-clack* of the train slowing on the tracks almost drowned out Royden Napier's hiss of displeasure.

"But this is Boxmoor Station!" he said, frowning up at the Marquess of Ruthveyn and snapping his newspaper shut. "Why the devil get off at Boxmoor?"

Ruthveyn stood, one hand braced on the door of their first-class compartment. "This was a mistake," he said over the slowing engine. "We have to go back."

"*Back* to Euston?" Napier cursed beneath his breath. "You came all the way to Whitehall yesterday to demand I roll out before dawn to accompany you on this *utterly essential* journey—your words, sir, not mine—and now you want to get off, turn round, and go home again?"

"Only briefly," said Ruthveyn. "We'll set off again in the morning."

"Oh, well pardon me!" Napier rammed the newspaper into his valise. "That's all perfectly clear now."

"With Mademoiselle Gauthier," Ruthveyn added. "We should have brought her to begin with. I wasn't thinking."

"And now you are? God save us!" Napier grabbed the back of the seat and hoisted himself against the lug of the slowing carriage. "I'm getting off, all right. But I'll not be coming back again, Ruthveyn—nor will my valise full of documents. If you wish Lord Bessett's involvement in this great goose chase of yours, you can bloody well fetch him down to Whitehall."

"We should have brought her along," Ruthveyn repeated, having listened to Napier's invective with but half an ear. "I shouldn't have left her alone, Napier. Moreover, she might be of help to Bessett. She might . . . I don't know. She should have come, that is all."

"And how would that look to the rarefied citizens of Belgravia?" Napier demanded. "My haring off to Yorkshire with the prime suspect in tow? Somehow I do not think Sir George's political headaches would be much mitigated by that."

The train had stopped, and up and down the line, doors were slamming amidst the porters' cries. Ruthveyn snatched his own valise from the rack, shoved open the door, and alit, never looking back at Napier.

"Ruthveyn," he shouted after him. "I bloody well mean it! If you're going to Yorkshire with me, this is your last chance."

But the marquess had paced off a straight line to the ticket agent's window.

"Two please," he ordered, "on the next train to London."

* * *

The massive white mansion in Belgrave Square looked somehow colder than she remembered it, Grace thought, stepping down onto the pavement. With a few words of thanks, she pressed the fare into the jarvey's hand.

He squinted down from the box. "D'ye wish me to wait, miss?"

One hand on her hat, Grace cast her eyes up at the gray skies. "Yes, if you don't mind," she said. "Just turn down Halkin Street. I might be half an hour."

"Aye, miss."

He touched his whip to his hat brim, then the carriage clopped away, leaving Grace alone in the colorless square. Already the trees were losing their foliage, and the grass was fading to a wintry shade of green. Feeling small against all the grandeur, Grace pulled her cloak snug and went up to ring the bell.

She was rewarded by a familiar face. "Trenton!" she cried. "How lovely to see you. Might I come in?"

The old butler looked wary and a little wan, but he smiled all the same. "Mademoiselle," he replied, finally holding the door wide. "It has been some weeks."

Grace had begun to tug off her gloves. "I have missed you all terribly," she said. "How is Miss Crane? Will you tell her I've come to call?"

"My pleasure, miss," he said, but he looked a little pained. "Will you wait in the small parlor?"

"Certainly," she said, turning to follow.

It was then that she noticed the faint smell of solvent. Inside the small parlor, the gold jacquard wallpaper had been stripped away, and the walls were now painted ivory. Above, the gold medallion had been removed from the ceiling and the gilt pier glasses taken down, giving the entire room an almost restrained look.

"Fenella is fitting out the room all afresh, I see," she

said, handing her cloak and gloves to Trenton. "I confess, I like it rather better."

"Miss Crane thought it ostentatious," Trenton confessed. "I don't believe she ever liked it."

"And Tess cannot have mourned the passing of those mirrors," said Grace, smiling. "It seemed she spent half the morning polishing them."

Trenton's face fell. "I regret to say Tess is no longer with us, miss," he replied. "Indeed, much of the staff has been let go."

"Let go?" Grace was shocked.

"I fear so. Miss Crane said that as she did not mean to entertain, and the children were now gone, the new staff weren't needed."

"The new staff?" Grace paced farther into the room. "What new staff?

"The staff hired since Mrs. Crane's time," said Trenton behind her. "The *last* Mrs. Crane, I should say."

Grace spun around, still holding her gloves. "Do you mean Ethan's mother?" She looked at him curiously. "But that was eons ago. Who would be left?"

"Just three of us, miss," said Trenton a little mournfully. "Indeed, I think that more recently Miss Crane has decided to let the house go and remove entirely."

"Remove? Remove to where?" But Grace knew the answer to that question as soon as it left her lips.

"Back to Rotherhithe," said Trenton. "I am not sure precisely where. She says she misses it, and—oh, but there! One mustn't carry gossip. Let me see if Miss Crane is in. I am not . . . perfectly sure."

On a rising swell of panic, Grace realized she had very nearly come too late. Fenella must mean to marry and move into Josiah Crane's house. It was the only thing that made sense.

Grace hastened after him. "Trenton." She settled a hand on his frail arm. "I *must* see Fenella. I cannot tell you how important it is. Do not let her suppose things that . . . well, that simply are not true. Do not let her turn me away, please. I beg you. Tell her—why, tell her I said I shan't leave until she sees me."

"Yes, miss." But he looked unconvinced.

Grace felt suddenly unwell again. It was the smell, she thought. "Trenton," she said before he left the room, "might I wait in the sitting room? I think the smell of paint is turning my stomach."

For an instant, he hesitated. Then a hint of sympathy passed over his face. "Certainly, miss." He gave a little bow. "Just show yourself up."

As the elderly butler vanished into the nether regions of the house, Grace crossed the grand marble foyer and went up the broad, semicircular staircase to the upper landing. Here she paused to look around, one hand sliding along on the balustrade as she paced from one end to the other.

It felt positively eerie. The last time she had been up here, Ethan had lain dead in his study across the corridor, and she had stood weak-kneed against the sitting-room wall, oblivious to the policemen and servants surging around her. But that awful night, thank God, now seemed a lifetime away.

Grace turned and paced back toward the sitting room, suddenly wishing she had the gift of sensing emotion as Anisha and Adrian did. Surely this house surged with unseen anger—all of it directed at Fenella now. And the poor woman was walking into the teeth of it, unawares.

The sitting-room door stood open as it always did. Grace strolled inside only to find that it, too, was in disarray. All the paintings were down, and a set of scaffolding stood in one corner, as if this room was soon to be painted, too. Mr. Holding's favorite chair was gone, along with the glass cabinet containing his display of stuffed game birds—a thing Grace had always found vaguely loathsome.

Too restless to sit, Grace removed her hat and laid it on the tea table with her gloves, then began to wander the room. How foreign it all seemed to her now, with the landscapes down and everything seemingly upturned. And though she could not disagree with the changes Fenella was making, it struck her as odd that such a thing should be done so shortly after Mr. Holding's death. It seemed . . . a little disrespectful, perhaps.

In the back of the room, the scaffolding stood like a bare tree against a wintry sky, but not quite against the wall, as if it were in the process of being moved. Curious, Grace peeked round it.

The large gilt-framed portrait that had hung over the fireplace was tucked behind it, propped against the wall in the shadows. But it looked strange, somehow. Absently, Grace tipped it forward with one finger, and was instantly horrified. The sitter's face had been slashed by two long strokes down the middle, and a third cutting all the way across, leaving pieces of canvas to flop impotently. On a gasp, Grace tipped it back again.

But now the cuts were obvious to her. What in God's name could have possessed someone? What depth of hatred could drive someone to do such damage to an inanimate object?

The portrait, she recalled, was of Ethan's mother in her youth. Mrs. Crane had been a lovely young widow when she had married into the Crane dynasty, and never had Grace heard an ill word spoken of her. Indeed, by all accounts she had been a fine woman, proud of her family and her domestic accomplishments.

But someone had clearly hated her.

Someone had hated Mrs. Holding enough to slice her face nearly to ribbons. Grace caught her hands together and tried not to wring them. Something just was not right. The work being done in the house went beyond renovation or removal. And why renovate at all if one meant to go? And why slash an old and meaningless portrait to bits?

Unless it held some meaning that others could not so readily see.

On impulse, Grace went to the mahogany secretary opposite the hearth and slid open the top drawer, her hand suddenly shaking. The wooden tray that had always held a supply of Ethan's personal stationery was empty now. But the left-hand tray still held a thick, creamy pile of Fenella's monogrammed letter paper.

Grace pushed the drawer shut with her fingertips, a cold, ugly suspicion running like a shiver up her spine. Good Lord. How many evenings, she wondered, had they all sat here together, quietly reading or playing whist after dinner: Ethan, Fenella, Josiah, and she? And how many letters had Fenella written, seated at that very desk?

Ethan's study was just across the passageway. Grace had spent little time there, but she knew without looking that had she ever pulled open his top drawer, she would have seen a tidy stack of Crane and Holding letterhead to one side and Ethan's personal stationery on the other, the latter lightly used.

The second stack—*this* stack—had always been kept here for Fenella's convenience. Because Ethan both craved society's approval and yet feared its disdain. Because he felt awkward and unpolished, and left the handling of all things social to his sister. The sister who wasn't his sister at all, but his stepfather's daughter.

For reasons she could not explain, Grace went back to Mrs. Holding's portrait and knelt to one side to better look at it. Ethan's laughing gray eyes looked steadily back at her—albeit from separate bits of canvas now. Nausea churned in her stomach, and she set her bloodless fingertips to her lips.

Just then, there was a faint sound. Grace rose and turned to see Fenella on the threshold, still attired in deepest mourning, a jet brooch at her throat and tiny jet earbobs quivering upon her earlobes.

Fenella's hands, too, were caught before her. But she looked oddly bloated—almost matronly—and her heavy auburn hair was in disarray, which was most unlike her.

"Grace," she said, little warmth in her tone. "This is most unexpected. I am not at all sure you ought to be here."

Something like anger swelled in Grace's chest. "Why, Fenella?" she asked. "Why may I not call upon someone I once accounted a dear friend? Is it because the police still call me a murderess? Or is there another reason?"

"I cannot like your tone," said Fenella, stepping fully into the room. "I think it best we let the police do their jobs and reserve our opinions—and our friendship—until then."

Grace thrust out a hand. "What happened to Ethan's mother's portrait?" she demanded, stabbing her finger at it.

Fenella flinched as if struck. "It was damaged by the workmen," she replied. "We had no further use for it anyway."

Quivering with indignation, Grace paced toward her. "*Mon Dieu,* Fenella!" she whispered. "That is his mother! What are you doing to this house? What is in your mind?"

"Better to ask yourself what it is I have *undone,*"

Fenella retorted. "Ethan is dead, Grace. He is not coming back. And this—all this ostentation!" Here, she lifted both hands heavenward. "The gilt and the marble, and even this very house!"

"Fenella, what are you saying?"

"That *I am a Crane!*" Fenella gritted. "We are not Holdings. We never were. We dragged ourselves up from nothing—and on the way, yes, mayhap we stooped to drag the Holdings from bankruptcy—but always, always Cranes knew who and what we were. They did not need a monstrous mansion in Westminster or a page in Debrett's."

"But this makes no sense!" Grace bit out. "How could you be so ungrateful? Ethan made all of you rich!"

"And at what cost?" Fenella's eyes were afire now. "Oh, Ethan knew how to sell things, but he never troubled himself to learn anything of shipbuilding. And Josiah, like his father, has his cards and his dice to occupy him. So we all flit round to our dinner parties whilst the soul of Crane Shipbuilding is hired out to draughtsmen and carpenters, and the money spent on monstrosities like this."

"So you are undoing it all, are you?" Grace backed toward the door a step. "You begin by turning off Mrs. Holding's old servants and tearing Ethan's house down around your ears. And then what, Fenella? Do you rename the business Crane Shipping?"

"It *was* Crane Shipping, you little fool!" Fenella hissed. "The word *Holding* was just an appeasement—to her and to Ethan!" She thrust a tremulous finger at her stepmother's portrait.

"And who is going to run it?" Grace cried. "You? *Mon Dieu,* have you any notion how ludicrous that sounds?"

It was the one thing Grace should not have said.

"Do you think for one moment I cannot?" Fenella's

visage blazed with hatred. "By God, I can keep a set of books in my sleep, but Papa and Ethan thought me good for nothing save marrying off—or worse, hosting dinner parties and writing his prattling letters to people I could not have given a damn about."

She lurched almost threateningly nearer, and realization struck Grace like a hurtling knife. Fenella was insane—perhaps had been so for a long while. "I did not say you weren't capable." She held one hand out almost defensively. "Fenella, calm yourself. I am your friend, remember? I never said you were incapable."

"No, but like everyone else, you thought it," Fenella raged. "Papa would rather have had another man's get at the helm than to hand the family jewels to his own daughter."

"Fenella, Ethan was your brother," Grace whispered. "He gave you *everything*. He loved you."

"He was *not* my brother!" she cried. "And Mrs. Holding—my dear stepmamma with her knitting and tatting and 'a-woman's-place-is-in-the-home' nonsense! After she came round, I wasn't allowed to put so much as a toe over the threshold of Swan Lane. And look what has come of it!"

"Swan Lane," Grace muttered. "That's where you were last week."

"That's where I've been *every* week, for God's sake," said Fenella. "Someone has to be at the head of this business! Between Josiah gaming it away and Ethan draining the coffers on tomfoolery, the company hasn't two sous to rub together. And you have the audacity to suggest I cannot manage my own family's business? That I should stand idly by while I am passed over again and again, and one man after another allowed to run it to ruin?"

Grace was beginning to feel genuine fear. She cut a

glance over one shoulder, hoping to see Trenton in the corridor. She realized a little sickly that she was backing her way out the door.

"Fenella," she said. "You are very bright. Have I not always said so? I am perfectly sure you could manage on your own."

"Oh, don't you patronize me, you fancy French brood-mare!" Fenella's eyes blazed. "That's all you ever were to Ethan, Grace—just a means to an end. He wanted an heir off you—a male heir—because a female would be worthless. Well, I shan't have it, do you hear? Another man without an ounce of Crane blood, sitting in my grandfather's chair and leaving me with nothing but cast-off scraps and platitudes? Just as Ethan did these last ten years. Just as my father did when he married *that woman*. Well, I have had enough of it."

Grace felt her knees sag. Good God, it was true. Fenella had killed Ethan. She had killed him to prevent him from marrying. To keep them from having children.

She set her hand on the doorjamb to steady herself. "Fenella, you should think of Josiah," she said. "He can help you. He is a Crane."

"Yes, but *he's weak*," she spat. "Just like his father before him."

Grace had backed into the corridor now, almost onto the balcony. A horrific thought struck her. "Fenella, where is Josiah?" she asked, almost tripping over her hems. "*Tell me*. What have you done to him?"

Fenella's full mouth turned up into an almost beatific smile. "Poor Josiah is ill," she said. "So ill. Too ill to be out gaming—or even to be in the office. But someone must go, mustn't they? I think the staff will grow accustomed to me. After all, I own the controlling interest."

Grace could not get her breath. She felt the balustrade

strike the small of her back. "You put that note under my door!" she whispered. "You wrote that letter and hid it in my things!"

"Live by the sword, die by the sword, Grace!" Fenella laughed richly. "Ethan should have written his own bloody letters, shouldn't he? Well, I have sent his regrets to his last little tea party ever."

Grace cut a glance to her left. The stairs were but twenty paces away. "*Mon Dieu,* Fenella, why now?" she whispered.

Fenella seized her by the shoulders. "Because this time I wasn't going to wait and risk it," she hissed, giving Grace a vicious shake. "You'd have been with child soon enough, by the look of you. No, this time I could not wait."

"You . . . oh, Lord." Grace's hand came up to cover her mouth. "You killed her! You pushed Ethan's wife down those stairs."

"It was a terrible, terrible accident." Fenella's face was so close Grace could see the spittle hanging off her lip as she rasped out the words. "But she had to go. The silly cow was with child. It was to be a surprise for Ethan. Well, I surprised *her*!"

With that, Grace found herself shoved hard. She fought for balance. "Stop, Fenella!" She grabbed Fenella by the arm with all her strength. But the black bombazine tore, and Grace's hand struck a cracking blow across Fenella's jaw.

"You little bitch!" Fenella's mouth twisted with hatred. "You were never my friend! You weren't even Ethan's—"

"Stop!" shouted a voice from below. "Miss Crane, unhand her now! This is the Metropolitan Police."

Fenella's eyes narrowed to inky slits. "You bitch!" she hissed, seizing Grace's throat.

"Fenella Crane!" The booming voice was Royden Napier's. Grace could hear his feet starting up the staircase. "You are under arrest. Release her and step away. I am armed."

"No!" cried Fenella, tightening her grip and shaking Grace like a rag doll.

Just then, from one corner of her eye, Grace saw movement in the shadows. *Someone creeping up the back stairs*. Trenton?

Grace clawed back, one hand finding Fenella's jet brooch and ripping it away. The second caught at the front of her gown, tearing it again. Frantically Grace fought, but the black was edging round her vision.

Fenella's strength was driven by madness. She was pushing Grace, the balustrade like a fulcrum at the base of her spine. She felt herself tipping backward and flailed out with one arm, finding nothing but empty air.

Grace could see nothing but the white of the ceiling above. She forced down the panic. She was not going over. *She was not*. Not without a bloody fight, by God.

Ruthlessly, Grace seized a fistful of Fenella's hair and dragged her face back until they were nose to nose again. "If I go," she gritted, "then by God, you go, too, Fenella!"

With that, she lashed one arm about Fenella's waist. Suddenly, there was a mighty crack of wood. Something snatched Grace, dragging her back from nothingness. The balcony gave way, and Grace let Fenella go. Grace hit the floor, landing with an arm and a leg dangling in thin air.

"Hold tight, I've got you," a voice rasped against her ear.

"Nooo!" screamed Fenella. It was a cry wrenched straight from hell.

Grace blinked away the blackness. Fenella hung two

feet below the splintered rails, dangling from Adrian's arm, her feet flailing like some crazed marionette.

"Hold still, damn it!" Adrian grunted, clutching Grace round the waist and Fenella by the wrist.

But Fenella did not hold still, and it was an impossible predicament anyway. She jerked again, her eyes wide with fear, or perhaps with hate. And then her hand slipped from Adrian's. She sailed down to the marble foyer in a voluminous cloud of black bombazine, her head landing with a crack, then bouncing to strike again.

Grace screamed. Adrian's other arm came round her, dragging her back from the edge. Somehow, she got to her feet, shivering, and threw herself into his arms.

"I have you, love, I have you." He buried his face against her but an instant.

"Adrian!" she cried. "Oh, thank God."

"I have you," he rasped. "I will never let go. Don't even ask it of me."

Blinking back tears, Grace drew back, still shaking. "Fenella?" she whispered.

Adrian craned his neck over what was left of the balcony. "Napier," he said over the edge, "is she . . . ?"

But Royden Napier had already knelt in the middle of the white marble floor, two fingers beneath Fenella's ear. Her arms were spread high, like an angel unfurling her wings, her rich red hair fanned out between them.

Together they hastened down the stairs. Blood glistened like gemstones in a crescent-shaped spatter, one droplet running down Napier's cheek. He looked up as they approached, his eyes bleak and knowing.

"She is gone," he said.

Without releasing Grace's hand, Ruthveyn bent to one knee and felt Fenella's wrist for a long, uncertain moment.

Then he let it go. The back of the hand bounced a little as it struck the marble, the fingers splaying open to reveal a knot of Grace's hair.

"Snow, Napier," said Adrian hollowly, staring down at the white, blood-spattered marble. "White, white snow. And rubies glistening all around."

EPILOGUE

The Wedding Gift

*L*ord Ruthveyn suffered the interminable months until his wedding day with his usual burning impatience, even as he appeared as outwardly calm and unruffled as ever. At his intended's insistence, nothing was said of their betrothal to the greater world, while amongst friends and family, the ceremony was tentatively set for "sometime in the spring," ostensibly to allow the worst of the weather to clear—even as one or two less charitable people maintained it would likely take that long for his bride to reconcile herself to her fate.

Grace, however, had already embraced her fate, and perhaps a little too exuberantly, for as March edged toward April, and that dreaded window to the soul remained blessedly shut, she clambered hastily from bed one morning to be greeted by the sight of her chamber pot—the bottom of it, specifically—and to the vision of her morning chocolate coming up again.

She sat back down on the edge of her bed, clammy, colly-wobbled, and almost deliriously happy. Grace might manage to be patient, but the heir to the marquessate of Ruthveyn clearly could not. Lady Anisha—already on record as having predicted a son born hale and healthy in the autumn—chortled with glee upon being summoned to her brother's study to consult the charts at last in order to choose the most auspicious wedding date.

As soon as the door shut after his sister, Ruthveyn helped Grace gingerly to her feet and pulled her into his arms as if she were made of spun glass. "*Grace,*" he whispered. "Oh, my love. The die is cast."

Grace merely laughed and kissed him hard.

"I hope, Adrian, that you don't mean to pack me in cotton wool for the next few months," she said long moments later, "for I had other—far more *exuberant*—notions."

But his solemnity did not lift even as he brushed his lips lightly over her cheek. "You have made me," he said, "the happiest man on earth—and a fortnight hence, I shall be twice as happy as that."

At that, a mood of seriousness fell across them both. "*Alors,* you are resolved, then?" she asked, a ghost of a smile passing over her face. "You are not afraid?"

"I have been resolved, I think, since almost the moment we met," he said, staring down into her eyes. "Whatever happens, Grace, wherever life takes us, *we* were meant to be. We simply were. Because this is fate."

And so it was that on a sunny, mid-April morning, the newly minted Marchioness of Ruthveyn found herself caught in one embrace after another as the wedding guests flooded up the steps of her husband's Mayfair mansion, where the wedding breakfast was to be held.

The last to arrive was Royden Napier, who came a little sheepishly up the stairs, his dark brows in a knot. Lady Ruthveyn received his felicitations with all the grace she could muster, then politely excused herself to attend to two of her most important guests.

"Well, Ruthveyn, you have done it," said Napier, as they made their way toward the grand ballroom, which had been set with tables and festooned with flowers for the occasion. "My heartiest congratulations."

"Don't look so solemn, old chap," said Ruthveyn evenly. "The honeymoon phase never lasts long, does it? There is yet hope, I daresay, that she will stab me in my sleep and make all your dreams come true."

"I rather doubt it," said Napier glumly. "She looks radiantly happy."

Together they watched as Grace, still in her wedding finery, knelt to kiss Anne and Eliza on their cheeks while Mrs. Lester stood smilingly, if a little stiffly, in the background.

"She is reconciled with the family, then?" Napier murmured. "I confess I am relieved. They made a pretty pair of angels, those two, tossing their rose petals up the aisle at St. George's."

"It was Grace's dearest wish to have them in attendance," said Ruthveyn solemnly. "Not that she isn't fond of Tom and Teddy, mind. But angelic they will never be."

Just then, Lord Bessett approached, a glass of champagne already in hand, a lovely blonde on his arm. "Afternoon, Napier," he said coolly. "I think you've not met my mother, Lady Madeleine MacLachlan."

The introductions were swiftly made, with Napier bowing politely over Lady Madeleine's hand. Geoff was polite but stiffly formal, Ruthveyn noted, with all the cold hauteur a wealthy young nobleman could muster. He still mistrusted Napier, as did Ruthveyn himself. Still, there was yet something of the diplomat left in Ruthveyn, and he knew no better balm to Grace's reputation than to have the assistant police commissioner on the guest list at her wedding.

"So is it true, Mr. Napier, that Josiah Crane has returned from the Mediterranean?" asked Lady Madeleine, as if to fill the awkward silence. "What a fright that poor man has had."

"Indeed, he returned just this week, ma'am, his health much recovered by warmer climes," said Napier. "It seems the small doses of arsenic his cousin was using to debilitate him have done no permanent damage. I beg your pardon, Ruthveyn. I have not had an opportunity to mention his return to your bride. I should hate her to meet him unawares."

"You needn't worry about it in the least," said the marquess. "Grace has always liked and trusted Crane. Only my sister—misguidedly, as it happens—was able to convince her he might be a cold-blooded killer."

"Perhaps Lady Ruthveyn did not believe it of him," said Napier charitably. "But she did not believe it of Fenella Crane, either—nor did I, come to that."

"Ah, well." Ruthveyn kept his voice equivocal. "Grace has a gift for judging men's characters. With women, she is less certain."

"Aren't we all," muttered Napier under his breath.

Geoff, whose gaze had been scanning the crowd, seemed to return himself to the present. "That reminds me, Ruthveyn," he said. "I was supposed to tell you that Sutherland wishes to speak with you and Grace if you have a moment before the meal and the toasting begin?

Something important, I believe. You will find him near the dais."

"Thank you," said Ruthveyn smoothly. "Lady Madeleine. Gentlemen. If you will excuse me."

He bowed and took his leave of them, suddenly anxious to return to his bride. He found Grace by the head table with Anisha, who was helping Safiyah Belkadi shore up a floral arrangement that was listing starboard and threatening to topple into an ocean of table linen.

He slid a hand beneath Grace's elbow. "Let Nish deal with that," he said under his breath. "Sutherland wishes to speak with us."

"Yes, of course."

Grace went willingly across the ballroom with him, her hand warm and secure upon his arm. He knew, even if she did not, that they were soul mates. That they had been destined for this, and that nothing, not even the Gift, would ever come between them. Still, he wished he could have proven it to Grace—or at least have proven to her that it did not matter to him what their future held. They were as one, and this was their destiny.

"Ah, there you are!" The Reverend Mr. Sutherland beamed at them in what could only be called avuncular joy. "May I offer again my felicitations, and my best wishes for a long, happy, and fruitful union."

"I am sure it will be," said Ruthveyn, clasping the Preost's hand in his. "Thank you, sir, for all your help and encouragement."

"Dear me, that sounds rather fainthearted, Ruthveyn! I intend you to have something more enduring than encouragement." He held a roll-shaped parcel wrapped in colorful paper behind his back. "So, you sail soon for Calcutta! You will be going home at last."

"Yes, for a time," said Ruthveyn, casting an affectionate glance down at Grace. "My bride—in collusion with my sister—insists we leave straightaway."

Grace wished to leave at once, he knew, before she was too far gone with child to go at all. And though Ruthveyn scarcely shared his sister's certainty that in India he would find the sort of guidance that would enable him to control the Gift, he was more than willing to try it. He was also oddly pleased to know his son and heir would be born there, in the same house in which he'd grown up.

"Well, I wished you both to have this before you left England," said Sutherland, presenting the roll to Grace with a dramatic flourish. "It will make, I daresay, for some interesting conversation during the long weeks at sea. And I believe you will take much comfort in it, too, Ruthveyn. I finished it just yesterday."

"You finished it?" said Grace, smiling at him. "But this looks like a print. Or a rolled drawing. Have you some artistic bent, Mr. Sutherland, that you have been hiding from us?"

"No, indeed!" Sutherland's eyes twinkled. "No talent at all, save for persistence and keen eyesight! Now, I know it is a little odd—and it isn't properly framed as yet—but I wish you to go ahead and open it."

"Why not?" Grace cast an uncertain look at her husband. "My love, will you do the honors?"

A few amongst the chattering throng turned at the sound of the paper tearing. Paying them no heed, Ruthveyn laid it on the nearest table and gingerly rolled out a thick sheet of parchment.

"My God," he said, his eyes trailing over the branches and columns of neatly etched names. "It is . . . why, it is a family tree."

"Look, Adrian!" said Grace, setting her finger down

upon their linked names. "It's *our* family tree! Here we are—and forevermore shall be."

"Yes, but here is perhaps the second-most-interesting marriage on the page, my dears." Mr. Sutherland leaned across the table and pointed at a set of lines near the top.

"The devil!" said Ruthveyn. "Why, it is Sir Angus Muirhead."

"Just so!" Sutherland paused to beam at them both. "And it shows us where, in 1660, Sir Angus married one Anne Forsythe—and it shows that they, too, were distant cousins."

Grace's eyes widened. "*Mon Dieu,* you found him!" she said. "You finally found him!"

"Indeed, but more importantly, if you trace this line back—" Here, his index finger did precisely that, following the names almost all the way back to the top, "—then you will see that both Anne and Angus were descended from the same line as was Lady Jane McKenzie."

"Lady Jane McKenzie?" Grace had narrowed her gaze, trying to follow the small print up the document.

"Sibylla's mother," he clarified. "You can see all just here."

It took Grace a moment to digest everything, her wide blue gaze locked with Ruthveyn's. "*Mon Dieu,* we are cousins!" she said, grabbing both her husband's hands.

"Well, perhaps eighth cousins three times removed," Sutherland clarified. "I'm not at all sure that constitutes kinship in any real sense."

But when the happy couple did not break their locked gazes, he cleared his throat sharply. "Well, I see Bessett motioning for me," he murmured. "I know you will wish a moment to yourselves before the festivities begin."

Grace snapped from the trance first. "Oh, thank you, Mr. Sutherland!" she cried, turning to plant a firm kiss on his cheek. "Oh, I could not have—indeed, *we* could not have—" She halted, set a hand to her belly, and blinked back tears, "—we *none* of us could have had a better, more meaningful wedding gift than this."

As Ruthveyn cleared the strange knot from his throat, Sutherland looked suddenly awkward, his gaze going back and forth between them. "I knew you were both fretting over it," he confessed. "And finally—with a big magnifying glass and a long night—I found him."

"But where?" asked Ruthveyn

He knew Sutherland had searched high and low for the records of Sir Angus and traveled twice back to Scotland in his efforts—once in the dead of winter, which was madness. He had pieced together much of Grace's family history over the months, both French and Scottish, but the final link had eluded him.

"I finally found his name written in the margin of one of the old Forsythe family Bibles, on a page with its corner turned back such that it looked like Angus *Muir*," said Sutherland. "And he hadn't a title then, so it was easy to miss. But when I turned the corner up, there was the rest of it. It seems that after the bridge collapse, he healed, returned briefly to Scotland to marry, and must then have been knighted later. It isn't at all clear."

"But it *is* he?" Grace whispered. "You are sure? It is certain?"

"Aye, it's he, my lady," said Mr. Sutherland. "And he was your great-grandfather many times over. Once I had the name right, everything else fell into place. We had most of it—just not in pieces we could put together."

At that, Ruthveyn snatched up the drawing and took Grace by the hand. "Sutherland, you are a prince among men," he said, setting off toward the ballroom doors.

Grace cast an eye over her shoulders at the guests, who

seemed already to be enjoying themselves. "Wait, where are we slipping off to?" she asked.

"To the conservatory for a moment," said Ruthveyn fervently, relief and joy flooding through him. "I want to look at this in a good light."

Once inside the glass walls, Ruthveyn spread the parchment back out on the tea table near Milo's cage. The parakeet toddled back and forth on his perch, cocking his head to survey the document with one beady eye.

They sat down together, tucked snugly on the rattan chaise, their eyes reading up and down the columns and branches of impossibly small names, many of whom were as familiar to Ruthveyn as his own. It looked right to him. It looked *perfect*. And now it was clear to see just how Grace's family branched off, with Sir Angus and Lady Anne the last Scots above a long line of French descendants.

At last, Ruthveyn turned to her, happier in that moment than he had ever been in the whole of his life. "Do you realize what this means, my Grace?"

Her eyes danced. "Yes," she said, her mouth curling into that slow smile he loved so well. "It means you can never, ever be perfectly sure what I am thinking. Or what I'm about to do next."

"Oh, I know what you are going to do next," he said, his voice low.

"Indeed?" She crooked one eyebrow. "And what would that be?"

"You are going to throw me down on this chaise," he said, "and have your wicked way with me." And then Ruthveyn caught her in his embrace and fell into the softness of the cushions, tumbling her over him, wedding finery and all.

Laughing, Grace caught herself on her elbows as she fell. "Ah!" she said, her eyes going soft with desire. "Until now, I wondered if it mightn't all be a parlor trick—but you really *are* psychic."

And then she kissed him, slowly and thoroughly.

"*Pawwwk!*" said Milo. "*British prisoner! Help, help, help!*"

At Avon Books, we know your passion for romance—once you finish one of our novels, you find yourself wanting more.

May we tempt you with . . .

- **Excerpts** from our upcoming releases.
- Entertaining **extras**, including authors' personal photo albums and book lists.
- Behind-the-scenes **scoop** on your favorite characters and series.
- **Sweepstakes** for the chance to win free books, romantic getaways, and other fun prizes.
- Writing **tips** from our authors and editors.
- **Blog** with our authors and find out why they love to write romance.
- **Exclusive content** that's not contained within the pages of our novels.

Join us at
www.avonbooks.com

An Imprint of HarperCollins*Publishers*
www.avonromance.com

Available wherever books are sold or please call 1-800-331-3761 to order.

FTH 0708